P9-DMZ-808

Praise for
No One Ever Asked

"Humble. Powerful. Awakening. *No One Ever Asked* unapologetically invites its reader into a journey of historical significance and soul discovery. A trek which, once taken, you won't come back from."

— MARY WEBER, author of *The Evaporation of Sofi Snow*

"Emotionally resonant and brimming with hope, *No One Ever Asked* is an intimate portrayal of a community in chaos. As Katie Ganshert employs alternating perspectives and vastly different viewpoints, she dives deep into fraught themes of race, adoption, social justice, infidelity, friendship, and more. This gripping story is written with sensitivity and grace, and it will stay with readers long after the final page is turned. A heart-changing, transformative work!"

— NICOLE BAART, author of *Little Broken Things*

"*No One Ever Asked* is that rare breed of story that lingers in your heart and mind long after the final page is turned. Gut wrenching and achingly authentic, this story lays bare the profound intricacies of racial tension. Katie Ganshert is a gifted wordsmith with an uncanny ability to elicit the emotions her characters are experiencing in the reader. This evocative and incisive human drama will not leave you unmoved—a cautionary tale infused with hope. With a handful of stellar novels already to her credit, Ganshert has raised the bar once again. *No One Ever Asked* has my highest recommendation."

— REL MOLLET, relzreviewz.com

Praise for
Life After

"Katie Ganshert is a skilled writer who wrestles earnestly with the clashing forces of faith and fear. *Life After* will hook you on the first page."

— LISA WINGATE, *New York Times* best-selling author
of *Before We Were Yours*

7/19

"Ganshert uses masterful pacing, engaging characters, and believable dialogue to bring readers along . . . tackling big issues powerfully."
    —*Publishers Weekly* Starred Review

"Another emotionally gripping page-turner from Katie Ganshert, a novelist who consistently writes with honesty and insight. *Life After* plumbs the depths of all that gives our existence meaning. Well done."
    —SUSAN MEISSNER, award-winning author of *Secrets of a Charmed Life*

"Katie Ganshert has made her mark by writing compelling stories about resiliency and faith. In her latest, she draws us through the aftermath of trauma, examining the soul's miraculous ability to not just survive but to thrive—even in the wake of tremendous suffering. The result is an emotional journey that prompts us to question the greater purpose behind every moment we are given."
    —JULIE CANTRELL, *New York Times* and *USA Today* best-selling author of *The Feathered Bone*

NO ONE
EVER
ASKED

BOOKS BY KATIE GANSHERT

The Art of Losing Yourself

A Broken Kind of Beautiful

Wishing on Willows

Wildflowers from Winter

Life After

NO ONE EVER ASKED

A NOVEL

KATIE GANSHERT

WATERBROOK

No One Ever Asked

Scripture quotations and paraphrases are taken from the following versions: Holy Bible, English Standard Version, ESV® Text Edition® (2016), copyright © 2001 by Crossway Bibles, a publishing ministry of Good News Publishers. All rights reserved. Holy Bible, New International Version®, NIV®. Copyright © 1973, 1978, 1984 by Biblica Inc.® Used by permission. All rights reserved worldwide.

Although the plot of this book is inspired by recent events, the characters and their experiences are fictional and any resemblance to actual persons is coincidental.

Trade Paperback ISBN 978-1-60142-904-9
eBook ISBN 978-1-60142-905-6

Copyright © 2018 by Katie Ganshert

Cover design by Mark D. Ford

All rights reserved. No part of this book may be reproduced or transmitted in any form or by any means, electronic or mechanical, including photocopying and recording, or by any information storage and retrieval system, without permission in writing from the publisher.

Published in the United States by WaterBrook, an imprint of the Crown Publishing Group, a division of Penguin Random House LLC, New York.

WATERBROOK® and its deer colophon are registered trademarks of Penguin Random House LLC.

Library of Congress Cataloging-in-Publication Data
Names: Ganshert, Katie, author.
Title: No one ever asked : a novel / Katie Ganshert.
Description: Colorado Springs : WaterBrook, [2018] | Includes bibliographical references and index.
Identifiers: LCCN 2017048918| ISBN 9781601429049 (softcover) | ISBN 9781601429056 (electronic)
Subjects: | BISAC: FICTION / Contemporary Women. | FICTION / Christian / Romance. |
    FICTION / Sagas.
Classification: LCC PS3607.A56 N66 2018 | DDC 813/.6—dc23
LC record available at https://lccn.loc.gov/2017048918

Printed in the United States of America
2018

10 9 8 7 6 5 4

For my daughter.
You have made my world so much bigger.

The world is wrong. You can't put the past behind you. It's buried in you; it's turned your flesh into its own cupboard.

CLAUDIA RANKINE

Brown v. Board of Education

On May 17, 1954, the *Plessy v. Ferguson* decision of 1896, which legalized state-sponsored segregation, was overturned. In a unanimous decision, the Supreme Court stated that separate educational facilities were inherently unequal.

At the turn of the twenty-first century, education for black students was more segregated than in 1968.

Prologue

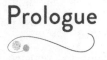

An earthquake started it. The one in Haiti back in 2010. All those images in the media afterward had done their job. Entire buildings not just toppled but flattened like sandcastles at high tide. Lifeless bodies left in the rubble. Small, brown children, streaked with blood, covered in ash. A cross left standing in front of a ravaged church building, and upon it a white Jesus, arms splayed wide in an offer of salvation.

Camille Gray had stared at that particular image the longest. She was not a woman of passivity. When she was moved, she was moved to action. And so—though she had never been to Haiti herself—she rolled up her sleeves, gathered a team of volunteers, and five months later gave the town of Crystal Ridge its very own, citywide 5K. The media around the event produced pictures in sharp contrast to the ones that inspired the run.

Bright-eyed children sporting Hope for Haiti T-shirts and wide, happy smiles. Adults of varying shapes and sizes, some who had trained and others who more obviously hadn't, pinning race bibs to their fronts. A giant banner at the finish line on Morton Avenue, right in front of the Pickle Pie Deli. Water tents and food carts and a live band and an ambulance on standby, just in case.

That year's 5K raised twenty thousand dollars and left Camille with the euphoric feeling that came after a job well done.

It was obvious to everyone. The race must continue.

The following year, with the Haiti earthquake long since gone from the news, the people of Crystal Ridge ran for Crystal Ridge. Camille—a longstanding PTA mom—gathered together other PTA moms and decided the money would be split among the seven schools that made up Missouri's highest-ranking district. Thus creating the Crystal Ridge Memorial Day 5K, an event the town looked forward to with increasing anticipation every year.

Everyone, that is, but Juanita Fine.

Friends and family called her Nita and often joked at the irony of her surname, as Nita was never actually fine with anything. Least of all, hordes of people standing on her front lawn, unfolding lawn chairs on the curb and cheering on people who were running to raise money for a school district that seemed to have plenty.

Juanita lived in the only house that remained in the city's business district. It had been her father's house before her and his father's house before him, and she saw no reason to surrender it to developers. Sometimes she suspected the town's annual race was nothing more than subterfuge—a plot to chase her away—because her two-story brick home sat on Morton and Main, with a grocery store on the left and a law office on the right. And every year, that law office was one of the race's biggest sponsors. Which meant every year there was loud music playing outside her home and a slew of volunteers handing out water and cheering the runners along as they stampeded across her grass. And every year she made a phone call to the local police department to file a complaint.

Last time, she spent twenty-seven minutes telling a female police operator that Chewbacca had ruined her rosebushes.

Chewbacca.

That was another thing. The runners dressed in costumes.

This year the Crystal Ridge Police Department had finally provided Nita with a stack of bright orange cones, to which she fastened signs that read in bold lettering: Stay Off the Lawn!

She had planned to sit on her front porch swing and wave her cane at anyone who dared defy those signs, except this year there was a twist. Not only were there adults in costume, but great plumes of pink powder polluted the air, forcing her and her asthmatic lungs inside to watch from the window, rapping the pane whenever any of the onlookers toed her property line.

Most of them ignored her.

So she watched, increasingly irate, as volunteers along two oblong tables snagged plastic bottle after plastic bottle, squeezing their contents into the air, creating bright cotton-candy puffs that rained down like fairy dust. Just beyond them were the water pistols. Young folk wearing headbands brandished them like proud soldiers as they shot streams of pink water at the runners. And just beyond them, the Crystal Ridge marching band—banging their drums as they marched in formation. Thankfully, away from her.

At 4:22 p.m., a cluster of racers approached, each one wearing a rainbow-colored tutu. Even the boys. In fact, two of them—full grown, large-bodied boys—wore leotards. They were out of their minds. All of them.

Nita scowled as a spray of pink hit her driveway.

Enough was enough.

She pushed open her front door, let in the cacophony of sound, placed her hands on her hips, and glared with the full force of her disapproval, as if doing so could make all of them stop. But nobody did. Nobody noticed her at all. The tutu-wearing runners kept running. The volunteers continued tossing clouds of pink into the sky. The marching band kept marching farther away.

But then the minute hand changed from 4:22 to 4:23, and something happened nobody could possibly ignore. Something happened that had never happened in the town of Crystal Ridge before, at least not that Juanita Fine could remember. Something that had been brewing ever since that horrible town meeting last July.

A startling crack burst through the noise like a car backfiring. For a split second, in the infinitesimal span between the sound and the processing of it, Nita thought one had.

Until it happened again.

The crowd scattered. Onlookers trampled her cones. Tables upended. Bottles of pink cornstarch flattened underfoot like sandcastles at high tide. And through all the chaos, a blood-curdling, terrifying scream rose above the others.

One that went on and on and on.

Even after everyone was gone and all that remained was yellow police tape and a bright crimson stain on her green grass, Juanita Fine could still hear it.

PART I

Newton's First Law: Objects in motion stay in motion with the same speed and in the same direction unless acted upon by an external force.

One

Before

Wipers squeaked against the windshield, smearing raindrops across the glass. The rhythmic sound filled the car as Anaya Jones idled in the driveway. Her hands trembled like her great-grandfather's. Even though he died when she was in first grade, she would always remember the exaggerated way they shook at the dinner table whenever he used silverware.

She turned the key, and the wipers stopped at a thirty-degree angle. All that could be heard was the pitter-patter of rain as she sat behind the steering wheel. A satchel lay open on the passenger seat—the new one her mother gave her before her first day of student teaching. The flap was open, revealing a corner of the science curriculum manual stuffed inside and a sparkly picture a student had given her from art class. Silver glitter would probably speckle the bottom of her satchel in the weeks to come. It wouldn't go away. And neither would this.

The shaking in her hands moved into her arms.

Anaya picked up the satchel, removed the half-empty cup of cold gas-station coffee from the cup holder, and stepped out into the cool rain. The screen door squealed on its hinges as she pulled it open. It took a good three tries before she could manage the lock.

Inside, the house was quiet.

It still smelled like last night's dinner.

Auntie Trill slept on the sagging couch, four-year-old Abeo wedged between her and the backrest, tracking Anaya's movements with wide-awake eyes. Her uncoordinated attempts with the house key must have woken him.

She placed her finger to her lips and tiptoed past him into her room, where she set the coffee and the satchel on her desk and pulled a men's sweatshirt over her head. She sat on the edge of the bed—her body like wet cement as she pressed the sleeve to her nose and inhaled an achingly familiar scent—one that would forever be associated with regret.

What happened, Anaya?

Her heart thudded in response to the question.

It beat into the darkness like a jungle drum.

The front door opened.

"Our kids deserve to go to a school that's not failing." Mama's voice carried into her bedroom. "And if they think they can turn us away without a fight, then they don't know what a mother gonna do for her child."

Anaya peeked through the crack of her bedroom door.

Mama had come home talking on the phone, her voice loud in the early morning silence. "We ain't responsible for no tuition."

With a moan, Auntie Trill raised up a listless arm and batted the air.

Mama pulled a face. One that clearly said, *This ain't your home.* It wasn't either. Auntie Trill's apartment was being fumigated, so she and her youngest were staying for a couple of days. "That's exactly what I'm saying. They gotta follow the law."

Abeo had popped his head up now. Anaya could see it from her spot in the doorway.

Mama rubbed the top of his head, gave some mm-hmms and some uh-huhs to whoever she was talking to, then said goodbye.

Auntie Trill sat up next to her son, her face lined with sleep, her head wrapped in a silk scarf. "You're fighting awful hard to send your boy to a school filled with a bunch of rich white kids."

"I don't care if they're pink with purple polka dots and richer than Oprah Winfrey. I'm not gonna stand by and watch my son fall through the cracks." Mama handed a white paper bag to Abeo. By the look on his face, you'd think it was Granny's homemade cinnamon rolls instead of stale pastries from a hospital cafeteria. "Darius needs to be challenged, and he needs to get away from them boys."

"And away from his daddy's school?"

"It's not his school anymore, Trill."

Grief came like a wave—sudden, engulfing.

"Anaya!"

She stepped back from the door, into the darkness of her room, just as

Mama came inside. Her attention moved to the bed, which wasn't rumpled with sleep, but neatly made. "Are you sick?"

"Headache."

Mama's expression softened with knowing. Only she didn't really know. "I didn't see you yesterday."

Yesterday.

What an innocuous word. And yet, it hovered between them, bloated with all the emotion that came with it.

Yesterday.

An anniversary not meant to be celebrated.

Mama stepped forward and wrapped Anaya in a hug. She smelled like hospital food and exhaustion. "You okay?"

No, she wanted to cry.

She wasn't okay.

Something was seriously wrong.

What happened, Anaya?

The doorbell rang.

Mama put her hand on Anaya's cheek, her brow furrowing. "Baby?"

"Aye, Anaya!" Auntie Trill called down the hallway. "Marcus is at the door."

Her stomach turned to stone.

"Are you two fighting again, because he looks like . . ." Auntie Trill poked her head into Anaya's bedroom. "Well, he looks a whole lot like you do."

"Thanks."

"I have to get to the salon. Can you watch Abeo for me?"

"Sure."

"I'm gonna change for work," Mama said, giving Anaya's arm a squeeze.

Anaya nodded, hating that Mama needed to go to another job. Hating the dull pain in her ankle that served as a reminder of all that had been lost. It hurt worse when it rained, and right then, as she shuffled robotically to the front door, the rain was falling harder, gathering in puddles around Anaya's car.

Marcus stood on the front porch rolling a hat between his hands. When he looked up, his eyes looked as tortured as her soul. "I am so sorry."

●●●●●

The phone buzzed in Jen Covington's sweat-slicked palm, turning her pulse manic.

We're getting off the plane.

Having read the text message over Jen's shoulder, Jen's best friend clutched her arm, and the two shared a breathless look—one that encompassed every prayer, every hope, every hard, impossible emotion felt in these last three years.

"*We,*" Leah whispered.

And just like that, a flood of tears welled in Jen's eyes.

It was happening.

After all the loss and all the waiting and all the political red tape, after the horrible unknown and the fight of her life, Jen was finally going to be a mother.

Not just in theory. Not just on paper.

But in real, actual life.

A ball of emotion swelled in her throat—hot and thick. Adrenaline coursed through her veins, clamping down on her jaw, setting a tremble in her muscles. Ever since Nick told her the news over FaceTime two days ago, she had kept a piece of her heart locked away. Over the past two days—while Leah made phone calls and organized a meal train and brought over spring clothes that would fit a seven-year-old girl because all the clothes they bought in the beginning had been for a child much smaller—Jen braced herself for the other shoe to drop, because the other shoe always did. But now they were here. Nick's text was the proof.

We're getting off the plane.

In a cluster of celebration stood Leah's husband and their two young children, friends from church, Jen's in-laws, and her mother—her brimming-with-excitement, teary-eyed mother. Nobody said anything about the two who were missing. Jen refused to think of them and focused instead on the people who were here, holding balloons, brandishing handmade signs.

Welcome Home, Jubilee!

With Leah's round, hard belly between them, she continued clutching Jen's arm. She held on tight while Jen shifted her weight from one foot to the other, her breath shallow in her chest, her underarms clammy with sweat, her mind spinning with unformed thoughts. Nick and Jubilee had already gone through customs in Dulles. All they had to do now was walk through the jet bridge and the terminal.

Her eyes searched the crowd.

Leah stood on tiptoe, looking around at the travelers walking toward them. An elderly woman pulling a floral carry-on. An Asian couple and a little girl skipping between them with a Hello Kitty backpack jouncing around on her shoulders. A man in a wheelchair wearing a cannula and a Wake Forest baseball cap, being pushed by a gentleman with a build like a linebacker.

Suddenly, Leah's grip tightened.

Because suddenly, there he was.

Her husband.

And there she was.

Her daughter.

Hand in hand.

Nick caught Jen's eye through the distance.

The cluster of family and friends around her shifted. They held up their signs and began to cheer.

The little girl lifted her head.

Nick pointed in their direction.

Leah let go of Jen's arm and covered her mouth. And Jen, unable to hold her own weight, dropped to her knees.

Nick whispered something to the girl Jen had loved so desperately from afar these past three years. Jubilee hesitated for the smallest of seconds, and then she raced down the airport terminal. With one hand clutching the waist of her jeans, she ran straight into Jen's waiting arms. Their bodies collided, knocking Jen back. But she didn't fall. She absorbed the impact as Jubilee wrapped her skinny arms around Jen's neck and her skinny legs around Jen's waist. With a sob tearing loose from the deepest part of her soul, Jen stood and pressed the small girl against her.

The nightmare was over.

Her prayers had been answered.

Her daughter was home.

And Jen would never, ever let her go.

These were the words she whispered—over and over again. Jen poured them, with all the love in her heart, straight into her little girl's ear.

●⬮●₌⬮●

Camille Gray placed her hands at her temples and lifted, watching in the mirror as the furrow between her eyebrows stretched and smoothed away. Now if only she could make her face stay like that.

"What are you doing?" Paige asked. She sat on the bathroom rug wearing her favorite cat pajamas, her freshly washed hair cascading in blond ringlets down her back. She'd paused from combing through her doll's matching mane, an arrangement of American Girl outfits and accessories on the floor all around her.

"I'm traveling back in time, to a land before wrinkles." Camille leaned closer to the mirror. She didn't think she'd spent her life furrowing her brow, and yet, at forty-three, the line had etched itself into her skin. She released her face. The furrow sprang back into place. "Your mother's getting old."

"Not old, Mommy. Wise," Paige chirped.

Camille chuckled. Like her, Paige had a long memory. At kindergarten roundup—over two years ago now—when Paige kept pointing out the fact that Camille was the oldest mommy there, Camille had jokingly insisted that she wasn't the oldest; she was the wisest.

Her daughter uncrossed her legs and came to the vanity, then placed her hands on the countertop and lifted herself up so that her bare feet dangled above the tiled floor. "Your dress is pretty."

"Thank you, sweetheart."

"Your earrings are simply beautiful."

Camille smiled down at her, uncapping her lipstick. Paige was clearly angling for something.

"Would you like to wear my tiara?"

"That might be overdoing it a little, don't you think?" Camille leaned close to the mirror again so she wouldn't smudge.

A knock sounded on the door behind them.

She spotted her husband in the mirror's reflection and did a double take. She'd been doing that a lot lately. Two-and-a-half months ago, they celebrated Neil's forty-seventh birthday. When he'd caught sight of the picture Camille snapped of him blowing out the candles in his cookie cake, he asked with legitimate horror, "Am I really that bald?"

He wasn't.

It was a bad angle.

But the next day he joined a CrossFit gym and turned into one of those people they used to make fun of. He even bought a shirt with one of those CrossFit jokes only people in CrossFit could understand. Neil dove in as if exercise and the Paleo Diet might bring his thick hair back. It didn't. It did, however, bring his college body back—the one he had when he and Camille first met and he was on a rowing scholarship at Brown. The transformation happened fast, as if the extra pounds he'd been carrying around his middle for the past ten years had been nothing more than a new style he'd decided to try on for a while—an unfortunate accessory he thought looked good but never suited him to begin with.

"You ready yet?" he asked, his expression set in mild irritation.

"I just have to slip on my shoes." She rubbed her lips together, then dropped the lipstick into her bag and zipped it shut, the skin around her mouth tightening. It was hard not to feel irritated with his irritation. Yes, she'd promised not to get caught up at this afternoon's meeting, but it wasn't her fault it went longer than planned. Kathleen was still distressed over the locker-room incident, and Rebecca Yates had chosen the very end of the meeting to make her surprise announcement. It would have been rude for Camille to leave without joining in the celebration.

And yes, maybe she was still a tad annoyed with Neil's after-CrossFit comment early this morning—something he said in passing on his way to the shower, as if he were commenting on something as innocent as the weather.

I'm really sick of the rain.

Only Neil didn't say he was sick of the rain. Supposedly, he was sick of his job—a career they'd built their entire lifestyle around. Could he really blame her for the hint of snark that had come with her reply?

"I'm really sick of Taylor's attitude. Should we quit them both?"

Camille slipped her feet into a pair of nude high heels and hurried past the piano room, out to the kitchen, where Austin arranged dominoes on the island countertop, standing them at attention in an intricate design.

"Ooh! Can I knock it over?" Paige asked, climbing onto one of the stools, bumping the island as she did so.

"Paige!" Austin barked.

"Move back a little, honey," Camille said.

"But I'm not touching anything."

"You just ran into the counter, and the dominoes are on the counter. It's called a chain reaction, Paige, and it doesn't have to start with one of these." Austin picked up another domino and set it in place with laser focus.

"Camille." Neil pointed to his watch. "Our reservation was at seven."

She grabbed her purse and looked into the living room, where their eldest sat wedged in the corner of the couch, one long, lean leg crossed and wrapped around the other as she texted into her phone.

"Taylor," Camille said.

Taylor looked up—impossibly young, perpetually annoyed.

"Make sure your sister is in bed no later than eight. I don't want her getting sick again."

Paige scrambled off the stool, bumping the island all over again.

Austin yelped and held up his hands as if doing so would stop the dominoes from wobbling.

"But Mom, I really, really want to watch *The Wizard of Oz*."

"Honey, it's too late for you to start a movie. And the flying monkeys scare you."

"No, they don't. Not anymore! I watched it over at Faith's house, and I didn't even get a little bit scared." She clasped her hands beneath her chin. "Pleeeeeease."

Camille shook her head, her attention back on Taylor, who was supposed to be in charge. "She already took her bubblegum medicine. Don't let her talk you into taking any more. Austin needs to floss his teeth before he goes to sleep. All that food gets stuck in his braces, and if he doesn't floss, he's going to get cavities."

Taylor stared at her with heavily lidded eyes.

"Don't forget to set the alarm as soon as we leave, and absolutely no YouTube."

"Mom," Taylor said. "I'm six*teen*." She stressed the final syllable, as though the age implied all manner of adultness and maturity, when in fact, it implied everything opposite.

Neil wrapped his arm around Camille's waist and nudged her toward the door, bringing the familiar scent of expensive cologne with him. "They will be fine."

"Can I watch *some* of the movie?" Paige asked, trailing them.

"Tomorrow, sweetheart. I'll watch the whole movie with you."

"Promise?"

"Pinkie swear." Camille held out her little finger.

Paige entwined hers with her mother's, temporarily mollified.

Camille kissed her daughter's forehead, inhaling the sweetness of her strawberry shampoo, and whispered, "Be good for your sister. And make sure she sets the alarm."

"Camille," Neil said.

"I'm coming."

As she stepped into the garage, the clattering sound of falling dominoes followed her. For some reason, it stayed. On the silent drive to the restaurant. As the waiter led them to their table. As they looked at the familiar menu and lifted their glasses of Beringer, toasting twenty-one years of marital bliss.

Two

June: Twelve Months Until the Color Run

Knock 'em dead.

Anaya ignored Marcus's text message and the feelings it invoked—seriously, why was he texting her?—as the people inside the conference room erupted into a round of good-natured hilarity.

Or maybe I should say . . . may the force be with u.

His second message came with an upside-down, smiley-faced emoji, and it was at once so unexpected and familiar, she had to bite the inside of her cheek to hold back her own laughter. It bubbled up in her throat like a cathartic release. An ice pick breaking apart a frozen tundra of anxiety as the laughter in the conference room lost its muffle, took on clarity.

A door had opened.

And just like that, Anaya remembered herself—where she was and why she couldn't flirt with Marcus. She sat up straight and pulled a small bottle of hand sanitizer from her purse. She squirted the gel into her palm, then vigorously rubbed it into her hands and over her wrists as a young woman with bright blue eyes and thick blond hair and skin that glowed with confidence came into the waiting area, a man escorting her. He wore a suit and had apple-red cheeks. He shook the young woman's hand before she stepped outside into the warm sunshine.

She hadn't noticed Anaya sitting there at all, exchanging the bottle for a tube of lotion, hurriedly moisturizing her sanitized skin.

The gentleman in the suit spotted her. "You must be . . . Anaya?"

She stood and shook his hand. "Uh-*nigh*-uh," she corrected.

"Right. Anaya. I'm sorry about that."

"It's fine," she said. But even as she said it, her voice sounded stiff. Overly formal. Especially compared to the laughter moments ago. It had nothing to do with the way the man had mispronounced her name and everything to do with the fact that she was here at all. The Crystal Ridge School District administration building.

"Tim Kelly, principal at O'Hare Elementary. Ready to come on back?"

Yes, she was.

She'd been working through a packet of interview questions with Mama for the past two weeks, ever since she got the phone call. With a nod and a shaky breath, Anaya followed Tim Kelly into the conference room, hoping the slick of cold sweat beneath her underarms wouldn't show against the white silk of her blouse. She straightened her pale-pink pencil skirt—an outfit she would never wear on the job, or anywhere else for that matter, but had splurged on once she started filling out applications.

A woman sat inside, alone at the conference table.

As soon as Anaya walked in, the woman stood to introduce herself. "Cindy Ellis, assistant superintendent here at Crystal Ridge."

Cindy Ellis, assistant superintendent, had the distinct look of a woman who was once fat but had recently lost a lot of weight and didn't really look the better for it.

"Would you like some water?" Cindy asked. Not waiting for an answer, she reached for the pitcher at the center of the conference table and poured Anaya a glass, then indicated one of the open seats.

Anaya sat down with a quiet "thank you" and carefully placed her portfolio in front of her.

"Usually, we do interviews for elementary positions with all the principals, but since this is so late in the year and we are interviewing for one specific position, it's just us." Cindy set the glass of water to the left of Anaya's portfolio. "We're very impressed by the glowing recommendation you received from your cooperating teacher, Kyle Davis. And of course, it doesn't hurt that you're already familiar with our district."

Anaya twisted her fingers in her lap, her acrylic nails so bright pink, they were almost fuchsia. ReShawn did them yesterday in Auntie Trill's salon while Anaya got braids. ReShawn was Auntie Trill's oldest but not actually Anaya's cousin, since Auntie Trill wasn't technically Anaya's aunt. She was Mama's best friend and Anaya's godmother. Anaya had asked ReShawn for something more subtle—like a French manicure—but ReShawn scoffed.

Don't let them make you forget who you are.

The advice had annoyed her.

Anaya liked a French manicure as much as she liked fuchsia. And she wasn't going to forget who she was. Not ever again.

"We'd love to know, Anaya. What makes you interested in teaching for Crystal Ridge?"

The paycheck.

But Anaya could hardly say that. Nor could she mention the fact that the district she pictured herself teaching for was in no position to hire. As she looked at the apple-cheeked Mr. Kelly and the gaunt Ms. Ellis, she wondered if either had anything to say about South Fork, its loss of accreditation, and all the talk of student transfers. The people of South Fork certainly had plenty to say. Mama, most especially.

"I admire the way the district strives for excellence," Anaya answered, "and expects excellence from every student. I want to be part of an atmosphere that fosters success."

Mama always said her lip twitched when she lied. Anaya wondered if it was twitching now.

"You used to be quite the track star." Cindy looked down at a copy of Anaya's resume. "Our athletic director told me you broke every single collegiate record there was to break."

Anaya's hands clasped tighter in her lap.

"What an unfortunate injury."

Unfortunate.

It was hardly the right word, but she nodded anyway and waited for Ms. Ellis to ask how the sport shaped her—as a person, as a teacher. Or maybe Ms. Ellis wanted to know how the injury itself had shaped her. Anaya had an answer prepared for both.

Instead, the woman crossed one leg over the other and folded her hands on her knee. "Have you ever considered coaching?"

Anaya blinked. "Track?"

"Our girls' district varsity coach retired this past year. I hear there are some really talented girls on the team. One in particular. To have someone like you as the coach would be wonderful."

Anaya's ears flushed. "Someone like me?"

"Someone who has competed at the level in which you have."

"I don't have a coaching license."

"Oh, those are easy to get," Tim Kelly chimed in. "I'm sure the district would cover the cost."

"Of course," Cindy said. "And you'd receive a nice coaching stipend every year."

Anaya looked from Cindy to Tim. Both needed to work on their poker faces. It was suddenly very obvious. Her cooperating teacher's letter of recommendation had gotten her here. Coaching track would ensure that she stayed. While this was far from her first choice, Anaya definitely needed to stay.

Three

The back door of the moving truck slid open with a sound like rolling thunder. Jen reached her arms overhead, twisting to stretch her muscles after the twelve-hour drive. Her mother was still climbing out of the driver's side of Nick's car, gripping the plant she insisted Jen bring on the long journey. Jen's bottom felt like jelly and probably looked like a flattened pancake as she squinted down the row of nearly identical split-level homes with single car garages and green, sloping lawns.

Her new neighborhood.

The only sign of life? A black-and-white cat with large, luminous eyes staring out from beneath a row of boxwoods across the street. And a kid several houses away, popping wheelies on his bike.

"It's a cute neighborhood," Jen's mother, Carol, said in a thick southern drawl—one that seemed to grow thicker the farther north they drove. "Smaller than your home in Clayton but probably as good as you're gonna get in this area. The property values looked sky high on Zillow."

Nick rubbed his chin and studied their belongings the way one would study a chessboard, trying to figure out the best way to begin. Boxes and furniture had been crammed inside the van so intricately, they formed a three-dimensional jigsaw puzzle. "Well, Juju-bee, what do you think?"

He draped his hand across Jubilee's skinny shoulder. She stood there, her braids already fuzzy, sucking on her two middle fingers. The first few weeks home, she had sucked them raw. As soon as they started packing up the house in North Carolina, the habit had returned in full force. "Should we go check out your new room, see where we'll put your bed?"

Jubilee uncorked her fingers. "Bunka-bed?"

Bunka-bed.

Ever since she saw her twin cousins' bedroom and the fun wooden ladder leading up to the bed on top, she'd suffered a serious case of bed envy. Actually, *envy* was too tame a word. She'd suffered a jealous rage. And when neither Jen nor Nick gave in, Jubilee showed them both by getting hold of a permanent marker and defacing the pretty white daybed Jen had carefully painted and assembled when they were still waiting to bring her home.

"Bunka-beds?" Nick scooped Jubilee up into the air and tossed her over his shoulder, tickling her ribcage as he did.

She burst into a fit of hysterical giggles.

"How are we supposed to fit bunka-beds through that door?" he said, continuing his tickling as he carried her toward the house. "We'd have to cut a hole in the roof and lower it in with a rope."

Playful distraction.

Nick had mastered the technique, because Nick was made to be a daddy. Jen watched him unlock their new front door and carry their laughing daughter inside with a deep, theatrical laugh of his own.

"Of course," Mom said, "there's a reason the property value is so high. Did y'all know Crystal Ridge is the number-one ranked school district in the whole state of Missouri?"

"You might have mentioned it." Once. Or five hundred times.

"Number one." Mom looked at Jen beneath raised eyebrows, and when she didn't seem properly impressed, her mother continued. "Missouri's no small state, sugar."

"No, it isn't."

"Then why aren't you more excited?"

"Because we're not sure where we're sending Jubilee in the fall."

"Come again?"

"We might not enroll her in Crystal Ridge."

Mom's eyes grew irritatingly large. "You're yanking my chain."

"I'm not yanking anything."

"Where in the world would you enroll her?"

"South Fork."

"Jennifer. South Fork?" Carol, of course, knew all about South Fork. Because Carol had spent an inordinate amount of time house shopping online for her daughter as soon as Jen broke the news that Nick had accepted the managerial position at Schnucks, a supermarket in Crystal Ridge. "Why on earth would you send her there?"

"Because, when it comes to Jubilee and school, we have to consider all kinds of things."

"Like what?"

"Diversity."

Mama huffed. "Diversity."

"Crystal Ridge hardly has any." The small percentage they did have were mostly Asian and Indian. She and Nick didn't want Jubilee being one of the only black kids in her class. She needed mirrors. People who would look like her. "South Fork does."

"But isn't that the wrong kind of diversity?"

Jen cocked her head. "The wrong kind?"

"Please promise me you'll pray long and hard about it before you make any decisions." With a dip of her chin, she wrapped her arms around the potted plant and headed to the front door.

Sometimes the stress Jen felt in her body seemed like the black-and-white snow on the old boxed television set in her childhood living room—an army of angry ants, scuttling across a white screen. Daddy would mutter curses under his breath as he moved the rabbit-ear antenna around in search of reception. Whenever his search failed, he'd give the side of the television a hardy whack, as though he might beat the static away. It never seemed to work.

The kid popping wheelies fell over in a loud crash.

The cat darted out from the bushes, around the side of the house—a small bell on its collar jingling as it went.

Jen opened her mouth to call out to the boy, to make sure he was all right. But he stood up sheepishly and quickly pedaled away, leaving her alone in the evening sun. She stared at the unfamiliar street number on the side of the mailbox standing sentry at the end of the driveway.

1749.

Winding Hill Road.

Quickly, without giving herself any time to really consider the ramifications, she typed her new address into a text message and shot it off to the recipient. She had no idea if he'd get it. No idea if his number was still the same.

"That entryway is a lot smaller than the pictures let on."

Jen's pulse hiccupped.

She quickly pocketed her phone, ignoring the curious look her mother gave her as she did.

"You're awfully jumpy," she said.

"I didn't hear you coming."

Mom came back to the truck and stared for an extended moment at the puzzle of belongings before releasing a long, drawn-out sigh. "Oh, Jen."

"What?"

"How am I gonna live with you so far away?"

"Mama."

"And just when I finally have a granddaughter." Her mother shook her head. "And y'all spent the last two months hiding her away."

"Not hiding her away. Cocooning." It was an important ingredient to the attachment recipe. One Mom couldn't seem to understand. Nor could she understand why it wasn't good for Jubilee to expect presents every time her memaw came to visit. And yet, Carol couldn't seem to help herself.

"Now it's just me and your father—who's been a miserable old coot ever since he retired."

Dad's misery seemed to predate his retirement, but Jen kept the thought to herself.

Without warning, Mom wrapped Jen in a tight hug. For as long as she could remember—before Young Living and DoTerra—her mother would rub lavender behind her ears whenever she finished her after-shower lotion. The smell engulfed her now. Just like her mother's arms.

They squeezed so tight, Jen could hardly breathe.

Four

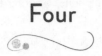

Camille pressed her sandaled feet on the floor of her Highlander and reared back against the seat. "Taylor, they're braking!"

Taylor tapped the brakes too hard, then lifted her hand off the steering wheel and gestured to the car in front of them. "I can see their brake lights, Mom. I'm not blind."

"Hands on the wheel."

Taylor wrapped her fingers around the steering wheel at a perfect nine and three, her knuckles whitening. Apparently ten and two was outdated.

Camille commanded her muscles to relax. But they refused. Probably because this was a horrible idea. Especially in light of the ominous feeling sitting in the pit of her stomach. When her children were babies and the feeling struck, she would creep into their rooms and place her index finger in front of their tiny, puckered lips to make sure they were breathing. Now she checked batteries. Namely, the ones in the carbon monoxide and fire detectors on every level of the house.

All of them were working.

She made sure to lock the doors before they left. She'd packed plenty of sunscreen to avoid sunburn. All three of her children knew how to swim and swam well.

But still the ominous feeling remained.

It stalked the edges of her mind, hovering malevolently as cool air blew from the vents. Of course, her daughter couldn't be like most of her friends— content to sit shotgun while their mothers played chauffeur and they texted on their phones. Not so with Taylor. In fact, her daughter's eagerness to obtain a driver's license ran in direct opposition with one of Camille's most strongly held beliefs—namely, that sixteen was a perfectly ridiculous age for anyone to be operating a motor vehicle.

Her fingers dug into leather. "You're getting really close to those cars."

Taylor glanced in the direction Camille indicated, where parked cars lined the side of the road. Instead of moving farther away from them, the Highlander drifted in the direction of her gaze.

"Taylor!"

Taylor jerked the SUV to the center of the lane, the set of her shoulders high and stiff. "You know, it's really hard to drive when you criticize everything I do."

"It's really hard not to criticize when you're about to hit things."

"I'm not going to hit anything."

"Everyone just relax!" Paige commanded from the backseat, holding up her arms as if she were stepping between a pair of boxers in a ring. "Nobody's gonna die. We're going way too slow to die."

This, thank heavens, was true. It was the one thing Camille could count on. Her rule-following eldest might not be a natural behind the wheel, but she did take the speed limit very seriously.

"Yellow means stop."

"I know," Taylor muttered, slowing to a stop at the traffic light.

Camille sank back against the leather seat, thankful for the short reprieve.

"Listen to this," Austin said, reading from the book he checked out from the library yesterday. "In 1945, six US Navy bombers disappeared, along with the crew sent to rescue them. Before the twenty-seven men vanished into thin air, one pilot reported, 'Everything looks strange. Even the ocean.'"

"That's fascinating, honey."

"It's the only place on earth besides the Dragon's Triangle where compasses don't point to magnetic north."

"You're such a nerd," Taylor said.

"Taylor," Camille reprimanded.

Austin was unfazed. "Some people believe the lost city of Atlantis is underneath."

"What's the lost city of Atlantis?" Paige asked as the radio transitioned from the weather forecast to *Lonnie at Lunchtime*. Lonnie had a deep, made-for-the-radio voice. When Camille first met him in person to plug the Crystal Ridge Memorial Day 5K several years ago, she'd been shocked to discover that he was actually a small man who wore moccasins and had a soul patch.

"We're back," Lonnie said, *"and ready to talk about this perplexing transfer law."*

"It's not a real city," Taylor said.

"Shh!" Camille turned up the volume, her stomach tying into knots.

"Ever since the Department of Education gave South Fork schools a big, red F, stripping the district of its accreditation, a group of mothers have been fighting for the right to send their children to a district that's not failing. The high court has spoken, and it looks like the mothers have won. The question on everyone's mind is, what now? There's no instruction manual, folks, but everyone seems to have an opinion. Call me up, listeners, and let's chat. I'm Lonnie at Lunchtime, *covering the latest community controversy, and I want to know: What do you think about this one?"*

●●●●●

"I'm going to the bathroom," Taylor said as soon as they walked through the pool gate of the Crystal Ridge Country Club.

"Didn't you go before we left?" Camille asked.

"You're monitoring my urination now? Awesome. Would you like me to start a chart so it's easier for you to keep track?" Taylor scowled with the full force of teenage hormones and stomped away.

Camille wanted to stomp back. These days, her eldest made her want to stomp quite a lot. She couldn't tell what was more dismaying—Taylor's animosity or the animosity Camille felt in return. Was it normal to have such strong feelings of dislike for your own daughter?

She pushed the feelings down—swallowed them into the pit of her stomach, right next to the ominous one she couldn't shake—and walked toward her waving friend. Kathleen had saved them a couple of lounge chairs and was currently beckoning them over from the other side of the sparkling pool, holding her wide-brimmed, floppy hat on her head as though some nonexistent wind might blow it away.

Paige skipped ahead, her flip-flops smacking against the hot pavement while Austin shuffled behind, his nose stuck in his book.

"Honey, why don't you go say hi to Bennett?" Camille encouraged, setting their beach bag beside the chair as Kathleen removed the towels she had draped over it.

Bennett was Kathleen's middle son and currently showing off for Kathleen's oldest. Cody was going to be a senior and had the kind of face and build Camille would have swooned over at Taylor's age. Taylor's best friend, Alexis, seemed to be swooning now. She certainly laughed loud enough as Cody shoved Bennett into the pool and told him to get lost.

"Austin." Camille wagged the can of SPF 30 at her son. "We came here to swim, not read."

He folded the corner of the page to hold his spot.

Paige gasped. "That's a library book!"

Austin set the book in the beach bag and peeled off his T-shirt, revealing skinny white arms and some red pimples on his back. She'd talked to Neil about calling a dermatologist, but Neil had scoffed.

He's getting to be that age, Camille. I had them too. They went away. Don't make it a big deal.

"You look frazzled," Kathleen said, sliding her sunglasses down her nose.

"I let Taylor drive." She fished a second bottle from the bottom of the bag—SPF 50—and began spraying Paige, who had already removed her bright-pink cover-up and stood with her arms held out to her sides. Austin finished with the SPF 30 and dropped it on top of the beach towels.

Paige's body rocked as Camille rubbed the white spray into her shoulders. "Mom thinks Taylor's the worst driver in the whole world."

Kathleen laughed.

"I think no such thing, missy," Camille said, her attention sliding to the bad driver. Taylor had slipped out of the clubhouse and was heading toward Cody and Alexis. Camille watched as Taylor took off her shorts. Her shoulders and arms remained covered by the long-sleeve, lightweight cover-up Camille had purchased for her a couple of weeks ago.

Kathleen saw the cover-up as further evidence of Taylor's uncommon responsibility. A teenager who cared about the dangers of skin cancer. Camille knew it had more to do with self-esteem. While most people would die for a runner's body like Taylor's, she suspected her daughter was insecure about her chest. Or lack thereof.

"Mo-om," Paige whined, giving her leg an impatient wiggle.

Camille finished her spraying, then patted Paige's side—a nonverbal cue that she was free to go.

She ran off to the shallow end, where Dane—Kathleen's youngest—was swimming about with a snorkel and flippers, and very quickly began coaching him on the proper way to accomplish an underwater handstand. Dane was going into third grade, which meant he was one year older than Paige. Cody was one year older than Taylor. Both sets of children would—of course—grow up and get married. Their families would vacation together every summer in the Dominican, and Camille and Kathleen would officially be two of the best grandmothers of all time. At least, this was their plan.

"Why don't you have *Neil* give her driving lessons?" Kathleen said.

"He can't. Not with his work schedule."

"You're a saint."

"Taylor would beg to differ."

Across the pool, Cody did a running cannonball into the deep end, sending up a fountain of water that had Taylor and Alexis shrieking and pulling up their knees. Cody surfaced with a grin, shaking the water from his hair like a wet dog. It had turned a rich golden in the sun, his skin as tan as Taylor's nut-brown legs.

Austin jumped into the pool where it was waist deep. He sucked in his stomach against the cold, his hands hovering above the water as he waded over to Bennett. Camille didn't miss the way Bennett frowned at Austin's approach.

It had the knots in her stomach tying tighter.

She and Kathleen met at a women's Bible study at their church, and quickly hit it off. At the time, Cody was in first grade at Lewis and Clark Elementary. Taylor had just started kindergarten at O'Hare. Both women were getting their feet wet with the PTA, and both women had drooling baby boys on their hips—Austin and Bennett. It didn't seem possible that this year those boys were both going into middle school.

Camille had mixed hopes. Maybe Austin would finally have a best buddy—that one tight connection he could never seem to make in elementary school. But then, sometimes Bennett treated her son like a convenient friend— someone he'd hang out with when it was just the two of them but ditched as soon as anyone "better" came along.

This past spring, just when Camille had worked up the nerve to talk to Kathleen about it, the locker room incident happened with Cody, and Kathleen grew extra defensive about her children. Besides, Camille could never be sure she wasn't imagining Bennett's surly attitude. Case in point: the two were currently splashing each other good-naturedly in the pool.

Camille grabbed a stick of gum from her bag and sank back against the lounge chair. "Lonnie was talking about the South Fork transfer on the drive over."

"Did you watch the news last night?" Kathleen asked.

"I try to avoid it these days."

"A student at South Fork High stabbed someone yesterday. The man's in critical condition at the hospital."

Camille shook her head. That was exactly why her stomach was tying into knots. South Fork was one of the most violent districts in the entire state of Missouri, and suddenly, because of some poorly written law, those students had the option of coming to Crystal Ridge. She looked at Austin and Bennett, who were still splashing in the pool. Come August, they'd be walking the halls with much bigger, more mature eighth graders. She stuck the stick of gum in her mouth. "I can't imagine they would come here. I mean, we're their biggest rival, and there are two other districts just as close."

"I'm sure some of them will come to our schools."

"Have you talked to Jill?"

Jill was Kathleen's second cousin and the vice president of the school board, which made her their informant in all things district related.

"I guess the superintendents in the area are meeting sometime today to come up with a game plan." Kathleen snagged her Chick-fil-A lemonade off the ground, the ice inside rattling as she took a long pull from the straw.

Across the pool, Cody was attempting to grab Taylor's foot and drag her into the water. Alexis watched with a look of irritation, as though she wanted Cody to grab *her* foot, not Taylor's.

"You know that dream I had the night before 9/11?" Camille asked.

Kathleen raised her eyebrow—a gesture soaked in amusement. "The clairvoyant one?"

"Laugh all you want, but I didn't get anything out of order." Her memory was sharp as a tack. She dreamed she was watching the news and everything was fire and chaos and she felt panicked and horrified. It was a dream that happened before those towers fell, no matter how much Neil and Kathleen and anyone else she told the story to insisted she must have had it after.

"I woke up this morning with the same feeling now as I did then."

"Impending doom?"

Camille tossed the crumpled wrapper at her friend.

"I'm sure everything's going to be fine," Kathleen said. "The school board and our superintendent will make sure everything works out."

"You're right."

"Of course I am. Now tell me about this idea of yours."

"Oh, right. I was thinking. What if next year we turned the 5K into a color run?"

"What's a color run?"

"You know—those paint races, where the runners get covered in a bunch of color as they go. My cousin from Denver ran one. She posted a bunch of really cool pictures on Facebook afterward."

"That sounds fun."

"Doesn't it?" Camille smiled. "I'll bring it to the table at tomorrow night's meeting. Which, by the way, is going to start a half hour later than planned."

"Then maybe I'll actually be on time."

"Mo-ommy!" Paige walked toward them, dripping wet and clutching her stomach.

Camille sat up. "What's wrong, sweetheart?"

"My belly feels gooey."

"Uh-oh," Kathleen said. "Impending doom."

Five

"I'll need you to fill out this form, sweetie. Don't forget to turn that top page over and answer the questions on the back." The receptionist slid the clipboard over the counter as Jubilee tugged the hem of Jen's shirt.

She made her hand into a fist, stuck out her pointer finger, and jabbed herself in the arm, looking up at Jen with big, wanting-to-know eyes. Was she going to get a shot? It was the same question Jubilee had been asking all morning. The same question Jen continued to dodge.

With the clipboard and pen in hand, she found a seat near the play area and nodded toward the bins of toys, where a little girl with pudgy fingers and wispy brown pigtails sat building a tower out of oversized Legos.

"You should go play."

Jubilee didn't budge.

She stood resolutely in place, stress oozing from her pores and seeping into Jen's. It had been a traumatic twenty-four hours, thanks to the big production Mom made out of her goodbye the night before. This morning, Jubilee woke up dysregulated and unhappy with almost everything—the itchy tag on the back of her shirt, the oversized dollop of toothpaste on her toothbrush, the lack of a swing set in their new backyard.

"I hate dis oatmeal."

Don't eat it, then, Jen had wanted to snap.

Instead, she slammed the silverware drawer shut and rummaged through a box on the counter for the can opener. That was when Nick suggested they reschedule the doctor appointment for a time they could take Jubilee together. Her waspish thoughts turned into biting words.

"I can handle a doctor appointment, Nick."

She was a nurse after all.

But now, with her irritation no longer hot to the touch, she had serious reservations. Jubilee was terrified of doctors, and Jen had a hard time handling

Jubilee's fear. Over the past couple of months, Jen had discovered that she had a hard time handling a lot of things.

Jubilee shuffled over to a bin of picture books.

Jen stared at the top section of the form. Pregnancy and birth. It wanted to know things like weight and length, the type of delivery, whether there were any complications. If Mom drank alcohol or smoked cigarettes, and if there were any health concerns during the pregnancy.

Beneath that, Family History: *Check if the child or immediate members of the child's family have had the following illnesses or problems.*

The words settled in Jen's soul like wet snow. With a resigned breath, she filled out Jubilee's name and the sparse details she knew when the front door to the pediatrician's office opened with a swoosh of humidity. A woman walked inside holding the hand of a little girl. They had matching blue eyes and matching pointed chins and matching long hair swept up into matching messy buns. The girl wore a bright-pink swimsuit cover-up and flip-flops. The woman wore cutoff jean shorts and a loose-fitting tank and a tan leather tote over her sun-kissed shoulder.

She knew the receptionist by name. They laughed together as she removed one of the masks in the small basket on the front counter and placed it over her daughter's mouth, looping the strings around the backs of her ears.

The mother-daughter duo found two seats across from Jen, and the woman's eyes met hers in that awkward way eyes sometimes meet—whenever a person was caught staring. Only instead of looking quickly away like she hadn't noticed, the woman spoke in a familiar, friendly tone, as if they weren't strangers. "It's a shame to be in here when it's so nice out there."

Jen nodded, hoping the gesture didn't look as stiff as it felt.

"I'm Camille." The woman came out of her seat to reach out her hand in a gesture so reminiscent of Leah, Jen's heart squeezed. Leah was a hand shaker too and had introduced herself in the exact same way the first time they met all those years ago.

"I'm Jen."

"This is my daughter, Paige. I'm pretty sure she has strep throat. It always starts the same. A stomachache and a headache. Is that your daughter there?" She nodded toward the pigtailed toddler building the Lego tower, her mother on the other side of the waiting room, typing furiously into her phone.

"No, actually. That's my daughter."

Jen watched, wondering what would come after the flicker of confusion, the scramble to make two mismatching pieces fit. It wasn't curiosity or disapproval but a slow-moving pleasure that left Camille with her hand pressed against her chest. "She's absolutely beautiful. What's her name?"

"Jubilee."

"Where is she from?"

The question came like a scrape against vinyl. It always did. Why did Jubilee have to be from anywhere? Sometimes Jen got the urge to answer with something snarky—like Des Moines or Minneapolis—but then she would reprimand herself for the unkind thoughts. "Liberia."

"Liberia. Wow. You don't happen to know Deb Zykowski, do you?"

"We're new to town."

"Ah. So that explains the southern accent."

"Is it that bad?"

"It's that charming. What neighborhood did you move to?"

"Winding Hills."

Camille lit up like a tree at Christmas. "That means Jubilee will be going to Kate Richards O'Hare Elementary. That's where Paige goes. What grade?"

"Second."

Camille's countenance went even brighter. She turned to her masked daughter. "Did you hear that? Jubilee is going into the second grade at O'Hare, just like you."

Paige looked neither impressed nor unimpressed with the news. She sat in the back of her chair, arms casually resting on the armrests, wiggling her toes like she didn't have a care in the world.

Jen wondered if she shouldn't explain to Camille that Jubilee's place of education was still undecided.

"I know I'm biased, but if you ask me," Camille leaned forward conspiratorially, "O'Hare is the best elementary school in the district. I love that it's smaller than the others. A two section school. The rest are all four. It gives it a family feel, you know? My oldest daughter's at the high school, and my son is officially a middle schooler now, a fact I'm trying hard not to think too deeply about. Both went through O'Hare from kindergarten through fifth, which makes me an O'Hare veteran."

"I've heard really good things."

"There's going to be a new second grade teacher this year. Mrs. Pennelin had to move back home quite suddenly last month to take care of her mother. It was sad to see her go. My other two both had Mrs. Pennelin in second grade and loved her to pieces. But I'm sure whoever they hire to replace her will be just as wonderful. O'Hare only hires the best."

"That's . . . great," Jen said.

"I hope you're not too worried about the transfer situation."

"The transfer situation?"

"Oh. Well, one of the nearby districts lost their accreditation earlier this year. The students have the option of transferring to an accredited district. It has things in a bit of flux at the moment, but I'm positive it'll get worked out. We have an excellent school board. Our superintendent is always on top of things. He'll look out for our kids."

Camille touched her daughter's hair, an instinctive gesture that looked as natural as breathing. "We should get our girls together for a playdate. Get you plugged in. I'd love to introduce you to Deb. She adopted two girls from China when she was almost forty, bless her heart. Her youngest is best friends with Paige. She had a cleft palate, and the older one had a heart defect. Faith was only ten months and Hope was almost two when they came home. Both girls had to have multiple surgeries."

"Wow." The thought left Jen's head spinning.

"They celebrated six years home two weeks ago. When did Jubilee come home?"

"This past April."

"Oh, wow. So it's very new. That settles it; you have to meet Deb. Are you busy tomorrow night?"

"Um . . ." Jen shifted in her seat.

"Sorry. I'm talking a mile a minute. I promise I'm not normally this overwhelming. I'm just so excited we got to meet like this." Camille pulled a pad of cupcake-shaped sticky notes and a purple gel pen from her tote. "Every Memorial Day, a group of us PTA moms organize a 5K for the city. We're having a meeting tomorrow night at my house to start discussing next year's run, and Deb will be there with her two youngest. The ones adopted from China. You should come! I promise it's much less of a meeting and much more of a social hour."

The door opened. A nurse stepped out. "Jubilee Covington?"

And just like that, Jubilee's entire body went rigid.

Camille scribbled a number on a Post-it note and handed it over with a smile. "If you can't come tomorrow, that's no problem. Either way, call me. We'll get the girls together for a playdate."

Jen nodded distractedly, slipping the note into her purse. She went over to Jubilee and took her hand, but Jubilee began to shake her head and dig in her heels.

Heat flooded Jen's face.

"She's not a fan of the doctor," she explained with a falsely lighthearted laugh, hating that she felt compelled to explain anything.

"Oh, neither is Paige," Camille said sympathetically.

The little girl sat with her legs swinging back and forth, looking perfectly at ease.

Jubilee tried yanking her arm away.

Jen could feel Camille's stare on her back like a laser beam. With a plastic smile fixed in place, Jen tightened her grip on Jubilee's arm and began walking her forward.

•◦•◦•◦

If not for Camille's utter confidence in the staff at Dr. Porter's office, she might have slid out into the hall to make sure nobody was being tortured to death. By the sound of it, you would think someone was breaking the child's legs.

"Okay, Paige," the nurse said, holding up the long white swab. "You know the drill, right?"

Paige nodded primly and set her hands in her lap. It was as though the hysterics in the next room had turned her daughter extra stoic.

The nurse swabbed the back of Paige's throat.

She gagged softly. Tears welled in her eyes, but she quickly blinked them away, slid off the examination table, and sat in Camille's lap.

The nurse gave Paige an affection tap on her nose. "This will only take a few minutes, and then we'll know."

With a swell of pride, Camille wrapped her arms around her daughter and kissed the crown of her head. Swabs weren't fun, especially not when your throat was already tender and you had to cut a fun day at the pool short in order to get one.

"All that noise is making my head hurt," Paige said.

Camille placed her hands over her daughter's ears. "I'm sorry, honey."

"Why is she being so loud?"

"I think she must be scared." Camille drew Paige's legs to the side and leaned her back against her chest.

"She doesn't sound scared. She sounds mad."

Camille silently agreed. At the moment, Jubilee didn't even sound mad as much as she sounded feral. Poor Jen. She had looked so flustered when the nurse came out and called Jubilee's name. This must have been why.

"Will I have to get my tonsils out?" Paige asked.

"We'll have to wait to see what Dr. Porter thinks."

"I hope he lets me keep them."

"Even if they're making you sick?"

"They are attached to my body, Mom. I don't want anyone to saw them off."

"Nobody is going to saw them off. The doctor will take them out while you're sleeping. You won't feel it at all, and when you wake up, you get to eat all the ice cream you want."

"Seriously?"

"Just ask Austin."

"Never mind, then. I want these puppies gone."

Camille laughed. Where in the world had Paige learned the phrase *these puppies*?

Her phone chirped inside her bag.

When she fished it out, Kathleen's name lit the screen. Camille hit the Talk button and pressed the phone against her ear. In the other room, the screaming had turned into distressed moans.

"Is Paige crying?" Kathleen asked.

"No. It's a little girl in the other room."

"It sounds like a dying cow."

Somehow Camille doubted Kathleen had any idea what a dying cow sounded like. "Are you still at the pool?"

"I brought Bennett and Austin home with me to get out of the sun. I didn't want them to be wiped out for the game tonight."

"You brought me home too, Mom!" That was Dane, and he didn't sound too happy about the arrangement.

"Cody and Taylor stayed at the pool. How's Paige?"

Camille stroked her daughter's corn-silk hair. "We're waiting for the nurse to come back with the results."

"So that means you're sitting down?"

"Yes." Camille's skin flushed. "Why?"

"I just talked to Jill."

"And?"

"They chose us."

"What?"

"At the meeting today. The superintendent of South Fork made the announcement. Apparently, this transfer law requires them to provide transportation to a nearby district. It's us, Camille. They're going to bus their students to Crystal Ridge."

Six

Jen felt like the Tin Man from Oz as she opened the box marked Family Pics and pulled out the framed eleven by sixteen that had hung in their old home—a photograph of the three of them, smiling together in the airport terminal. Leah had snapped it. Jen ran her thumb across her frozen smile—the Proverbs 31 woman, the one from the Bible, who laughed without fear of the future, because that future would hold her daughter.

Now here she was, sitting in that future, the makings of bruises on her legs where Jubilee kicked her, surrounded by fun-sized candy-bar wrappers and blank beige walls and boxes she didn't have the energy to unpack. She raised another 3 Musketeers in mock salute. To the mother who went to every adoption class, attended every seminar, quoted the adoption guru Karyn Purvis like a Bible scholar quoted Scripture, and possessed all the arrogance that came with too much knowledge and not a lick of experience.

She stuffed the chocolatey nougat into her mouth when a rummaging sound came from downstairs.

Jubilee was up and on the move.

With her hand against her lower back, Jen stood from her spot on the bed and made her way into the kitchen. Her daughter was standing on the counter, digging in the cupboards with a blanket wrapped around her waist.

"What are you doing?"

Jubilee turned around, a box of Cheez-Its in hand as a strong, unmistakable scent hit Jen with full force. Her sore muscles tensed. "Jubilee, did you have an accident?"

Jubilee shook her head.

Jen nodded at the blanket. "Can you take that off?"

Jubilee shook her head again. Proof that she was lying. That she had, in fact, wet her pants. The blanket might be covering the visual evidence, but it could not mask the incriminating smell. It filled the kitchen with an odor that had become all too familiar.

"You need to go upstairs, take off your shorts, and get into the bath."

"No accident!"

"You did too have an accident."

Jubilee's head shaking moved into her hands. She waved them in the air and the blanket fell away, revealing a wet stain on her shorts.

Jen took her hand and pulled her off the counter. "Come on. Let's get into the shower."

Jubilee's body slid to the floor like a rag doll.

Freaking out over needles, Jen understood. That hysteria at least made sense. This, however—wanting to sit in her own urine? Refusing to get clean? The illogicality of it had Jen's blood pressure rising. For an infinitesimal moment, she relished it. Tangible proof that she wasn't made of tin. A human heart beat inside her chest after all.

But then Jubilee began to flail and scream, and Jen's blood pressure rose to dangerous heights. She bent over to pick Jubilee up just as her daughter reared back and spit. A glob of white saliva stuck to Jen's cheek.

Sound and time froze.

Mother and daughter stared at each other in shocked, still silence.

Jen touched the sticky goo with her fingers, and something snapped—broke like the walls of a dam holding back a river of rage. Months' worth of rage. Or maybe years. It rushed out of her in a deranged wail—a scream without words that rivaled every horror film put together. And there were no watching nurses to stop her. No friendly stranger with an adorable matching daughter listening in the next room. It was just them alone in this new house with no witnesses. The blood-curdling sound rattled the walls and excoriated her throat—so frighteningly loud and long it had Jubilee ducking away, scrunching up her shoulders and covering her ears.

When it ended, Jen bellowed, "That is how *you* sound!"

She dragged Jubilee up the stairs and deposited her outside the bathroom. She glared at the little girl with snot and tears running down her face and pushed her words through clenched teeth. "Take off your clothes, and get into the bath."

Jen stalked back down the stairs, her entire body shaking as she sat on the couch, bent over her knees, and curled her hands around the back of her neck. She should go to her daughter, repair the breach her outburst had just caused.

Take Jubilee into her arms. Do what Karyn Purvis would do and rock her like a baby. But Jen was afraid she would hurt the baby. Jen was afraid she would shake it to death.

So she stayed where she was, curled into the fetal position while Jubilee cried upstairs, until the sound of a lawn mower kicked to life. Jen sat upright. It was a sound that wouldn't be so loud, except for the open window behind her.

Horror turned the lava in her blood to igneous rock.

Everything went cold and dead.

She had just thrown an adult-sized temper tantrum. Loud enough for the entire neighborhood to hear. Loud enough for the entire town of Crystal Ridge to hear. And her living room window was wide open.

•❀•❀•

By the time Nick got home from his first day of work, Jen had eaten three more fun-sized candy bars. She could practically feel the fat cells multiplying on her hips. Mercifully, the scale was packed away in one of the many scattered boxes.

As soon as he walked in the door, Jubilee catapulted herself into his arms, clinging to him like Jen clung to Leah's words on the phone. *Yelling does not make you a bad mom. It just makes you a mom who's had a bad day.* Jubilee buried her face in his neck as he walked through the living room into the kitchen, where Jen was sautéing garlic in a pat of butter—a smell that was as comforting to her as the taste of her mother's homemade mashed potatoes.

"I got four ouchies today," Jubilee said, pointing at the brightly colored Band-Aids on each of her thighs.

She also spit in mommy's face.

But Jubilee didn't mention that.

"Four ouchies? Oh man, Juju-bee. I'm so sorry." Nick kissed Jen's cheek. "That smells delicious."

"Da doctor is bad."

"The doctor is trying to make sure you stay healthy. And you know what? I'm pretty sure you won't have to get anymore ouchies for a long time." Nick looked over the top of Jubilee's head and mouthed the word, *Right?*

Jen lifted her shoulder and moved the minced garlic around in the pan, watching as the butter browned and bubbled at the edges.

Nick set Jubilee on her feet. "Why don't you get out your markers and draw me a picture of your day."

Draw him a picture of her day. What kind of a superhero dad was he? And why did Jen sometimes resent him for it?

He waited until Jubilee was gone, then snagged an apple from the bag on top of the refrigerator and passed it from one hand to the next. "What's up?"

What was up.

Oh, nothing much. She was just going crazy. That was all. In fact, today she screamed like a psychotic banshee—so loud she was probably already a scary story that the neighborhood kids would tell. *"Stay away from the Covington home. I heard there's a mean ghost lady who lives inside."* Maybe the nice man who was outside pruning his rosebushes had already called CPS and someone would show up and take Jubilee away. Maybe she wouldn't be sad if they did. It was a horrible thought. One that made her feel ungrateful and mean.

"Jen?"

She turned off the burner. The garlic stopped sizzling. "I want to go back to work."

"Okay."

But it wasn't a supportive *okay*. It was a wrinkle-your-nose, pull-back-your-chin, I-don't-think-you're-in-your-right-mind *okay*.

Well, maybe she wasn't in her right mind.

But his response still made her feel prickly. It made her feel like an agitated porcupine. "Pretty soon, Jubilee's going to be in school full time. What am I supposed to do—sit around in this house all day?"

"I'm sure you're not going to have as much time as you think."

She dumped the sautéed garlic into the pasta sauce and brought the buttery pan to the sink, where she began to scrub it with a ferocity bordering on manic.

Nick came over and shut off the faucet. "Babe, for as long as I can remember, you've wanted to stay at home. One of the reasons I took this job was so that you could stay home."

"So I'm not allowed to change my mind?"

"Of course you are. I'd just like to understand why."

She was suffocating. That was why. Today's events had turned into two hands wrapped around her throat. Yes, she had talked about this for years. Quitting her job. Staying at home to raise their children. It was everything she thought she wanted. Everything she had desperately prayed for. But now? Now the idea of being in this house, her life revolving around that particular girl while she grappled with these particular feelings, made those two hands squeeze and squeeze and squeeze until she couldn't breathe anymore.

"I'm sorry. I thought it was what I wanted, but I don't think I'm cut out for it." She wiped at her forehead with the back of her wrist, pushing aside her bangs. "And Jubilee needs to go to South Fork."

"Whoa. We should probably talk about that one a little."

"What's there to talk about? She needs to be around kids who look like her. I don't want her feeling more different than she already is." And also, Jen wanted to avoid the enthusiastic woman from the pediatrician's office from now until eternity, and she wouldn't run into her at the drop-off line in South Fork.

"I completely agree."

"Crystal Ridge is ninety-five percent white."

"I don't think it will be next year."

"What do you mean?"

"It's all anyone could talk about today at the store. I guess South Fork lost their accreditation last January, and parents have been fighting to get their kids transferred to an accredited school ever since. Today the superintendent at South Fork announced that any kids wanting to transfer would be bussed to Crystal Ridge."

"Really?"

"Really." With a gentleness that pierced her, Nick turned Jen around and pulled her into a hug. He smelled like everything good and familiar—more comforting than all the sautéed garlic and mashed potatoes in the world. "If you want to go back to work, it'll be easier if Jubilee goes to our neighborhood school."

Seven

Announcement on the Crystal Ridge district website:

> South Fork District Superintendent, Dr. Robert Joiner, announced today that South Fork will provide transportation to the Crystal Ridge Community School District for students wishing to transfer out of the South Fork District. According to state law, unaccredited districts must cover the transportation costs for students to one accredited district in the same or an adjoining county. Neither the board nor the superintendent had a role in this decision. Please note, the Crystal Ridge Board of Education has no authority to supersede a ruling of the Missouri Supreme Court.
>
> We invite you to attend a public meeting in the high school gymnasium from 6:00–7:30 p.m. on Monday, July 9. This meeting will be an open forum in which the board will answer questions and address concerns about the transfer process.

Camille scrolled down the page in search of more information, but there was nothing more to read. That was it. A short announcement and a public meeting that wasn't for another two weeks.

"Camille?" Neil popped his head into the office. "Have you seen my phone?"

It couldn't be true. South Fork couldn't just choose them without their input. There needed to be collaboration. A call for a vote. Instead, their voices had been completely erased from the equation.

"Camille?"

She blinked up at her husband.

"Austin and I should have left five minutes ago." He was looking at her like it was her fault. Like she purposefully gave Paige strep throat so she could call Neil home early from work and force him to take their son to his baseball game. And to top it off, she went and hid his phone to make the whole ordeal that much more bothersome.

"Did you check your car?"

"Yes. And the kitchen, and my briefcase, and the couch cushions . . . ," he said as he put on his watch—the sporty one she got for him last Christmas.

"Did Paige take it?" Their youngest was in the habit of snagging their phones when they weren't looking and snapping several—usually hilarious—selfies. Sometimes one turned out so impressively well that Camille would print it on a small, square canvas and hang it in the art room in the basement.

While Neil went in search of Paige, Camille rolled the chair away from the desk and went into their bedroom to help him search, her mind chewing over the announcement, disbelief morphing into outrage. As she got down on her knees to look beneath the bed, she began compiling a list in her mind of legislators and politicians she and every other concerned parent would call to let them know how absolutely unacceptable this was. She would put it together and email it out tonight.

Camille stopped her searching.

Didn't Neil have that important meeting today?

Anytime he had an important meeting, he wore a sport coat to work. His phone was probably hiding away in one of the pockets.

Sure enough, she found it in his lightweight, navy-blue sport coat. As soon as she pulled it out, it vibrated in her palm. She turned it over and saw a text message. It was a single emoji—the eye-rolling one. And it came from someone named Jas.

Jas?

Curious, she hit the message with her thumb. The text message appeared, along with the one before it and the one before that.

Hairy Gary is fighting 4 the guns.

R u serious?

As a heart attack. Pretty sure he doesn't even know the difference b/w a rifle & a shotgun.

Camille scrolled up. The messages kept loading. Loads of them. Mostly one or two liners. A couple of those supposed-to-be-funny Chuck Norris memes. One was a group picture. Camille didn't know anyone in it except Neil.

Everyone was dressed in workout clothes, smiling at the camera as they flexed their muscles in coordinating poses, her husband included.

"Paige said she never took it."

Camille quickly jabbed the Off button and spun around just as Neil came into the closet doorway.

"Any luck?"

She held up his phone with a smile. "Coat pocket."

"Oh, right." He came inside the closet and took it from her with a quick, perfunctory kiss on the cheek. "Thanks. I'll make sure to record him when he's up to bat."

Eight

"He died last night."

"That poor man," Deb said.

Rebecca Yates placed some stuffed mushrooms on her plate. At four-and-a-half months pregnant, her belly was starting to pop. "He was only fifty-four years old. He left behind three kids and eight grandkids."

The four women—all long-standing committee members for the Crystal Ridge Memorial Day 5K—exchanged pointed looks as Paige came skipping into the kitchen, Faith and Hope following after her like a pair of hungry ducklings.

"It's time to take my medicine," Paige announced, stopping in front of the refrigerator.

Camille grabbed the measuring spoon and carefully poured out the correct dosage of amoxicillin—thick and pink and smelling like bubblegum.

Paige drank it down, then licked her lips before placing the spoon into the sink. "Okay, let's go up to my room and play American Girl dolls. My Nana got me a new mermaid outfit. It would look *really* silly on Felicity. Who wants to put it on her first?"

Faith and Hope shot their hands into the air.

The ladies waited until the girls fell out of earshot before continuing the worrisome conversation.

"Patrick thinks the kid will be tried as an adult," Rebecca said, moving on to the fruit-and-cheese platter. Patrick was her husband and a police officer for the Crystal Ridge Police Department. "He's already been in on multiple counts for drug possession and vagrancy."

Rose Hawthorne—the oldest of the women and also PTA president at the high school—poured herself a glass of wine. She had two stepkids in college and a daughter going into her sophomore year at Crystal Ridge. "These are the students coming to Crystal Ridge in the fall."

Rebecca swallowed her bite of mushroom. "Not if we have anything to say about it."

"I'm not sure that we do," Deb said.

"Of course we do," Rebecca replied, her tone filled with exasperation.

It was an exasperation Camille should feel too. An exasperation she had felt as soon as she read the announcement on the website yesterday. But then she found that long text conversation on Neil's phone, and she'd been distracted ever since with a question that wouldn't stop circling her mind.

Who was Jas?

"I'm concerned about class sizes," Rose said.

"Same here." Rebecca raised her eyebrows. "I mean, what's going to happen if every single South Fork student decides to take the State of Missouri up on this law? How are we supposed to accommodate an entire district of students, especially when so many of them are failing?"

"It's a lot to ask of our teachers."

Deb slid onto one of the stools. "The more we talk about this, the more worried I get."

Was Jas short for Jason? Some buddy from Neil's CrossFit gym? They seemed to share a mutual love for hunting—a sport Camille had a hard time understanding. The whole thing was entirely too redneck for her corporate exec of a husband. Of course, she grew up in Southern California, where hunting wasn't a thing. Where people didn't have a bunch of guns in their garages. A sticking point that had caused arguments between them when they brought Taylor home from the hospital.

Camille wanted to get rid of them.

Neil had scoffed. "They're locked in a safe in the garage. You think our newborn is going to crawl inside and crack the code?"

So the guns remained—hidden away and rarely used. Between the demands of his job and three kids underfoot, life didn't afford many opportunities for hunting excursions.

Rebecca moaned. "These mushrooms are to die for. Somebody needs to stop me, or I'm going to gain sixty pounds with this baby."

"Oh, stop," Deb said. "You hardly gained any weight with Emma."

"That was eight years ago. My metabolism isn't what it was then."

Rose lifted her glass of wine. "Welcome to pregnancy in your midthirties."

A knock sounded at the door, followed by a swoosh of noise as the new arrivals removed their shoes in the foyer.

"Sorry we're late," Kathleen called, coming around the corner into the kitchen brandishing a pan of her signature Scotcheroos. "But I brought something to make up for it."

"Just what I need," Rebecca muttered.

Bennett and Cody trailed into the kitchen after their mother.

"My eldest is dying of boredom, and my middle got a new video game and is desperate for someone to play it with."

Bennett held up *Call of Duty*, a version Camille didn't recognize. "Is Austin downstairs?"

The muscles in Camille's chest went tight. She wasn't sure she wanted Austin playing something so violent, but she also wanted Bennett to want to be here, and at the moment—holding up his new game—he looked bright and excited.

Cody took off his baseball cap and ran his hand over the top of his blond hair. "I texted Taylor and asked if I could tag along with her and Alexis. She didn't seem too annoyed with me."

Camille smiled, perhaps a little indulgently. "You know you're always welcome," she said.

Taylor and Alexis shuffled into the kitchen, and Bennett disappeared into the basement with his new video game.

"Speak for yourself." Taylor grabbed Cody's hat and plopped it on her head. She looked adorable. And a little bit too . . . Victoria's Secret catalog, with her too-short shorts and her lightweight long-sleeve shirt with a wide neckline that fell over her bare shoulder.

Sex.

The word stole into Camille's mind like a thief, and for one panicked moment she wondered if Taylor was having it. She wondered if she was having it with Cody. It came so out of the blue that she wanted to laugh at the absurdity. Taylor and Cody were church kids. They went to FCA every Wednesday night. And Taylor was only sixteen. Her sixteen-year-old daughter was not having sex. For goodness' sake, she only got her period two years ago—an age not uncommon for runners but mortifying to Taylor nonetheless.

"We're going for a walk," Taylor said, heading for the door.

"Where to?" Camille asked.

"I don't know. Around."

"Do you have your phone?"

Taylor shot Camille a withering look—because of course she had her phone—then walked out into the humid evening, Alexis and Cody following.

"So what did I miss?" Kathleen set the Scotcheroos in front of Rebecca and winked. Then she turned to Camille, seemingly unfazed by the flirtatious vibe between their two teenagers or that downstairs, their two eleven-year-olds were shooting people to death in some *Call of Duty* virtual reality. But then, Kathleen had always been the more laid-back parent between the two of them. "Is next year's 5K all planned?"

"Our plans have been sidelined by the transfer news," Rose said.

"And the stabbing in South Fork."

Kathleen leaned in, her voice lowered. "I heard that it was gang related."

Camille got out a butter knife and began cutting the Scotcheroos into equal-sized squares, an image of her husband flexing for the camera with a bunch of people she didn't know stuck in her mind. Since when did her husband flex?

It was like the time they rented *Napoleon Dynamite* on DVD. Neil had laughed hysterically while she found the entire thing spectacularly stupid. Not ha-ha stupid either but legitimately dumb. She remembered looking at him and thinking: *I don't understand your sense of humor.*

She had the same alarming thought now, only bigger. Because this wasn't about Neil's sense of humor; it was about him. This stranger who texted Chuck Norris memes and poked fun of someone called Hairy Gary with a mystery friend named Jas.

"You're awfully quiet." Rose gave Camille a nudge with her hip. "Is everything okay?"

"I'm fine." She felt them all staring as she finished cutting the Scotcheroos. "I'm just concerned, like everyone else."

"You're not usually so docile when you're concerned," Kathleen teased as Rose poured her a glass of wine too. "Hey, didn't you invite that woman from the doctor's office?"

"I never heard from her," Camille said, momentarily distracted from her distraction. She'd really hoped Jen would call. The woman had seemed so reserved. Camille had a soft spot for people like that. She always wanted to pull them under her wing, coax them out of their shell. Maybe it was because they were too often mistaken for stuck-up, when usually they were just shy. Or maybe she simply liked being the person who got to talk the most in a relationship.

Whatever the case, there was a moment this afternoon when Camille considered calling Dr. Porter's office to see if they might give her Jen's number. She didn't have Jen's last name, but surely anyone would know who Camille was talking about the second she mentioned Jubilee. Camille was pretty confident nobody in Dr. Porter's office would be forgetting that patient anytime soon. And equally confident that no matter how much everyone in that office loved Camille, they wouldn't hand out patient information.

"Who's the woman from the doctor's office?" Rebecca asked.

"Someone I met in Dr. Porter's waiting room yesterday when I brought Paige in for her strep test. She just moved to town and adopted a little girl the same age as Faith and Paige."

Deb perked up. "Where from?"

"Liberia."

"*Liberia,*" Rebecca parroted. "That's in west Africa, isn't it?"

"She's only been home a couple months."

"Oh man, those early days are such a fog. I can't imagine having to move in the middle of them." Deb served herself a Scotcheroo, placing it carefully on a napkin. "I would have loved to meet her."

"Hopefully, you'll still be able to." Deb was the only other mom in the group with kids at O'Hare. The other ladies had children who went to different schools in the district. "Her daughter's going to O'Hare."

Rebecca stuck a toothpick in another mushroom and raised her eyebrows ominously. "If O'Hare has any spots left."

Nine

Ever since Anaya was a baby, Mama would take her to Auntie Trill's salon whenever it was time for another press and curl, which happened every second and fourth Saturday of the month. The two women would set their babies side by side, swapping notes on their size and their skin tone and the texture of their hair, until those two babies grew into little girls with box braids and strong opinions, jumping rope and playing hopscotch outside the front window.

When Anaya turned eleven and told ReShawn she would rather die than have her hair detangled one more time, ReShawn dared her to cut it off. Anaya, feeling brave and bold and rebellious, took Auntie Trill's clippers and, to Mama's great horror, gave herself a buzz. Had she known how mercilessly the neighborhood boys would tease her, she never would have gone through with it. But she hadn't known, and it was a good thing, too—because if she'd never gone through with it, she never would have become Auntie Trill's shampoo girl.

Every Sunday at church, while her mama was lifting her hands, asking Jesus to come and set to right all the world's wrongs, Anaya was praying that He would make her hair grow fast, just long enough to cornrow so Auntie Trill could put in crochet braids. When her prayers were finally answered, Auntie Trill struck a bargain.

I ain't doing your hair for free.

And so, Anaya agreed to work for it. At first, it started with shampooing. Auntie Trill had the unfortunate habit of scheduling three appointments at once, which meant there was usually one customer in her chair, another under the dryer, and another at the sink. Auntie Trill didn't need any hands for the woman under the dryer, but she couldn't shampoo and braid at the same time. So she taught Anaya how to shampoo, deep condition, and massage so well that the women in the chair would close their eyes and moan their approval.

Eventually the shampooing turned into answering the phone between washes, scheduling appointments, sweeping the floor, and helping walk-ins find the perfect moisturizer for their kinky 4C curls.

All for nine dollars an hour.

An amount that had ReShawn turning up her nose. To her, the salon felt like an obligation—a millstone around her neck, because Auntie Trill wasn't quiet about her desire to pass the business to her one and only daughter. The louder Auntie Trill got about it, the more ReShawn stayed away. And whenever she did come, she was always wrinkling her nose and telling her mother to stop using that tea tree oil.

To Anaya, the salon wasn't a job so much as it was . . . home. A safe haven filled with everything good and familiar, from the slow jam of old-school R&B music Auntie Trill loved to play to the burst of laughter that came whenever she or one of her customers broke out into an impromptu groove session. It was the place people went to hear the latest neighborhood news, and if you asked Anaya, tea tree oil smelled exactly like nostalgia.

She worked there in high school, she worked there through college, and she kept on working there now, while she waited for her phone to ring with news about the position at Crystal Ridge. It had been fourteen days since the interview, and Anaya's thoughts had stuck themselves on a torturous loop of vacillation. So had her prayers. She needed the job so Mama could stop working so much and resume night classes. But how could Anaya take the job?

Currently, Whitney Johnson sat in Auntie Trill's chair, wincing and grimacing because of her tender head, while Anaya used her fingertips to massage old Cynthia Martin's scalp. Cynthia sang in the choir at church. She used to slip Anaya candy from her purse with a conspiratorial wink in the lobby. She had soft hands that always smelled like Nivea Creme, and at the moment they were snapping to the slow beat of Marvin Gaye's "Let's Get It On." She was either oblivious to or pretending not to hear Auntie Trill and Whitney chattering away about the only thing the people of South Fork seemed capable of talking about these days—the uncertain future of their school district and the students who attended.

"My cousin works at the district office, and she said the place has been flooded with parents asking about the transfer ever since school let out."

"It costs money for each student who transfers. Don't these fools know where that money's coming from? Just 'cause it's free for them don't mean it's free. We gonna feed our tax dollars into a rich district that don't need any while our own schools go bankrupt, and then what?" Auntie Trill shook her head. "And all these people walking around like their prayers been answered."

Mama was one of those people.

Whitney scrunched up her eyes for a short second—another one of her winces. "Maybe a little competition is exactly what this district needs. It'll force the administration to finally get off their hind ends and do something."

"They ain't gonna be able to do nothing with all that money going out."

"Trill, parents gotta do what's best for their child." Cynthia opened her eyes just long enough to shoot Anaya an encouraging wink, because that was exactly what Anaya's mama was doing for Darius—something Mama and Auntie Trill kept arguing about.

"What's best for their child? We need to start doing what's best for the whole community, not just what's best for our own children."

Anaya picked up the bottle of deep conditioner, trying not to think about what Daddy would say if he were still alive. Of course, if Daddy were still alive, Darius never would have started hanging out with those boys; he wouldn't have needed a fresh start. If Daddy were still alive, Anaya probably wouldn't have busted her Achilles tendon and they wouldn't be under the financial strain that they were now. Nor would Mama be put in the awful position of having to choose between her son and her community. It wasn't fair. A mother shouldn't have to feel the desperation that came when her bright child was stuck in a school that offered zero college prep classes. A school that had overcrowded classrooms and underpaid teachers, many of whom were subs, because subs didn't require health insurance. A school that might as well be a pipeline to the Missouri prison system, especially for boys without fathers.

Boys like Darius.

Boys like Armand Davis, the seventeen-year-old who stabbed and killed his abuser. Of course, the media wasn't spinning it that way. They were making Armand out to be a violent thug instead of a mentally impaired kid who'd spent his whole life in and out of foster homes. A kid who needed a doctor, not a prison cell.

"Mmm-mmm, I love the smell of that conditioner," Cynthia said. "It's like being on a warm beach surrounded by sunshine and coconuts."

Anaya smiled.

"I gotta get me that shirt."

She glanced down at her T-shirt, surprised. She was wearing the black scoop-neck Darius got her for her birthday. The one that said Made in Wakanda. It had quickly become a favorite among her collection. "You're into Marvel?"

Cynthia gave her eyebrows a saucy lift. "I'm into Black Panther."

Anaya's smile cracked wide open.

"What are you two grinning about over there?" Auntie Trill asked.

"Happier things than what you two are frowning about over there," Cynthia called back.

Anaya helped Cynthia sit up. She wrapped a plastic cap over her head and brought her to one of the dryers, where she would sit so the conditioner could soak in, nice and deep. As Anaya helped the old woman get situated, Cynthia patted her hand. "What's this I been hearing about you and that young Mr. Wright getting back together?"

The words pushed Anaya off a cliff. As she fell, she smelled sweat and felt the fast pulse of dance music. She shut her eyes, blocking out the sudden, intrusive memory before it could crystallize.

"Is it true?" Cynthia asked.

"No ma'am."

"Well, that's too bad. I was hoping for more to smile about."

"They been spending a lot of time together." This came from Auntie Trill, who had snuck up behind them to help get the dryer placed just so over Cynthia's head.

"We're not spending time together. I volunteer at the youth center."

"Mm-hmm. You sure volunteer a lot."

Yes, she did, but it had nothing to do with Marcus. In fact, if there were another youth center in South Fork, she'd gladly volunteer there. But there wasn't. And her interview for Crystal Ridge made her feel like a giant sellout. When she volunteered at the youth center, she felt like less of one.

"Here's what I have to say about Marcus Wright," Whitney said. "If you don't snatch that boy back, he's gonna move on."

"And you won't hear me complain if he moves on with my ReShawn, neither. That girl needs a man who loves the Lord. Not the men she has prowling around her while she's working at the airport. I tell you what, she is on a slippery slope."

Anaya walked away from the loud dryer, away from Auntie Trill and Whitney going on about how hard it was for a black woman to find a decent man these days. She went to the front of the salon and squirted a dollop of hand sanitizer into her palm. Her hands were more than clean, but the habit had turned into a compulsion. Her phone vibrated against the front desk.

The number on the screen turned her breath shallow.

With a look over her shoulder, she slipped outside onto the sidewalk—where the salon sat between a liquor store and a gun shop that never conducted background checks.

"Hello, this is Anaya."

"Anaya, hi!" The greeting was friendly, the voice familiar.

It was Tim Kelly, calling on behalf of O'Hare Elementary.

•❛•❜•

When Anaya was little, her daddy told her a story. It was about a farmer whose horse ran away, but then it came back and brought another horse with it. All of a sudden, the farmer had two. The next day, the farmer's son tried to ride the new horse, but it bucked him off, and he broke his leg, leaving the farmer without a worker. A week later, the emperor's men came to gather every able-bodied man in the village to fight in a war. The farmer's son was spared because of his broken leg.

After every twist of events, Daddy would say, "Good news, bad news. Who's to say?"

When he finished, Anaya wanted to know if the story came from the Bible.

"No, sunshine," Daddy said. "It's from China."

After he'd kissed her on both cheeks and the tip of her nose too, she stared up at the ceiling, wondering how her daddy went and got a story all the way from the other side of the world when he'd only ever lived here in South Fork.

Now Anaya had her own version of the story.

A girl wanted to teach in South Fork, where her daddy taught because he loved his community and held the belief that when you loved something, you poured yourself into it. But South Fork didn't have the money to hire a new teacher. So the girl applied for a job at a different district—the antithesis of the community she wanted to serve—and because of a glowing letter of recommendation, she got an interview. South Fork lost their accreditation, and now the very ones the girl had always pictured herself teaching had the option of coming to her.

Good news, bad news. Who's to say?

Certainly not Anaya. She only knew that at the moment, despite everything Auntie Trill had to say this afternoon, Anaya wanted them to come. She wanted Darius and all the rest to join her so she wouldn't feel so alone.

She walked inside the house and found Mama asleep on the couch.

Anaya bent over and kissed her cheek.

Mama's eyelids fluttered and then opened. The coffee brown of her irises went soft and warm as a slow smile spread across her face. "Hey, baby doll," she said, her voice croaking like a frog.

Anaya folded her arms over the back of the couch and set her chin on her hands. "I got a call from Principal Kelly."

Mama sat up, quick as a lightning bolt. "And?"

"I got it."

"You got it?"

Anaya nodded.

Mama practically hurdled the couch. She wrapped her arms around Anaya and rocked her back and forth in an exultant dance. "Oh, thank You, Jesus. Thank You, Jesus. Thank You, Jesus."

Anaya couldn't help herself. Mama's joy was contagious. For the first time since Tim Kelly's phone call, she felt herself smile.

"It's been a rough couple of years for all of us, but the clouds are parting, and the light is starting to shine through." She grabbed Anaya by the shoulders. "My baby is gonna teach second grade at O'Hare Elementary."

"And coach the varsity track team."

Tears welled in her mother's eyes. "I know it's not what you envisioned, but it's a good way to keep doing what you love. You deserve this, baby. You've worked so hard, and your father would be proud."

The words twisted Anaya's heart.

Because Mama didn't know the whole story.

With a teary smile, she pulled Anaya into another rocking hug. And as she swayed back and forth, back and forth, the refrain played on.

Good news, bad news. Who's to say?

Ten

The small crowd of parents sat in camping chairs, clapping as Camille's son walked up to the plate. He looked skinny, and also nervous.

"Come on, Austin!" Kathleen called. "Swing hard, buddy."

It was the final game of the tournament, the bottom of the fifth. Two outs. Malone & Strut was down by one. The bases were loaded. Bennett had just had a rare strikeout and threw his bat, which nearly got him kicked out of the game. Kathleen's husband, Rick, was calming him down off to the side, and Neil was nowhere to be seen. But Camille couldn't think about that now. She couldn't think about the South Fork transfer or the strange text messages on her husband's phone. All she could think about now was her son and the way his heart was probably racing.

She fisted her hands over her knees and leaned forward. "Come on, Austin," she whispered under her breath.

Please, Lord, let him get a hit. Let him be the hero, just this once.

Austin took a few practice swings while the pitcher waited at the mound. The opposing team wore hunter green. They were sponsored by Schnucks. Austin wore red and gray. They were sponsored by Malone & Strut, a law office located on Main Street. Rick was a divorce attorney. When Camille first met him, which was several years before he made partner, she'd asked, "Why divorce?"

Rick had shrugged and said, "Job security."

"Well, you won't be getting our business," Camille had replied in a jovial tone, one that hid her underlying smugness. It was a smugness that wasn't appropriate, and neither was the joviality. Marriage wasn't a competition, and divorce wasn't funny. The job security Rick joked about wasn't a joke. It was a sad reality. The thing was, it had never touched Camille. Not personally, anyway. She came from a long line of healthy marriages. Neil wasn't so fortunate. His grandparents were divorced. Neil hardly knew his grandfather. Growing up, he couldn't spend time with his grandmother without hearing her speak bitterly about the man or his new wife. The experience made him adamantly against the whole thing.

So adamant, in fact, it was one of the first points they established after he got down on one knee and popped the question. Divorce was off the table. It simply wasn't an option.

Whatever they were going to face in their marriage, they would face together. If something so horrible came along as to require counseling, they would go to that together too. And therein lay the source of her smugness. Camille Gray's marriage had always been a given—like the sun rising in the east and setting in the west. You didn't have to fight for the sun. Nobody sat up at night worrying that it might fall off course.

Perhaps that should have been a warning.

Camille had taken her marriage for granted, and things taken for granted were all too easily neglected.

Kathleen whooped again as Austin stepped inside the box.

The pitcher wound up and let the ball go.

It flew over home plate, straight into the catcher's glove.

"Striiiike!" the umpire called, a little too enthusiastically.

Camille's heart sank. *Come on, Austin. You at least have to swing.*

"It's all right, kiddo," Rick shouted, clapping as he returned to his seat beside Kathleen. "Make sure to swing at those good ones."

The catcher threw the ball back to the pitcher, and after checking the runners at first and third, he wound up again.

This time, Austin did swing. The ball cracked off the bat and sailed into the air. Camille jumped from her seat, ready to let out an ecstatic cheer, but the ball landed just foul of the first base line. Kathleen groaned. Camille sank back into the chair—her heart thudding in her ears.

The count was now 0-2.

She clasped her hands together, her muscles coiled.

Please, Lord. Please, Lord. Please Lord . . .

The pitcher threw the ball.

Austin swung and missed.

Camille's thudding heart sank into her toes.

"Tough break," Rick said, clapping her on the shoulder as the runners on base jogged to the dugout. "At least we have one more inning to get 'em."

Yeah. One more inning.

Camille watched listlessly as the boys took their positions in the field. Bennett ran out to first, because Bennett was athletic like Cody and Dane. He usually hit doubles and triples. Kathleen and Rick didn't know what it was like to have an Austin. Sometimes *Camille* hardly knew what it was like to have an Austin. Her son alternated between right field and the bench. Right now, he was on the bench—sitting with slumped shoulders, his hat pulled low over his face.

A surge of anger broke through Camille's listlessness. Where was Neil? He promised he would be here. Austin always did better when his father came. Whatever pep talk Neil gave him before the games seemed to set at ease the worst of Austin's nerves. But he wasn't here now, and it was already the last inning.

She removed her phone from her purse and dialed his number.

For the past two weeks, they'd been like their son at the plate—a whole lot of swinging and missing, no matter how hard they tried. Miscommunication. Misreading cues. Much of it revolved around the South Fork transfer—which had Camille hard at work and Neil hardly caring. In fact, the less he seemed to care, the more riled up she got. So much so that she had contacted every legislator and administrator there was to contact—some more than once—pausing only to organize the annual Fourth of July block party.

"Hello," he answered, his voice terse.

Camille stood from her seat and walked a few paces away, where Rick and Kathleen wouldn't hear. "Where are you?"

"At work."

Really? That was it? No explanation? No apologies or excuses? "You told Austin you were going to be here at his game."

"And you told me you were going to pick up my mother for the closing."

Camille's stomach dropped to the ground, right next to her heart. She had completely forgotten. For the past several months, her mother-in-law had been living in a retirement home. It was only recently that Neil was able to convince her to put her house on the market. It sold quickly, and today Camille was supposed to drive her to the bank for the closing. Neil mentioned it a couple of nights ago, but immediately afterward Lacy Cunningham texted about O'Hare's newest hire.

Lacy had identical twin boys in Paige's grade. She avoided being a room mother but volunteered for things like classroom parties and the winter carnival. Her youngest cousin had interviewed for the second-grade position, but she didn't get the job. Someone named Anaya Jones did. Lacy had taken the whole thing rather personally.

The closing for her mother-in-law had fallen right out of Camille's mind.

Eleven

Jen rubbed shea butter between her palms, letting it soften before she slathered it on Jubilee's skin. Thirty minutes ago she'd been covered in sidewalk chalk. Now she was squeaky clean from a bath. Earlier a little neighbor girl had joined her outside. The two of them decorated the driveway with flowers and hearts and rainbows while Nick broke down boxes in the garage and Jen unpacked the last of the kitchen.

The low-key evening had been so blessedly normal. There was no spitting, no screaming, no accidents, no lying. It came as a reprieve. A much-needed reprieve—like a breath under water. Maybe Leah was right. Maybe everything was going to be okay.

"So," Jen said. "What did you and your new friend talk about?"

"She said you not real."

Jen stopped her rubbing. "What?"

"She tell me you are not my real mama."

The words filled up the space in the small bathroom, squeezing out all the air. Jen sat back on her heels, a dollop of shea butter melting in her hand. Jubilee wasn't the first kid to hear something like this. Jen had read stories from other adoptive moms online. Still, there was nothing quite like hearing it from the mouth of your own daughter.

"Why do you think she said that?" Jen asked.

Jubilee lifted her bare shoulder.

Jen came up on her knees and rubbed the shea butter there. When she finished, she held out her hand. "Touch."

Jubilee poked her knuckle.

"See. I'm real, aren't I?" The question reminded Jen of her favorite bedtime story as a child: *The Velveteen Rabbit*.

"Real isn't how you are made," said the Skin Horse. "It's a thing that happens to you."

Jubilee smiled a shy sort of smile and spread her hands wide over her belly.

When she first came home, it had been so alarmingly distended. "But I not grow in your tummy."

Right.

And that was what the little neighbor girl had meant when she used the word *real*, not understanding the implications—as if a mother were only really a mother when she conceived and carried and delivered a child. Jen must only be pretending.

Sometimes she felt like she was.

Often she had these moments where she was looking down at her life—at her interactions with Jubilee—and she would have this thought, like none of it was real. Her. Them. Here together, in Missouri. At any moment she would wake up three years younger in her bedroom in Clayton and think, *What a strange dream.*

"You're right, Jubilee. You didn't grow in my tummy."

Her shy smile turned into a frown.

"Do you know where you did grow?" Jen lifted Jubilee's chin and pressed her other hand against her own chest. "You grew right here. In my heart."

•◦•◦•

One look at the calendar and Camille's skin flushed with feverish vindication. There, on the square marked July 7, was a note about the possibility of a tournament game—should Austin's team make it that far—Paige's sleepover at Faith's house, and nothing at all about the closing.

Camille had been so bothered—so consumed with the uncharacteristic brain lapse ever since she got off the phone with Neil—that she hardly noticed when Austin's team took the lead in the bottom of the sixth, nor could she join them for a celebratory dinner at Maria's Cantina afterward. Austin went with the Malones, and Camille drove home.

And here was proof that her mistake was actually his.

He was mad at her for something that wasn't her fault.

The garage door opened.

A few seconds later, her husband walked inside with his briefcase and car keys, his suitcoat draped over one arm and his tie loosened around his neck.

Camille pointed at the calendar. "You didn't write it down."

"I didn't think I needed to. Not when I talked to you about it in person two nights ago."

"I've told you a hundred times, if something is important, it needs to be written down on the calendar. Especially right now. I have a lot going on at the moment."

"So do I. That's why I needed you to be there for my mother this afternoon. It took a half hour just to calm her down, Camille, and another two for her to ask the attorney and the Real Estate agent all of her neurotic questions."

"If it was such an inconvenience, you should have called me."

"My mother called you."

"Your mother always calls me, Neil! I have a million and one things to take care of—three of those being our children. I can't be expected to take care of her too. I'm not superwoman."

"Oh please. You love being superwoman." His words came out so contemptuously, Camille took a step back. He'd never spoken to her like that before. "You love being the one everybody needs. Well, today I needed you, Camille. Your husband. Remember me?"

"You didn't write it on the calendar."

"Never mind the calendar! I asked you for one thing—*one thing*—and you blew it off like it didn't even matter."

"I didn't blow it off. I've been taking care of our children! All day long, while you're at work or CrossFit, that's what I'm doing. Taking care of our children. And does anyone ever thank me for it? No! We have a teenage daughter who treats me like dirt. She's determined to get her license, and she's a horrible driver. And who has to do all the driving with her? Me, that's who. Because you're always at work."

"Oh, that's right. Camille the martyr."

"I am not a martyr."

"Are you kidding me? It's your second favorite role, right after superwoman."

"You're a jerk."

"Maybe I am, but at least I'm an honest one. At least I can admit to my shortcomings."

"Really? Then who's Jas?" The question tumbled out, impossible to take back. She couldn't undo it, nor could she unsee the way all the color drained from her husband's face. But now that it was out, she refused to regret it. Camille pulled back her shoulders and jutted her chin. "I saw all the text messages, and I have to say, they were awfully chummy."

"You were snooping on my phone?"

"I wasn't snooping, Neil. It was an accident. I saw them when I was helping you find your phone, so don't make this about some invasion of your privacy. Who is Jas?"

"A friend from the gym."

"A guy friend?"

Neil held up his hands and took a few disgusted steps back. "You know what? I'm done."

"You're done? What is that supposed to mean?"

"It means that right now I can't be here with you." With one final shake of his head, Neil turned around and walked out the door, leaving Camille standing there—alone and trembling.

Twelve

Neil didn't come home. Camille had lain awake, staring at the ceiling as nine turned to ten and ten turned to eleven and eleven turned to midnight. She finally fell into a fitful sleep somewhere around one, with dreams soaked in anxiety. The terrible kind, where her children were falling into alligator-infested waters and she was desperately trying to hold on to them, but there was only one of her and three of them and no matter how tightly she held on, they kept slipping out of her grip.

She woke at four-thirty with a loud, startling gasp, then lay back down as darkness turned to dawn and soft morning sunlight filtered through their bedroom windows.

It was Sunday morning. The house should be bustling with activity. Everyone should be awake, showering and getting ready for church. Instead, it was just her, alone in the cavernous house. Taylor slept over at Alexis's. Camille almost always said no when she asked, because Alexis had her own car and she didn't trust that the two wouldn't sneak out and drive somewhere in it. How did she know Alexis wasn't as horrible at driving as Taylor? And where in the world would they be off to past midnight? This time Camille surprised them both by saying yes. She could spend the night.

Then she texted Kathleen, asking if she wouldn't mind having Austin overnight as well. Kathleen, of course, said yes and wanted to know if everything was okay. Camille hadn't technically lied when she answered with a vague "mother-in-law drama." Now she lay in the king-sized bed, immobilized—as though any movement would make this whole thing more real.

Neil hadn't come home last night.

It was the first time in their twenty-one years of marriage that he hadn't come home.

It left a panicked feeling in Camille's chest.

She and her husband weren't the sort of couple who got into yelling matches. And say one did come, she never imagined they'd be the type who walked away from it.

That wasn't who they were.

Was it?

She didn't know anymore, and that—in and of itself—felt like falling into alligator-infested waters all over again. Someone had tossed her off a cliff she didn't know was there, and she was flailing in midair, trying to stop the whole thing from happening.

How couldn't she know?

This was the man she'd shared her life with for the past twenty-six years, twenty-one of them as husband and wife. They met her freshman year at Brown, in Economics 101. He was the teaching assistant and the first thing she noticed about him was his fingernails—broad and neatly trimmed and tan, like his skin. She stared at them as he handed her a syllabus, struck by the perfect, pale half moon at the bed of his thumbnail. When he passed, she stared at her own—smaller, less pronounced, but there just the same. The girl sitting next to her—the one who kept twisting the hairs in her eyebrows—had them too.

Lunula.

Camille didn't know at the time that the white half circles had a name. She only knew that she found them oddly comforting. Because in this, everyone around her was the same. And somehow that commonality made her bold decision six months earlier to attend a college so far from home less foolish.

She had no way of knowing that the TA with the broad fingernails had noticed her that first day too. That while she was wrestling with a strong and unexpected bout of homesickness, he was wrestling with his own set of nerves. Neil had never been a TA before. Back then, he wasn't yet accustomed to leading a conference room full of junior execs. Camille didn't notice any tremor of doubt or uncertainty in his voice when he asked his first question, so she had no way of knowing that when she raised her hand, it gave him a boost of confidence that set the tone for an engaged class.

It was a confidence Camille assumed came with him.

Neil Gray—a senior with a rowing scholarship—tall and lean and so much more mature than the freshman boys on her dorm-room floor. She was flattered when he asked if she'd lead an Economics 101 study group. Eager to take up the role as assistant to the assistant. And only partially surprised when at the end of the semester he asked her to dinner at an off-campus steak house. Afterward, he made her head spin with a kiss that obliterated every other kiss that came before. Only a *man* could kiss like that, and Camille had never been kissed by a man before.

Her friends teased her about their rhyming names.

"You can't marry him, Camille," Sloan had said one night as they watched *Friends* on their small, boxy television. Sloan was Camille's roommate sophomore year. She had a nose ring and wore her hair short like a pixie. "The two of you are so obnoxiously in love. Add rhyming names to that equation, and you'll become the butt of every joke."

Camille had laughed. In truth, she secretly loved that their names rhymed. She secretly loved the idea of the two of them being so obnoxiously in love—their coupledom so nauseatingly cute—that others would poke fun at them in an attempt to cover their jealousy.

Sloan would not sway her. Camille's heart was his.

And he had promised to cherish it. To love and protect it.

For the past twenty-one years, he had.

Now though, as she lay staring at sparkling dust motes in the stream of sunlight, she wondered if his promise came with an expiration date.

Who was Jas?

The question taunted her.

He never answered it. It was the question that had him throwing up his hands and walking away. It was the question that made the panicky feeling in her chest grow. It expanded like a balloon, squishing her heart to the side.

If only she could rewind time. Go back to last night and forget about what was or wasn't written on the stupid calendar. Give him a hug when he walked into the house instead of putting on her boxing gloves. Swallow her pride and apologize for forgetting.

What was that verse in Proverbs?

"A gentle answer turns away wrath."

A gentle answer would have diffused the situation. Neil would have forgiven her, and they could have joined Austin's baseball team at Maria's Cantina because Neil could never pass up their *queso*.

But she couldn't rewind time. That was one thing her superwoman self hadn't figured out. The ugly fight that ensued could not be reversed.

The only other one she could remember being as ugly came eleven years before, when Austin was a baby with colic. Camille would be up in the middle of the night, rocking him—wanting to shake him—letting Neil sleep because he had to be at work the next morning, all the while silently resenting her husband. Until one day, all that resentment exploded—word vomit and emotional bile all over her shocked, clueless, could-sleep-like-the-dead husband who wasn't even aware that Austin had been waking up in the night. He wasn't aware because she never told him. She never asked him for help. But she shouldn't have to ask, should she? Neil should know that their firstborn was the exception, not the rule. Babies didn't typically sleep through the night. Neil should know that she was exhausted.

She had expected him to be a mind reader, a task every bit as impossible as superwoman.

Maybe Neil was right. She was a martyr.

Camille rolled over and placed her hand on the smooth, unrumpled comforter on Neil's side of the bed.

Where had he slept last night?

The question turned her insides to stone.

A rumbling sound interrupted the dark turn of her thoughts. It was the garage door.

Camille bolted upright so fast her head spun. She threw the comforter off her legs and shoved her arms into her robe, using the sleeves to swipe beneath her eyes so she didn't look like a raccoon.

She walked into the kitchen just as Neil walked in, his short, thinning hair disheveled. His eyes bloodshot. The sleeves of his dress shirt rolled up his forearms. His tie missing altogether.

"Where were you?" she asked.

"The office."

"All night?"

He didn't answer. He shuffled into the living room and took a seat on the edge of the couch.

Camille crept after him, unsure what to say. Afraid to make much noise as he buried his face in his hands and rubbed at his eyes. When he looked up, she was sure he was going to apologize. He shouldn't have left. It was a horrible thing to do.

But that wasn't what he said.

"I'm not happy."

All the breath rushed out of her in a whoosh, as if Neil had punched her in the gut when she wasn't looking.

He wasn't happy.

He dragged his hand down his face—his palm scratching like Velcro against day-old whiskers that weren't usually there. "I haven't been happy for a while."

"Okay." It was a breathless word, because Camille wasn't breathing.

"I think I need some time. Some space."

Time.

Space.

He was saying these things—using these words—without meeting her eye. He poured them all on the floor.

"Neil."

He looked up at her then, with familiar hazel eyes.

"Are you cheating on me?" She waited and watched. Camille had an odd sixth sense about the truth. Her two younger sisters called her the human lie detector. It was a sixth sense that came in handy with a teenager in the house. She wasn't sure how she did it; she just did. When it came to people she knew, she could always tell when they were lying.

But as Neil looked her in the face and said, "No, of course not," Camille had no idea at all if he was telling the truth.

•◦•◦•

Neil turned her into a liar. When her kids came home on Sunday and asked where their father was, she looked them straight in the eye and said he had to go on a last-minute business trip. Then she locked herself in the bathroom and hyperventilated.

She almost called Kathleen. She needed to talk to someone. She needed to tell a friend that she couldn't breathe. That she'd been thrown into the middle of *The Twilight Zone*.

What was going on? How could he just leave?

This was silly. Couples fought all the time. He didn't have to leave over it. And what about all those things he used to say about divorce? Was it still off the table? She had no idea. He told her he wasn't happy and then asked for something as elusive and intangible as space and time.

What did that even mean? What did he need space from? Her, or the children too?

The whole thing left Camille alternating between fury and desperation. When the latter hit, she would pace around her bedroom with the phone, wondering if she should call him, beg him to come back. But then the fury would come, and she'd slam down the phone because—forget him. He was the liar. He was a selfish jerk. He wanted time and space? Well, he could have it. He could have all of it in the world. And when he snapped out of it and realized what he'd done and came crawling for forgiveness, she would watch with icy indifference. She would make him feel all the misery and distress she was currently feeling.

The anxiety of it all drove her to WebMD, where she concluded that Neil had a brain tumor. Her uncle Gordon died of a brain tumor when he was fifty-four, and the last year of his life, he hadn't been himself at all. It was the hardest part of his death—the tumor in his brain stole Gordon's identity. Her husband must have a brain tumor, and she was sitting there at her computer when she should be taking him to an oncologist and demanding an MRI.

That was when she would pull up his number on her phone and start pacing again.

Call him, you idiot. Call him before it's too late.

But what if she did and *Jas* answered?

He never said whether *Jas* was a woman or not, but she had to be. Otherwise, he would have answered the question. Now every time Camille closed her eyes, she pictured them together.

It made her nauseous.

It made her insane.

And she had to hide it all beneath a smile for the sake of her children.

The whole thing was an out-of-body experience. Watching herself chase after Taylor, who almost left this morning for cross-country without a water bottle. Watching herself answer text messages about tonight's public meeting at the high school. Watching herself drive Paige to swimming lessons. Watching herself sit beside Austin on a bench in the shade while he explained scientific laws as his sister worked on her backstroke in the pool. Last week he'd swapped his Bermuda Triangle book for one about Isaac Newton.

"That means that an object in space could go forever and ever and ever, without stopping, because there's no gravity to act against it."

"What about when it reaches the end of the universe?" she heard herself ask.

"The universe doesn't end, Mom. It's expanding."

"Into what?"

Austin shrugged and then shut the book. "When's Dad getting back?"

The panic hit so hard then, she nearly gasped out loud at the uncertainty of it all. The unknown. She was the object floating in space, untethered by the one thing she'd counted on as surely as she counted on gravity.

Her husband being there.

Thirteen

Kathleen gave Camille a wide-eyed, slightly accusatory look as she moved closer, squeezing past a row of knees. The gymnasium was packed with bodies and simmering like a pot about to boil. It was hot and cramped, and Camille felt light-headed. She'd never suffered from claustrophobia before, but at the moment everything seemed to spin and shrink at the same time.

"Where have you been?" Kathleen asked.

"Fighting with Taylor. She wanted to come, but I needed her to stay home to watch Paige." Camille took the empty foldout chair Kathleen had saved for her. They'd been set in rows on the gym floor—extra seats in addition to the bleachers.

"All the legislators are here."

Up front, the Crystal Ridge School Board sat at a long table, each member with a separate microphone and an identifying placard. The board president, Keith Staley—a hefty man with sweat marks already under his arms—nervously pulled at the whiskers in his goatee while Kathleen's second cousin, Jill Yvech, stared icily at the men in suits lining the front row.

"Jill said they wanted to share the floor tonight, but the board won't let them."

"Why not?"

"Because everyone is livid, and the board wants someone to wag a finger at. Rick says it's like a nasty divorce and we're the poor children stuck in the middle. That's why he's not here. He deals with enough drama in his day job. He didn't have the energy for more. All he cares about anyway is football, and we're pretty sure Cody's spot is secure. Where's Neil? Is he working late again?"

The question incapacitated her.

Because she didn't know.

She had no idea if Neil was working.

She had no idea where Neil was at all.

He left. He just left.

"Camille?" Kathleen leaned away from her, her brow knitted together in appalling concern, as though Camille might at any second throw up all over the gym floor. "Is everything okay?"

Neil left me.

The words stuck in her throat, impossible to say out loud. They didn't belong to her. She wasn't someone who got left by her husband. That was Let-Herself-Go Lorraine, who lived off a diet of fast food and wore the same three baggy shirts on repeat, one of which had a hole in the armpit.

Or Drama Queen Connie, who was so mortifyingly honest about her marital problems on Facebook it made everyone uncomfortable. It made everyone want to look away. Only they couldn't because Drama Queen Connie was a train wreck. Nobody had been surprised when she announced that her "loser of a husband walked out and was refusing to pay alimony."

Camille wasn't like that.

She did Pilates at the YMCA two times a week. She was surprisingly good at Zumba. None of her clothes had holes in them, and the only things she posted on Facebook were cute pictures of her children.

And still . . .

Neil left.

What was she going to tell the children? Everything inside her froze into sharp ice at the thought. Paige would cry and cry and cry, and Austin would bury himself in violent video games like *Call of Duty* and become a terrorist, and Taylor would find a way to blame Camille. She would act out. Maybe she'd start having sex. She'd get pregnant and wouldn't be able to run track in college, and somehow she'd blame Camille for that too. Only it wasn't Camille's fault.

All she'd done was forget to pick up her mother-in-law.

Neil, on the other hand, was most likely having an affair. It was the only explanation. Men didn't leave for something so arbitrary as happiness, did they? She was sure men didn't care about happiness unless they found someone who made them extraordinarily happy.

But that couldn't be it either. Neil wasn't a cheater. And if he were, it was further proof that he had a brain tumor. For crying out loud, his conscience suffered whenever Camille sampled a grape in the produce aisle. How would it survive an affair? She imagined him kissing another woman in the way he used to kiss her. How long since he'd kissed her like that?

Kathleen snapped her fingers in Camille's face.

Camille blinked.

"What's going on with you?"

"Sorry," she said, giving her head a little shake. "I have a terrible headache."

It was true. She did. The kind of splitting headache she got whenever she tried quitting coffee. But she'd had her two cups this morning, so maybe *she* was the one with the brain tumor. Maybe she would die and Neil would be free to marry his gal-pal from CrossFit. Some woman called Jas would take Camille's place. She and Neil would move the gun safe into the house, and then she would teach all Camille's children how to hunt.

"Well, take some Advil and snap out of it. This is too important for headaches."

Kathleen was right.

This was vitally important.

Her children didn't know it yet, but their father had ripped their entire world out from under them. She couldn't let their education be ripped out from under them too.

Not if she could help it.

Fourteen

They were running late. Mama had to stay past the end of her shift because two of her coworkers didn't show. By the time she rushed home, she had no time to shower. Now she was self-consciously patting her hair, positive it smelled like hospital cafeteria food, as the two of them made their way down the hall, toward the distinct sound of booing.

Anaya's skin prickled.

A stack of pamphlets was scattered across a table outside the gymnasium. She snagged one and slid past two different cameramen, and all their gear, clogging the doorway.

The gymnasium was packed. Every seat was taken. Fifteen minutes past six, and the atmosphere was heated—like a teakettle about to whistle.

"Just to be clear," a large man sitting at a long table with several others said into his microphone. The placard in front of him read Keith Staley. "This will not happen at the expense of our tax dollars. The South Fork district must pay tuition for every student who chooses to transfer. We will receive that tuition on a monthly basis."

"What happens if South Fork doesn't pay?" someone shouted.

"We have been assured that if that were to happen, their government aid would come to us."

Several cries came from the crowd—too indecipherable to address. Anaya and her mother stood off to the side, squeezing next to the overflow of attendees.

"Next speaker, please," Keith said.

A woman in a purple Crystal Ridge Wildcats Wrestling T-shirt standing at the front of a long, single-file line moved up to the microphone. "My name is Diane Greer, and I'm head of the high school booster club. I'm wondering if South Fork students will be playing on our sports teams."

"South Fork students will become Crystal Ridge students, and as such, they will have all the same opportunities every other student has."

Several objections bubbled up from the crowd. Then someone commented that maybe the football team would finally win some games this year, and the objections turned into laughter.

It made Anaya want to take Mama's hand and walk away. But Mama had planted her feet and stared intently at the line of people waiting to speak. Instead of becoming shorter, it grew in size as one after another stepped up to the microphone. They had questions about class sizes and additional support staff and special education. Test scores and whether or not the incoming students would put Crystal Ridge's accreditation at risk.

When Keith Staley explained that class size would be set at the recommended desirable levels—and once capacity was reached, Crystal Ridge would not be required to take any more transfers—someone from the crowd yelled, "Then lower the capacity!"

Mr. Staley either didn't hear or pretended not to.

Anaya removed the small bottle of hand sanitizer from her purse and rubbed the gel into her hands. She imagined her skin thick, impenetrable. She imagined the angry words bouncing off her. She told herself they weren't about Darius. Because if these people knew Darius, they would want him to be a part of their school. And not just because he was good at football, but because he was funny and smart and kind.

An auburn-haired waif of a lady introduced herself as Rebecca Yates. She had two children at Truman Elementary and, as she put it, an unexpected surprise on the way. She smoothed her hand over her shirt, revealing a small round bump where a flat stomach should have been. "In August, I'm going to send two of my children to you, and I have to say, I'm very concerned about their safety. My husband is a police officer. He's well acquainted with the crime rate in South Fork. Only two weeks ago there was a fatal stabbing. And if that were the only thing, then okay. But that isn't the only thing. We aren't talking about a bunch of kids with poor grades. We are talking about a pattern of violence, and as parents we'd be foolish not to be concerned about that."

The crowd began to cheer.

It seemed to embolden Rebecca Yates. "I want to know what the safety plan is going to be when school starts in August. I want to know if there're going to be metal detectors installed. I want to know if the behavioral records of each South Fork student are coming with them, just like their medical records are coming with them."

The cheering grew louder.

Anaya and Mama exchanged a look.

What would they say about Darius's behavioral record? Would anyone see past it? Would they understand that a record was just a record? It came without context, without explanation. It didn't say anything about the fact that Darius had recently lost his father. That he'd been hurting and upset and impulsively young. A record wasn't a person. Darius's record was not Darius.

Anaya closed her eyes.

Her skin was thick. Her skin was impenetrable. These people could not hurt her. These people did not know her. These people were going to send their children to her.

"We ought to be able to send our children to school without worrying that they will be shot or stabbed or offered drugs!" Rebecca shouted over the roaring approval, her face red and impassioned. "I'd like to know what your plans are to protect them from that!"

Anaya felt sick to her stomach.

She wasn't naive. She'd known there would be concerns and pushback. But this? She and her mother had come expecting an angry house cat and instead found themselves inside a cage with a hungry tiger. The crowd turned into a living creature—one that grew an extra hissing head every time Keith Staley attempted to cut the other one off.

They demanded a special session be called with the governor.

They refused to be the Band-Aid for South Fork's problem.

Over and over again the message was overwhelmingly and painfully clear. *They* were not welcome. *They* needed to stay where they belonged.

Anaya's ankle throbbed, and her heart too. As thick and impenetrable as she imagined her skin to be, at the end of the day, it was still flesh. And flesh had this terrible way of bleeding.

A woman with long blond hair and sun-kissed skin stepped up to the microphone. She wore the kind of outfit that looked expensive and fashionably casual. "Hello, everyone," she said. "I'm Camille Gray. I have three children in the district. A student athlete who's going to be a junior, a son going into sixth grade at the middle school, and my youngest will be in second at O'Hare."

Anaya could feel Mama's glance.

Second grade at O'Hare.

"I'm part of the PTA, as well as president of the Crystal Ridge Memorial Day 5K committee. I love this community, and as someone who loves this community, I'd like to address the mother who spoke in the beginning—the one who brought up race. I think I speak for everyone here when I say that if these students were all white with the exact same records and challenges, we'd be every bit as concerned."

The crowd began to clap. A few people whistled.

"I don't care about skin color. I don't even *see* skin color. This isn't about race."

"It's about trash!"

The anonymous male shout from the crowd came like the slice of a knife. The sharp sting made her wince.

Camille Gray lifted her chin and kept on going. "This is about commitment to education and a drastic difference in values. Just look at the statistics. Sixty-three percent of their seniors didn't graduate last year. Very few parents volunteer in their schools. I'm sorry for the condition of the South Fork District. I truly am. But I think we'd be foolish to think that mentality won't make an impact here."

The clapping escalated.

Anaya wanted to plug her ears.

She wanted to shield her mother from all of it—her strong, resilient mother, who worked two jobs and came home bone weary but still made time to fight for her children. Who refused to let Anaya drop out of college last year when she lost her track scholarship. She didn't have the luxury to shop around for a district, and she couldn't come into the class to volunteer. She was too busy making sure her children had a roof over their heads and food on the table.

How could anyone look at her life and dare accuse her of not valuing education? She loved her children—wanted what was best for her children—as much as, if not more than, every other mother in this gymnasium.

And the students who were going to get on a bus at six in the morning for the sake of a better opportunity were absolutely committed to their education. They weren't part of the small percentage that gave South Fork a bad name.

Crystal Ridge was going to get many of South Fork's top students—another reason Auntie Trill hated the transfer.

"I know this has been an emotional evening," Camille Gray continued. "Many of us are upset. But that's only because we didn't have a say in this decision. No one ever asked how we felt about this. Don't we live in a democracy? We should get to vote. We voted for all of you." She motioned to the row of legislators dressed in suits. "Why didn't we get a chance to vote for this?

"A lot of people are talking about doing the right thing, which is easy to say. But what about all the decisions and choices that led up to South Fork losing their accreditation?" She turned to the approving crowd and the cameramen standing inside the doors. "This isn't our mess to clean."

Fifteen

Anaya and her mother drove home in a silence heavier than the moon. The meeting scheduled for an hour and a half had gone way past, but Mama and Anaya couldn't find a way to leave. It was as if they were incapable of moving. Paralyzed. So they just stood there and listened. Afterward, a woman from Crystal Ridge had come up to them and apologized. She was shaking and appalled. But by then Anaya had gone numb. She couldn't even remember the woman's name now.

When they stepped inside the living room at half past nine, they found Granny asleep on the couch and the local news playing on the television. A sound bite from the Crystal Ridge gymnasium played inside their living room.

"Turn it off," Mama said, her voice quivering. "I don't want Darius to hear any of it."

Anaya jabbed the power button.

The house went quiet. There was nothing but the heavy breathing of her great-grandmother.

"I'll get her to bed," Anaya said. "You go on to sleep, Mama."

Mama didn't object. Maybe because she had to be up in four short hours. Or maybe because tonight had zapped all her energy. She squeezed Anaya's elbow and walked away like a soldier weary from battle, like the things said in that gym had sunk deep into her bones, making her whole body sag.

Anaya lifted Granny to her feet. She wound the old woman's arm around her shoulder, wrapped her own arm around Granny's thin waist, and walked her to her room. She was light and frail, yet even as Anaya bore her weight, her grandmother had an unmistakable strength.

The kind carved from a life of adversity.

Granny was six months old when the stock market crashed in 1929. She was raised in the Great Depression, a daughter of a hardworking sharecropper. As a little girl, she sat at the feet of her great-grandmama Hettie Horton—a freed slave from Jackson, Mississippi—absorbing stories she would one day pass on to Anaya.

The mattress creaked as she tucked that strong-as-steel woman into bed and kissed her forehead.

According to Hettie, when her father got free at the end of the Civil War, he was promised forty acres of land and a mule—restitution for centuries of abuse. But President Andrew Johnson didn't follow through on his promise. He returned all the land under federal control to its previous owners—the very enslavers who scarred the back of Hettie's father.

And what did the government do?

With the southern economy in shards, state governments enacted strict codes to ensure free labor would continue. They arrested newly freed slaves by the droves for things like vagrancy and loitering—Hettie's father included. But where was he supposed to go—a displaced man with a daughter and nothing to his name? He was labeled a criminal, and as such the thirteenth amendment no longer applied. Convict leasing became the new order of the day, and the powers that be did what they could to criminalize the formerly enslaved. They put them in jail. They put them back in chains. All the while propagating the same mentality Camille Gray spoke tonight.

This isn't our mess to clean.

In one fell swoop, they washed their hands of all culpability. They acquired amnesia, as though the past never happened. Meanwhile, their willful blindness ensured the problems would continue into perpetuity.

It's about trash!

Anaya's arms trembled.

Nobody booed the man who shouted it. Nobody objected at all. She was trash. Latrell and Darnell next door were trash. Little Abeo. All the kids who came to the youth center. Her brother, Darius.

Trash.

This was what the world told them. Maybe not with words as bold as that man's, but the message was the same. In every media outlet. In all that was missing from the history books. Every time another school district like South Fork failed, with run-down facilities and too-crowded classrooms, brimming with students the same color as Anaya. The same color Camille Gray insisted she did not see.

All of it sent the same message.

This is what you are worth.

Too many believed it.

And Anaya hated them. In that moment, as she stood inside Granny's room, she hated every person in that gym with a hatred so visceral it made her body quake. She should ask for forgiveness. Get down on her knees and repent. Add her hatred to the list of things she'd already repented of, the list of things she continued to repent of.

But all of it stuck in her throat like bile.

There was a picture frame on Granny's dresser—a photograph of her daddy's father. Granny's only son. Marching in a line, holding a sign that said I Am a Man, with his head held high as a crowd of angry onlookers jeered, livid that he had the audacity to say he was human.

As Anaya shut off Granny's light, she couldn't help but wonder about those jeering people. She knew what happened to her grandfather and Granny. Many of the men in that line—her grandfather's friends—were still alive today. So what about the angry onlookers? Where did they go?

Across the hall, Mama knelt on the floor with her hands clasped on her bed and her head bowed in prayer.

The bile in Anaya's throat turned into a hard lump.

It's about trash!

She wondered if the refrain was echoing through her mother's prayers like it was echoing through Anaya.

●❀●❀●

Jen's phone buzzed with a message from Nick: That was unbelievable.

Uh-oh, Jen typed back.

When it came to Nick, *unbelievable* was never a good thing. He only ever used that word when something was unbelievably bad.

On my way home now, came his response.

Jubilee was already in bed. Jen had to lie with her for forty-five minutes before she fell asleep. When her breathing finally turned deep and rhythmic, Jen tiptoed away, wincing every time a floorboard creaked. The first month home, Jubilee would startle at the slightest sound. She refused to stay in her bedroom alone. So Jen and Nick took turns sleeping on the trundle they would pull out from under Jubilee's daybed. Thankfully, Jubilee hadn't woken up tonight.

Jen came downstairs to tackle the massive pile of laundry that kept expanding on their basement floor. She sat cross-legged with the news on, her phone beside her, trying to find matching socks, when the word *transfer* caught her ear. She picked up the remote and pointed it at the television, upping the volume.

A female reporter with Channel 6 News stood outside in the dark while people filed out of the high school gymnasium behind her. "It was a packed house tonight here at Crystal Ridge High, at a meeting that went an hour longer than planned. And one thing was very clear. Emotions were running high."

Several clips played on the screen—making a montage that was indeed *unbelievable*—before cutting back to the newsroom. "Citizens aren't the only ones in disagreement about the transfer law," the news anchor said. "Here's a closer look at what some of our decision makers have to say."

The same reporter stood outside again, this time in the daylight, speaking with a man who bore a resemblance to Barack Obama. According to the bar stretching across the bottom of the screen, his name was Dan Green, and he was the vice president of Missouri's Board of Education.

"Do you think the concern is over a flood of students coming in, or do you think it's more about the fact that these are low-income, black kids coming into a mostly white district?" the reporter asked.

Green arched a brow. "Melissa . . . I don't think you need to be Sherlock Holmes to figure this out. All the pieces create a telling picture."

The screen panned to a quick shot of a run-down school building. Several cars whooshed past while students—almost all of them black—got on and off a cluster of yellow buses. Then it cut to a different man, also in a business suit. Apparently, he was Jen's state representative. He stood with his hands in his pockets, squinting against the sun. "Anybody who makes this about race is intellectually lazy."

PART II

Newton's Second Law: Force equals mass times acceleration. (In other words: The bigger something is, the harder it is to move.)

On November 14, 1960, six-year-old Ruby Bridges became the first black child in the South to attend an all-white school. She was escorted to the doors by federal marshals and would become the public face of desegregation.

As soon as Bridges entered, white parents pulled their children out. They refused to send them to a school where a black child was enrolled.

Sixteen

August: Ten Months Until the Color Run

Camille: Hi, ladies. I'm sorry to bail last minute, but something came up and I can't make it tonight. I talked with Kathleen. She said she can host the meeting at her house. She has the list of sponsors from last year.

●❦●❀●

Color Run Meeting:

Rose: I can't believe she canceled. She never misses these meetings.
Deb: I think it's Paige. She had a meltdown at the park this morning. All because the strap of her sandal broke. I've never seen her so upset in my life.
Rebecca: You know she wasn't upset about the sandal.
Kathleen: Cody says Taylor hasn't been herself.
Deb: Those poor kids.
Rose: Divorce is horrible. I remember thinking how much easier it would have been if Tony would have died instead. And I didn't even have kids back then.
Deb: Do you really think they're getting a divorce?
Rebecca: Patrick saw him at the Coffee Hound with another woman.
Rose: What?
Rebecca: He said she was very exotic looking and in her *midtwenties.*
Kathleen: I could kill him.
Deb: I don't understand. I thought they were happy.
Rebecca: He's obviously cheating. Men don't walk out unless they're cheating.
Rose: Does Camille know?

Rebecca: I'm not going to tell her.

Rose: Well, someone should. She deserves to know if her husband is having an affair.

Deb: Do you think he's going through a midlife crisis?

Rebecca: My uncle went through one of those. He sold the house, and my aunt didn't even know about it. Moved to Australia. Started highlighting his hair.

Kathleen: I seriously want to murder him.

Deb: I think we should start a prayer chain.

Kathleen: She hasn't been going to church.

●●●●●

A feeling of accomplishment blossomed in Jen's chest. All because she ate the leftovers. She wasn't being wasteful. She finished all the pasta in the refrigerator.

Well done, you.

She turned on the faucet and began rinsing the bowls in the sink, the phone pressed against her ear. "Nick and I went to talk to Principal Kelly yesterday to see if Jubilee could be in her class."

"And?" Leah said.

"He didn't look at us like we were crazy when we explained to him why it was important."

"That sounds promising."

"On our way out, we ran into that woman. The one I met at our new pediatrician's office. We have a playdate tomorrow at some new splash pad downtown."

"That's great, right? You need to get out. Make some friends. I'm sure once you do, you'll start feeling more like yourself."

More like myself.

She wasn't sure who that was anymore or that making friends had anything to do with it. She looked out into the backyard, where Jubilee sat beneath a bush, digging in the dirt. She would probably get a tick. They were awful this summer. One would crawl into her hair—which was so thick that finding her scalp was nearly impossible. It would latch on, unnoticed, for who knows how long, gorge on her blood, and balloon into the size of a grape.

The thought made her shudder.

She should call Jubilee out from under there, but Jen couldn't bring herself to do it. She didn't want to risk distracting her. Not when she was finally entertaining herself.

Jen sighed. "Nick isn't sure about her."

"Why not?"

"Because of that town meeting last month. He was appalled by the whole thing. She was one of the people who was very . . . *opposed* to the South Fork transfer."

"Oh."

Camille Gray had been quoted in several news articles, one titled "Racism: Alive and Well in Midwest Suburbia." It seemed to level the playing field between them. Jen's daughter threw a massive, raging fit at the doctor's office. Camille Gray had been accused of racism. When they ran into each other yesterday, there was a brief moment wherein Camille looked as embarrassed to see Jen as Jen was to see her. It was a brief moment that had Jen experiencing an acute bout of pity for the woman. So much so, it was Jen who brought up the playdate.

She shut off the faucet and shook the water from her hands.

She could hear Lila laughing in the background. The dog barking. His name was Kenan. Leah and PJ were Tar Heel alumni and big-time fanatics. They even named their sheltipoo after the Tar Heel football stadium.

"I miss y'all," Jen said.

"We miss you too."

Seventeen

Kids squealed and ran around in swimsuits and swim trunks, dodging the water as it shot every which way. Jubilee stayed close by Jen's side. She held tightly to her hand as they made their way to an open picnic table. As soon as they found one, Paige dropped her emoji-themed beach towel on the bench and dashed toward the fun.

"Stop!" Camille called after her.

The little girl froze midstride, then reluctantly turned around and came back. Camille dug inside her large beach bag for sunblock and made quick work of spraying her down.

"Don't forget," Jen heard Camille mutter under her breath. "We came with a friend."

This elicited a sigh so heavy, Paige's shoulders lifted and fell in an exaggerated heave. Then she turned to Jubilee and, with a look of such long suffering, asked if she wanted to go run in the water together.

Jen's stomach tightened with uncertainty.

This was quite possibly a horrible idea.

But Jubilee nodded shyly, and together the two girls ran through the maze of laughing children, beneath the canopy of a giant red-and-blue polka-dotted mushroom, a wall of crystal-clear water enveloping them.

Jen smiled at Camille—hoping it didn't look awkward on her face. Leah said she needed to make a friend. She needed to stop hiding away in her house. Nobody remembered or cared that she had screamed like a banshee. *They probably thought it was the TV,* Leah had said, clearly not understanding how loud and psychotically Jen had screamed. She'd been avoiding her neighbors ever since—a hard task as the ones across the street were almost always outside working on their lawn. But Camille wasn't her neighbor, and friends did things like smile, so that's what Jen did as she sat at the table beneath the shade of an umbrella.

"This is nice," she said.

"Isn't it? I've been pestering the city to put one in for years. It's much safer than a swimming pool and half the upkeep. They finally listened and had it installed this spring." She lifted her hand and waved at someone on the other side of the large nonslip play area; then she turned to Jen with slightly pink cheeks and intense focus—as though whatever they were about to discuss was imperative. "So, how are you settling in?"

"Pretty good. We have everything unpacked, anyway."

"Good for you."

Jen attempted another smile.

"You certainly came at an unusual time. I hope you're not getting the wrong impression about Crystal Ridge." Camille wore oversized sunglasses, which made reading her expression difficult. But it seemed to Jen that she was looking at her in a beseeching sort of way. As though Jen's opinion meant more than it should. "We're usually drama-free. I really hate that the media is making this school issue about race. The media is always making things about race these days."

"I haven't really been following the news too closely," Jen said.

"Good. None of it's true. I mean, Paige's best friend is from China. And there are minorities who go to Crystal Ridge. They have the same concerns the rest of us have. This has absolutely nothing to do with anyone's race."

Jen wasn't sure what to say.

"So . . ." Camille straightened, keeping a close watch on her daughter as Paige hopped around from one sprinkler to the next, pointing to where Jubilee should hop too. "Is Jubilee all ready for school?"

"I think so. We got everything on the supply list at least."

"That supply list. Ugh. It's a bear, isn't it?"

"I had to go to three different stores to get it all. And I think I'm going to have to get a part-time job to cover the expense."

Camille smiled. It was a bright, dazzling smile that showed off straight white teeth. The kind that made Jen feel charming and funny. "Do you work?" Camille asked.

"Not right now. I just got my nursing license to practice in Missouri. I'm hoping to find something."

"A nurse. How wonderful. Have you ever thought of working at a school?"

"I . . . well, no, I guess I haven't." She was a pediatric nurse back in North

Carolina, before Jubilee came home. She worked in an office much like Dr. Porter's, and never—in all her years—had she encountered a patient as violently opposed to shots as her daughter.

"Would you like to?"

"Do you know of a job opening?"

"Yes, I do! The nurse at the high school is expecting. She's due at the end of this month, and I know for a fact they haven't found a long-term sub to replace her yet. I don't think she's going to come back, either. I have a feeling she's gonna want to stay home and snuggle that baby."

A cold feeling hugged Jen's chest.

Snuggle that baby.

Hadn't that been Jen's plan for so long? But then, her baby was seven years old. She still wet her pants and talked so incredibly loud at early hours in the morning that it left Jen grinding her teeth.

"I'd be happy to put in a word for you. It'd be perfect, really. You'd have the same schedule as Jubilee. Summers off. Winter break. Spring break. Do you want me to say something to the principal? I don't mean to brag, but I do have a good amount of clout."

"Um . . . sure."

Camille flashed another one of those dazzling smiles, then returned her attention to the chaos of running, squealing children. "Oh dear. My little CEO."

Jen followed the direction of Camille's gaze, where Paige had pulled Jubilee into the grass and was leading her through a series of dance moves.

"I apologize in advance. She can be quite bossy."

"They seem like they're having fun."

"Paige went to Camp Broadway last week. It's through a theater company here in town. They did the whole bit—singing, dancing, acting. Between you and me, I think her personality is more suited for directing."

Off in the distance, Paige modeled for Jubilee how to do a Charleston-esque kicking maneuver. Jubilee tried to mimic it and toppled over. After a few more failed attempts, Paige threw up her hands and marched over to the table.

"Can we go to the park?" she asked.

"No, sweetheart. We didn't come here to play at the park. We came to play in the water with our new friend."

"But I already talked to Jubilee, and she wants to go to the park too."

Camille tipped her glasses down her nose and instigated some sort of unspoken staring contest, wherein Paige narrowed her eyes but cracked first.

"That's what I thought," Camille said. "Now go play."

She spun around and marched back to the big mushroom.

Jubilee was still standing in the grass.

"That was impressive," Jen said.

"I can always tell when someone is lying. It's one of my secret talents." Her face fell when she spoke the words—like a rope losing slack. Or a deflated balloon. It left Jen experiencing another one of those odd acute bouts of pity.

"If you want to lend that talent my way, I'd gladly take it."

Camille turned and looked at her.

"Jubilee struggles with lying. We're never really sure how to handle it. If you have any advice, I'm all ears."

This seemed to be the right thing to say, because Camille Gray came back to life.

•❖₂❖•

Nick: How'd the playdate go?
Jen: Good. The girls really seemed to hit it off.

•❖₂❖•

"See, honey?" Camille said, in a voice that was probably too encouraging. "That was fun with Jubilee, wasn't it?"

She adjusted the rearview mirror so she could get a good look at her daughter.

Paige wrinkled her nose. "Her hair smells funny."

Eighteen

Darius dipped his head and took in the meticulous lawn, the colorful flower bed, the clean brick of the building, the shiny new playground with an expansive field, tennis courts, a baseball diamond. He let out a low whistle. "We're not in Kansas anymore, Dorothy."

"What does that make you," Anaya said. "Toto?"

"Nah, I'm the Lion. After he got his courage."

"You didn't have courage when the flying monkeys came on the screen. If I remember right, you wet yourself the first time you saw 'em."

"Look. Those things were not monkeys. They were . . . blue-faced, red-lipped, creepy little winged . . . humanoids." Darius shuddered. "They still give me nightmares."

Anaya shook her head and pulled into a parking space.

Darius grinned at her. He had the kind of contagious smile that made everyone around him smile too. Even if they didn't feel like it. Even if their stomachs were churning with nerves. "What am I supposed to do with the box?"

"Untie it and carry it in."

She grabbed a plastic bag from the backseat. There were eight rolls of tinfoil inside—each for ninety-nine cents at Dollar Tree. She looped the handle over her wrist and headed toward the front double doors painted royal purple—the official color of the Crystal Ridge Wildcats. After years as a black-and-orange South Fork Falcon, purple felt traitorous. But she found the intercom anyway and gave it a buzz.

A burst of static crackled the air.

Anaya drew back.

"You're supposed to submit your transfer request at your home district, ma'am. Not here."

Anaya cocked her head. "Transfer request?"

"All students wishing to transfer to Crystal Ridge need to fill out the appropriate paperwork in South Fork, ma'am."

Suddenly, it clicked. This woman thought Anaya was a South Fork mother, and judging by her tone, she wasn't happy to see her.

"I'm not transferring anyone. I'm Anaya Jones, the new second grade teacher? I don't have a key card yet, but I spoke with Principal Kelly, and he said I could come by."

"Oh! Oh my goodness. Yes, of course. Come right in!"

The lock unlatched with a buzz.

Anaya grabbed the handle and pulled the door open for Darius, who walked toward her, his entire six-foot-two-inch frame obscured by the large, unwieldy refrigerator box they'd snagged from Sears. Anaya paid one of the delivery guys five dollars to secure the thing to the roof of her small car. Darius wasn't working with Uncle Jemar today, so she made him come with her.

"Don't smash the corner!" she yelped, opening the door wider so that her brother had more room to maneuver the box inside.

"You wanna do this?"

The cardboard scraped against the sides of the doorway, and then, miraculously, Darius succeeded. The large box was in the building. Anaya raised her arms and cheered as a woman came out from the front office. She gave the two of them—and the box—a baffled sort of look, then stepped forward to shake Anaya's hand.

"I'm so sorry about the mix-up. With the transfer deadline this afternoon, it's been an absolute zoo around here. Parents don't have a clue where they are supposed to go to submit transfers. My name is Jan McCormick. I'm the school secretary." Jan McCormick looked to be on the downhill side of middle-aged, with a face that might have been pretty had her eyes not landed so close together. "It's so nice to finally meet you."

"You too," Anaya said, although she had a hard time meaning it after being on the receiving end of Jan's condescending tone. "This is my brother, Darius."

"Hi, Darius." Jan shook his hand too.

"Mr. Kelly said I was welcome to stop by and see my classroom."

"Of course you are." She gave the box another perplexed look.

Before Jan could ask about it, Principal Kelly stepped out into the entry-way. Unlike the first time they met, he wasn't wearing a suit and tie. He'd exchanged the formal attire for a pair of khaki-colored cargo shorts, a white golf shirt, and black flip-flops. His nose was red and peeling, as though he'd spent a day out in the sun without any sunblock.

"Anaya! So great to see you. And this must be . . ."

"My kid brother, Darius."

"Right. Darius. Tall kid," he said, giving Darius a much more enthusiastic handshake than Jan McCormick had. "You play sports, Darius?"

"Football, sir."

"Will you be joining us in the fall?"

"Depends on the lottery, sir."

"Right. The lottery."

The deadline for transfer submissions was three o'clock. At three, the administrators at both districts would have the enrollment process underway. A lottery would determine which of the transfer students got in and which would have to transfer elsewhere, since there were more transfer requests than spots available in the Crystal Ridge District.

"What's with the box?" Mr. Kelly asked, bending his head to the side so he could get a better look at Anaya's bag. "And the rolls of . . . tinfoil?"

"My sister's making a time machine," Darius answered, in a sort of mocking, amused tone that made her want to slug him.

She didn't feel free to do it in front of Mr. Kelly or Jan McCormick.

Mr. Kelly's eyes twinkled. "A time machine?"

"It's an idea I came across earlier this year. A fun way to teach history. I thought I'd give it a try." When she first read about it, she'd been struck by its brilliance and had fun imagining the way her students' eyes would light up when she revealed it. Of course, she imagined kids like Abeo and Cynthia's grandson Tavian, who sometimes accompanied Cynthia to Auntie Trill's and always had a knock-knock joke to share.

The phone rang in the front office.

Jan McCormick excused herself, then bustled inside to answer it.

Darius picked up the box, and he and Anaya followed Mr. Kelly down the hallway. Their shoes squeaked against the shiny linoleum. The air was cool and smelled like Pine-Sol.

"You'll be happy to know our PTA has a new-teacher fund."

"A new-teacher fund?"

"To offset the cost of setting up a classroom. It's quite generous, if I do say so myself. Jan will be happy to explain how it works. Your room is here in the north hallway. Reach the T, turn left. First door on your right." Mr. Kelly stopped.

And Anaya stepped inside . . . her very own classroom. Large and mostly empty except for a computer station and twenty new desks, polished and pushed to one corner. There were two large bulletin boards on one wall, an interactive whiteboard on another. Two rows of cubbies, empty and as clean as everything else. An entire row of windows, where plenty of natural light streamed inside, and an exit door in the back that led out to one of three playgrounds.

"What do you think?"

In a little less than a week and a half, this classroom would be filled with twenty second grade students. She desperately hoped at least some of them would be South Fork transfers. Kids at South Fork deserved a room like this. They deserved a time machine too. Anaya would give it to them, and more. With the help of the PTA's new-teacher fund, she would make this classroom the coolest classroom in the whole state of Missouri. "It's perfect."

"I should have your class list ready on Monday."

Darius set the refrigerator box inside.

Mr. Kelly slid his hands in his pockets. "I know it's been a crazy start to the year, but I think it's gonna be a great one."

Nineteen

"Why you eatin' like a bird?" Granny's voice dripped with disapproval.

The coverage of the controversial town meeting last month? The anger it stirred up in the residents of South Fork? Granny didn't get too riled about those things. She said it was the same old stuff; nothing new under the sun. But the minute someone didn't take seconds of her cooking? Watch out.

Mama scooped up a forkful and took a bite. Anaya wondered if she tasted it at all.

Today was Friday.

Parents were told they could expect a phone call from an administrator on Friday.

The wait was making Mama crazy.

Uncle Jemar wiped his mouth with a napkin and leaned back with a groan. He'd eaten two full plates. Since Daddy died, Granny had taken to feeding Uncle Jemar twice as much. As he set his hands over his belly, Anaya thought it was starting to show. "Ain't nobody make biscuits and gravy like you, Granny. But don't you tell Estelle I said so."

"I'll send you home with leftovers."

He shook his round, bald head. "And let my wife know I've been cheating?"

Mama's phone rang.

Granny didn't allow phones at the dinner table, so Mama practically hurdled the table and the chairs in an attempt to snag it off the counter. When she got ahold of it, she frowned at the screen and sent the call to voice mail.

"Girl, you trippin'," Uncle Jemar said.

Mama raised her eyebrows. "Excuse me?"

"Wanting to send my nephew to that school after such a shameful meeting. I tell you what I'm gonna send there. I'm gonna send my foot. They all talking about how this ain't nothing to do with race. Yeah, okay. And Neil Armstrong really walked on the moon."

Darius coughed and caught Anaya's eye.

"You two go on and laugh. It don't matter. I seen the evidence. There ain't no way that boy walked on the moon. Look at the shadows if you don't believe me. Watch the footage in slow motion. They got the whole world fooled."

Uncle Jemar was a conspiracy theorist, and this was one of his favorites. The problem was, whenever he got talking about them, it made it easy to dismiss anything else he had to say.

"Jeremiah be rolling over in his grave, seeing his son at that school."

"You hush now." Mama wagged a paper towel at him, her expression cross. It was the same thing Auntie Trill kept saying, and Mama didn't like hearing it from her brother-in-law any more than she liked hearing it from her best friend.

A lot of South Fork parents reconsidered after the public meeting that went viral. Between that and the superintendent making such a hard sell to get parents to stay, a good percentage had changed their minds.

Not Mama.

According to Mama, Dr. Robert Joiner was all wind and no follow-through. She said his promises were too little too late. Anaya had been relieved, no matter what Daddy was or wasn't doing in his grave.

Mama's phone rang again.

This time she didn't send the call to voice mail. She flapped her arms in the air to quiet Uncle Jemar, who was still going on about Neil Armstrong and the moon, and pressed the phone against her ear, answering with a breathless hello.

She nodded. "Yes . . . I understand . . . Thank you."

Anaya couldn't read Mama's expression.

Until she put the phone back down and looked up at Darius with a smile brighter than the sun. "My baby's going to the best high school in the whole state of Missouri."

* * * * *

After dinner, Mama went to work, and Anaya ended up here—at the courts. Two of them were squeezed between First Immanuel and the youth center, and every Friday evening Marcus was there, doing what he could to keep the boys of South Fork safely occupied on a night that gave itself too eagerly to trouble.

He dribbled at the top of the key, passing the ball smoothly back and forth from palm to palm—a sight that dredged up bittersweet memories that were better left undredged.

It was the summer before Daddy died. The youth center's very first three-on-three basketball tournament. The day Anaya laid eyes on the finest man she'd ever seen—with rich caramel skin and beautiful eyes and a swagger that said he knew what the ladies were thinking.

He talked a big game, but he played an even bigger one. Every girl at the tournament noticed him.

"Ain't he fine?" ReShawn said, nudging Anaya's shoulder with her own.

"Who?"

"*Who?* Girl, you know who. You been staring at that boy for a minute."

Anaya jutted her chin and looked away.

Stubborn.

He swished a three and held his cocked wrist in the air, catching her eye across the court as he did.

"He's the reverend's nephew."

Anaya raised her eyebrows. "For real?"

"Mm-hmm. Rev says his nephew wants to follow in his footsteps."

"He wants to be a preacher?"

"Rumor has it he's fixing to take over at the youth center."

When it was Anaya's turn to play, she felt his eyes on her the whole time. It made her hyperaware, so much so that she may have shown off a little. When the game ended, he sauntered over. She was standing on the sideline swigging water with her teammates—Latrell and Darnell, brothers who grew up next door and sandwiched Anaya in age.

Apparently, mister preacher boy already knew them.

They gave each other some dap and came together in back-thumping hugs. When it was over, Marcus acknowledged her with a "sup" nod, followed by a quick but not so subtle up-and-down look that made her wish she wasn't sweating in a pair of basketball shorts.

"Anaya, this is my boy, Marcus," said Latrell, the older of the two brothers. "Marcus, this is my homegirl, Anaya."

She gave Marcus a nod of her own, trying to play it cool.

"You play college ball?" he asked.

"Does it look like I play college ball?" Anaya motioned to her vertically challenged height.

"You move like you do."

"Nah," she said, thankful she was too brown to blush.

"Anaya runs," Darnell said. "She aight."

"*Aight?*" She gave Darnell a friendly shove. "Fool, I run laps around your sorry butt."

"Pshh, girl. Please."

But it was true. When they were in high school, she used to smoke him in the mile.

Marcus looked impressed, and as the conversation unfolded, she observed that he was shyer—quieter—than he first appeared and had the adorable habit of nibbling on his left thumbnail. Her team ended up playing his in the championship game. He smelled way too good for a boy who'd been playing basketball all day. A shock of electricity hit her every time their bodies touched, which was a lot given the fact that they were guarding each other. She wondered if he felt it too. If chemistry like that could be one-sided.

Her question was answered when he asked if he could walk her home. He didn't hold her hand, but he may as well have with how often their knuckles brushed. Each time, the electric shock hit her just as it had on the court.

That was three years ago.

Anaya shook her head.

Auntie Trill was right. The gossip running around town was justified. She was spending more time than usual at the youth center these days. And over the past few months, Marcus was attempting to dip their toes back into friendship. Anaya wondered why. Did he really want to be friends—and only friends—or was he fishing for something more? Was it even possible for them to be friends?

One thing was certain. He wasn't going to wait around forever. Pretty soon, one of the girls vying for his attention would actually snag it, and Anaya would be forced to watch the romance unfold.

As if sensing her thoughts, Marcus picked up his dribble. Their eyes met and held. He straightened from his crouched position and gave her that same nod he had all those years ago—only it wasn't cocky so much as curious. He was always waiting for her reaction. This was how he treated her now. Like a startled fawn, and one wrong move would have her darting back into the safety of the forest.

Anaya nodded back, thankful again that her dark tone covered the heat pooling in her cheeks. Despite herself, she still loved him. She was too weak not to.

Twenty

The egg cracked against the counter and slid from the shell, hitting the hot frying pan with a loud hissing sizzle. While the water warmed in the teakettle, Camille's breakfast crackled and popped against melted butter, reminding her of that 1980s commercial.

"This is drugs. This is your brain on drugs. Any questions?"

Yes, actually.

But not about drugs.

Her questions were for Neil. Namely, how could he?

It was the first Saturday without her children, and every sound magnified the emptiness of her cavernous home. Yesterday, she packed them each a suitcase, and they left to their father's new apartment in the city. He had an apartment now. Neil—her husband—had an apartment.

The unfolding nightmare that had become her life continued to march onward. Over the past couple of weeks, Neil had been asking to take the children for a weekend. Camille wanted to scream. To tell him tough luck. He didn't get to have their children for the weekend. This was not going to be their life. But the kids missed their dad, and as angry as she was at Neil, she refused to make this any harder on them. She had to be the bigger person. She had to be the woman in the Bible, the one King Solomon praised because she let her baby go. She loved her baby too much to see the child torn in two.

The egg continued frying in the pan, browning at the edges.

"This is drugs. This is your brain on drugs."

Rebecca talked about drugs at the town meeting. She'd been castigated by the media for it as harshly as Camille had been castigated. So much so that the two women found a brief, close-knit camaraderie in the aftermath. It gave them something to bond over. For the first time since the inception of the 5K and all the planning that had happened between the first run until now, they got together for coffee—just the two of them. And for one passionate hour, they vented their frustrations over being so unfairly portrayed.

"I'm not an idiot," Rebecca had huffed. "I'm well aware that there are drugs in Crystal Ridge already."

"Of course you are," Camille consoled.

"I only meant that there will be more if these kids come. Do you know how many of them have been brought in for drug possession? And we're not talking about a small bag of weed, either."

For some reason, Camille thought it sounded strange. Hearing pregnant Rebecca say the word *weed*.

When their outrage was spent, the conversation fizzled. They grappled for a topic to fill the space—kids, mostly—but Rebecca's children were very into Cub Scouts and 4-H and Camille's were currently distraught. Neil had been the elephant in the room, sitting between them as they sipped their coffee. But Camille refused to address it. So they stumbled along awkwardly for another half hour before calling it a day.

She and Rebecca hadn't gone for coffee since.

Camille scooped the egg onto a plate, then stared at it with contempt. Neil preferred his sunny-side up with extra pepper. How many eggs had she made for him through the years? And now what? He left like none of them mattered. Like she was as easy to discard as the twenty pounds of weight he'd been carrying around his middle.

She dumped the egg in the trash compactor and walked to her bedroom. Everyone was talking about her. She could feel the way people stared whenever she went out in public.

This was another thing that infuriated her.

Neil was turning her into an agoraphobe. Camille had never—not once in her life—been the least bit hesitant to get out of the house. But now? She'd found an excuse every Sunday to avoid church. She couldn't bring herself to go to the last 5K meeting. The only reason she'd picked the splash pad for Paige's playdate instead of inviting Jen and Jubilee to the country club to swim was for the strict purpose of avoiding as many people she might know as possible.

It hadn't worked.

Laura Ransom was there, with her two towheaded toddlers. Camille hated the extra note of kindness that had been in Laura's wave. Neil had made her into an object of pity.

Poor Camille.

Did you hear her husband left her?

The whispers followed her everywhere she went, even now. She shuffled into the bathroom and stared at herself in the mirror. No wonder everyone was concerned. Her cheeks had turned gaunt, and the thinness was not becoming. It accentuated her age.

She ran her hands down her hair, thick and blond and naturally wavy. While most men fixated on the more obvious female anatomy, it had been Camille's hair that turned Neil on. When they first started dating, he called it her crown of glory.

She never cut it.

She had it trimmed of course, but never more than that. For the past twenty-six years, she kept it the same long length—halfway down her back.

All for him.

Her upper lip began to curl in the mirror's reflection. Her left eye twitched. A wild, untamed thing bucked and kicked inside her, like a bull in a chute. It needed to get out. It needed to do something.

Camille grabbed a pair of scissors sitting on the vanity and let the beast have its way. She hacked at her hair, letting it fall in long clumps against the tiled floor. She cut it all off in a fit of rage that did not stop until the teakettle had long been whistling.

⚬ ⚬ ⚬ ⚬ ⚬

Camille's short hair, which was styled in a sleek bob barely long enough to tuck behind her ears, came as a giant shock. When Neil dropped the kids off yesterday afternoon, he stared—his mouth agape—until Camille barked at him to stop.

She gave it intermittent pats as she drove with the windows down and Paige chattered in the backseat. She was going on about all the things she had done with her father over the weekend. Board games. Mini golf. The zoo. Swimming. Dinner at a hibachi grill. Apparently, he'd gone and squeezed every fun summer activity into the span of two days.

Camille kept her face appropriately schooled, pretending to relish Paige's words when each one felt like a whip against raw skin.

"I can't believe it's you, Mom. I keep thinking you're somebody else."

"It's really me." As though to prove it, she patted her hair again.

On Saturday, after her sanity returned and panic set in, Camille did her best to even her hair out, swept the shorn locks into the garbage, then drove forty-five minutes to Saint Charles all so she could go to a salon where nobody would know her.

Thankfully, no one did.

And so far, nobody had bothered to ask how her weekend had gone. Nobody knew about her crazed breakdown in the master bathroom. Or that she ended the night in their basement wine cellar, opening up every bottle of Neil's most expensive wine and giving it a taste before dumping it down the drain. Some she'd given more than a taste, which was why she woke up yesterday with a pounding headache and a tongue so dry, it felt swollen in her mouth.

It wasn't her finest hour.

She was in no hurry to repeat it, but in two weeks her children would be leaving her again, and she would have to find a better way to cope. She pinched the bridge of her nose, trying not to think about it. She told herself that in two weeks this nightmare would be over. Neil would wake up and come to his senses.

She slowed to a stop at the traffic light. Beside her, a woman was peering into the side view mirror, attempting to pop a zit on her chin. Camille stared at her, fascinated by her lack of discretion, when a low-riding vehicle pulled up behind them.

The driver had thick cornrows that looked like fat, black caterpillars on his head, and he was playing rap music so loud, the base vibrated the steering wheel against her palms. Every other lyric contained a four-letter word and a well-known racial slur.

Appalled, Camille quickly rolled up the windows and peeked back at Paige, who had long been in the practice of asking what unfamiliar words meant. Camille didn't want to try to explain that one.

Thankfully, Paige didn't notice, and Camille's phone began to ring. The screen said *Deb*.

Camille answered with a hello so overly cheerful, it was obvious she was compensating.

"Hey," Deb said. "How are you?"

"Great. Just driving Paige home from piano lessons."

"Have you checked your email today?"

"Not yet."

"Class lists came out." If a week-old party balloon had a voice, Deb's would be it. "Paige and Faith aren't together."

Camille's heart sank. "Who has who?"

"Faith is with Mrs. Webb. Paige is with the new teacher, Miss Jones."

Of course.

Of course it couldn't be the other way around. If it were the other way around, Camille wouldn't think twice about going into Mr. Kelly's office and asking for a transfer. In fact, she'd be quite thrilled to do so.

See, her actions would tell the world, *she wasn't racist.*

Racist people didn't want their children to have black teachers. Anaya Jones was a black teacher, and Camille wanted her to be Paige's. It would, however, look awfully suspicious if she went into Mr. Kelly's office and asked for Paige to be transferred out of Miss Jones's class. It would, of course, have nothing to do with skin color. But nobody wanted to believe that.

She flipped her blinker and turned down Windamere Avenue.

She wanted to ask Deb if she'd consider transferring Faith into Paige's class, but it would be wasted breath. Technically, transfer requests weren't allowed. Principal Kelly's public stance was essentially the same refrain Camille had said to her children on more than one occasion. *You get what you get, and you don't throw a fit.* But in Camille's experience, there were always exceptions. The problem was, Deb wasn't the type to ask for an exception. She hated to be a bother, and she would most definitely see a transfer request as such. Even though it wasn't. Camille would have been happy to make the request for her, and she had no doubt it would be granted. A transfer would require nothing but a simple swap that would take Jan McCormick two seconds to accomplish.

"Faith is pretty bummed."

"Yeah." Paige would be too. She peeked at her in the rearview mirror. Now that she wasn't talking a mile a minute, her expression had changed. She was staring out the window with a look so lost and faraway, Camille's throat tightened in alarm.

"Of course, they can still eat lunch together. And play at recess. And we will do plenty of playdates."

"Yeah," Camille said again.

"You know I'm here, right? If you need to talk about anything?"

"Yes, of course. Thanks, Deb."

As soon as they hung up, Camille dropped her phone onto the consul and turned onto her cul-de-sac, feeling scratchy and mean, like she was seven again and her mother was making her wear that awful wool dress from her aunt Cora. The feeling was swiftly interrupted by an unusual sight—flashing red-and-blue lights. A police cruiser sat in the driveway across the street. Neighbors had gathered outside. They stood on their front lawns in small pockets, whispering excitedly to one another.

"What's a police car doing here?" Paige asked.

"I'm not sure." Camille slowed to a stop in front of the neighbors next door. "What's going on?"

"Someone tried breaking into the Robersons' house. They busted a window and everything."

"Are you kidding?"

"No. The alarm went off. All the dogs in the neighborhood started barking."

"Did they catch who it was?"

"It looks like they got away."

Camille glanced back at Paige, who heard every word. Someone had been prowling around their neighborhood. A burglar attempted to break into the Robersons' home on a Monday afternoon with Austin and Taylor across the street.

Alone and unprotected.

● ● ● ● ●

Camille: What is the code to the gun safe?

Neil: Why?

Camille: Because the neighbor's house was burglarized, and the
        criminal is still at large. Somebody has to protect our children.

Camille's phone began to ring. The call was immediately, and aggressively, sent to voice mail.

Neil: Please call me.

Twenty-One

Paige's new teacher reminded Camille of that actress with the hard-to-pronounce name. Lupita something. Only she wasn't quite as slim, and instead of short hair Anaya Jones wore hers in tiny, long braids pulled back in a thick ponytail. She had regal-looking cheekbones and straight white teeth, an athletic build, and a face entirely too young to be a teacher.

Or maybe Camille was just getting old.

She was certainly nervous and uncommonly self-conscious as she walked with Paige to her new classroom. It was Unpack Your Backpack night at O'Hare Elementary, and they had come early. When they reached the classroom door, it was only halfway open and decorated with the words *Superhero Headquarters* and an array of superhero logos.

And indeed, it was.

One bulletin board was covered in green with a large 3-D Hulk at the top and letters that read "Our Work Is Incredible." Another showcased a darkened skyline made up of black rectangular skyscrapers with yellow rectangular windows and twenty small capes flying overhead with twenty neatly written names. "Miss Jones's Super Second Graders." Off to the left, an entire corner of the room had been made into its own reading wonderland with beanbags and black walls and peel-and-stick stars and a vertical banner that said "A Good Book Will Take You to a Galaxy Far, Far Away." An impressive collection of Funko Pop Star Wars lined the top of the two bookcases.

Paige loved Funko Pop.

But these weren't what caught her daughter's attention. Her eyes were fixed on a large, mysterious object near the exit door.

"What's underneath that sheet?" she asked.

"It's a secret," Anaya said with a tantalizing wink as she stood from her seat behind her desk and stuck out her hand to shake Paige's. "I'm Miss Jones, and you would be . . . ?"

"Paige Amelia Gray."

Miss Jones straightened, her attention landing on Camille, and for one blip of a second, her expression faltered, revealing it for what it was—a mask. The kind that was so well done, it came as a shock when it slipped out of place.

"I'm Paige's mother, Camille," she said, injecting confidence into her tone as she stepped forward for a handshake of her own. She refused to sound self-conscious, even if she felt it. "She's very excited to be in your class this year."

"No, I'm not."

"Paige!" High-pitched laughter bubbled from Camille's throat. "I'm so sorry. It has nothing to do with you. She's upset that she's not in the same class as her best friend."

Miss Jones nodded coolly.

"Anyway, I know we're here a little early. I don't want to bother you. We came to set out the goody bags the PTA made for all the students and wanted to introduce ourselves before we got to work. I'll be your room mother this year. If you need anything—anything at all—let me know. I'm happy to help."

"Thank you."

Camille tightened her grip on her daughter's hand and, with a stiff smile, pulled her into the hallway, where she'd left the box of goody bags earlier this morning. Each one was tied prettily with purple ribbon and had a picture of a wildcat on the front. She and Deb had spent the last three nights stuffing them. Thankfully, Deb didn't ask about Neil. They were too busy postulating about the neighborhood robber.

"I bet it was a silly prank that got out of control," Deb had offered.

Camille didn't think so.

She certainly wasn't going to take any risks. Which was why she called Rebecca and asked if Patrick knew of any good firearm classes she could take around the area. If a robber tried to break in, he wouldn't find Camille defenseless.

Paige lifted the box onto the table outside Miss Jones's classroom. Camille supervised, trying not to think too hard about Anaya's icy greeting. She probably recognized Camille from the unsavory media coverage. They certainly replayed the clip of her at the public meeting often enough. The unfair portrayal left Paige's new teacher with an equally unfair impression.

As Camille watched Paige organize the goody bags, she told herself it was nothing. So what if Miss Jones didn't like her? As long as she treated Paige

fairly and kindly, it didn't matter. And besides, there was a good chance Camille was misinterpreting the entire exchange. She'd walked into the classroom
paranoid. Of course she would have paranoid thoughts. Maybe Anaya had the
kind of personality that took a while to warm up.

An unfamiliar black woman and her daughter turned down the hallway,
hand in hand. The little girl had a bounce in her step and a head full of braids
and colorful beads that clacked when she walked.

Camille smiled extra big at them both.

"Are these for us?" the mother asked.

"They sure are," Camille said.

The woman encouraged her daughter to take one, then prompted her to
say "thank you" after she did.

"You are quite welcome," Camille said.

The mother-daughter duo walked inside the classroom.

"Wow," the little girl said, elongating the word in a wonder-soaked way.

Camille watched inconspicuously from the hallway as Anaya's eyes went
wide and warm at the sight of them, blowing Camille's personality theory to
smithereens. "I wondered if the Nia on my class list was the same Nia who
came into my Auntie Trill's salon."

The mother and Anaya fell into a laughing, enthusiastic hug.

All Camille got was a stiff handshake.

She turned her attention back to the goody bags, but it was hard not to
eavesdrop. The women had the kind of voices that carried.

"Look Nia," the mother said. "You know Miss Jones."

"Mama says you give the best head rubs in the whole state of Missouri."

This had Nia's mother slapping her thigh. "She sure does. She sure does.
Oh girl, I can't tell you what an answer to prayer this is. I've been so nervous,
wondering if I made the right decision. It's like the good Lord done took me by
the shoulders and said, 'Relax, daughter. I got you.'"

"That blesses me more than you know."

"What's under that sheet?" Nia asked.

"It's a secret," Anaya answered. It was the same answer she gave Paige, but
it sounded warmer somehow. Like it wasn't just a secret but a secret between the
two of them.

"Can we unpack my backpack now?" Paige asked.

Camille blinked.

Paige had finished setting out all the goody bags, and the hallway was slowly starting to fill with parents and children.

They walked inside just as another family arrived. Lacy Cunningham, with one of her two identical boys. Her husband must have the other. Was she still upset that her cousin hadn't gotten the job? Secretly, Camille found herself wishing she had. Miss Jones didn't seem to like her, and as much as Camille tried to tell herself she didn't care, of course she did. Her children's teachers always liked her. Camille was their unspoken favorite.

"Look, Paige, Jubilee is sitting at your table group. And Sarah is sitting in the group right behind you. You have lots of friends in your class."

Paige couldn't seem to catch Camille's enthusiasm.

Or any of her classmates' for that matter.

As children came in—wide eyed and wonder filled—Paige sat solemnly in her new seat and got to work on the instruction sheet in front of her. She put her pencils in her pencil case and her art supplies in her supply box and wrote her name on each of her pocket folders.

Paige Amelia Gray.

She worked her way through the directions as more and more families arrived. Every kid took special notice of the large mystery object beneath the sheet, and every kid wanted to know what was hiding under there.

With two more instructions left to go, Leif Royce walked in, making the muscles in Camille's abdomen clench. If only they'd gotten through the list a little quicker, they could have avoided him altogether.

Leif was a goliath of a man who clasped his son's skinny shoulders with two meaty paws. Gavin always looked in need of a bath, like Pigpen from *Peanuts.* Perhaps that was unfair. It wasn't like he had a cloud of dirt following him around, but he sure could use a mother to wipe his nose. Unfortunately, Gavin didn't have one. She died several years ago, leaving Gavin and his brother, Derek, alone with their bear of a father.

Derek was one grade below Taylor. Back in middle school, he had a crush on her that was so severe, it bordered on obsessive. Neil had to intervene, and afterward he'd commented that he wasn't sure Derek Royce was "all there."

In Camille's opinion, none of the Royce family was.

Leif had a habit of telling inappropriate jokes that made everyone cringe.

He was the one at the public meeting who yelled "It's about trash!" as Camille addressed the crowd. She hated him for saying it. Mostly because his words came to be associated with her. But she hadn't said anything about trash. That was all Leif. Honestly, if the media wanted to talk about racism, they should talk about him.

Thankfully, Jen and Nick Covington walked in as soon as he did, saving Camille from having to carry on any sort of a conversation. She waved enthusiastically from the front of the classroom, catching Jen's attention.

"The girls are sitting next to each other," Camille said as the small family made their way toward her. She shook hands with Nick. "Camille Gray. We met very briefly outside the school a couple weeks ago."

"Right," he said. "Our daughters played at the splash pad."

"Yes, they did. Paige had a wonderful time."

"So did Jubilee."

"I hear you're one of the new managers at Schnucks, which means you might be my new contact person."

"Contact person?"

"For the Crystal Ridge Memorial Day 5K. Schnucks has always been one of our biggest sponsors. I'm hoping the trend continues."

"I think that could be arranged, especially considering my wife's new job."

"I haven't gotten it yet," Jen said, nudging her husband with her elbow and turning to Camille. "You weren't kidding about your clout."

"Did you get an interview?"

"Tomorrow. The principal made it sound very casual."

"That means you got it." A feeling of satisfaction stole through her. A pleasurable warmth in the midst of too much cold. It made her want to loop her arm around Jen's and keep her right there, by her side.

Nick crouched beside his daughter—who wore braids not nearly as neatly done as Nia's—and began helping Jubilee with the list. Unlike Paige, she needed someone to read it for her.

Beside them, Gavin wiped his nose on the back of his hand. He started pulling items from his bag and stuffing them inside his desk without attempting to read anything on the instruction sheet while Leif stood behind him like a bodyguard, his thick, hairy arms tightly crossed in front of his chest.

Anaya Jones was making her rounds, stopping at every desk to introduce

herself. The closer she came to Leif, the more nervous Camille became. She felt
as though someone should warn her. But then, Leif's David Duke T-shirt was
probably warning enough. Honestly, what in the world had Principal Kelly
been thinking when he put Gavin Royce in Anaya's classroom?

"Hello," Anaya said as she reached their table group. "You must be
Jubilee."

Jubilee nodded shyly, her two middle fingers stuffed inside her mouth.

Jen gently removed them and encouraged her to say hello.

"We're thrilled that Jubilee is in your class," Nick said.

"Well, I'm thrilled to have her." Anaya gave Jubilee the same radiant smile
she'd given Nia before turning to Gavin Royce and his intimidating father.

Her attention flicked to his T-shirt.

"You must be Gavin," she said. "I'm Miss Jones, your new teacher."

Gavin Royce shook Anaya's hand with the same one he'd been using as a
Kleenex.

A muscle in Leif's face twitched.

"When do we get to know what's under that sheet?" Paige said.

"On the first day of school. Right now, it's still under construction."

This heightened the intrigue.

Paige led Jubilee and several others over to investigate; they all studied the
sheeted object in the same way her children studied wrapped presents under
the Christmas tree.

Anaya didn't linger.

She gave Camille, the Covingtons, and Leif Royce a friendly enough nod,
then headed back toward her desk, where she struck up a conversation with
Nia's mother.

"They should stick with their own kind."

The words belonged to Leif, and he didn't mumble them either. He spoke
so loud, in fact, there was a hiccup in the conversation. Anaya and Nia's mother
stopped talking.

"This district is going down the drain."

"Excuse me," Nick said. "What did you just say?"

Camille could feel her face catching fire—a molten heat that crept up her
neck, pooled in her cheeks, and spread into her ears.

"I think I spoke clear enough."

"Yeah, you did. I guess I was hoping I misheard."

Camille imagined that old show, *Lost in Space,* and the robot that flashed red. *Danger, Will Robinson! Danger!* When it came to men like Leif, it was best not to engage. But nobody had given Nick the memo.

"It says on the district website that everyone is welcome, regardless of religion, race, and ability."

"I'm not the website."

Several parents watched the exchange, shuffling their feet nervously.

"That's obvious. But last I checked, this is a Crystal Ridge school. Which means your rude comments aren't welcome here."

Leif hitched his crossed arms up a notch, his eyes narrowing into slits.

Camille looked at Jen.

Someone needed to tell her that Nick should tread carefully.

Twenty-Two

Mama said the quickest way to get over your nerves was by praying over the people who were making you nervous. Right then, it was a bunch of seven-year-olds. So as the wall clock ticked down to the morning bell and the air all around smelled of fresh pencil shavings, Anaya walked from one desk to the next, running her fingers over each nameplate as she prayed.

Her fingers stayed longest on Gavin Royce—the boy with the snotty nose and a father with a heart full of contempt. She reminded herself that he didn't choose his dad any more than a person could choose where they were born. All these kids in her classroom had been dealt a particular hand, and that hand would determine so much of their future. So much of who they became.

Unless . . .

"Unless someone like you cares a whole awful lot, nothing is going to get better. It's not."

The quote came from *The Lorax,* one of the many books her father used to read to her when she was little and Darius hadn't yet come to be. Daddy loved books. He would put his ear to their spines like they were whispering things. Sometimes he would open them and smell the pages.

"You smell that, Anaya?" he'd say.

"Smell what, Daddy?"

"Possibility."

He studied religion and literature at Howard and often said it was the latter which saved him. He was joking, of course. It was Jesus who saved him. Daddy knew that. He just liked to get Mama riled up.

Daddy had his own Lorax philosophy, only it didn't come in a catchy rhyme. *Be the change where you're at.*

Anaya was pretty sure he meant South Fork, but she wasn't there. For better or worse—God's sovereign will or because she lived in a fallen world—this was where she was. So with her father's words clutched determinedly to her heart and a fresh round of butterflies swooping in her stomach, she walked down the wide, sunny hallway toward the commons, where all twelve classes sat in neat lines behind their grade-colored dots.

Red for kindergarten. Orange for first grade. Yellow for second. She glanced down the row of Yellow 2, doing roll call in her mind. It didn't take a minute to realize that three students were missing. All three were her transfer kids.

Nia. Dante. Zeke.

Her attention swept over the other lines, then landed on Principal Kelly, who walked toward her. "The bus with the O'Hare kids went to the wrong school. As soon as they get here, I'll escort them to your classroom."

He moved along before she could ask any questions—like how long? And where had they gone? And had they gotten off the bus? Did anyone help them as they stood in the crowd, confused because wherever they were didn't look like the right place? It made the knots in Anaya's stomach pull tighter.

She invited the students who were sitting in line to follow her. As soon as they reached the classroom and found their desks, Paige Amelia Gray's hand shot up in the air.

"Yes, Paige?"

"When do we get to see what's under that sheet?"

"Soon."

"Can I pull it off when it's time?"

"I wanna do it!" Gavin interrupted, setting off a chorus of objections.

Anaya held up her hands—a call for quiet—and began walking them through the morning routine. Backpacks in cubbies. Papers from their take-home folder in the apple-red inbox tray. Popsicle sticks out of the attendance cup, into the hot or cold lunch cup. It was a much tamer way of taking attendance than some of the teachers she had through the years—her favorite being Mr. Vogel, sixth grade homeroom, who would call everyone's name like a drill sergeant. They'd stand at attention and yell, "Here, here!" Followed by their own special handshake Mr. Vogel made with each of them at the beginning of the term. It worked like magic. Whatever stress Anaya had carried into the classroom during sixth grade slowly fell away. She grew up putting her daddy on a pedestal. That was the year he nearly got usurped.

She didn't think that kind of roll call would translate to a place like this, so she stuck with the cups and herded the children back to their seats, where they would begin each day with a writing prompt. Today's? A summer memory. She was careful not to say a *fun* summer memory. She wanted her students to feel free to write whatever memory was on their hearts—whether it was fun or not.

As sharpened number-two pencils scratch-scratch-scratched against paper, Anaya stared at the attendance form on her computer screen, immobilized by the three Popsicle sticks that hadn't been touched, when a knock sounded on her door.

Principal Kelly stood outside with Zeke, Dante, and Nia.

The little girl's eyes were puffy and red.

Like a mama duck, Anaya gathered them to her bosom and squeezed them tight, then helped them get situated, eager for the rest of the class to stop staring. By the time Nia sat down, she'd developed a loud case of the hiccups.

It was only natural then that when the time finally came to uncover the mystery object, Anaya chose Nia to be her special helper. Several kids objected—Paige Gray loudest of all—but their excitement to see what was underneath trumped their disappointment at not being picked.

Nia stood proudly in front of them—the bus fiasco temporarily forgotten as she removed the sheet with a dramatic flourish.

The class broke into a round of rapturous excitement, making all the time Anaya spent wrapping that box in tinfoil worth it. Every single second.

"What is it?" a little Indian girl named Aaishi asked.

"This, my young superheroes, is our very own time machine."

"Get outta town!" Gavin Royce exclaimed.

And something inside Anaya's heart went soft and warm.

The tension that filled her room after Gavin's father's words on Unpack Your Backpack night was nowhere to be felt. Here, in her classroom, nobody cared about transfer students. These children weren't threatened by South Fork. They were just a bunch of seven-year-olds who still wanted to believe that it was possible to travel back in time.

●●●●●

A group of girls gathered to jump rope on the playground blacktop. Nia was the star of the show—the only one who knew how to do double dutch. Several classmates wanted her to teach them how while Paige Gray watched with crossed arms. When it was her turn, the ropes got tangled up in her feet. So she grabbed Jubilee's hand and the hand of another little girl who wasn't in Anaya's class and pulled them away to the monkey bars. Paige was really good at the monkey bars.

"You're going to want to keep a close eye on her," Mrs. Webb said.

"Why's that?"

"Her parents recently separated."

"Oh."

"It came as a huge shock to everyone."

Twenty-Three

That night at the dinner table, Nick asked Jubilee about her first day of school.

"Who did you eat lunch with?"

"I don't remem-ba," she said with a shrug.

"Did you sit with Paige?" Jen asked.

Jubilee shook her head. "She say no."

Jen and Nick exchanged a look of concern. Did Paige exclude Jubilee at lunchtime?

Nick set his fork down. "What do you mean she said no?"

But Jubilee didn't extrapolate. She scooped up a bite of rice with her fingers and stuffed it into her mouth. She still wasn't accustomed to using silverware, especially not when it came to things like rice. And the whole phenomenon of chewing with her mouth closed felt light-years away.

"We play on da monkey bars," she said with her mouth full.

"Who played on the monkey bars?"

"Paige and me."

"Oh." Jen's muscles relaxed. "You and Paige played together at recess?"

Jubilee nodded and reached for the soy sauce.

Meanwhile, in another house, Camille and her youngest sat at the kitchen counter, writing out American Girl doll invitations for Paige's eighth birthday party. This year, Camille had every intention of going all out. If her little girl wanted pony rides, Camille was going to find a way to get them.

"You know what would be fun?" Camille said. "If you invited party guests to dress up like it's the 1950s. I could make you a poodle skirt."

"Like the one Grandma sent me for Maryellen!" Maryellen was Paige's favorite American Girl doll, and on every special occasion—even ones that didn't typically include presents—Camille's mother sent Paige American Girl doll outfits in the mail. She hated living so far away from her grandchildren. This was her way of compensating. For the Fourth of July, Camille's mother sent the poodle skirt because Maryellen harkened from the 1950s—an era that would make for an adorable party theme when it came to seven- and eight-year-old girls.

Paige carefully wrote out Faith's name on the first invitation.

"Who else do you want to invite?"

She began ticking girls off on her fingers. "Hope, Emma, Madison, Avery, Brooklyn, Zoe, Aaishi, Sarah, Violet—"

"What about Jubilee?"

Paige scrunched her nose.

"Paige, honey. I'm sure Jubilee would love to come to your birthday party."

"But she sucks on her fingers like a baby, and she eats with her mouth wide open. When she chews, you can see all the food inside."

"That's a silly reason not to invite someone to your party." Camille reached across her daughter and grabbed the invitation on the top of the stack. "Here, make this one out to Jubilee."

⚬●₅⚬₅⚬

Paige's Birthday Party Invitation

You're invited to a
1950s American Girl Party
to celebrate
Paige Amelia Gray's 8th Birthday!

Saturday, September 22nd
at 1:00 p.m.
1246 Ashbury Court in Crystal Ridge
RSVP to Camille by Mon, Sep 17th: 321-464-2917

Please bring your favorite doll!

●⚬₅⚬

Jen Covington got the job. For the next twelve weeks, while the high school nurse went on maternity leave, she was going to manage the health and well-being of the 456 students at Crystal Ridge High School. She would have to remember to send Camille a thank-you card.

After her first day of work—Jubilee's fifth day of school—her daughter excitedly pulled something from her backpack, laying to rest the unease Nick and Jen were beginning to feel whenever their daughter talked about her school day. It was impossible to tell whether or not Jubilee was being excluded.

"Look what I get!" she said, proudly waving the pink-and-blue party invitation in the air.

"It was nice that Paige invited her," Nick said later.

"Yes, it was."

As they huddled around the sink to brush their teeth, neither expressed the concern on both of their minds. How, exactly, would Jubilee handle all the stimulation that came with an eight-year-old's birthday party?

●●●●●

To: graypartyof5@msn.com
From: jones.anaya@crystalridge.k12.mo.us
Subject: Paige
Date: Thursday, September 6

Dear Ms. Gray,

I would like to speak with you about something concerning Paige. Please call at your earliest convenience.

Thanks,
Anaya Jones
2nd Grade Teacher
Kate Richards O'Hare Elementary

Twenty-Four

Camille aimed the gun and pulled the trigger.

There was a loud crack. A powerful kick. Her steady hands. And the cathartic release that came with the sight of that bullet hole, exactly where she'd aimed it.

"How are you doing that?"

Camille wasn't sure. She only knew that the instructor had finally moved on from the mind-numbing boredom that was gun law and gun safety to the part she'd been itching to get to—marksmanship. Turned out, Camille was a natural.

She felt vindicated with every pull of the trigger.

Take that, Jas, whoever you are.

Take that, burglar, wherever you are.

Take that, Neil, you traitorous slimeball.

Bam.

Bam.

Bam.

She hit the target every time. Maybe not the center of the bull's-eye, but impressively close.

"I'm imagining the target is Neil's head."

"Let's refrain from talking about targets being people's heads," the instructor said. His name was Alvin. It didn't fit him at all. He looked much more like an Ashton or a Channing or a Zac. "At least while you're in my class."

Camille grimaced, mildly apologetic.

"If you knew her husband, you wouldn't care," Kathleen said.

Flashing one of his deep dimples, Alvin helped Kathleen get set up and take aim. Her shot missed the target entirely.

She wasn't a natural.

"I think you should hire a private investigator. Rick has a list of them, and he'd be happy to share."

"I'm not hiring a PI."

"Why not?"

Because her husband wasn't cheating! He was simply having a small psychotic break, and soon he would come back with profuse apologies and dozens upon dozens of roses and she would make him pay, but only for a little while. By this time next year, the whole thing would be nothing more than a distant, slightly perplexing, sometimes humorous memory.

"You should think about the kids," Kathleen said. "If he files, you're going to want to have ammunition."

"He would never try to take the kids away from me."

"You didn't think he'd ever leave, either." Kathleen delivered the words gently, but they still made her ulcers ache.

Camille was positive she had them. Either that or stomach cancer. Her symptoms aligned quite frighteningly with those listed on WebMD. She chose to think optimistically and diagnosed herself with ulcers instead.

She certainly had enough stress in her life for them—with Neil taking their children on exciting excursions every other weekend, leaving her alone to lick her wounds, then dropping them off afterward like she wouldn't have to deal with the fallout. Paige, asking when Daddy was coming home. Austin, folding more and more into himself, and Taylor, growing more antagonistic. It couldn't continue. They couldn't remain in this limbo Neil had thrown them into. They needed answers. Yet she was terrified to push for any. She was terrified that if she did, he'd give her an answer she didn't want, and they'd go from being Rick's friends to Rick's clients. Every time she thought about it, her stomach took a quick step off a sharp cliff.

Right now, they were still sharing a bank account, credit cards. What would happen if he divorced her? Would she be humiliated, jilted, *and* destitute? Yesterday afternoon the doorbell rang unexpectedly, and Camille had been so illogically convinced it was going to be a man in a black suit serving her dissolution papers that she'd hidden in the bathroom and hadn't answered.

Camille placed her arms exactly as Alvin instructed and lined up with the target. This time the bullet sailed directly into the center of the bull's-eye.

Alvin whistled.

The two women took a seat at the picnic table, their guns locked on safety as he walked out to adjust the targets.

"Juanita Fine called the police on me yesterday," Kathleen said.

"*What?*"

"Rebecca told me about it on the phone last night. Patrick was laughing like a hyena in the background. He thinks Juanita is hilarious. Apparently, I parked in her grass."

"Did you?"

"I parked in front of her curb. Maybe a hair on the curb. I don't know; I was in a rush. The tires were definitely not in her grass. And anyway, that part of her lawn doesn't even belong to her. It belongs to the city. That woman needs to take a chill pill."

"She's very protective of her yard."

"Well, I nominate you to tell her that the 5K is going to be a color run this year."

"I nominate Deb."

They both laughed.

There was a brief, comfortable lull in conversation as their beefcake of an instructor moved one of the targets several paces back.

"Cody wants to ask Taylor to homecoming."

"Really?"

"Do you think she'd say yes?"

"If she doesn't, I'll say yes for her." But even as Camille said it, the ache in her stomach burned hotter. She thought she'd overheard Taylor telling Alexis the other day that Cody was a jerk.

"I keep telling him he'd better hurry up, before someone else asks her." Kathleen batted at a pesky fly and twisted her lips to the side. "I don't know, Camille. The other day, he told Rick he might quit."

"The football team?"

Kathleen shook her head, not because the answer was no, but because she didn't know what to do about it. All summer long, Cody counted on being the starting quarterback for the Crystal Ridge Wildcats. But then the transfer happened, and Darius Jones showed up, and suddenly Cody's spot wasn't quite so secure.

"The coach told him that he wasn't starting tomorrow."

"Man, Kathleen. I'm sorry." She reached across the table and gave her friend's hand a squeeze. "If it makes you feel any better, Darius's big sister thinks my daughter is a bully."

"What?"

"She emailed me this morning. We spoke on the phone. She says she's concerned because Paige is excluding some girls at recess."

"Did she say who?"

"One of the transfer students. And Jubilee Covington." Camille hated, hated, *hated* that one of the two girls was Jubilee. Her heart sank the second Anaya said the name. Maybe that was why she hadn't received an RSVP from Jen regarding Paige's birthday party invite.

"See, that makes me mad. Both are new this year, right? I'm sure it has nothing to do with exclusion and everything to do with comfort level. Paige doesn't know those girls."

"That's what I said. I mean, her class has always been tight knit." Camille picked up her new handgun as Alvin made his way back to them. "I still have to talk to her, though."

○●●●●○

As soon as Camille stepped inside the house, Taylor made a beeline for the door, her hair damp from her postpractice shower.

"Wait a minute. Where are you going?"

"Library."

"Again?"

"I told you. I'm working on a French project."

"Does this project involve a boy?"

Taylor rolled her eyes so hard, there was only white.

Note to self: spy on eldest at the library.

Just like she should spy on her husband at CrossFit.

No.

Nope.

She wouldn't do it. She refused to be that woman.

"I can give you a ride if you want."

"Alexis is driving. She's already out front." As if to prove it, Taylor held up her phone. There was a text from Alexis that said Here! "Sure would be nice if I had my own license so my friends wouldn't have to be my chauffeur."

"We'll practice this weekend."

"Sure we will," Taylor said, stepping outside.

"Make sure you're home in time for dinner," Camille called after her.

Taylor slammed the door.

And on that note, Camille headed up the stairs to check on her less sarcastic, less hostile children. Austin was sitting on his bed, flipping through a book about chess, stopping occasionally to jot a note on a pad of paper.

She tried not to feel concerned as she watched him. Camille had a hard time understanding her son. She had always been a part of the popular crowd, just like Taylor was a part of the popular crowd. Granted, Taylor didn't seem to care about being a part of that crowd half as much as Camille did at that age. But still, she was part of it. Paige was outgoing and charming and would most likely be the *leader* of the popular crowd. But Austin? Austin was a loner. Austin was introverted, and lately his introversion bordered on antisocial.

She wanted to talk to Neil about it, but Neil was the one to blame. And besides, any time she did talk to Neil about Austin, he became exasperated and said things like, "He's not you, Camille."

To which she usually replied, "Thanks for stating the obvious. And excuse me for wanting to talk to my husband about our children."

"That's *all* you talk to me about."

It was an unfair comment Neil had muttered once upon a time. She was so furious with him, she had turned on her side and gone to sleep. In the light of morning, it didn't feel worth rehashing. So she forgot about it altogether. But maybe she shouldn't have. Maybe she should have paid that comment more attention.

Austin looked up from his notebook. "Hey, Mom."

"Hey, honey." She leaned against his doorjamb. "How was school?"

"Uneventful."

This had been his answer every day since the first day. So far, it seemed to be true. There hadn't been any fights or any sign of the violence many of them worried about at the public meeting back in July. There was a small skirmish in Austin's homeroom yesterday, but Camille didn't hear that from Austin; she heard it from Kathleen. Apparently, Bennett and Maxwell Teague had an altercation. But that was nothing new. The two of them had been having altercations since kindergarten, when Maxwell stuck his wet finger in Bennett's ear and Bennett reacted by slugging Maxwell in the stomach. The principal at Lewis and Clark must not have communicated to the principal at the middle school the importance of keeping the boys apart. Poor Mrs. Fullerton was in for a long year.

On the other hand, the kids from South Fork appeared to be on their best behavior.

Rebecca kept saying it was the calm before the storm and just you wait. Camille was starting to suspect that Rebecca would rather have the violence for the sake of her own vindication than avoid the violence for the sake of her children's safety.

"Did you know that the number of possible unique chess games is greater than the number of electrons in the entire universe?"

Stop being weird! she silently shouted.

She wanted to grab Austin's book and throw it out the window, send him outside to play baseball like every other boy in the neighborhood. But she would never do that. She would not pressure her son to be someone he wasn't. She would let him be exactly who God created him to be. She would let him march to the beat of his own drum, even when that marching scared her to death.

"That's a lot of chess games," she said instead.

"An insane amount," he replied, his attention returning to the notebook.

Frowning slightly, Camille left him to map out one of those infinitely possible chess games and headed into Paige's room, where she sat on the floor undressing her Maryellen doll. As much as Camille didn't want to, she needed to talk to her about the concerns Miss Jones brought up on the phone earlier today.

"Hey, Mom," Paige said. "How did the gun shootin' go?"

"Your mother's a pretty good shot." Camille sat on the edge of her daughter's canopy bed, watching Paige straighten Maryellen's hair, unsure what was worse: having a son who was too easy a target for bullies or having a daughter who might actually *be* a bully.

"Honey, are you nice to all your classmates?"

"Of course," she said, with such utterly confounded sincerity Camille knew it wasn't true.

"So you don't leave anyone out?"

"What do you mean?"

"At recess, do you tell other kids they can't play with you? Like Jubilee?"

"I played with her on the first day."

"And since then?"

Paige stopped unbuttoning Maryellen's shirt. "I don't like when she tries to hold my hand."

"Honey, you and Faith hold hands all the time."

"Not anymore. That's baby stuff."

"What about Nia? Do you leave her out?"

"I hate her."

The strong, matter-of-fact words came like a slap across Camille's face. Since when did her daughter hate anyone? "Paige, we don't use that word in this house. And you have to be nice to Nia."

"Why?"

Because otherwise, you're going to look like a little racist! The thought came irately—like a rage-filled scream in her head. Camille slid off the bed and joined Paige on the floor. "Honey, you know why. We learn why every Sunday at church."

"We don't go to church anymore."

"Yes, we do. We've just taken a small break. We'll go back this weekend." Camille reached into Paige's lap and took her hands. "Babe, we're nice to everyone because Jesus tells us to be kind. We treat others how we want to be treated."

"Well, maybe someone should tell Miss Jones what Jesus says because she's not nice at all!"

Camille drew back at the sudden outburst.

Paige's face turned pink, and she was doing that thing she did whenever she didn't want to cry—where she pulled her chin toward her neck and sucked on her lower lip and the vein in her temple began to throb.

"Paige."

"I hate second grade!" she yelled. "Miss Jones lets Nia do everything, and she never lets me do anything! All the girls love her and hate me, and I don't want to go back to church unless Daddy comes too!"

Whatever restraint Paige was holding on to snapped in half. She burst into tears so violent, her shoulders heaved.

Camille didn't have any words. All she could do was pull her broken daughter into her lap and rock her back and forth, wiping away Paige's tears and hating her husband.

Twenty-Five

L<3vy: Did u hear abt Cody & Taylor?
Dax: Cody & Taylor? I thought he was hooking up w/Alexis.
L<3vy: Was.
Dax: ??
L<3vy: He asked her to homecoming & she said no.
Dax: He asked Alexis?
L<3vy: No, Taylor.
Dax: Yikes.
L<3vy: You know who she likes, right?
Dax: Not Cody.

The Liberia Adoption Facebook Group:

September 15 at 3:48pm

Jen Covington: Hey, Friends. I need advice. Our daughter was invited to a birthday party. It's for a little girl in her class. Jubilee was VERY excited when she brought the invitation home. To be honest, my husband and I were excited too. It's a relief to know she's making friends. She really wants to go. The problem is, she's only been home five months, and when she gets overstimulated, it turns into a nightmare. Any advice? RSVP due date is in two days, and I still don't know what to do.

Ruth Barnes: Man, that's hard. Do you know if they're opening presents at the party?
Likes: 2

Jen Covington: I have no idea.

Ruth Barnes: I would find that out beforehand.

Jen Covington: What if they're opening presents?

Ruth Barnes: Don't go.

Meredith Thompson: Go in with a well-thought-out exit strategy, and be prepared to pull that eject handle even a couple minutes in. Staying for the presents or to watch the kid blow out the candles is not worth the resulting 24-hour night-mare you may have to endure as a result of staying a minute too long.

Likes: 4

Dixie McLaughlin: Low expectations. Like Ruth said, find out the schedule from the kid's mom and prepare her step by step. Go through what she can expect at each transition, be prepared to leave, and come up with a reason ahead of time. Use lots of connection to keep her regulated.

Likes: 5

Carmen Hart: I don't think you have to miss out on the party just because they are opening presents. Like Dixie said, if you know what's coming and prepare her ahead of time, she might surprise you. We have to give our kids a chance to surprise us.

Likes: 3

Amanda Collins: If they are opening presents, maybe when you and Jubilee pick out a gift for the birthday girl, you can get Jubilee the same thing. That way, when she gives the present to birthday girl, she won't feel like she's losing something. Our kids have lost enough.

Likes: 3

Ruth Barnes: Whoever started the whole "let's open presents at the birthday party" tradition must have hated mothers.
Likes: 10
> **Amanda Collins:** LOL!
> **Dixie McLaughlin:** They sure never adopted a kid with trauma!

●●●●●

Camille drove the Highlander into the garage and shifted into park. The back was laden with groceries. She bought more than usual, mostly because she needed something to do. An excuse to avoid the house. She didn't want to feel its emptiness.

Emptiness was a horrible thing to feel.

It reminded her of Austin when he was five and he'd get the word confused. *I feel empty,* he'd say. The first time he said it, Camille had been quite alarmed. Until she figured out he really meant he felt bored. Well, Camille didn't feel bored. She really did feel empty. Just like the house she didn't want to go into.

Her phone vibrated on the console.

The name *Jen C* popped up on the screen.

Grateful for the distraction, she snatched it up and pressed the phone to her ear with an exuberant, "Hello!"

"Hey, Camille. It's Jen." There was a brief pause. "Jen Covington."

"Jen! It's so great to hear from you. How's the job going at the high school? Taylor hasn't been to your office, has she?"

"No. Not yet."

"Well, good. She's always had a pretty sturdy immune system. Of course, if you know of any medicinal cures for sarcasm, I'm all ears."

"Hah. I don't think that one's been invented yet, but I'll let you know if I hear anything."

"Perfect. So, you're liking the job?"

"So far. There's a lot of kids to keep track of, but I'm slowly wrapping my mind around it all. No two days are the same, that's for sure."

"Well, that's good to hear." Camille pushed the button on the garage door opener. It rumbled to life behind her, slowly squeezing the sunlight away. "Because a little birdie in my ear told me that Joelle is getting ready to hand in her resignation. Apparently, she's one smitten new mama."

"That's great." Jen's voice carried a false sort of note, like it wasn't really great at all—an interesting contradiction. Was she not being honest about her enjoyment as the new high school nurse? "I'm really happy for her."

"And you," Camille said.

"Yeah, me too. Hey, I'm calling about Paige's birthday party."

"I hope you and Jubilee can make it."

"I think we can. I . . . well . . . Do you mind if I ask what's going to happen at the party?"

Camille's brow furrowed. "What's going to happen?"

"The order of events, I mean. I'm sure this is a weird question, it's just . . . Jubilee's never been to a birthday party before, and I want to help prepare her. Ahead of time."

"Oh, of course. Well, the theme is American Girl doll. But please do not take that to mean you have to get her an American Girl doll present. She has plenty, and the accessories are not very budget friendly, if you know what I mean. Barbies are ten times cheaper and just as popular around here. Now, if Jubilee has an American Girl doll, she is more than welcome to bring it along. Or any doll really. It doesn't have to be American Girl."

"Okay."

"It's going to be a 1950s theme. Paige's favorite doll is Maryellen, and she's circa 1954. So if you have anything 1950ish to wear, great! Of course, plenty of girls will come in jeans and T-shirts, so absolutely no pressure to dress up."

"Okay."

"The girls will play for a half hour or so. Maybe longer. It all depends on how long it takes before they start getting squirrelly. There will be a bounce house. Paige is obsessed with bounce houses. A snack table, of course. After that, the girls will get to decorate matching girl-doll T-shirts. Isn't that adorable? It's an idea I found on Pinterest. One will fit them, and the other will fit their doll. Paige wants to have a tea party with the cake, which will take up a chunk of time. And then whenever that wraps up, the girls can spend the rest of the time playing."

"So . . ." There was another pause, as if Jen were trying to process all that Camille just told her. "You won't be opening presents *at* the party?"

"Oh goodness, no. Third child in and I've learned my lesson there."

This seemed to come as a great relief. "Okay. Great."

Camille smiled. It was her first genuine one of the day. "Does this mean you and Jubilee can make it?"

"Y-yes. We'll be there."

Twenty-Six

There was a toy aisle at Target that used to make Jen cry. An explosion of pink and glitter, tiaras, dress-up clothes, and plastic tea sets. Jen would be shopping for Clorox or lightbulbs, come across the aisle, and want to curl into a ball and weep a river of tears that would sweep all the pink away.

Now the aisle made her nervous.

She faced it like a soldier headed into battle or a boxer staring at the ring—knowing soon she'd have to climb inside and face her opponent.

Paige's birthday party was tomorrow, and Jen RSVP'd yes. They would be going. And while Camille insisted that Jubilee didn't need to dress up like she belonged in the 1950s, Jen had spent the past several days in a craze searching for a poodle skirt that would fit her seven-year-old. She'd also driven to the nearest American Girl store, which was thirty minutes away, and spent an exorbitant amount of money she and Nick didn't have to spend, all so Jubilee could take a doll to a party. Not any old doll, mind you. An American Girl doll. A Truly Me doll, with dark brown skin like Jubilee's and short, curly hair.

Jubilee named her Baby. Not particularly creative, but that was the name she wanted.

Now they just had to buy Paige a present, and since they weren't opening the presents at the party, Jen most certainly would not be spending more exorbitant money to get her an American Girl doll gift.

A Barbie would have to do.

Beside her, Jubilee danced on her toes, bubbling over with excitement. Ever since Jen told her she was going to Paige's party, she could hardly contain herself. That was making Jen nervous too. It wasn't even party day, and already Jubilee was dysregulated. She thought about Meredith Thompson's advice and wondered if she shouldn't pull the eject handle now.

"Remember," Jen said. "All the presents at the party are going to be for

Paige. Whenever you go to a birthday party, the presents are for the birthday girl."

Jubilee nodded.

"We're going to pick out a gift for Paige, and Mommy will let you get a matching one. That way, when you give Paige her present, you don't have to be sad because you already have the exact same one."

"Like bunk-a beds!"

"Sure. Like that."

She knew it flew in the face of traditional parenting. She knew her parents would wholeheartedly disapprove. Her mother would wax on about the dangers of spoiling even though she spoiled Jubilee worse than any one of them, while Dad would complain about the everybody-gets-a-ribbon mentality and how it was solely responsible for the decline of their country.

Well, they didn't have to know about this.

This wasn't any of their concern.

And her parents were hardly the picture of parental success.

Just look at Brandon.

Her heart constricted at the thought of her brother. It had been five months, and she hadn't heard a peep. Not one single peep. He hadn't even sent a congratulatory text. Hey, I heard you're a mom. Congrats! He never replied when she texted him her new address either. But then, maybe Brandon didn't have a phone anymore. Maybe Brandon wasn't even alive.

Jen batted the disturbing thought away and led Jubilee to the Barbie section.

•❦•❧•

Paige raced down the stairs dressed in a black-and-white poodle skirt that matched the one Camille's mother sent in the mail for Maryellen. She catapulted herself into her father's arms as if it had been years instead of six days.

As he caught her with one hand, a large gift bag slung over his elbow, Camille noticed that he looked tan and fit—like the separation was suiting him.

"How's my big eight-year-old?"

Camille wanted to tell him to put Paige down. She was too old to be held like that. But Paige wrapped her arms and legs so tightly around her father's neck and waist, Camille wasn't sure he'd be able to extricate himself. "Are you staying for the party, Daddy?"

"No, Bug. I can't stay. I just wanted to stop by and give you your present."

Paige stuck out her bottom lip.

Neil gave it a tap, then set her down. "What a pretty skirt."

Paige twirled in a circle. "It's called a poodle skirt. Do you see the poodle here? Mommy's friend Rose made it for me."

"That was awfully nice of her."

"And Mommy did my hair." Paige patted her curls, which Camille had pulled up into a side ponytail identical to Maryellen's. "She put rollers in and everything."

"Well, your mother has always been quite the mommy."

The muscles in Camille's jaw tightened. She hated that he was standing there in the foyer so casually, as though it wasn't the same one he'd walked out of two months ago. She hated that he had the audacity to ring the doorbell. But most of all, she hated that such a flippant comment about her motherhood could make her heart squeeze as tightly as it did.

"Do I get to open my present now?" Paige asked.

Neil held up the gift bag. It was lime green and pink with matching tissue paper, and for an unsettled moment, Camille wondered who wrapped it. There was certainly no way Neil had put it together. Jas probably did—over a breakfast of turkey bacon and egg whites. Neil probably didn't like his eggs sunny-side up anymore. They probably put the gift in the backseat of Neil's Audi and went to CrossFit together, and when they finished, she handed it over with a kiss on his cheek. "Oh, darling, don't forget Paige's birthday present. It's such a lovely day, maybe we can go hunting when you get home."

Camille's jaw clenched tighter.

"Your grandmother helped pick it out," Neil said.

She huffed.

He shot her a look.

Sorry, but there was no way Neil's mother had anything at all to do with Paige's present. She couldn't even choose which beans to buy at the grocery store. It was the one silver lining of Neil's uncharacteristic betrayal. Camille was under no obligation to help her mother-in-law decide between store brand and Bush's.

Paige ripped out the tissue paper with little regard for the pretty arrangement and let out a high-pitched scream. "You got me Logan!" She yanked the Logan doll out from the bag. "Mom, Daddy got me Logan!"

"I see."

"Thank you, thank you, thank you!" Paige threw herself at her father in another overzealous hug. "Faith is bringing Tenney today. She told me at school. I hope she brings her guitar too. Do you think somebody will get me Logan's drum set?"

Neil and Camille spoke at the same time.

Just as he was saying, "I guess you'll find out at the party," Camille said, "Nobody is going to get you that drum set."

Camille frowned at him. "We're not opening presents at the party."

"What?" Paige exclaimed.

"Honey, that's not something we do. You know that."

"We did it for my birthday party in kindergarten."

"That's because there were only five guests."

"But Sarah's mom let her open presents at her birthday party, and it was the funnest part of the whole thing! Everybody loved it."

"Paige—"

Tears welled in her daughter's baby blues. There had been so many tears lately. So many manic, uncharacteristic tears. "You said the birthday girl gets to pick what she wants to do for the whole day. You told me that last night. You promised! And I really, really, *really* want to open presents at the party. Please, Mom. Please?"

"Okay, Paige. Settle down. If it's really that important to you, we can open presents at the party."

Twenty-Seven

Jen felt gross. None of her clothes fit her well anymore. Her entire body was jittery, and Jubilee's braids were already fuzzy, and they weren't even inside yet. Her daughter was skipping up the manicured lawn toward a house three times the size of their own, wearing a poodle skirt that was a little too big and slightly frayed, because beggars could not be choosers. Paige's present was tucked under one arm, and her new doll was tucked under the other as Jen whispered frantic prayers behind her. Half pleading, half demanding.

Please, Lord. Let this go well.

The front door opened.

Camille stood in the doorway looking like she belonged on the cover of *Better Homes & Gardens.*

This is what a mother is supposed to look like, Jen thought.

"I'm so glad you could come," she said, waving them inside. "And with your very own doll! Oh, how wonderful."

Jubilee beamed and held up the wrapped Barbie.

"You brought a present. How incredibly thoughtful of you. Paige will be so excited."

"It's a—"

"Oh, don't tell me! I want to be as surprised as Paige." Camille made a big fuss of covering her ears. "The presents go right over there, on that table. All the girls are out in the back, playing. Mothers too."

Jen pictured a bunch of well-dressed, thin mothers in tailored clothes, running around with tiaras and fairy wands.

Jubilee walked through the foyer, into an opened piano room, where the table Camille had pointed to was brimming with presents—all large and wrapped in fancy paper with fancy pink ribbons.

Camille stopped Jen with a touch on her arm. "I wanted to tell you before things got underway. There's been a slight change of plans."

"Oh?"

"Paige was insistent on opening presents today." Camille rolled her eyes in a lighthearted way, as if to say, *You know kids.* But no. Jen didn't. It turned out, she didn't really know kids at all.

"She's going to open her presents at the party?"

Camille shrugged, the gesture just as lighthearted as the eye roll. "Apparently."

Jen's stomach churned. This was hardly a slight change of plans. She and Nick hadn't prepared Jubilee for this. How could Camille be so inconsiderate?

Pull that eject handle even a couple minutes in.

They weren't even a full minute in, and her heart was screaming *Eject!* But Jubilee was waving excitedly for Jen to follow her to the open patio doors, which let in a warm breeze and the happy laughter of little girls.

We have to give our kids a chance to surprise us.

Was this one of those times?

"I really am sorry," Camille said. But she didn't sound sorry. In fact, a hard edge had crept into her tone. It was as though the woman could sense Jen's turmoil, only instead of feeling sympathetic, she got defensive.

"That's okay. It should be fine."

Please, Lord. Let it be fine.

Her body pumped with stress and cortisol as she encouraged Jubilee to set the present on the table. "Remember," she said, "we have your matching Barbie right here in Mommy's purse. Okay?"

Jubilee nodded.

The stress and cortisol pumped harder as Jen followed her out onto a large upper deck. Beneath was a nice patio and an expansive backyard. There was a table filled with fancy finger food, and a castle bounce house and at least fifteen little girls running around with dolls of their own, dressed in bobby socks and saddle shoes and poodle skirts that weren't frayed.

She caught sight of Paige, dressed in an outfit every bit as perfect as her mother's, as well as a glittery birthday crown. She didn't have a fairy wand, but she did have a light saber, and currently she was pointing it at two little Asian girls in matching vintage party dresses.

They both fell over in the grass, as though the birthday princess had struck them dead, and the three burst into a round of hysterical giggles.

"Yoo-hoo, Jen!" someone called from below.

Jen put her hand up to her forehead like a visor and squinted at one of the mothers she met at Unpack Your Backpack night, right after the tense encounter Nick had with that awful man.

"Can I go play?" Jubilee asked.

Jen nodded and followed her, astonished at the way she ran down the steps, unafraid to join the girls who all seemed to know each other so well. Jen sometimes felt this way about Jubilee—usually when she was doing something less praiseworthy, like willfully wetting her pants or throwing her spoon across the table. It always came in a rush—this startled, shocked feeling. *Who are you?* She was a stranger with strange behavior. Jen wondered if other moms felt the same way, but then she thought about Leah, who said things like, "Oh, I was the exact same way at that age," whenever Lila threw a fit over something silly, like not getting to wear big brother Noah's Spider-Man costume through the sprinkler.

"How are you?" the woman asked when Jen reached her.

Jen scrambled for a name, but came up completely blank. "I'm doing well. You?"

"Soaking up the last of this warm weather."

"It's nice," Jen said lamely.

Another woman joined them, just as familiar. Just as nameless. Only this time, Jen knew who she belonged to. She was the mother of the two matching Asian girls zapped by the lightsaber. Camille had introduced them. Again, at Unpack Your Backpack night.

"Deb," she said, shaking Jen's hand.

Jen could have kissed her.

"I'm sure it's hard to keep track of all the names."

"A little."

"How's the new job going at the high school?"

"Oh." She didn't know Deb knew she was working at the high school. Camille must have told her, which made her wonder what else Camille had said. "It's busy."

"I'm sure."

"You work at the high school?" the other woman asked.

"I've been filling in for the nurse while she's on maternity leave."

"What are things like there?"

"What do you mean?"

The mystery woman leaned closer, like whatever she was about to share was confidential. "With the transfer students? The two schools have always been rivals. I'm sure it must be quite . . . tense."

"I don't really notice, to be honest."

This didn't seem to be the juicy answer the woman was looking for.

Thankfully, a few others joined the conversation, taking Jen out from the spotlight.

"Camille is brave," someone said.

"Tell me about it. I always cap Riley's parties at eight. That's all the little-girl emotion I can handle at one time."

"I think she must have invited everyone in Paige's class."

"And then some."

Jen looked around at all the girls. Besides Jubilee and Deb's two and a little girl named Aaishi who looked Indian, the party guests were white. There were no transfer students. Jen's attention wandered to the snack table, and her heart gave a jolt. Jubilee was eating food. She was sitting on a woman's lap, eating food. Jen quickly excused herself from the conversation and hurried over.

"I'm sorry about that," she said to the woman as she approached.

"Oh, I don't mind. She's such a little sweetheart."

But Jen minded.

Jen minded very much.

Because she knew what this could lead to. Jen had firsthand experience.

The whole thing had a name: indiscriminate affection, a term she and Nick had learned all about. What it was, why it happened, the correct way to discourage it. The problem was, those books and articles never accounted for the fact that your heart might start pounding and your voice might start shaking and your thoughts might get too tangled to remember exactly the right thing to say. Those books also didn't say how oddly others would look at you, like you were an overpossessive mommy who just needed to relax.

"I think she was getting upset because the bounce house was full." The nice, oblivious woman nodded toward the castle, which was being supervised by a teenager with bare feet and legs that went on for days. She wore a tiara and a bored expression and a pile of blond hair on top of her head in a messy bun.

"So I invited her over here with me. She is such a cuddle bug. Emma doesn't let me anymore, so I'll take all the cuddles I can get." The woman gave Jubilee an affectionate squeeze as Jen's mind scrambled in every direction, searching for a way to get Jubilee off this woman's lap without causing a scene. Without a repeat of what happened at their church back in Clayton—when Jubilee clung to another stranger's neck and refused to let go.

"I want you to be my mommy!" she had screamed.

And everybody in the church lobby stopped and stared while Jen had to pry Jubilee away.

How quickly the woman had gone from charmed to horrified. How easily Jen could tell what she'd been thinking: *What is going on in your home?* Earlier that morning, Jubilee defaced her daybed with a permanent marker. And Jen—big, bad meanie that she was—took every coloring utensil from Jubilee's room.

"You can play with them at the kitchen table," Jen said, "where I can supervise you."

Jubilee picked up the tin piggy bank on her dresser and hurled it at Jen's head. It missed, thankfully. And with a calmness Jen hadn't felt, she picked it up off the floor and took that too.

Of course Jubilee had wanted that woman to be her new mommy. That new mommy didn't make her do hard things, like pick up her room or take a bath when she didn't feel like it. That new mommy didn't take her piggy bank or her markers. So what if she was a perfect stranger? Two months ago, Jen had been a perfect stranger too.

Thankfully, none of that happened now.

Jubilee announced that she had to go potty.

Jen nearly melted into a puddle of relief. First, because Jubilee didn't pee on the woman's leg, and second, she had her excuse. She hurriedly ushered Jubilee away.

"Remember what we talked about, honey," Jen said, once they were inside the bathroom. "If you are scared or upset or you need a hug or you want to sit in someone's lap, you come find me, okay? That's what mommies are for."

When they returned to the backyard, the teenager with the tiara approached. "There were too many kids in the bounce house a little bit ago, but there's room now. Would you like a turn?"

Inside, Paige was jumping with Deb's two girls, all three of them holding on to American Girl dolls of their own. Jen stood off to the side, watching through the black mesh windows. As soon as Jubilee crawled in, Paige collapsed in an exaggerated heap. "I'm so hot I might die. I need lemonade. Mixed with Sprite! Who wants to try my special lemonade-Sprite concoction?"

Faith and Hope raised their hands.

Paige giggled because Faith raised her doll's hand too.

And before Jubilee hardly had the chance to stand, the three girls left. As Paige slid out and landed on her bottom in the grass, Jen experienced a sudden and intense wave of mutinous dislike.

Jubilee stood alone inside the bounce house, Baby dangling in her hand—and for a second it seemed like she understood the full weight of what had just happened. It seemed like she understood what Paige had done. But then she tried a few tentative jumps, and a large smile spread across her face, revealing a mouth full of mismatching teeth. She jumped higher and higher, spinning in circles.

"Mama!" she shouted. "Dis' is so much fun! Come in! Come jump!"

Jen pictured it.

She—a full grown woman—slipping off her shoes and crawling inside. All the mothers in their expensive clothes, pausing from their conversation to stare at Jen's large bottom as she went in. She would be a hot, sweaty mess in two seconds flat. She would probably sprain something, like her back, and Camille would need to call the ambulance, and Jubilee would never be invited anywhere again.

"C'mon!" Jubilee yelled, tossing Baby into the air and catching her in both arms.

"I'm too big," Jen called. "The bounce house is for little girls."

It wasn't true, of course.

The bounce house could have held her, even with the extra pounds she seemed to be carrying on her body these days.

Jubilee looked disappointed.

Thankfully, it didn't last. She was having too much fun jumping around like a maniac to pout for long. Jen watched—a spectator of her daughter's joy—her muscles slowly unwinding. Maybe this would be okay. Maybe Jubilee's first birthday party would turn out a success.

Please, Lord, let it be true. Please, please let this be a good day.

But then the birthday girl marched through the backyard, telling everyone to go into the living room because it was time to open the presents. The hope expanding in Jen's soul burst like a popped party balloon.

She tried to trick Jubilee into thinking it was time to go, but Jubilee was no fool. They hadn't had any cake or tea yet. They hadn't decorated the dolly-and-me T-shirts. Jen had explained at least a dozen times this past week that they would get to decorate dolly-and-me T-shirts. Jubilee really wanted to decorate dolly-and-me T-shirts. And if they left now, Jen was certain Camille would take the early departure very personally.

So they ended up in the giant room with a cathedral ceiling and canvased pictures of the family in coordinated outfits, watching Paige sit on her throne—a plastic, blow-up pink princess chair that probably fit her best two years ago. All her party guests sat crisscross on the floor while the mothers stood behind with their phones out, capturing the birthday girl as she opened whatever present they'd purchased.

None of them seemed to be having a minor panic attack at the last-minute change in party plans. None of them seemed to notice that Jen was. So far, all the presents had been American Girl, and all the girls wanted a good look. Camille had the bright idea of passing them around so everyone had a chance to see.

Eject! Eject! Eject!

But it all happened so fast. Paige tore through her presents, and suddenly they were being passed around. And Jubilee was sitting far away, out of Jen's reach, growing visibly frustrated. Because to her, this wasn't taking turns. This was loss after loss after loss for a girl whose life had been defined by it. *Here, look at this toy. Oh, but you can't have it. None of these are actually for you. Nothing is ever actually for you.*

It was horrible.

And Jen's underarms were beginning to sweat.

And Jubilee let out a frustrated growl.

And a mother standing beside Camille stared for an extended moment.

"Jubilee," Jen called softly, hating the way her voice shook as she did. She crooked her finger. "Come stand by me."

Jubilee shook her head, her arms crossed tightly in front of her chest.

Camille handed Paige the Barbie-shaped box Jen had wrapped earlier this morning. Jubilee had danced around her with her matching Barbie in hand while Jen cut and folded and taped.

Now Jubilee sat up straight as Paige tore off the paper. When the Barbie was revealed, there was a moment of nothing. No *ooh*. No *aah*. No, *Oh, this is exactly what I wanted!*

Jubilee knocked into a girl behind her as she scrambled up to her feet and barreled through the circle of party guests. She dug inside Jen's purse with overeager hands and pulled out her matching Barbie. "Look, Paige. Dey match!"

Paige Gray—the mutinous monster—looked at her mother and said, "I already have this."

"Honey, there's no such thing as too many Barbies."

"But I have this exact same one."

"Paige, say thank you, sweetheart."

Paige looked at Jubilee with heavily lidded eyes. "Thank you." Then she tossed the Barbie into the pile of glittery pink paper wrappings and opened the next gift. It was an American Girl rabbit and hutch that had Paige jumping up from her seat, hugging it to her chest. "Oh, I adore rabbits!"

Jubilee threw her Barbie.

It nearly hit Aaishi in the back of the head.

"Jubilee!" Jen yelped, hefting her into her arms with a strength born of adrenaline just as Camille caught Jen's eye. She at least had the good manners to look stricken. This was, after all, her fault. Opening presents was not a part of the schedule. Opening presents was not something Jen and Nick had prepared Jubilee for. They wouldn't have RSVP'd yes if they had known Paige would be opening presents.

"Is everything okay?" Deb asked, touching Jen's arm with cool fingers.

"Yes, it's fine. We're . . . we're going to use the bathroom."

She began to walk Jubilee toward the kitchen, rubbing her back and swaying, trying to calm her daughter before her whimpers turned into wails and everybody stopped and stared. She needed to get Jubilee away from all the stimulation—away from all the presents. She needed to calm her down before this escalated any further.

But the farther away they got, the more Jubilee began to panic.

By the time Jen had her inside the nearest bathroom, the door shut and locked as though the extra security measure would serve as a sound barrier, Jubilee's noodle body had gone into full-throttle thrashing, and Jen's heart beat so frantically she thought it would burst through her chest like that gruesome scene from *Alien*.

"I no wanna go!" she screamed. "Don't make-a me go!"

Jen had to restrain her.

She had to restrain her feral daughter in Camille Gray's bathroom while everyone stood outside and listened. As Jubilee screamed and jerked and spit, Jen sat behind her on the bathroom floor, wrapping her body around her daughter's and holding tight. She rocked her back and forth, back and forth until Jubilee stopped fighting and her screams turned into sad, pitiful moans.

Jen continued to hold her. She continued to rock her.

Trapped inside Camille's bathroom.

Utterly and completely alone.

Twenty-Eight

"That was intense."

"That was *insane*."

"I've never seen a child act like that."

"Do you think something's wrong with her?"

"It was like she was possessed."

Camille ignored the gossiping mothers and their hushed, solicitous tones as she cleaned up the wrapping paper. No doubt the conversation would turn to her marriage as soon as she walked out the patio doors. No doubt that if this had been six months ago and someone else's marriage, she would have jumped into the fray. She did it at PTA meetings. She did it at birthday parties. She'd even done it at Bible studies.

Gossip cloaked in prayer requests.

She balled up a scrap of thick, glittery pink paper with a matching glittery pink bow. All that effort, crumpled into a halfhearted ball and stuffed inside a trash bag. And all these presents, carefully selected and much too expensive. Soon enough, Paige would get tired of them all. They'd end up in a trash heap or donated to Goodwill. In ten years, her youngest would move out. Go off to college. Probably resent Camille as much as Taylor resented her. And Camille would be all alone. Her life would turn into one long, never-ending weekend without the children.

And without them, who was she?

A cold shudder moved down her arms as she finished picking up the last of the scraps. The party guests and several mothers were outside again. Not all of them cared to gossip. They'd already had their tea, and Paige had blown out the candles. The girls had finished decorating their dolly-and-me T-shirts. The time was five to three. Five minutes until the end of the party. And yet nobody seemed poised to leave.

"I really wish Madison wouldn't have seen it. She's so impressionable. Did you see the way she was hitting and kicking her mother?"

"Madison would never do that."

Oh, shut up! Shut up, all of you.

The girl had a meltdown. Right then, Camille wanted to have one herself. She wanted to tell them all to stop their judging when it had been Camille's fault. She'd seen the panicked look on Jen's face when she told her they would be opening presents. She just hadn't cared then. She'd been too annoyed to care. After all, it was Paige's party, and Paige was distraught because her father left. He left them all. And couldn't Jen see that? Couldn't the woman cut her some slack?

She thought Jen was overreacting. She thought Jen was making a mountain out of a molehill.

But she wasn't.

Camille tied up the trash bag and set it in front of the dishwasher. She dialed Jen's number while tapping her finger against the countertop. Her wedding ring sparkled up at her like a cruel joke.

The phone rang in her ear.

Once.

Twice.

Three times.

And then voice mail.

She hit End.

"Camille?"

Camille turned around.

It was Pamela Trentwood, the worst of the gossipers. She had three children. A girl-boy-girl combination, just like Camille. But her husband wasn't quite as successful, her house wasn't quite as big, and her daughters weren't nearly as sought after. From the second Camille greeted Pamela at the door, Pamela had slathered on the sympathy, like she secretly relished it. Well, Camille *secretly* hated her.

"Would you like me to put on another pot of coffee?" Pamela asked, tapping the side of her empty cup.

No, actually. I'd like you all to leave. It's three o'clock, can't you see? I'm almost positive I said the party would end at three.

"I don't mind," Pamela said.

"It's fine. I can do it." Camille reached for the stainless-steel canister on the counter, where she stored the coffee beans.

Pamela set her cool hand on Camille's elbow. "It's been a fabulous party."

"Thank you."

"You've always thrown fabulous parties, but I think you've outdone yourself this time. I'm sure you wanted to make it extra special for Paige."

"I'm sure I did."

Pamela raised her eyebrows.

Camille pulled out the grinder and plugged it in. She dumped in some beans and hit the power button.

"It's too bad that girl caused such a fuss," Pamela said over the loud noise. "I hope Paige isn't upset."

"I doubt she is."

"I love your hair, by the way."

"Thank you." Camille let go of the button and began searching the cupboards for another filter, hopeful she wouldn't find one.

"My sister chopped her hair off when she got a divorce too."

Camille stopped her searching. "What was that?"

"I was just saying, my sister did the same thing. After her divorce. I think a lot of women do it after a breakup."

"There hasn't been a breakup. We're not getting a divorce."

"Oh, but I thought . . ." Pamela's face crumpled with forced confusion—an impressive feat, considering all the Botox she had injected into her forehead. "Didn't Rebecca see him with that other woman?"

• • • • •

How did the party go?

The question belonged to Dixie McLaughlin on the adoption Facebook page, and for the past half hour, as Nick bathed and lotioned their daughter, Jen sat in front of her computer, staring at it with burning eyes and a hollowed-out chest. She offered a bare-minimum response, and the replies were rolling in.

Oh, sweetie. That's terrible.

We've all been there.

You aren't alone.

How maddening! People just don't get it.

Warrior on, Mama. This gig isn't for the faint of heart.

No. No, it wasn't. This gig was for women like Dixie, who had not one, but two children from Africa. Another daughter adopted from foster care, as well as a sixteen-year-old foster kid with a newborn baby. All living under her roof. Not to mention goats, chickens, and a llama. Jen had one kid. One. And she couldn't seem to handle her at all.

Her phone began to chirp.

It was Camille again. The sight of her name on the screen had Jen unwrapping another Dove chocolate and stuffing it in her mouth. She tucked it into the pocket of her cheek and sucked hard.

She should have hit the Eject button as soon as Camille told her about the presents. But that would have seemed psychotic and extreme. Jen didn't want to look psychotic or extreme. In the end, she cared more about what Camille Gray thought of her than she did about the well-being of her child.

And now Jubilee would have to pay.

If her daughter was excluded before Paige's party, how much more would she be excluded now? Her throat tightened at the memory of all those appalled mothers—all those wide-eyed, staring children. Every single girl in Jubilee's class had witnessed the fit.

Except for Nia, the transfer student with beads in her hair.

Nia hadn't seen it because Nia wasn't there.

Nia wasn't invited.

Why wasn't Nia invited?

Jen's thoughts turned dark and judgmental.

She sent Camille to voice mail, hit the caps lock, and began shout-typing.

WHY CAN'T ANYTHING BE EASY?

She and Nick had prayed and prayed about this party. They worked so hard to prepare Jubilee, so ever-loving hard. But none of it mattered. The party had gone the opposite of well. It went as horribly unwell as a party could go. So unwell, in fact, her brain was already starting to suppress it. She couldn't remember what she said when she carried Jubilee out of the bathroom on that long, mortifying walk to the front door. She couldn't remember if she'd apologized. She couldn't even remember if she grabbed Baby. Her brain was shoving it down—deep, deep down—to a place she didn't ever want to visit again. But she knew how this worked. It wouldn't stay there forever. For the rest of her life, it would pop up at random, unexpected times like a mortifying jack-in-the-box, making her burn with embarrassment. Making her entire body shudder.

WHY CAN'T ONE BLASTED THING GO RIGHT?

With each typed word, each slam of her finger against a key, her anger bubbled. It was always there now, lurking right under the surface like a crocodile waiting for its next prey. Jubilee would spill her milk. The crocodile would snap. Nick would leave his socks on the floor. The crocodile would snap. Her thoughts would scream and rant and rail. An internal fit ten times the size of Jubilee's.

And then her mother's voice would come—familiar, reprimanding.

We do not cause scenes, Jennifer.

I CAN'T DO THIS. I CAN'T BE HER MOTHER.

You were never supposed to be a mother at all.

The whispered thought came like a cruel slap across an all-too-tender face. She closed her eyes as a hot tear tumbled down her cheek. She closed her eyes just like God had closed her womb. He closed her womb because He knew she wasn't fit for this particular job. But she hadn't listened. She barreled ahead. Couldn't get pregnant? Couldn't sustain a pregnancy? No biggie. She and Nick would adopt. This was God's plan, she told herself. But what if it wasn't? What if He was trying to tell her to stop and she didn't listen and now here the three of them were?

Her lips trembled. Her hollowed-out chest was caving in.

You were never supposed to be a mother at all.

Jen swiped at her cheeks and put her fingers back on the keyboard. She typed familiar words into Facebook's search bar. She went to a site she hadn't visited since she and Nick were matched with Jubilee. As soon as they got that precious referral picture from their adoption agency, Jen didn't need to visit this site anymore. Jen had a daughter. But before then, when she had no face to pin all that yearning on, she went with heart-shaped googly eyes. She went with a bleeding wanting heart.

Now?

Her heart felt dead. And somehow raw.

Second Chance Adoptions.

There was a little boy at the top of the page. Vincent. Six years old. Originally from Haiti. Home for three years. In need of a new family. A second chance.

Three years.

Jen hadn't even hit the six-month mark yet. *Get through the first six months,* people said. *Things get so much easier after the first six months.* Six months was getting closer, and Jen was only sinking deeper.

Six months.

While these people—the people who adopted Vincent from Haiti—had struggled for *three years.* Fought for *three years.* And still, they lost. Now he was here, smiling widely on the screen, tempting her in a way she never thought she would be tempted. She didn't want this struggle to be her life. She didn't want this to be her life at all.

Well, maybe it didn't have to be.

She closed her eyes, blood whooshing in her ears.

What would happen once Jubilee got too big to restrain? What would happen if she started to sense Jen's resentment? What if Jubilee ended up exactly like Brandon? She pushed the question down—deep, deep down—and stuffed another chocolate in her mouth.

This didn't have to be her life.

She had a way out.

Vincent's face was proof.

Soon he would have his second chance. A new family would adopt him. A family more equipped to handle Vincent's needs. And for the family that adopted him from Haiti? He would become a memory. A hard phase that they went through. They would feel guilty, of course. They would feel like failures. But soon enough those feelings would melt away and it would be like he never existed at all.

"Hey."

Jen jumped. Her hands jerked off the keyboard. She quickly closed out the internet before her husband could see.

"Whoa there. I didn't mean to scare you."

"Sorry. I didn't hear you."

"You were very involved in whatever you were looking at." Nick swiveled Jen's chair around. As soon as he saw her, his face went soft with compassion and concern. He pulled her up to standing and wrapped her in a hug. Her heart was still pounding so hard, she wondered if he could feel it. But he didn't say anything. He kissed the top of her head and whispered, "You're a good mom."

She shook her head.

"You are, Jen."

They were the same words Leah spoke. The same words Leah told her often. But at the moment, Jen couldn't believe them. Good mothers didn't resent their children. Good mothers didn't wish them away.

"I know today was hard."

"It was horrible."

"But now we know. We know how to handle parties."

"After today, she'll never be invited to one."

"Kids that age have short memories." Nick rubbed her back in slow, soothing circles, then pulled her away, firmly clutching her arms. "We're doing a good job."

He was. *He* was doing a good job.

Not her.

"Jubilee's ready for her goodnight kiss. I can go lie down with her after."

Jen sniffed and wiped her face dry; then she shuffled across the hall, into the doorway of her daughter's room. Jubilee lay in bed, her face visible in the soft glow of her night-light. Her eyes were wide and white—two blinking orbs that stared at Jen, a robot of a mother.

"I'm sorry, Mama," she said.

"For what?"

"For being bad."

The words uncorked her. Jen lurched out of the doorway to her daughter's bedside. "You are *not* bad."

Mama was bad.

Mama was rotten.

Because here was a child who had spent five years of her life in an orphanage. Who had to fight for every scrap of food—never mind toys—because you only got one meal a day, and when bellies were hungry, kids didn't have the luxury of sharing. A child terrified of the dark because for far too long, she had slept in pitch black. Hot, humid, fetid pitch black where children soiled themselves and whimpered into the void. And hers had been one of the better orphanages. At least there, the boys and girls had been locked into separate rooms at night. Not all of them did that. Some locked fifteen-year-old street boys in with six-year-old girls, and the stories Jen heard made her skin crawl.

This had been Jubilee's reality. And still, Jen's heart went hard and mean whenever that trauma surfaced. It was like Jen got amnesia and forgot about the past altogether.

"I love you," she said, willing it to be true.

"I love-a you too."

Jen bent over and kissed Jubilee's head and said apologies of her own, apologies in her heart. *I'm sorry I'm not better. I'm sorry I'm not the mother I thought I was going to be. I'm sorry I'm not the mommy you deserve.*

When she reached the doorway, Jubilee called her name.

Jen turned around.

"Was Jesus wit me in da orphanage?"

Jen wanted to tell her yes. Of course He was. Jesus was with her always. But the words stuck in her throat. How could she say them when sometimes she wasn't sure if Jesus was with them now?

Twenty-Nine

Any second now, he would walk out the front doors. Camille knew because she'd logged onto the gym's website and checked the times. Now she sat in her Highlander, gripping the steering wheel with sweaty fingers, spying from an insurance company's parking lot across the street at six o'clock in the morning.

Didn't Rebecca see him with that other woman?

The question kept reverberating in her mind like a giant booming gong, one that Pamela Trentwood hit with glee, and it wouldn't stop vibrating. The sound kept going and going and going—one long, uninterrupted wavelike succession of clattering noise.

Rebecca had seen Neil with another woman.

She had seen her husband with someone else, and she didn't tell her. She told Pamela, but not her. It was enough to make Camille's stomach revolt.

The front doors opened.

Camille ducked, positive he would see her. Of course he would see her. He'd recognize the SUV right away. But he didn't look across the street. And he was holding the door open for someone else.

A woman walked out, a gym bag strapped across her shoulder.

She was tall and slender and exotic, with black satin hair pulled up into a ponytail longer than Camille's had ever been. Her body was perky everywhere a female body was meant to be—and she was young.

Much, much too young.

Camille's throat tightened.

Don't kiss her. Please don't kiss her.

She squeezed her eyes shut, then peeked through one of them, watching as Neil walked shoulder to shoulder with this woman who looked way too feminine for hunting and Chuck Norris.

They stopped in front of his car.

The woman laughed at something Neil said. She laughed like her husband was a regular comedian and threw her gym bag into the Jeep beside his Audi.

She drove a silver, doorless Jeep Wrangler.

Camille imagined Neil riding shotgun, his foot up on her dashboard as the wind ran through his thinning hair.

Please don't kiss. Please don't kiss.

The woman said something.

Neil said something.

Then he lifted his hand in the air for a high five.

An actual high five.

The woman gave him one.

Their hands came down and stayed together for a lingering moment.

Then she smiled.

And he smiled.

And they got in their cars and drove away.

●●●●●

Camille to Kathleen: I take it back. Please tell Rick I would like the name of a really good PI.

Thirty

Anaya's day started with pajamas and a bloody nose. Actually, it started with Paige Gray in her pajamas reeling back in her chair and shouting, "That is disgusting!"

Indeed, it was.

Gavin Royce was bleeding all over, and it was day one of Spirit Week. Day one was pajama day. He pinched his nostrils together, but it wasn't doing a whole lot of good. The blood found its way through, and so far it had gotten all over his hands and his T-shirt and was making a puddle on his desk.

He didn't seem too upset about it. In fact, he seemed to just sit there and let it happen.

The other children weren't quite so calm.

Anaya plucked a handful of tissues from the Kleenex box on her desk, hurried over, and attempted to stanch the flow.

Everyone but Gavin had gotten out of their seats.

"Back in your chairs, please," she said in her mama's voice—kind but without an inch of slack.

"Is Gavin dying?" Zeke asked. He was wearing a pair of shark slippers designed to look as though the two sharks had eaten his feet.

"No, honey. He just has a nosebleed."

A horrible, horrible nosebleed.

So bad, there was no way she could send him to the office by himself. If she did, the school hallway would look like the scene of a massacre.

"Tilt your head up, sweetheart," she said, hoping that might squelch the flow.

"Ib I do dat, I dwallow doo buch blood."

"Okay. All right." She walked Gavin over to her desk, keeping a firm hold on the back of his head and the clump of Kleenex over his nose, already soaked with red. She plucked another clump and added it to the others. "Class, I'm going to run Gavin to the nurse's office really quickly. You all know the morning routine. Please move your sticks, and start right away on your writing."

With that, she hurried Gavin to the front office.

As soon as they walked inside, Jan McCormack lurched out of her seat. She made a big fuss, became a mother hen, and told Anaya she would take it from here. She'd better go wash her hands.

When Anaya looked down, she understood why.

They were covered in blood. Just like his T-shirt had been. His Confederate flag T-shirt.

She slipped into the staff bathroom to wash it off with soap and water, reminding herself that Gavin didn't buy his own clothes. Gavin probably didn't even know what the flag represented. Gavin was actually a very simple, very endearing little boy with a short attention span and atrocious handwriting.

By the time she returned to her class, a good five minutes had passed and her students—her lovely, well-behaved students—were all sitting at their desks, writing away. Even Dante—who needed a wiggle seat to help him sit still—sat on his knees, his elbow crooked in that odd way of a left hander, his bottom lip tucked under his two front teeth as he concentrated hard on the task in front of him.

Anaya beamed with pride.

Except for the cold lunch cup tipped over on its side, all was in perfect order. Hardly a month into the school year, and they had the morning routine mastered.

"Well, I think such responsible behavior earned you all an extra recess."

They looked up from their papers, smiling at one another in shared excitement.

"Let's stand for the pledge."

Everyone rose together, chairs scraping against the industrial carpet as they set their hands over their chests and recited the Pledge of Allegiance. When they were done, they sat back down and continued their writing. The attendance cup was empty. Anaya righted the sticks in the blue cup, counted the ones in the red, and plugged the attendance into her computer when Paige came up to her desk.

"Miss Jones?"

"Yes?"

"Are you gonna clean up that blood?"

The blood.

She jumped out of her seat like it had morphed into hot iron, grabbed the Clorox wipes in her bottom desk drawer, and hurried over to sanitize the area, embarrassed that she'd forgotten to clean it up right away.

Just as she was finished cleaning, she noticed that the desk across from Gavin's was empty. She stopped. Straightened. Looked around the room.

"Where is Jubilee?" Anaya asked nobody in particular.

The class looked around.

Anaya turned in a circle, as though Jubilee were playing a funny game of hide-behind-the-teacher, then marched over to the time machine and flung open the door. There was just the beanbag and the flashlight and a stack of picture books about Native Americans.

No Jubilee.

Had someone accidentally moved her Popsicle stick? Was she absent? But no, Anaya remembered seeing her this morning in Supergirl pajamas. She remembered thinking that her hair looked semipresentable today, mostly because of the large headband she was wearing.

"I like your hair, Jubilee," Anaya had said. "It's very pretty."

And Jubilee looked down in that shy way of hers, hiding her smile.

"Did she use the restroom?" Anaya asked, louder this time.

Nobody answered.

They all looked around at one another, until Sarah's hand slowly rose up into the air. "I saw her go out the door."

"That door?"

Sarah nodded.

Anaya raced over and flung it open, letting in the dreary morning air. She leaned outside and scanned the grounds. The playground. The basketball courts. The baseball field. The fence, and the wooded area beyond.

All of it was empty.

"Everyone stay in your seats." She propped the door open and stepped outside, her breath growing more and more desperate with every second that ticked by.

"Jubilee!" she called.

Nothing.

She moved farther away from her classroom. She was a shepherd leaving her flock for the one lost sheep. Mama loved that story from the Bible more than any other. She loved that Jesus cared most urgently about the lost one. At the moment, Anaya could understand why.

"Jubilee!" she yelled again.

Nothing answered but the wind.

Anaya had lost a child.

A student in her classroom had run away under her watch.

Panic was beginning to strangle her just as a glimpse of movement high up on the jungle gym caught her attention.

"Oh, sweet Jesus, thank You." She exhaled the praise on a pent-up breath. It was Jubilee. She was peeking out at her from the top tier of the jungle gym. Anaya cupped her hands over her mouth and called into the wind.

But Jubilee didn't come.

Anaya waved her hand in an exaggerated motion. "Come on in, honey. Before it starts to rain."

Jubilee ducked out of sight.

Thunder rumbled overhead.

Anaya looked over her shoulder at the students staring out the windows and jogged out to the playground, her ankle smarting. "Jubilee, honey. We need to go back into the classroom."

Jubilee remained in hiding.

Anaya climbed the ladder two rungs at a time.

The little girl sat at the top with her legs pulled up to her chest, her head buried in her knees.

"Sweetheart, can you please take my hand? We need to get inside before it starts to storm."

On cue, the clouds let out an ominous grumble.

Jubilee didn't move.

Meanwhile, her students were inside the classroom. Unsupervised for the second time this morning.

"Jubilee, whatever's going on, I promise you are safe and you aren't in any trouble. I just need you to take my hand so we can go inside."

Jubilee hesitated, then she took Anaya's hand.

Together they ran back to the class. They barely made it inside before the clouds opened up and unleashed the rain.

Anaya was just getting her students settled when the nurse came in with Gavin, his face scrubbed clean, his bloodstained T-shirt swapped out for a clean one that said Kate Richards O'Hare. Anaya's knees were still shaking from the adrenaline.

Thankfully, nobody felt like sharing with the nurse what just happened. Hopefully that particular adventure would remain Yellow 2's secret. She couldn't believe she almost lost a kid one month into her first year of teaching.

As soon as the nurse left and Gavin was seated, Anaya brought Jubilee back to her desk. She needed to know why the girl ran off. She needed to know so she could make sure it never, ever happened again. But Jubilee wouldn't say. She hardly lifted her eyes to Anaya at all.

Anaya took her lovingly by the shoulders. "Listen, Jubilee. I need you to promise me that you won't ever run away like that again. If you're scared or upset, you come talk with me about it, okay? I'll help you feel safe."

Jubilee nodded.

And Anaya—not sure what else to do—let her return to her desk. Later, when the class was doing literacy centers and Anaya sat at the bean-shaped table in the middle of a guided reading group, Nia raised her hand in the air. She was wearing a pink, fuzzy robe.

"Do you want to read the next page?" Anaya asked.

"No, ma'am. I want to tell you why Jubilee ran away."

"You know?"

She nodded emphatically. "I heard it with my own two ears."

"What did you hear?"

Nia looked around—at Gavin to her left, Sarah to her right, the rest of her busy classmates behind. Then she leaned over the table, as close as she could get. "Paige called her a bad name," she whispered.

"What was the bad name?"

"I'm not allowed to say it. If I did, Mama would wash my mouth."

Anaya frowned.

"I can say what it starts with though."

"Okay."

Nia stood and walked around the table. She leaned in to Anaya's ear, her breath warm and sweet like syrup. She cupped her hands and whispered, "It's the mean word that starts with an *n*."

●●●●

"She said she heard Paige say it."

Principal Kelly frowned. "But Paige is saying she didn't?"

"I spoke with all three girls. Jubilee confirmed what Nia told me. When I asked Paige, she denied it."

"Hmm."

Anaya took a deep breath. She wanted Principal Kelly to stand up. To howl. On her behalf, and their behalf, and every other person's behalf who had been on the receiving end of that word. But he didn't stand or howl. He just sat there looking mildly uncomfortable, like he ate something for breakfast he shouldn't have.

Meanwhile, she shook. Her entire body trembled.

Principal Kelly picked up a confiscated fidget spinner and began spinning it over his thumb. "You didn't hear it?"

"No, I didn't hear it. But why would Nia lie?"

"Didn't you say Paige has been leaving Nia out?"

Heat crawled up her neck.

It's just a scratch, Anaya. Nothing but a scratch.

"With all respect, sir, I don't think Nia would make up this particular story just to get Paige Gray into trouble."

Kelly rubbed his chin. "Right. Of course. It's horrible if it's true. It's just hard to move forward when we don't have any adult witnesses. It's one girl's word against another's."

Two girls' word against another.

And both of those girls happened to be black.

"There's really not much we can do," he said.

"Call her parents in."

Kelly's cheeks—which were almost always rosy—went strangely white. Anaya could practically see what he was thinking. Camille Gray was MVP of the PTA. She did so much for the school, for the whole district. But what about Anaya? What about Nia and Jubilee? Why was he more concerned about Camille Gray than them?

"Why don't you send the girls down. I'll have a talk with each of them separately and see what I can find out. We'll take it from there."

Thirty-One

"How long will the application take to process?"

"Not more than forty-five days."

Camille nodded, a feeling of triumphant accomplishment swelling in her chest. In forty-five days or less, she would have a permit to carry. Never mind pepper spray or the sharp self-defense keychain Neil got for her once upon a time when he still cared. This was the real deal. This would keep the burglars far away. Somehow this would even show Neil. She wasn't sure how, exactly. She just felt that it would. The whole thing was a much-needed adrenaline rush.

"Your left hand, please."

Camille surrendered it.

The bulldog-faced woman in the sheriff's office began rolling each of her fingers in the black ink, then onto the card.

Camille's phone started to buzz on top of her purse, which she'd set on the floor. She glanced down and saw the number of O'Hare Elementary on the screen. It was one o'clock on a Monday.

"I'm sorry, but I really have to answer that."

The bulldog-faced woman stared at her with a grim expression.

"It's my daughter's school. It'll just take one second." She took back her left hand with an apologetic grimace and used the heels of her palms to get the phone to her ear.

"Hello, this is Camille."

"Hi, Camille? It's Principal Kelly."

"Oh. Principal Kelly." She hadn't expected him. She thought it would be the nurse, calling because Paige had strep throat again. Dr. Porter said one more infection and they would most certainly remove her tonsils. "How are you?"

"I'm doing all right."

Only he didn't sound all right. He sounded a little odd.

She smiled awkwardly at the fingerprint lady, held up her inky finger to indicate one second, and turned away—as though doing so might lend her some privacy.

"I, uh, wanted to let you know about a situation this morning at school involving Paige."

"Okay."

"Apparently, a classmate heard Paige calling another classmate a name." Principal Kelly paused. "A racial slur, actually."

"What?"

"I called the girls into my office and talked to each of them."

Paige was called into the principal's office? Paige had said a *racial slur?* Camille's mind spun. Or maybe it was the room. She cupped her forehead with her hand, then quickly pulled it away. She had ink all over her hand. "I can't imagine Paige even knows any . . ." She glanced over her shoulder, at the woman who was impatiently waiting. "Any of those kinds of words. She certainly hasn't heard them in my house. Should . . . should I come get her?"

"No, no. It's fine. I spoke with Paige about it. She's saying she didn't say it. Jubilee and Nia are saying she did."

Camille could feel the heat rising. Up into the tips of her ears. All the way past her hairline. Jubilee and Nia. But . . . Jubilee struggled with lying. Her own mother told Camille as much at the splash pad the month before. If the girls thought Paige was leaving them out, it was very reasonable to think they would try to get Paige into trouble. That had to be it. Her daughter would never ever use a racial slur.

"It's become a bit of a he-said, she-said situation, only without the he. Paige and I talked a little about the word and why it's never appropriate. I wanted you to be aware, in case she came home with any questions."

"I appreciate that."

"I'm sorry to be the bearer of bad news on a Monday."

"Please don't apologize. And please know, I will certainly be talking to Paige about this when she gets home. If she did say a word of that nature, it won't happen again."

●◦●◦●◦●

"I've made Mrs. Gray aware of the situation."

"And?"

"She was shocked, of course, and said she would be speaking with Paige."

"What about Jubilee and Nia? Shouldn't their parents be made aware of the situation?"

"By all means, you are more than welcome to call them in."

She was.

He wasn't going to do anything.

Except stand there like he was expecting a thank-you.

"I know this isn't the outcome you wanted. But there's really not much we can do. Since no adult heard it, our hands are tied."

Right.

Of course.

There's really not much we can do.

It was such a discouragingly familiar response.

•●●●●

Camille stared at Paige in the rearview mirror as she pulled away from the pickup line at O'Hare.

"How long is it gonna take to watch Austin play chess?" she asked, pulling her seat belt across her lap and setting her backpack on the seat beside her.

"I don't have any idea. This is my first time, just like you." Camille turned on her blinker and pulled out onto the road, waiting for Paige to say something, *anything,* about her trip to Mr. Kelly's office. But Paige didn't. She sat in the backseat in her emoji pajamas, moving her finger in the air as though counting something invisible.

"Paige?"

"Yeah?"

"How was your day?"

"Good." Her eyes—wide and innocent—met Camille's in the mirror. "How was your day, Mom?"

"Well, Paige, my day wasn't so great. I got a phone call from your principal today, saying he had to call you into his office. He said you called someone a mean name."

"I would never do that."

"Two of your classmates said that you did."

"Nia and Jubilee are lying."

And just like that, Camille knew.

Nia and Jubilee weren't lying.

Paige was.

She was lying now just like she lied four years ago, when Miss Patty caught her stealing Faith's midmorning snack at Our Redeemer Preschool. Camille had a very stern, very serious conversation with her about the wrongness of stealing and how that was no way to treat a friend. Paige sat there looking so utterly confused and perplexed by the accusation that if not for Camille's sixth sense about lying, she might have fallen for it.

"I would never take Faith's fruit snacks, Mommy. I love Faith."

"Miss Patty saw you do it, Paige."

"Well, Miss Patty must be lying."

She'd said it with such a straight face. Such an alarmingly straight face that Camille had been struck with a disconcerting thought. Her daughter was a pathological liar.

She had the same feeling now.

And for one terrifying moment, as Paige stared openly, almost defiantly back at her from the rearview mirror, Camille was certain that if not for Principal Kelly's phone call, she never would have caught the omission. They would have driven to Austin's chess match, Camille completely in the dark. And if she was this in the dark about her youngest, how could she possibly know any of them?

"You don't believe me," Paige pouted.

"Why would Nia and Jubilee lie?"

"Because they hate me."

A honk sounded behind her.

Camille had slowed to a stop at a light that wasn't red.

She punched the gas, the muscles in her shoulders knotting. Stress accumulating on top of stress. Neil leaving. The South Fork kids coming. The public meeting that had gotten out of hand. The way the media attacked her afterward, like she was some kind of evil villain. Pamela's vindictive words on Saturday. And her husband this morning, walking out of the gym with that gorgeous woman.

Now this.

Her daughter used a racial slur.

She used a racial slur, Jubilee Covington was involved, and Anaya Jones probably believed that Camille was indoctrinating her daughter with racist ideology at home.

"We're not done talking about this, Paige," Camille said, pulling into the middle school parking lot. They were not done talking about this in the slightest. Now, however, wasn't the time. She was not going to be late to Austin's chess match. She was not going to be late when this was the first time in his life that he'd ever asked—without any prompting on her behalf—to join something.

Thirty-Two

"She's insisting she didn't say it, but I thought you deserved to know."

Jen Covington sat in front of Anaya at the short bean-shaped table in an undersized second grade chair, her face as white as chalk. "How does a kid that age even know a word like that?"

"How does a kid that age know any bad word? They hear it from someone."

Jen's eyes met Anaya's. Maybe they were thinking the same thing: Where exactly had Paige Gray heard it?

"Mrs. Covington?"

"Yes?"

"I'm sorry for being blunt, but do you know how to talk to Jubilee about these things?"

The chalky-white of her cheeks tinged with pink. Anaya wondered if she would get defensive. She wondered if her feathers were going to get ruffled. My goodness, white people and their easily ruffled feathers. Well, she was tired of tiptoeing. She was tired of handling their egos with care when they hardly thought twice about her heart.

Jen looked down into her lap, where her fingers wrestled. "When we first moved to town, my husband and I talked about enrolling Jubilee in a South Fork school—at Lincoln Elementary."

"Lincoln?"

Abeo went to Lincoln.

Anaya had gone there too. And already the rumors were flying that by year's end, it was going to be shut down. Everyone was talking about it after church yesterday. Only two tuition payments in, and the district was already beginning to topple.

"Maybe we should have stuck with our gut. If we would have sent Jubilee to Lincoln, we wouldn't have to have this conversation with her."

"She would have heard it at Lincoln."

Jen's brow furrowed.

Anaya shifted in the small chair. "I was barely six years old the first time my father sat me down and talked to me about that word."

"That young?"

"My best friend and I were playing hopscotch outside her mama's salon. A Middle Eastern man who owned the liquor store next door got angry at us for marking up his sidewalk with chalk. He told us to clean up the mess, and then he spat that word at our feet. He added a few choice adjectives before the noun, *dirty little* being two I remember most vividly."

Jen flinched. "That's awful."

"We told my Auntie Trill, and she told my mother, and my mother told my father, and my father sat me down and we had a talk."

"What did he say?"

"He explained what the word meant and its long, sordid history in this country."

Anaya could remember it like it was this morning. Sitting in that hot box of a kitchen while Mama fried chicken over the stove. Daddy in his ribbed, white cotton undershirt, revealing a tattooed bicep that made Anaya proud— her name and Mama's, strung together in the shape of an infinity symbol. A year and a half later, he would have Darius's added.

Daddy didn't shy away from hard things. He shot straight with her. How the word started as a noun that meant black person and quickly turned into something derogatory. It was the word slave masters used when they cracked the whip against the backs of black slaves. The word an angry white mob yelled at a six-year-old girl just because she dared to walk into a school building with white kids. The word a group of white boys used against Daddy when he was eight as they pulled him behind a dumpster and took turns punching him until he spit blood.

"But, Daddy," Anaya had said, "how come Uncle Jemar says that word?"

Of course, Uncle Jemar pronounced it a little differently, and never as meanly as that man said it to her and ReShawn. But he still said it. Sometimes he even said it to Daddy.

"Your Uncle Jemar says it in solidarity—a nod to the shared experience of our blackness."

This was how Daddy talked to her, even when she was six. He didn't shy away from the hard, and he didn't shy away from using big words like *solidarity* either.

"I don't judge him for it. But, Anaya," Daddy said, getting real, real serious. More serious than she'd ever seen. "That word is intricately tied to the oppression of our people, and because of that, you won't ever hear me use it."

He didn't either.

Neither did she.

"You're gonna have to get used to talking about hard truths with Jubilee," Anaya said. "It's the burden of being a black parent."

Jen Covington sat there looking lost, like she didn't have any clue what she'd signed up for. "I'm not black."

"But you have a black daughter, and this won't be the last time she hears that word." Just like it hadn't been Anaya's when she was six. By the time she was ten, she started to lose track. A white boy on her soccer team who laughed afterward, then covered his mouth with his hand. A car full of teenagers shouting the obscenity out the window as she rode her bike to ReShawn's house. Once it happened when she and Mama were at the park together. A man muttered it under his breath as he pulled his two-year-old daughter away.

Anaya's heart howled in pain, and Mama grabbed her hand. She started rubbing it. She massaged it with her two thumbs like the man's words had been a physical wound.

"It's a scratch, baby. Just a scratch. You rub it. You rub it real good until the pain goes away."

"I feel so ill equipped," Jen said, bringing her hands up to her temples. "I mean, what kind of mother doesn't even know how to do her daughter's hair?"

It felt like an olive branch. A humble confession. An admittance that she had no clue what she was doing. Maybe that was where progress began. Anaya stood up and went to her desk. She unpeeled a sticky note from the top of her pad and wrote down a number she'd known by heart since she was four.

She set it in front of Jen.

"What's this?"

"The number to my auntie Trill's salon. She'll help you with your daughter's hair."

Thirty-Three

"You did such a great job," Camille said, pulling her son into a side hug. She didn't actually have a clue how great or not great he did. She barely understood the way the chess pieces moved. She only knew that he said "checkmate" in two of his three matches, and when he walked over to her, there was a buoyancy to his step she hadn't seen in a long time.

"I'm not as good as Edison. He can beat Mr. Faulkner without his queen."

The name was vaguely familiar, but only because Austin had mentioned it in passing a time or two last week. This made three, which was more than Austin mentioned anyone. "Why have I never heard of this Edison before chess club?"

"He transferred from South Fork."

"Oh."

"He's right over there with his mom. C'mon." Before Camille could object, Austin—her shy, socially awkward Austin—was dragging her over for an introduction. If only she could change her face really quickly. Put on some sort of disguise. Dye her hair. Anything to keep Edison and his mother from recognizing her as Camille Gray—the outspoken lady in the news.

Hello, Foot. Let me introduce you to Mouth.

As it turned out, Edison and his mother didn't appear to recognize her. Maybe they didn't watch the news. Or maybe it was her chopped hair. Or maybe they did recognize her and they didn't care. Whatever the case, Edison was wonderful. A short, scrawny kid with a gap between his front teeth, an endearing smile, and a barely-there lisp that came with each of his *s*'s. It was apparent almost immediately that he enjoyed Austin's company as much as Austin enjoyed his, which made Camille inclined to like him.

His mother's name was Tamika Harris. She was a petite woman with a gap-toothed smile like her son's.

"How's Edison adjusting to school?" Camille asked.

"Oh, he loves it here. It helped a heap when he learned they had a chess club. Edison's been playing chess with his granddaddy from the time he could walk. It's been a great way for him to make new friends like your son. Edison just loves Austin."

Camille's heart melted into a puddle of mush.

Edison loved her son.

Which meant she now loved Edison.

"They have gym and health class together. Edison said Austin made him feel very welcome the first day of school."

"Did he really?" she asked, swelling with motherly pride.

"Invited him to eat lunch. You should be proud of your boy."

"Thank you. I am."

"We weren't sure we should come, after all the fuss. I won't lie. It was hurtful what people were saying. But people like your family have made the transition as good as it could be."

Heat rose into Camille's cheeks. It was safe to assume that Tamika Harris didn't know who she was talking to.

"My boy taught your boy how to play chess a few weeks ago, on a free day in health class. He says Austin's a natural."

"That was very nice of him."

"Edison's a nice boy."

"Well, we'd love to have Edison over sometime."

Tamika Harris beamed. "He would love that too."

● ● ● ● ●

She was late picking up Darius. First thanks to the meeting with Jen and then thanks to her chat with the school librarian—an elderly woman named Mrs. Finch who looked like she should have retired years ago. Anaya asked if she could help her find books about racism.

"Racism?" Mrs. Finch had said.

"Yes," Anaya said back, a massive headache working its way from the base of her skull to her forehead. She was eager to put this rotten day to bed.

"We have a section on African American history. Is that what you mean?"

Not exactly. But she let Mrs. Finch lead her there anyway.

O'Hare was one of the top elementary schools in the entire state of Missouri, and somehow this was what Anaya had to choose from—an African American history section that condensed that history into two topics: slavery and the civil rights movement. There were also some short biographies on people including Harriet Tubman, Jackie Robinson, Rosa Parks, and Martin Luther King.

Maybe Anaya would have felt disappointed if she'd been at all surprised.

In all honesty, South Fork had condensed black history to the same four people, the same two eras—except South Fork schools hardly had any library. They certainly didn't have bright and shiny hardcover picture books that looked fresh off the press.

Anaya selected a stack and checked them all out. Then she filled out an order form for several more, and when she handed it over, Mrs. Finch didn't look excited so much as mildly uncomfortable. It was the same way Principal Kelly looked earlier today when Anaya came into his office and told him what happened.

"We will have to get these approved," Mrs. Finch said. "I hate having that persnickety budget. If it were up to me, I'd order them all."

Would she?

Anaya couldn't help but wonder, and it was the wondering that made the pain in her head throb harder. Some days she got so sick and tired of all the wondering. Did Mrs. Finch say that to all the teachers about every order form, or did she say it to Anaya about these particular books?

This was the thing about wondering: there was no way to know one way or the other. She only knew that something was always happening to make the wondering start. It was like phantom pain in a limb no longer there. You couldn't treat it. The wondering was there, forever lurking in the background.

Anaya pulled into the parking lot of the high school, up to the roundabout in front of the gymnasium doors. Her brother was waiting outside, but he wasn't alone.

He sat on a bench in front of a small flower garden—shoulder to shoulder with a vaguely familiar white girl in expensive running shoes.

They were sharing earbuds.

Something inside Anaya sparked with heat. She tapped the horn. "Get in the car," she called out the window.

Darius removed his earbud and quirked one of his eyebrows at her. "Hello to you too."

"I'm not playin', Dare," she said. "Get in the car."

Darius and the girl exchanged a look that made the spark of heat in Anaya burst into flame. The two gave each other a fist bump, like a couple of good friends, and then he grabbed his football bag and his backpack and walked over with a swagger in his step.

Anaya didn't want to see the white girl looking. She didn't want to see her ogling Darius with equal parts desire and fascination, like he was some mysterious, beautiful alien. With her teeth clenched and her eyes trained forward, she waited for him to climb in, and then she drove away so fast her tires nearly squealed against the blacktop.

"What's your deal?" Darius asked, clipping his seat belt into place.

"Who was that?"

"Just some girl from French class."

"What's her name?"

"Taylor."

That's when it clicked. She was vaguely familiar because Anaya had seen her in the news before, whenever high school sports came on. Taylor was Crystal Ridge's running star. A junior who was breaking all kinds of cross-country records. One of the girls Anaya would coach come springtime because she ran track too. The oldest daughter of Camille Gray.

Anaya started shaking her head.

"Do you have a problem with her?"

"Other than the fact that she's a white girl."

Her brother let out a low whistle. "Dang, Nay. I didn't know you were such a racist."

The car screeched to a stop, tires skidding against pavement.

Darius lurched forward, held back by the seat belt across his chest. Thankfully, nobody was driving behind them. The road was empty, and they idled in the middle of it.

"Are you trippin'?" Darius yelled.

"Am I trippin'?"

"Seems like a fair question right now."

"That white girl you were flirting with? Her little sister—her eight-year-old little sister—called one of my students the N-word today. So yeah, maybe your big sis is trippin' just a little."

Darius didn't say anything. He stared back at her with an obnoxiously passive expression on his face like he didn't get it.

"Boy, do you even know what her mama was saying at that town meeting?"

"I wasn't flirting with her mama."

"She thinks you're a thug," Anaya said.

"I don't care what she thinks. I don't care what her little sister thinks either."

"Are you kidding me?"

"We're friends, aight? She's going through a rough time right now."

"A rough time?" Anaya let loose a huff of unamused laughter. Poor little rich girl. Anaya could cry a river of tears over how hard her life must be.

"And for your information, she hates what her mama said at that town meeting. She ain't like that. She's glad I'm at Crystal Ridge."

"I'll bet she is."

"What's that supposed to mean?"

"C'mon, Darius. You know what it means."

"Nah. I wanna hear you say it."

"A girl like her is just scratching an itch."

A girl like her.

A girl like her.

A girl like her.

The phrase echoed from somewhere deep, deep down, stirring up a hot shame she didn't want to stir.

Darius stared at her mutinously. His full lips pursed. His nostrils flared. Then he yanked on the handle and swung the door open.

"Where you going?"

"I think I'll walk home."

Anaya should call out to him. Apologize for the things she was saying. But her hands were shaking, and the phrase kept on echoing.

A girl like her.
A girl like her.
A girl like her.
She needed to get away. She needed to breathe. So she shifted into drive and let her brother walk.

Thirty-Four

Tamika Harris was a talker, and Camille was not about to be rude. In fact, she went out of her way—boisterously out of her way—to make a good impression. Maybe then, once Edison's mother realized who Camille was, she would be more inclined to give Camille the benefit of the doubt.

All the effort had made her late, and Taylor wasn't answering her phone or responding to any of Camille's text messages. And Camille still needed to have a serious talk with Paige.

A racial slur, actually.

Mr. Kelly's shocking words kept blaring in her ears—over and over again—until she pulled up in front of the gymnasium entrance and saw Taylor sitting sullenly on a bench.

"Late much?" Taylor muttered.

Answer your phone much?

Camille swallowed the snotty reply and apologized through the open window. "I tried calling to let you know, but you weren't answering."

"My battery died." Taylor tossed her backpack into the backseat.

It landed on top of Paige.

"Hey!"

"Can I drive?" Taylor asked.

"No. Not right now." Taylor's driving was the last thing Camille could handle right now. Her nerves were too frayed.

"Of course not." Taylor threw open the passenger-side door. She climbed in and buckled her seat belt, her chin jutting in an unattractive underbite.

Her attitude made Camille want to scream.

A racial slur, actually.

Taylor turned on the music as they drove toward the parking lot exit. She found her favorite station and turned up the volume. They were playing a pop song with provocative lyrics.

Camille turned it off.

"I can't even listen to music now?"

"Not that kind."

Taylor shook her head, crossed her arms. Sank down in the seat. "You're unbelievable."

Camille made a sharp turn and pulled to an abrupt stop in one of the parking lot's farthest stalls. She took a deep breath—an inhale through her nostrils, an exhale through her lips. Then she shifted into park and turned to face her children.

"I think we're due for a family meeting."

Taylor groaned.

Taylor hated family meetings. She hadn't always hated them. Once upon a time, before the joys of puberty set in, she used to enjoy them. But then she turned fourteen and went into high school and became this glowering, eye-rolling stranger Camille didn't recognize.

"Taylor, if you don't start treating me with more respect, I'm going to take your phone away."

"Maybe I would show you more respect if you didn't treat me like I was eight."

"Stop acting like you're eight and I will."

"What's wrong with being eight?" Paige asked.

Camille took another deep breath and turned around farther to address her youngest. "You aren't telling the truth about what happened today."

"I didn't say anything."

"Paige." Camille stared at her. She stared at her like they were having a staring contest. She stared without blinking until her eyes began to sting and Paige looked down into her lap.

"I'm sorry," she said. "I didn't know it was such a mean word."

Taylor narrowed her eyes, her attention darting back and forth between her little sister and her mother.

"Where did you hear it?" Camille asked.

Paige fiddled with the zipper of her backpack.

Camille waited. She waited with righteous indignation for Paige to tell her what Miss Jones probably would never believe. Paige heard it from Gavin Royce, who heard it from his father. Or Paige heard it from the speakers of that lowrider that pulled up at the stoplight beside them the day a burglar broke into the Robersons' house across the street. Never mind that the driver was a black man. They weren't allowed to talk about the hypocrisy of that.

But when Paige finally spoke, that wasn't what she said.

"I heard it from Uncle Ray."

"What?"

"Oh my gosh," Taylor said, her voice filled with nauseating disgust. She turned around in her seat, away from her sister.

Camille wanted to hold tightly to her righteous indignation. She wanted to demand, *When in the world did you ever hear your Uncle Ray use that word?* But Camille couldn't. Because Camille knew.

Uncle Ray did use that word. He used it every Thanksgiving, when they flew to California to celebrate the holiday with Camille's family. Her Uncle Ray was passionate about his football team. So much so that he would jump out of his seat to yell at a running back or a receiver. More than once he used that word. Camille didn't like it. She didn't like it any more than she liked Leif Royce's derogatory comment at the town meeting. Camille wanted to tell Uncle Ray to stop, but he wasn't a little kid. Uncle Ray was from a different era. And besides, her kids were always in another room. She didn't think they ever heard.

"Listen to me, Paige. We do not ever, under any circumstances, use that word. Do you understand?"

"But, Uncle Ray—"

"Should not be using that word, either."

"Do you even know what it means?" Taylor asked, turning back around in her seat, staring at her sister with as much contempt as she stared at Camille.

"It's a word for people with brown skin," Paige said.

Austin was starting to catch on. His mouth was slowly opening, wider and wider, until it hung like that horrified emoji with hands on its cheeks.

"It's a very *mean* word for people with brown skin," Camille said. "And people use it when they don't like someone just because their skin is brown."

"So Uncle Ray hates people with brown skin?"

"Of course not." Uncle Ray didn't hate African Americans. Uncle Ray had been having coffee with his buddy Carl every Saturday morning for the past twenty years, and Carl was African American. Both were retired truckers.

Paige frowned. "I don't get it."

"Uncle Ray is from a time when people used that word. It didn't make it right back then, either. But it was more common. I guess it's a habit."

Taylor huffed. "Some habit."

"Like Pop-pop's smoking?"

"Yes, like Pop-pop's smoking."

Paige nodded, but a small, persistent divot remained between her eyebrows. "Mommy?"

"Yes?"

"Do *you* like people with brown skin?"

"Of course I do, Paige. I don't care about skin color. It's what's in a person's heart that matters."

"But you didn't want them to come here."

"Where?"

"To my elementary school."

"*Paige Amelia Gray,* that situation had absolutely nothing to do with the color of anyone's skin."

"But—"

"But *what?*"

"But all of them *have* brown skin."

To that, Camille didn't have an answer.

● ● ● ● ●

Darius: I need a ride.

Anaya: Boy, you ignore my phone calls for the past hour and now you need a ride? I COULD TAN YOUR HIDE.

Darius: Don't call me boy. And you ain't my mama.

Anaya: Where you at?

Darius: 1246 Ashbury Court

Anaya: ??

Darius: It's in Crystal Ridge. Just come get me. Please.

Anaya: I'm on my way.

Thirty-Five

The closer Siri brought Anaya to 1246 Ashbury Court, the bigger the houses grew and the more manicured the lawns.

Anaya was riled.

No, she wasn't Darius's mother. But she'd been pretending since she was six, when Mama came home from the hospital with her swaddled baby brother. She let Anaya sit on the couch and placed him gently in her arms. He looked up at her with his big, brown eyes, and she fell hopelessly, instantaneously in love. It was a love that never wavered, not even when he made her so mad she wanted to take Daddy's belt and give him a whupping of her own. Like right now, after driving around in a sheer panic for the last hour, calling his phone every two minutes, imagining all the horrible things that could happen to a boy like Darius. Not to mention—his real mama wasn't above tanning *her* hide if Anaya came home without her son.

"In two hundred feet, turn left on Ashbury Court," Siri said in her pleasant, mechanical tone.

Anaya slowed down.

She turned onto the cul-de-sac to the alarming sight of flashing red and blue.

Her heart stopped dead in her chest.

A police car was parked outside 1246 Ashbury Court, and her brother Darius—the bundled baby placed in her arms sixteen years ago—was standing on a fancy lawn with his hands slightly raised in the air, just like Daddy had taught them.

Like the defibrillator the paramedics used on her father's chest, the sight made her heart jerk back to life—so violently she could feel the electric shock in each one of her fingertips.

Anaya jerked her car to a stop at the side of the road. She needed to get outside. She needed to get to her brother.

Her Darius.

Her sunshine.

She tore off her seat belt, clawed for the door handle, and stumbled out into the late-afternoon sun. "Excuse me, sir," she shouted—frantic—at the officer, her hands up in the air too. "That's my brother, sir. Is there a problem?"

The officer turned around.

He was a middle-aged man with a short red beard. His hand was on the holster of his gun. "There was a complaint in the area about a prowler."

Anaya stepped between him and Darius, her entire body flushed with fear. "A prowler?"

"Yes ma'am. There's been some break-ins in the neighborhood recently. So you can understand why people are concerned."

"Yes sir. But this is my brother, sir. He's not a prowler." He was a good boy. The best boy. The boy with a thousand-watt smile and an arm like a rocket and a ready joke and hugs that could take the worst of Anaya's grief away.

"What are you doing hanging around this house, young man?" the officer asked.

"I was just coming by to say hi to a friend, sir," Darius said, his voice trembling in the same way it did when he was four and the thunder would come and he'd crawl into Anaya's bed at night and ask, "Why's the sky gotta sound so mad?"

"It's not mad," she'd say back. "It's just excited." Then she'd tuck his warm little body against hers, breathing in the scent of the coconut oil Mama rubbed into his hair every night after bath time.

The officer peered at the house—the large, mansion-like house—and sucked on his teeth. "Mind if I see some ID?"

•◦•◦•

There was a police officer standing on her front lawn. And a tall, broad black man. And . . . Camille squeezed her eyes shut. Then opened them again, unable to believe what she was seeing.

"What's my teacher doing here?" Paige exclaimed.

"That's Darius!" Taylor flung open the car door before Camille had a chance to pull to a complete stop in the driveway. She ran up to the police officer while a few paces away, the black man—the black boy?—stood frozen in place, his hands raised like he'd done something wrong.

Had they caught the prowler?

Was he about to break into their house and the police arrived in the nick of time? But then, Taylor had shouted a name. Darius.

Darius. Darius Jones, Crystal Ridge's new quarterback. The kid who took Cody's spot on the football team. The kid who was winning Crystal Ridge more games than they'd won in years. Anaya's younger brother. He was at their house. Miss Jones was at their house. A police officer was at their house.

"Wait here," Camille told Austin and Paige, then hurried out after her eldest.

"He shouldn't have to show you an ID," Taylor exclaimed. "He's a friend from school."

Heat flooded Camille's cheeks. She had never in her life heard Taylor speak rudely to another adult. To her, yes. Taylor treated her rudely all the time. But another grown-up? Never. Certainly not to a police officer.

"What's going on here?" Camille demanded.

The officer looked a little bashful, a little uncertain as he stood there holding a woman's purse. "Do you live here, ma'am?"

"Yes. This is my house. This is my lawn. My name is Camille Gray."

"Well, Ms. Gray, we received a concerned phone call about a half hour ago. I came to check things out."

Camille looked around the houses in her cul-de-sac. How many of her neighbors were looking out their windows right now, staring at the scene unfolding on the front lawn? They had become the neighborhood spectacle, and the boy—this boy her daughter called a friend—was still standing there with his hands in the air.

She wanted to yell at him to put them down. For goodness' sake, if he really was her daughter's friend, he had no reason to stand there in such a guilty manner. But then she saw his eyes.

In every mind, there was a camera, and there were moments in life when that camera clicked and a memory was captured like a photograph. Camille knew without knowing how she knew that this was an image she would remember forever. When she was arthritic and gray with age-spotted hands, she would be able to pull the photograph from her memory and see the police officer with the purse, Paige's second grade teacher, the flashing lights of the cruiser as her wide-eyed children stared out from the backseat of her Highlander, and the teenage boy with his hands lifted and a world of fear raging in his eyes.

"Well, sir, there's nothing to be concerned about here. Whoever made the phone call must've been mistaken. This boy is my daughter's friend."

The officer nodded. Then he handed the purse to Anaya.

He offered a polite apology—to Camille, not to them—and drove away, his lights no longer flashing.

Anaya was tight lipped and gray. She wouldn't meet Camille's eyes. She didn't offer an explanation. She didn't say hi to Paige. She took her brother firmly by his elbow and pulled him toward her car on the street, its driver-side door hanging open.

And just like that, they were gone.

Austin and Paige scrambled out of the car.

Paige's eyes were bright with excitement. Twenty-minutes ago they'd been streaming with tears. All because Camille told her she would have to write an apology note to Jubilee.

"She never apologized to me for screaming and spitting at my birthday party," Paige had said.

"Maybe she should have," Camille said back. "But I'm not Jubilee's mother. I'm *your* mother."

Paige had jutted her chin in such a perfect impersonation of Taylor that Camille saw her future flash before her eyes. Another hostile teenager under her roof, waiting to happen. "It's not fair," she grumbled.

Well, tough cookies. Life isn't fair.

Camille had bitten her tongue. It wasn't the time to start quoting her father. "When you hurt someone, Paige, you apologize. End of story. And today, you hurt Jubilee."

That was when the waterworks began. That was when Paige started begging for her daddy and Taylor made snide comments under breath.

"She's just trying to get out of it."

"I am not!" Paige shot back.

Now that same weeping eight-year-old stood in the driveway, her eyes completely dry. "What was my teacher doing here?"

Camille looked at Taylor, who was staring at the place Anaya's car had been. Her cheeks were pink, almost red. "Taylor?" she said. "Do you want to tell me what's going on?"

"I don't know."

"Did you know he was coming over?"

"No."

"He didn't text you or—"

"I told you, my phone is dead."

Camille rubbed her neck. "Darius Jones. He's the football player, right?"

"Yeah."

"I didn't know the two of you were friends."

"Do you need a list?"

Camille swallowed. She would not blow up. She would not blow up.

"We have French class together."

"French class. So . . . is he who you've been meeting at the library all these evenings?"

"It hasn't been *all these evenings.*" But Taylor's blush grew more pronounced.

Her daughter liked him.

Camille could tell that her daughter liked Darius Jones, the boy who had taken Cody's spot on the football team. Maybe this was why she said no to Cody's homecoming proposal. "Are you going to the homecoming dance together?"

"We're just friends, Mom, okay? But don't worry, I'm sure after tonight he won't speak to me ever again." With that, she marched to the car, hit the button on the garage door opener, and stomped inside.

Thirty-Six

When Anaya was six, she ran in a toy store. She was always running, even then. That day, she took off out of nowhere for no particular reason other than she was bursting with excitement. Christmas was in twenty-seven days, and Mama had a baby in her belly—a real live baby—and Daddy was letting her pick out a gift for ReShawn. She felt the tickle in her legs, so she ran.

Daddy yelled. He yelled so frighteningly loud, her six-year-old body skidded to a dead stop.

When she turned around, she was certain he was gonna be fuming mad. How many times did he and Mama have to tell her, no running in the house? What in tarnation would make her think a toy store was any different?

Only when she turned around, Daddy wasn't mad.

Daddy looked frightened.

He came to her, got down on his knee so they were eye to eye, then took her by the shoulders and said, "You don't ever run inside a store. Do you hear me?"

"Why not, Daddy?" she'd asked, even though she sorta knew. If she ran inside, she could get hurt. She could bang her knee or bump her head or break something that wasn't supposed to be broke, like those little glass figurines Granny kept in her living room window. The ones that made rainbows on the walls.

Daddy gave her shoulders a squeeze. "Someone might think you stole something."

Anaya didn't understand. She would never steal. The Bible said stealing was sinful. It was right there in the Ten Commandments. *Thou shalt not steal.* So why would anyone think she would? She didn't get it.

Until slowly, over the years, she did.

Like the time the police came in SWAT gear and raided the neighbor's house at one in the morning, dragging Latrell out into the yard. The commotion woke everyone in the neighborhood. Porch light after porch light flooded the darkness while Anaya and the rest of her family watched out the window—helpless to do anything as those officers roughed up Latrell and his mama screamed and screamed in her nightgown.

"Don't hurt my baby. Don't hurt my baby. Please don't shoot my baby."

They tased her. Then they roughed her up too.

A white cop and a black cop. Partners in law.

All for a bag of weed plenty of white kids carried in their backpacks.

Darius had been eight. He tried to watch, but Mama pulled him away. She brought him into the living room and held him close and yelled at Daddy to get Anaya away from that window. But Daddy couldn't pull himself away. How was he supposed to pull Anaya?

It rattled her for months after.

It rattled her still today as she sat in her bedroom, with Mama gone at her night class and Granny watching a rerun of *Black-ish* on the living room television. Anaya had just gotten off the phone with ReShawn. She told her what happened. She thought talking about it would help. But Anaya still trembled. She kept thinking about the way she handed over her purse, even though she knew it was a violation of her rights. That officer needed a warrant. But she also knew that if she told him so, he'd take her and Darius to the station and get one. It was easier—safer—to hand it over. When he started pawing through her things, he might as well have been pawing her.

But she just stood there, trembling like she trembled now.

Until Camille Gray pulled into her driveway and Taylor ran over to the officer, upset and unafraid, because why would she be afraid? Her little brother would never turn into a hashtag. That didn't happen in the world in which she lived.

But Darius?

Anaya closed her eyes. The tears still gathered. They pooled in the corner, and one tumbled down her cheek.

She was a freshman in college when Tamir Rice was shot down by a police officer. Darius was twelve, the same age as Tamir. When she heard the news, she felt the same exact way she'd felt all those years ago, when she watched the police drag Latrell and his mama out the house next door—a helpless, cold feeling deep, deep down in her bones.

She followed the story like a woman obsessed while her classmates and teammates went on with life like nothing horrible had happened.

It made Anaya's heart rage. Because *why*? Why weren't they angry? Why weren't they livid? Why weren't any of them demanding justice? He was twelve. Only twelve. And he was shot down dead by a police officer in a two-second span that killed first and cared later. He bled there in the snow for four minutes. *Four minutes* while those officers stood and did nothing. They shot him down, and they let him bleed alone and scared, all because he had a toy gun that boys across the country played with every day.

"He was reaching for it, though," her roommate said.

Yeah, and twelve-year-old kids threw rocks at cars too. Because twelve-year-old kids were kids, and sometimes they did foolish things, but that didn't mean they should be killed for them.

"I don't understand it," she'd told her granny. How could her roommate say what she said with so much indifference? She went to church every Sunday, for crying out loud. She said she was pro-life. Well, here was life. A precious twelve-year-old life. "Why don't they care?"

"Because, baby, when they look at Tamir, they don't see their little brother."

But she did.

She would always see her brother.

Anaya walked down to her brother's room, the floorboards of each stair creaking beneath her feet. There wasn't a way to get down to him without announcing her arrival.

The basement wasn't really a bedroom. It was just a long room, with a washer and a dryer on one side and Darius's bed and dresser on the other. He gave up his own room when Granny moved in. He said he didn't mind.

"It'll be like my own Batcave," he'd said with a wink and an elbow jab to Anaya, making sure she acknowledged his comic book reference.

Now he lay on his mattress with his head hiding under his pillow.

"Darius?"

He didn't say anything. He didn't even move.

Anaya sat on the edge of his bed and took the pillow off his face.

He didn't fight her.

He just turned away toward the wall. But not before Anaya saw the tears.

She set her hand on his shoulder. The last time she saw her brother cry was the day they buried their daddy six feet underground. "Do you want to talk about it?"

He took the pillow back from his sister and placed it over his head like a little boy wanting to shut out the world.

●●●●●

Taylor: U ok?
Darius: I'm good.
Taylor: You didn't seem like yourself in class.

Ten Minutes Later

Taylor: I'm really sorry abt last night. That was super awkward.
Taylor: I wish I woulda been home when you came.
Darius: Me too
Taylor: Does your sister hate me?
Darius: Nah.

Thirty-Seven

Anaya slipped inside the back door of the youth center and headed to the room designated for employees and volunteers, where Marcus installed lockers last summer.

School had been uneventful today. Pajamas had been exchanged for sports jerseys on day two of Spirit Week. Between the Kansas City Chiefs and the Saint Louis Cardinals, her classroom had been mostly red. Nobody got a bloody nose. Nobody ran away. Nobody used a horrible word. There had been no encounter with the police. But still, her fingers were jittery as she twisted the combination of her lock, like aftershocks from the earthquake that was yesterday. When she finished, she fished out her small bottle of sanitizer and squirted some into her palm. She rubbed and rubbed until it disappeared.

Someone tapped her shoulder.

She jerked around like a woman ready to defend herself.

"Whoa." Marcus took a quick step back and held up his hands.

Anaya tried to laugh, but it came out all wrong—breathless and high-pitched—and Marcus got that compassionate look in his eyes. The one that reminded Anaya of warm, freshly baked chocolate chip cookies.

"I saw you come in," he said. "I wanted to check on you."

"Why?"

"I heard what went down yesterday."

"What? How?" But as soon as she sputtered the questions, her eyes went narrow. *"ReShawn."*

"Don't be mad at her."

"Don't be mad? You know what, that girl can't keep a secret to save her life."

"Why's it gotta be a secret?"

"I don't want it getting back to Mama."

"You don't think she should know?"

"Just so she can worry? She got enough of that without learning her son was profiled by the police in some white, bougie neighborhood he had no business being in." She stuffed her purse inside the locker and slammed it shut. "He has a prior, Marcus. Do you know what that means?"

"Don't go there, Anaya."

But she did. She kept going there. Over and over again. If that officer had been on edge—if he would have felt threatened in any way—yesterday could have gone so much differently. And her brother, the boy with a record? The world would have thought he deserved it. They would have labeled him a thug and moved along like her entire universe hadn't been shattered.

"Darius is fine. In fact, with the stats he's putting up every Friday, I'd say he's more than fine. I'd say that in two years, he gonna be Division I, full-ride fine."

"And in three years, he could blow out his shoulder."

Marcus twisted his lips to the side.

Anaya knew she was being negative. But she also knew and *he* also knew—more than anyone—how quickly a life could turn. A heart could stop beating. A tendon could tear in two. Love could fall apart.

"Are you taking care of yourself?" he asked.

"Do I look that bad?"

"You never look bad, and you know it."

She tried to smile. She wanted to smile. But she couldn't smile.

"Look. All I know is you work in Crystal Ridge all day. You come here at night. And then you spend every weekend shampooing heads at Trill's. Nobody is gonna blame you if you back off, kick up your feet a little. Have a *Star Wars* marathon. Find a comic con and engage in some cosplay."

Anaya slugged him.

His cheeks dimpled as he lifted his hands to defend himself.

"I don't dress up in costume," she said, giving his arm another lighthearted slap. "And the Saint Louis Comic Com isn't until June."

He laughed. "That's gotta be the whitest convention in Missouri."

It wasn't a lie. If someone were to draw a Venn diagram of the black community and geek culture, there would be very little intersection, especially of the female variety. But the small pocket of intersection that did exist—in that space where fans grew up on superheroes like Storm and T'Challa and Luke Cage—Anaya relished. And Marcus teased. He'd always teased.

"So what," she said, bringing the conversation back around to his original point. "Are you sick of me or something?"

"Nah. But I wanna make sure you're all right."

"I'm fine."

And she wanted to be here. Not just because *he* was here. Not just because she felt guilty for betraying the district that had employed her father for twenty years. But because she belonged. When she volunteered at the youth center, she wasn't an outsider. She didn't have to function on two different levels like she did at O'Hare, where she wasn't just a new teacher learning the ropes but the black new teacher from South Fork, constantly aware of how she was being perceived.

It was exhausting.

"It's okay if you're not, you know."

Unexpected tears sprang to her eyes.

They came out of nowhere, and they seemed to surprise Marcus as much as they surprised her. His eyes went big; then he hooked one of his fingers around one of hers, and pulled her into a hug. His arms were strong, his chest solid, and he smelled like aftershave. It felt like home. It was too easy. Too familiar. And she was too weak.

She pulled away, but not far enough.

Their faces were close. So close she could see specks of honey in his brown eyes. Freckles. Marcus's eyes had freckles. And his lips . . .

"Anaya, I really think—"

She didn't wait to hear what he really thought. She was so tired of watching her steps. So tired of fighting what felt most natural. She stopped Marcus's thought with a kiss so sudden, it took him a second to respond. But when he did, the whole world came to life.

This was good. So intoxicatingly good.

It was their first kiss since . . .

And just like that, the euphoric bubble around them burst, popped by the cruel pin of memory.

Anaya put her hands on Marcus's chest and pulled away.

He took a few steps back, dragging his hands through his hair.

"This is a bad idea," she said.

"Why?"

"Marcus."

"I'm still in love with you, Anaya. Most days, I can't get you out of my head."

"Marcus—"

"Just listen. I know I wasn't the man I was supposed to be. I got selfish and impatient. I let you down. But Anaya, all of that? It's the past. We can start fresh, with a clean slate."

Start fresh.

With a clean slate.

Like none of it ever happened.

She worried her lip, teetering on the edge of a cliff without the self-control to keep herself standing on solid ground. It would be easy—so easy—to lean over and fall.

"Your brother's playing this Friday, right?"

"It's homecoming."

"Let me take you to the game. I'll even buy you one of those nasty sweet-and-sour suckers you love."

She bit the inside of her cheek to keep from smiling, but not hard enough.

Marcus could tell she was cracking. He put his hands together like a man in deep prayer and dipped his chin. Then he gave her those puppy-dog eyes no girl had a chance resisting, least of all her. "C'mon, Anaya. Say yes."

●●●●●

Dax: Cody quit.

L<3vy: What!?

Dax: Coach told him he wasn't starting again, so he walked out.

L<3vy: When?

Dax: Just now. I think he broke his hand punching a locker.

L<3vy: OMG. Did u hear who's wearing D's jersey on Friday?

Dax: For real?

L<3vy: Don't tell C.

Dax: Man. He lost his spot & his girl to the same dude.

L<3vy: She was never his girl.

Dax: He wanted her to be.

L<3vy: Then maybe he shouldn't have done what he did with Alexis.

● ● ● ● ●

Kathleen: Cody came home with swollen knuckles, and he's saying he quit the football team. Rick is furious.

Camille: Oh my goodness, Kathleen. Seriously?

Kathleen: I've never seen him this upset.

Camille: Ugh. I'm so sorry.

Kathleen: We're not going to the game.

Camille: I don't blame you.

Kathleen: He seems to think Taylor's going to the dance with Darius.

Camille: She's going with a group of friends.

Kathleen: Well, I thought you should be aware that maybe she's not.

● ● ● ● ●

Dear Jubilee,

I'm really really sorry. I shouldn't have called you that mean name. I know what it means now, and I promise to never ever say it again as long as I live. Will you please forgive me?

From,

Paige

Thirty-Eight

"Miss Jones! Miss Jones!" Little Gavin Royce raised his skinny arm and waved back and forth like little kids do whenever they discover their teacher exists outside the classroom.

Anaya lifted her arm and waved back.

She could tell he wanted to run over and give her a hug. Gavin gave her the sweetest hugs every morning. But the hulking figure of Leif Royce stepped through the gate, slapping his wallet against his beefy palm. He followed the direction of his son's attention, and the passive look on his face turned into a thundercloud. He set his hands on Gavin's shoulders a little too roughly and steered him toward the metal bleachers, past the rowdy student section. Away from Anaya, as Mama's voice played in her head.

It's just a scratch, baby.

"For you." Marcus was done charming the elderly lady working the concession stand. He had a popcorn in one hand and Anaya's sweet-and-sour sucker twirling in the other.

She could feel her cheeks dimpling with a smile.

She took Marcus's gift as the stadium exploded with the raucous sound of the Crystal Ridge marching band and the cheering crowd. Darius and his teammates tore through the large Let's Go, Wildcats! banner. Cheerleaders punched the air with purple pom-poms, and the Wildcat mascot turned impressive, enthusiastic cartwheels in the grass.

She followed Marcus to a spot in the stands. Mama couldn't make it because of her night class, Granny was in too much pain with the changing weather, and Uncle Jemar wasn't *'bout to give his money to no white-bread, rich school.* He was here, though. Outside the fence, watching from a distance. Uncle Jemar couldn't resist watching his nephew play.

And play, he did.

After the first quarter, the score was 21–0.

Darius threw one touchdown and ran in two.

The crowd was going wild. Marcus was whooping and hollering. Anaya sucked on her sucker, eyeing Taylor Gray at the front of the student section. She had a purple paw print painted on one cheek, a gold paw print on the other. She was also wearing Darius's jersey.

"Man, that kid can run. Nobody can catch him," Marcus said, sitting beside her. "Who you keep shaking your head at?"

Anaya nodded at Taylor.

"That's Darius's number."

"Mmm-hmm."

"C'mon now," Marcus said, giving her a paternal, amused sort of look. "Don't be petty."

Anaya took the sucker out of her mouth. She'd whittled it down to a thin, barely-there circle. "When ReShawn told you what went down the other night, did she tell you the whole story?"

"She said Darius got profiled by the cops."

"Yeah. In front of that girl's house." Anaya filled Marcus in, from Camille Gray's commentary at the town meeting, to the word Paige used against Jubilee on Monday. When she finished, Marcus was frowning.

"See," she said. "Don't be calling me petty."

"Are they going to the dance tomorrow?"

"I don't think so. Darius is supposed to work with Jemar all day, and he hasn't said anything about needing a tie or boutonniere."

At halftime, the score was 34–10.

Anaya had finished her sucker.

And she and Marcus got lost in conversation.

She told him all the things she hadn't been able to tell him. About her classroom and her students. All the quirks. All the funny stories. How awesome second graders were, even at Crystal Ridge. She told him how hard it was telling Nia's mama what Paige had said. How for a second she was terrified Nia's mother was going to pull Nia out of O'Hare, and how for a second Anaya wished she hadn't said anything. How selfish it was of her to want Nia to stay while her father's district crumbled and she made money while it fell. She told him about the time machine and her plans. Plans her father would be proud of. Plans to be the change where she was at.

She told him about coaching track in the spring too, and how Taylor Gray was supposed to be her star.

"You know who you should recruit?" Marcus said. "Shanice. She's here this year. At Crystal Ridge."

"Shanice?"

"Yeah, you know. She's at the center every weekend. Nose ring? Always wearing basketball shorts?"

"Oh, right."

"Remember that track-and-field event we did a couple years ago?"

"Remember? I organized it."

Marcus smiled. "Well, Miss Organization, do you remember how fast she ran the 400?"

Yeah. She did.

Shanice Williams had blown everyone else out of the water. Even the boys.

The marching band burst back to life. The football players ran back onto the field. Halftime was over.

Milliken v. Bradley

On August 18, 1970, the NAACP sued the state of Michigan on behalf of all minority children attending Detroit Public Schools. After hours of testimony on redlining, exclusionary zoning, and other disreputable tales of housing discrimination, a federal judge agreed with the plaintiffs. The government "at all levels" bore responsibility for residential segregation.

It was the first time a federal judge recognized the critical role city-suburb borders played in maintaining segregated schools and ordered a major metropolitan area to do something about it.

Thirty-Nine

Yellow 2's October News Flash

October is here, which means the heat of summer is finally starting to wane, the leaves on the trees are starting to change, and we are starting a new, comprehensive literacy unit!

Time Travel Adventures: I asked the students to choose a decade, any decade (we talked about decades in math). Yellow 2 voted, and the 1950s won in an impressive landslide. So we will be transporting to a pivotal time in our nation's history, and we're going to read and write all about it.

Guided Reading: Your child's guided reading book should be coming home every night in his or her guided reading bag. Each group is reading an appropriate-level nonfiction book about an important event, person, or place from the decade we're studying. By the end of these books, students should be able to identify text features (table of contents, index, glossary, headings, etc.).

Writing Corner: In second grade, students have to complete a graded informational writing piece. We're going to be writing biographies. Attached, you will find the rubric and the list of lesser-known heroic figures students can choose from for their report. All these heroic figures either lived during the 1950s or left a legacy that impacted the 1950s. Students will complete these in class.

October is National Bullying Prevention Month. Our guidance counselor, Mr. Keibler, will be visiting our classroom once every week to talk about bullying. Mark your calendar for Wednesday, October 31, for Yellow 2's Fall Festival. Please contact Camille Gray for details: 321-464-2917. She's in need of several volunteers.

Happy October,
Miss Jones

•°•°•

They walked inside to the sound of laughter and a Boyz II Men song that immediately hurled Jen back in time, to when she was eleven at her very first middle school dance, swaying back and forth with a boy whose head came up to her nose. His name was Aaron Sheller, and the whole time they danced, her best friend stood behind him, lip syncing all the lyrics into an imaginary microphone.

Although we've come,
To the eeeeeend of the road

Jen had felt as conspicuous then as she felt now, standing in the doorway as four women beyond the front desk turned to look at them.

The one holding a pair of sheers—Trill, Jen assumed—smiled a wide, welcoming smile. If she thought it strange that a white woman had walked into her salon, she hid it well. "Come on in. You're in the right place."

Jen and Jubilee stepped farther inside. The salon was small and oblong and smelled faintly of coconut and eucalyptus. It was comfortably warm and divided in two by a front desk. On one side—the side where Jen and Jubilee stood—was a wall lined with hair-care products, extensions, and a variety of beads and barrettes. Beside it, a couple of flimsy chairs and a chipped magazine rack with magazines Jen had never heard of before—*Ebony* and *Essence* and *Upscale.* On the other side, a manicure table, a shampoo station, a hooded dryer, and a salon chair. All but the seats at the manicure table were taken.

"Abeo! Get your hands off my soda."

A little brown hand disappeared behind the front desk, away from the can of Diet Mountain Dew perched there.

"I'm thirsty!" a young voice said back.

"Go get yourself a juice box, then. You know where they are."

The little boy darted out from behind the desk, into a back room. He was dressed in an all-blue Adidas track suit with three white stripes up the side.

"She getting her hair braided?" Trill called.

Jen nodded.

"Anaya's student, right?"

Jen nodded again, her ears going slightly warm. Anaya had told her aunt about them. Exactly what, she wasn't sure.

"I'm finishing up with my ten o'clock. Why don't you go on and pick out some beads for her braids. ReShawn will check you out."

A slender young woman who'd been sitting at the shampoo station pushed herself up out of her seat. She wore a fashionable pair of joggers and an autumn-green bomber jacket and gold earrings so large and dangly they almost reached her shoulders. Her hair was cornrowed up into an elaborate bun at the top of her head.

"What beads you getting, girl?" she asked Jubilee, setting her elbows on top of the desk as she chewed on a piece of gum.

Jubilee looked up at Jen. "I want purple, like Nia."

Jen nodded toward the wall, encouraging her to grab some.

She did, and brought them to ReShawn, who picked them up and hugged them to her chest. "Oooo. These are *my* beads. These are my beads, aren't they? Their gonna look so good in my hair."

One corner of Jubilee's mouth lifted in an uncertain smile. Jen hated that Jubilee didn't know what to do with the banter. Inexplicably, Nia leaped to her mind, with a hand on her hip, jutting her chin. *Those ain't your beads,* she could hear her say.

"I love me some purple." ReShawn quirked one of her carefully shaped eyebrows. "Did Miss Jones tell you my favorite color?"

"You know Miss Jones?"

"Know her? Girl, we like this." ReShawn crossed two of her fingers. They were long and slender. "I've known Miss Jones since we were babies."

Jubilee's eyes went wide. "Really?"

"Yes, really. We tell each other everything." ReShawn winked and rang up the purchase. As she took Jen's credit card and ran it through a little device plugged into her phone, Jen wondered if Anaya told ReShawn about the name Jubilee had been called at school.

Nick had been livid. Angrier than after the town meeting. Angrier even than after Unpack Your Backpack night.

As she told him what Anaya told her, she remembered thinking, *This is how a real parent should react.* Jen, on the other hand, sat in that too-short chair, blinking dumbly, unsure how to react at all. She was too overwhelmed by all the things she didn't know.

"Come with me, little queen. Let's get that crown of yours washed." ReShawn offered her hand to Jubilee, who hesitated for a moment before taking hold and walking with her to the shampoo station.

Note to self, Jen thought. A kid's braid included a hair wash.

She had no idea, and she was too embarrassed to ask. So last night, she'd taken out Jubilee's puffs, washed, conditioned, detangled, and meticulously moisturized before sectioning her hair into braids.

The little boy came out from the backroom with an apple juice. He sucked the box dry and watched ReShawn set Jubilee up at the sink, fastening a pink cape around her neck and gently undoing each plait.

"You can come on back," Trill called to Jen, who hadn't moved from her spot by the desk.

Grateful, Jen smiled. She wasn't sure where she was supposed to sit—at one of the two chairs by the magazine rack or back there, with the rest of the women. She took one of the chairs at the manicure table.

"Woo wee, her hair is thick," said the woman sitting at the overhead dryer. She wasn't using it. In fact, she didn't seem to be getting her hair done at all. She wore blue jeans and a Steelers jersey and sat on the edge of the chair with her elbows on her knees, a tan purse dangling between her ankles.

"Yeah," Jen said. "It is."

"It looks healthy."

That might have something to do with all the moisturizer Jen put in it last night.

The woman walked over and felt Jubilee's hair for herself as ReShawn took out the last braid. "Oooo, that's nice and soft. Whatever you're doing, you keep on doing."

The words inflated something inside Jen. She clung to them like a woman in need of a life vest. "I haven't quite figured out how to style it."

The woman waved Jen's words away. "That's what you got Trill for. She does the best braids in Saint Louis. So good I don't even try. Anytime my granddaughters need their hair done, I bring 'em here."

Abeo dropped his empty juice box in a small garbage can by the manicure table and began twisting the bottles of nail polish in the display case. One tipped and dropped onto the floor.

"Hey." ReShawn had just turned on the water. "You gonna buy what you break?"

Little Abeo reached inside his pockets and turned them inside out. "I ain't got no money."

The women laughed.

It was a laughter that melted into conversation. Their voices mixed with the music and floated around Jen, slowly unwinding her muscles. They talked easily, familiarly. About a football party at so-and-so's house, about ReShawn's new boyfriend (Trill didn't like him) and her job at the airport (Trill didn't like that either), about some encounter Anaya's younger brother Darius had with a police officer and how long before a guy named Marcus would propose, about husbands and kids and grandkids. They talked about Lincoln Elementary and whether or not it would stay open and South Fork's urgent need for a whole new school board. Trill had lots of opinions about that.

When she finished her ten o'clock, the ten o'clock stayed to get her nails done by ReShawn, and the conversation continued. Jen moved to the seat at the shampoo station.

Jubilee sat in the salon chair as Trill used a blow dryer to dry her hair as straight as straw. She couldn't stop staring at herself in the mirror.

When Trill turned the dryer off, a song came on.

A song Jen didn't know.

It was a song that had ReShawn and Trill catching each other's eye with wide, matching smiles. As if on cue, Abeo jumped up from the toy truck he'd been pushing around on the floor and yanked up his pants.

All the women hooted with laughter.

"It's his song," Trill said.

"Get it, lil man," ReShawn added.

And little Abeo did.

He started shimmying his shoulders and sliding his feet like a young Michael Jackson. The women hooted louder. They snapped their fingers and moved their heads back and forth to the rhythm, just like Abeo.

Jen felt herself smiling.

She looked at Jubilee, who was smiling too. That shy smile of hers, as ever so slightly, her shoulder bobbed in tune with the beat.

Forty

Anaya's body thrummed with life as she hung the self-portraits her students painted the day before. At the top of the bulletin board were precut, bright letters that said: The Beautiful Colors of Yellow 2.

Anaya stepped back and smiled.

On Monday, Mr. Keibler visited her class for his fourth and final lesson on bullying. The timing was perfect, given what had transpired beforehand. She spoke about it with him quite extensively at the end of last month, and unlike Mr. Kelly, Mr. Keibler had been both visibly and audibly disturbed. Hence, the book he read to the class yesterday.

"It's not dumb skin or smart skin, or keep us apart skin; or weak skin or strong skin, I'm right and you're wrong skin."

Anaya's soul had sung when she listened to those rhymes, so much so that she wanted to jump out of her desk chair and clap her hands. Lift her arm heavenward and shout *Amen!* like Mama when she was feeling the Spirit. Mr. Keibler wasn't afraid to point out their differences. He didn't act like they were shameful or embarrassing in that way adults sometimes did. He didn't pretend the kids couldn't see color. Of course they saw color. It was one of the first things they learned in preschool. The names of each one and *look here, let's separate them into groups.* Four-year-olds knew that brown wasn't peach and peach wasn't brown. They just didn't ascribe any meaning to it.

That had to be learned. And the world was all too eager to teach. It delivered lessons in a thousand subliminal ways.

Every single day.

When Mr. Keibler left, Madison wanted to know why their skin was different. So Anaya taught an impromptu science lesson on the wonders of melanin. They spent the rest of the afternoon mixing paint colors to match their skin tones and creating the portraits she hung now.

The atmosphere had been kinetic.

She could practically see the wonder bouncing from one student to the next, until all twenty were excitedly holding their arms next to each other, admiring their different shades.

It was an atmosphere that had been brewing for weeks—an atmosphere that made her excited and a little apprehensive. Especially after yesterday morning, when Madison raised her hand and asked what she asked.

Her students were learning things she had to wait to learn until freshman year of college, when she signed up for an African American Studies course. Too many kids in South Fork never got that far. They moved through elementary school and middle school and high school believing the lie of omission. That the really important people from history—apart from a very select, standard few—were entirely white. But here in her class? She wasn't making them wait for college. Here in her class, she got to watch Nia and Dante and Zeke and Jubilee take on a new sort of glow. All these people—all these heroes. And they had brown skin just like them.

Nia had been the most ecstatic of all of them. But then, that was Nia. She spoke with a hand on her hip and a confident jut in her chin. "Why don't she have a day? Christopher Columbus has his own day, and he didn't even do nothing good. But Nina Simone is a hero, and she don't have a day."

Nia had selected Nina Simone for her informational writing assignment.

"My mama said most people don't even know who she is."

Nia's mother was right.

Not enough people knew about the Nina Simones of the world.

So they had a class discussion about why. Twenty second graders were becoming critical thinkers, right before Anaya's eyes. Why were there holes in the things they were taught? Why were there missing spots? *What* were the missing spots?

"You always want to ask what's missing," Anaya said, tapping her temple. "It's just as important as what's there."

And all twenty students had nodded soberly, like they understood.

A throat cleared behind her, interrupting the memory.

Mr. Kelly stepped inside her empty classroom, smiling a little awkwardly, his cheeks redder than normal, and Anaya knew why he was there. She'd been bracing for it.

"Hi there, Anaya," he said.

"Hi," she said back.

"What's this here?" he said, studying the just-finished bulletin board. "Did they do these in art class?"

"They did them in here, with me."

An almost imperceptible furrow creased his brow.

He cleared his throat again.

Anaya's muscles tensed a little more with every hem and every haw.

"So . . . you're sticking with the curriculum, right?"

"Sir?"

"I want to make sure you're covering what's meant to be covered. Second grade is a big year. There's a lot to get through." Mr. Kelly rubbed his cheek. "And the standards at Crystal Ridge are, of course, very high."

"Have I given you any reason to believe I'm neglecting the standards?"

"No, no. I've just . . ." He wrapped his hand around the back of his neck. "I've received a few concerned phone calls from parents."

And there it was.

"Some of them have expressed concern over what the kids are learning. They're worried that too much is being changed around." He slipped his hands into his pockets and squinted at the bulletin board next to the self-portraits— the Incredible Hulk bulletin board, where she'd hung the students' finished reports. Gavin Royce had chosen Frederick Douglass. Mr. Kelly seemed to be reading the quote at the top of Gavin's paper. "Usually, we cover this kind of stuff in February."

A scratch, Anaya . . .

She waited for the sting to subside, then spoke with measured calm. "The students had to complete an informative piece in writing this year. As far as I can tell, the teacher has the freedom to choose the topic."

Mr. Kelly strolled several paces as she spoke. He casually opened the door to the time machine and peeked inside. "Sarah Land's mother called this morning. She said that Sarah came home yesterday, feeling bad about being . . . white?"

"We talked about that."

"You and Mrs. Land?"

"Me and Sarah."

"Oh."

"She *was* feeling bad. I helped her understand that we don't learn about our past to feel bad about it. We learn about the past so we can learn from our mistakes."

Sarah had come up to Anaya's desk during quiet reading time. She was holding a book about Ruby Bridges and blinking back tears. "How could they be so mean?" she had asked, sniffling.

It was a valid question, and Anaya gave her what she hoped was a valid answer. "You don't have to be a mean person to do mean things."

Sarah had pondered that for a while, and then they talked for a little longer. About all those big feelings—those bad and sad and mad feelings—and how Sarah could turn them into something good. She could decide that she would do better than her ancestors. She could be the change where she was at.

Anaya wasn't sure if Sarah understood.

But she gave her a hug, and Sarah wiped her eyes.

And then recess happened.

Sensitive Sarah Land—a follower not a leader—didn't follow Paige Gray to the monkey bars that day. Instead, she played hopscotch. She played hopscotch with two little girls with matching beads in their hair. Jen Covington had taken Jubilee to Auntie Trill's.

"She also expressed concern that you were teaching the kids about someone named Emmett Till. I wasn't exactly sure who that was, so I did a Google search. The pictures are quite . . . graphic."

"They are very graphic."

"Don't you think that's a little mature for second grade?"

"I didn't teach them about Emmett Till, Mr. Kelly. Madison came across him on her own at home when she was searching the internet for important events in the 1950s."

"Oh."

"I could hardly leave something like that unaddressed. I assure you, I did not go into any details."

Mr. Kelly's brow furrowed even more.

"Sir?"

He looked at her, his furrow impossibly deep.

"I'm not neglecting any of the district's standards. I'm just approaching some of them from a different angle. Maybe that's not such a bad thing."

Forty-One

Camille clasped her hands, craning to see. It was a chilly fifty-eight degrees, but her palms were sweating. Her underarms too. She always got nervous watching Taylor run. It was as though her lungs were incapable of expanding until she caught the first glimpse of her long-legged daughter rounding the corner, kicking hard toward the finish line with a comfortable lead.

This was the cross-country state meet, which ratcheted her nerves to a whole new level. It didn't matter that this was Taylor's third time; fifth if you counted track. Last year, Taylor placed seventh. Seventh as a sophomore. This year, Taylor had her sights set on the top five. Coach Mack told Camille in confidence that he thought she was capable of top three.

Camille was afraid to believe him.

Until she saw Taylor with her own eyes, halfway through the course, keeping pace with numbers one and two.

It did the opposite of settle her nerves.

"Mom," Austin said beside her. "I don't have to spend the night. I can just hang out."

"I already told you, Austin," Camille replied, her eyes glued to the top of the hill. Any second now, the front runners would appear. *Any second.* "If you and Edison want to hang out, he is more than welcome to come to our house."

"But he's already been to our house. He wants me to come to his."

"I said no."

"Why not?"

Because Edison lives in the ghetto! There was another shooting in South Fork last week. Camille fully supported Austin and Edison's budding friendship, but not at the expense of her son's safety.

"Dad, will *you* let me?"

A monster in Camille's chest snarled to life. Austin's father didn't get to make that decision. He forfeited that ability four months ago. But before she could say so, a runner appeared. A brunette, followed closely by two blondes.

Camille rose up on her tiptoes, her heart pounding.

Taylor? Was one of them Taylor?

The crowd broke into applause. A heavyset woman whooped and ran forward, jumping and clapping her hands. "C'mon, Vanessa! Push, baby. Push!"

Vanessa was the brunette, and she was losing her lead.

Not to Taylor.

Taylor wasn't part of the pack.

"Where is she?" Paige asked, jumping on the balls of her feet to see around the crowd of spectators. "Why isn't she in third anymore?"

Two more runners crested the hill. Contenders for fourth and fifth.

A Latino girl. And a redhead.

Camille's hands clenched into tight fists beneath her chin.

C'mon, Taylor, where are you?

It wasn't too late. If she showed up now—*right now*—she could start her kick and pass the two girls for fourth place. She could still make her goal, because her kick was impressive. Her kick had won her many races.

"There she is!" Austin said.

Camille's adrenaline surged.

Taylor had come over the hill, her face scrunched up in exertion, neck and neck with two others.

C'mon, Taylor. C'mon. Show us that kick, baby.

Paige started jumping and cheering, calling out encouragement.

Camille clutched Austin's shoulder.

Where's your kick, Taylor? Show us that kick.

But it didn't come.

The other two girls pulled ahead.

Taylor crossed the finish line at number eight.

Camille's thudding heart sank into her stomach.

Eighth place.

Taylor had gotten eighth place.

"Ouch, Mom." Austin extricated himself from her death grip. She had grabbed Neil's arm too. Their eyes met, and, like a hot potato, she let him go.

She turned away and pushed through the crowd toward her daughter, who was leaning over her knees, sucking at the air, nodding at her coach. He clapped her shoulder, then headed off to cheer for his other runners. He had three today.

Taylor shook out her legs, looking down at them like they were foreign objects instead of a familiar part of her body.

"Honey?"

Taylor looked up. Her cheeks were red, her lips pale, her forehead beading with sweat.

"You did great."

"No, I didn't. I did awful."

Camille opened her mouth to reply, but Taylor didn't wait. With heartbreaking tears in her eyes, she walked over to the tent where she and her teammates put their bags. She squatted and yanked at the zipper.

"Hey," Neil said, squeezing past a couple of women. "Is she okay?"

He was dressed in a pair of casual jeans and a heather-gray cotton pullover. It was an outfit Camille picked out for him after he lost his weight. Turned out, he lost that weight for another woman. And he had the audacity to ask if Taylor was okay.

No, Taylor wasn't okay. None of them were okay. Everything was falling apart. Camille and Kathleen were in an incredibly weird place because Kathleen was so worried about Cody. She seemed to hold Camille personally responsible for the fact that Taylor rejected Cody's homecoming proposal, as if Camille had any control over who Taylor liked. She didn't even have any control over who her husband liked.

Jen Covington—who was the full-time nurse at the high school now, thanks to *her*, no less—hated Camille's guts. So did Paige's teacher. Both of them might as well have dressed up as matching Elsas at Yellow 2's Fall Festival, given how coldly they treated her. Never mind the fact that she planned the entire party, even though her own family was in turmoil. Never mind the fact that Camille made Paige write an apology note. Never mind the fact that Camille had personally called Jen at least three times hoping to explain. The woman never answered; she never returned Camille's phone calls. She cut Camille off completely and became BFFs with Nia's mother. Their girls even had matching hair now. And somehow all of it was Neil's fault. Because everything started falling apart when he left.

"*Is she okay?*" Camille's voice trembled like it did the first time she had to give a speech in high school. Only this time, it wasn't trembling with nerves. "What do you think, Neil? Her father walked out on her."

His face went pale. "I didn't walk out on Taylor."

"Right. That was just me."

"Don't put this on my shoulders, Camille. She had an off day. It happens to everyone."

"It never happens to Taylor."

"It just happened right now."

"I saw you with her."

"What?"

"I saw you with Jasmine Patri."

His face went even whiter, confirming everything she already knew and all the things she only suspected.

"Or *Jas,* as she appears in your phone. You know, I've been wondering. Do you two have a nickname for me like you have for her ex-husband? Hairy Gary and Camille the Heel? Is that how you struck up a relationship? She was new to town and lonely, so she told you her sob story while you did burpees together? Maybe that's why you never invited me to CrossFit."

"You hate CrossFit."

"And she loves it. Just like she loves hunting and numbers. Aren't you two perfect for each other? The financial advisor and the accountant."

Neil narrowed his eyes. "Did you hire someone to investigate her?"

"I hired someone to investigate *you.*"

People were starting to stare.

Austin and Paige among them. They remained where they'd been when Taylor lost, watching in the same way they watched the police officer and Darius Jones on her front lawn.

She took a step closer and lowered her voice. "I don't even know who you are. We've been married for twenty-one years, and somehow you're a complete stranger." Because the Neil she knew? He would never have done this. Not to her, and certainly not to their children.

"I can't believe you hired a private investigator."

"I can't believe you're having an affair."

"It's not an affair." He ground the words between his teeth. "We go to CrossFit together."

"And have coffee dates."

"They weren't dates. She needed someone to help her with her finances."

"And you were all too eager to help."

"Yeah, well. It's nice to be needed every now and then."

"What is *that* supposed to mean?"

"You don't need me, Camille! You have everything under control. The whole world under control. You certainly don't need *my* help. Let's be honest here. The only reason you're upset is because you won't be able to send out your perfect little family Christmas photo this year."

His words smacked her across the face. So sharp, so unexpected, so cruel, she stood there in frozen, breathless shock. She hated him. She hated him with total and complete hatred, just like she hated Jasmine Patri.

In that moment, she hated them so much she felt capable of murder.

Neil shook his head, dragged his hands down his face. He looked disgusted. With her. With them. With all of it.

Well, yeah! she wanted to scream. She was disgusted too. And why didn't he just file the papers already? If he wasn't coming back, then what was he waiting for? But she couldn't say that. She was terrified of saying that.

"Tell Taylor she did a great job, all right? I'll see her next weekend."

Forty-Two

December: Six Months Until the Color Run

It was a relief to sit. To be away from the lobby, away from the fake smiles. Had they always been that way? Or just now that hers felt so fake?

She set her coat and purse on the empty seat beside her. Neil used to take the aisle seat. He would stretch one long leg to the side of the chair in front of him. Then Austin, then Taylor, then Camille, because Paige still went to kid's church, and Camille never minded sitting shoulder to shoulder with a friendly stranger. Now it was only her and her coat. Her kids were gone for another weekend with their father.

As people around her settled in, Camille pretended to look through her bulletin. It advertised the women's Christmas event next weekend, as well as the Christmas Eve services, which would be at three, five, and midnight. The words and numbers trembled in front of her; her hand was shaking. Camille grabbed it with her other and ordered it to stop, right now. The way she would her squabbling children. But it wouldn't stop. So she clasped her hands and shoved them between her knees.

The congregation stood to sing.

Then they sat to listen.

Camille had a hard time. Her pastor was preaching from Ephesians 6. He was pumping them up to put on their armor and prepare for battle. But Camille was too tired for battle. Camille didn't have the energy to strap on belts and breastplates and helmets.

She kept thinking about Christmas. They usually celebrated the holiday at home. She and Neil had been adamant ever since Taylor was old enough to understand Santa Claus that their children would wake up in their own beds on Christmas morning. They would open presents and stay in their pajamas and decorate a birthday cake for Jesus. Neil's mother would come over in the afternoon. They would eat an early dinner much too lavish for the six of them. Her mother-in-law would overstay her welcome, but when she finally did leave, they'd cuddle up downstairs to watch whatever Christmas movie best suited the ages of their children at the time. Last Christmas they watched *It's a Wonderful Life.*

This year, Camille would be getting on a plane with her three children and flying to California. They didn't go for Thanksgiving, so her parents insisted they come, which meant she would spend the holiday with her two younger sisters and their intact families. It was going to be the first time Camille saw any of them since Neil left.

She picked at a hangnail. She found out over Thanksgiving that he still took the kids to church. Not their church, mind you. He wasn't brave enough for that. But *a* church. She wondered how he could go. How could he sit there on Sunday morning and not suffocate beneath the pressing weight of his own sin? Didn't he feel any conviction at all? She didn't understand, and her anger had lost its edge. It came in fits and starts. But she couldn't sustain it. Inevitably, the red heat would ebb, leaving a gray, listless loneliness in its wake.

Despite everything, she wanted him back.

Not just because she was tired of being the object of pity. Not just because she loathed the weekends when he had the children and she was left to wander about in a house too big for one. But because she was starting to miss him. At night, alone in bed, she longed for him. *Neil.* At least, the Neil she'd fallen in love with.

As their pastor asked his congregation to turn to a psalm and Bible pages crinkled all around, Camille traveled back in time to when she and Neil were newlyweds living out the Song of Solomon, euphoric on love and the fact that they could consummate it whenever they wished. They could consummate it, and the angels would sing.

Her heart sure did.

A tangle of sheets. A lazy Saturday morning. A trail of kisses from her hipbone to her ribcage as overnight whiskers tickled her skin. Neil's strong hands, which had calluses because he still went rowing, and then the interruption of a phone call. A loud, piercing ring that stole the moment away.

Neil saw his mother's number on their caller ID and fell back into bed with a groan. "Why in the world is she calling us at eight o'clock in the morning on a Saturday?"

"Because you're her only child and she needs you," Camille said. His mother was a lonely widow. His father died when Neil was eighteen—a tragedy that left his mom overstepping all reasonable boundaries between a mother and her son. Back then, Camille found it heartbreaking. Back then, it had drummed up her sympathy. "You should answer it."

He did.

Neil sat on the edge of the bed, talking his mother through whatever crisis had befallen her. Camille slid behind him and wrapped her arms and legs around his torso. Neil slept without a shirt, and his skin was deliciously warm in the morning. She pressed her ear against his bare back, listening to the deep sound of his voice between each steady heartbeat. Even though his mother drove him crazy, he never lost his patience with her. His tone remained gentle and respectful.

After he said goodbye, Camille ran her fingers through his messy hair. It was still thick and a rich, golden blond from their honeymoon in Hawaii.

"You know what I love about you?" he said, bringing his chin to his shoulder.

"Do tell."

"You're nothing like my mother."

"Oh?"

"You're strong. And independent. Incredibly decisive."

"Some people call that bossy."

"I call it . . . appealing." He turned around and slowly leaned her back onto the bed, where they would enjoy the rest of their Saturday morning as husband and wife.

Camille swallowed the memory. It tasted like ash on her tongue. Somehow the things Neil loved about her became the things that drove him away. He didn't find her decisiveness, her independence, so appealing anymore.

"Stand up," the pastor said.

Camille blinked.

"If you're too weary to fight this battle on your own, if you don't even know the words to pray anymore. All you have to do is stand. We will gather around you. We will place our hands on you. And we will stand in the gap like we are called to do."

Camille's heart began to thud.

"Don't be afraid. This isn't a therapy session. You don't have to talk or make any confessions. All you have to do is stand."

Slowly, people did.

A few here and there scattered throughout the sanctuary.

"This is why we're called the body. When one member suffers, we all suffer. Let your weary soul be lifted."

Oh, her soul was weary.

And her heart was pounding.

Quicker and quicker.

Three rows ahead, a black man and a black woman stood. They were holding hands.

"Look around. You aren't alone."

The couple holding hands looked around.

Camille looked around too.

Several people were standing. Among them, an elderly black man toward the back. Another black couple across the aisle. They stuck out—the only black congregants in a sea of white.

And they were standing because they were weary.

Camille was sitting because she was afraid.

"If someone beside you is standing, I want you to go to them. Go, and pray strength and truth over them. Let's lift up our brothers and sisters who are tired and weary, church. Let's do what the saints were meant to do. Let's lift them up."

Forty-Three

January: Five Months Before the Color Run

Jen lay in bed with her shoes on, exhausted but glad to be home. Ever since Mom called her up and said in her singsong way, "I purchased your tickets!" Jen had been dreading the trip. It was hard enough living under the same roof as her parents for a week. Having to parent Jubilee under the same roof as her parents for a week had taken the whole thing to a new level. It was a relief to have it behind them—their first trip home, their first holiday season, and all its accompanying stress. She might have eaten her weight in Mom's homemade lefse to help her through it.

"I feel gross."

"You don't look gross." Nick tossed the last of his dirty clothes into the laundry basket and climbed into bed. "In fact, you look very, very un-gross."

He kissed her neck.

"What if I turn into my father?"

"You aren't going to turn into your father."

"I'm on my way to getting as big as him."

"You're nowhere even close."

"He wasn't always so heavy." Jen had seen the proof with her own eyes. Once upon a time—long, long ago—before type 2 diabetes, before Jen was even an apple in Mom's eye, her father had been quite the athlete. "Don't you think it's maddening how my mother worries about his health all the time when she's the one who keeps feeding him all the unhealthy food?"

"It is a little ironic." Nick crooked his elbow and rested his head on his hand. "I think it's more maddening that she lets Jubilee drink a carton of milk every day."

"It was good to see Leah though."

"Her kids are getting big."

"I almost told Mom about Brandon before we left." He'd finally contacted Jen via text message. His number hadn't changed.

"It's probably good that you resisted the urge."

"Do you think we made a mistake? Should we have sent him some money?"

"Jen . . ."

"I know, it's just . . ."

"He's your brother."

"He's my brother." Her invisible, nonexistent brother. Because her parents pretended he didn't exist. They acted like talking about the problem was the same as having the problem. "Do you think he'll ever get clean?"

"We'll keep praying." Nick turned over onto his back. They lay side by side, staring up at the same ceiling. He took her hand. "And you would still be beautiful."

"What?"

"If you got as fat as your dad."

Jen gave his stomach a playful thwack.

He let out a groan and rolled back over to his side.

"He's never taken care of himself, you know. Sometimes I think I might have learned that from him."

"So . . . ?"

"So I was thinking about a New Year's resolution."

"You're going to become one of *those* people, huh?"

"I was thinking of taking up running."

Nick quirked his eyebrow.

"I could train for the 5K."

"The one your BFF is organizing?"

Jen tried to thwack him again, but he blocked her. "Leah said she'd train with me. She said PJ and her and the kids could drive up for a visit the weekend of the race. Y'all could cheer us on."

Nick pulled her close. "I would love to cheer you on."

⁕⁕₌⁕₌

"I loved when my oldest could finally drive."

Everyone turned to look at Deb.

She shrank back a little. "Of course, I don't mean to imply you shouldn't be upset. You have every right to be upset."

"I can't believe he didn't even talk to me about it. He bought her a car for Christmas like it was no big deal, and then he took her to the DMV behind my back and got her a license." Camille was still fuming over it. "If something happens to her, it will be on *his* head."

"I'm sure nothing will happen to her," Deb said comfortingly.

"She's not old enough to drive."

"According to the State of Missouri, she is."

Camille shot Rose a sharp look. "Of course, Neil's nothing but a hero right now. According to Taylor, he hangs the moon. I really could kill him. Ugh. And after I went out of my way to take his mother out for lunch."

"You're a saint."

"I'm not a saint. I did it for Paige." And Camille was glad she did. Since moving into the retirement home, her mother-in-law was going downhill at an alarming rate.

"Were you at least able to relax in the California sunshine?"

Camille sighed.

Her time in California had not been relaxing.

Taylor talked to her aunts but acted like Camille wasn't there. Austin kept asking to FaceTime with Neil, and Paige cried at church because her one-year-old cousin's vegetable pouch exploded all over her pretty red dress before pictures, which meant Daddy wouldn't see how pretty she looked. Camille almost started crying too. It didn't help that her mother kept going on and on about how thin they all looked, as if Neil left them destitute and starving. Her sisters couldn't get over her hair, which had grown out some, but was still much shorter than they'd ever seen. And her dad and brothers-in-law kept patting her on the shoulder and saying things like "I'd like to knock some sense into him." Camille wanted to leave Neil and all conversation about him in Missouri. She certainly didn't breathe a word about the private investigator and all she'd learned about Jasmine Patri.

"Let's just talk about registration."

"Yes," Kathleen said. "Please."

"The New Year's resolution ads were a fabulous idea."

"Thank you, thank you." Rose took a regal bow. "Every year you freak out that we'll never be able to top the year before, and every year you freak out for nothing."

"I think everyone is really excited to have our very own color run. Speaking of which, I ran the numbers. We will save so much money if we do the color ourselves."

"Won't that be a headache?"

"Not if we get enough volunteers. We've never had a problem drumming them up in the past." Camille bent to reach inside the refrigerator and pulled out the hummus.

"Are you wearing a gun?" Rose asked.

"You can see it?"

"Am I not supposed to?"

Camille turned to Rebecca. "I must have it on wrong."

Rebecca stepped over baby Harper. "Here, let me see."

"Why are you wearing a gun right now?"

"I'm trying out Rebecca's harness. She thinks I should wear it. I think I prefer the special purse I bought."

"You won't be able to get to the gun as quickly if it's in your purse."

Rose wrinkled her nose. "Do you think you'll run into a situation where you'll need to get to a gun?"

"Someone broke into her neighbor's house in the middle of the day, Rose."

"That was over four months ago."

"And they haven't caught the burglar."

"So she's going to shoot a burglar? What happens if one of her kids surprises her and she thinks it's a burglar?"

"You guys are making me nervous," Deb said, her attention swiveling between Rebecca, who had removed the gun and was adjusting Camille's harness, to little Harper, sleeping soundly in her car seat on the floor.

She was all bundled up in pink fleece and a matching bow, her fist curled by her plump cheek as she suckled in her dreams. Camille read once that men's pupils dilated when they saw a naked woman and women's pupils dilated when they saw a newborn baby. She had no problem believing the scientific tidbit. Babies did funny things to her chest. Even when they were crying, Camille's heart still constricted with longing. She never thought, *Thank goodness that's not me anymore.* She'd take a tiny wailing infant over a hostile teenager any day.

Rebecca must have noticed Camille's adoring gaze. "You can hold her if you want. She needs to wake up soon anyway; otherwise she won't sleep tonight."

Camille didn't have to be told twice. She had Harper out of her car seat and nestled against her neck quicker than it took Rebecca to adjust her harness. Harper smelled like talcum powder with a hint of sour. Spit-up. Camille inhaled deeply. She actually missed the smell of spit-up.

"Remember when ours were all cute and cuddly and didn't hate our guts?" Camille said to Kathleen.

"I'm not sure I remember what that's like." Kathleen bit into another carrot. "Not with my oldest, anyway."

"Things aren't getting better with Cody?" Deb asked.

"You'd think it would, with the season over and done with, but the guys are still giving him a hard time."

"At least they didn't *win* state," Deb said, and then her face turned red. No doubt she felt horrible for suggesting the state championship loss was a good thing. Rose's daughter was a cheerleader, after all, and had taken the loss quite hard.

"Cody's taking his frustration out on us. Bennett worst of all. Rick's ready to ship him off to military school."

"Do you think he regrets quitting?"

"I don't know. I think it's all finally starting to hit him. He's a senior. He won't get another shot, you know? This was it."

"At least he has tennis in the spring," Deb said.

Kathleen gave Camille a pointed look. "So long as Darius Jones doesn't play tennis."

⁕⁕⁕

Anaya would be happy never to set foot in the Crystal Ridge High School gymnasium ever again. All the hostility and animosity that bred in the atmosphere back in July had turned into a ghost haunting the rafters. She could feel its cold presence pressing against her skin and wondered if she was the only one who could.

She finished writing her name on a name tag and stuck it as close to her shoulder as possible. She hated name tags. Not only because it created that awkward moment where eyes flickered toward chests but because people inevitably said her name wrong.

"Hey, A-nay-a," they'd say, like they were old buddies.

And she would smile and say hello back and let her name be butchered.

She worked her way through the bodies toward the bleachers, the ghost hovering over her shoulder. Crystal Ridge was holding a district-wide staff meeting to kick off the second semester. An attempt to rally the troops, snap them out of their Christmas-cookie comas, and share several PowerPoint presentations about the latest and greatest pedagogy. Anaya was anxious for it to be done so she could leave this place and head to her classroom, where it was easier to forget who employed her.

Halfway to her seat, someone grabbed her attention with a clap on the shoulder.

"Hey, Anaya." It was Troy Brewin, the head football coach. "How's my boy doing? Did he have a good break?"

Darius *wasn't* his boy. In fact, Darius didn't even like Coach Brewin.

"Hey, do me a favor. Make sure he's taking good care of that arm on the off season, will ya? A coach has to look out for his star." Troy gave his eyebrows a wag. "Speaking of which, I hear you've been busy recruiting one of your own."

"What's that?"

"Shanice Williams. I had her in gym class last semester. That girl can run. All the fuss about these transfers? I don't know about you, but I'd say it's doing us wonders." He gave Anaya a conspiratorial jab, like they were in on it together. Not a single thought for the fifty-plus teachers and staff out of a job in the South Fork district last month. It was like he didn't care about them. He probably didn't.

Troy lifted his arm. "Hey, Kyle!"

Anaya's throat constricted. She felt ill. Very suddenly ill.

Kyle Davis nodded at Troy Brewin, and then Kyle's attention flickered to her. Anaya student taught with him last year. He was standing beside a big-chested young woman with a tiny waist—a figure made evident by a top that seemed one size too snug. "Anaya, hey! I was wondering when we'd run into each other. How's your first year going? Everyone treating you well? Allow me to introduce you to my new student teacher, Ellie Sorrenson."

Ellie reached out her hand and shook Anaya's; then she shook Troy's. His attention lingered overly long on Ellie's name tag.

"Anaya was my student teacher last year."

"Wow," Ellie said. "You got a job in the district, huh?"

"Yes."

"You've got big shoes to fill," Kyle said. "Anaya's one of the best student teachers I've ever had."

Troy Brewin's smile turned into the Cheshire cat's.

Kyle picked up on the innuendo. "Hey, now. I didn't mean it that way."

Anaya's skin crawled. She tried to tell herself it was only a scratch, but her heart pounded like a drum. And Ellie Sorrenson stood there looking like she felt the sting too.

Forty-Four

Anaya had to hand it to the woman. She knew how to make a person's birthday special. A candy-bar wreath hung on the door of her classroom, and a pile of homemade birthday cards littered her desk. After they said the Pledge of Allegiance, Camille presented her with a large framed picture of a dandelion painting, the kind with the seeds that blew off in the wind. Only instead of spores, the painting was made up of twenty unique thumbprints, each one with the name of a student written below. Off to the side was the message:

> *Wishing you a Happy Birthday*
> *Love, Yellow 2*

They all sang her "Happy Birthday," waving their fingers back and forth like conductors of an orchestra, and then Camille left and Jan McCormick came in carrying a large bouquet of red roses. The class made a collective sound, as though they'd just witnessed two people kissing.

"Someone has an admirer," Jan said with a wink.

Anaya buried her nose in the rose petals, then plucked out the card, unable to contain her grin as she read the short poem.

"Are you smiling because those are from your boyfriend?" Nia asked.

"Maybe."

"What's his name?"

"Marcus."

Madison sat up on her knees. "My brother's name is Marcus."

"Are you gonna marry him?"

Anaya set the vase of roses on her desk and wiggled her left ring finger at Nia. It was naked, although ReShawn kept saying it wouldn't be by summertime. Every time she said it, it tied Anaya's stomach into knots. With excitement. And also dread. She couldn't shake the feeling that soon—very soon—the other shoe was going to drop.

"How old are you?" Madison asked.

"Twenty-three."

"That's old," Gavin said.

"That's not old," Paige corrected. "My mom is forty-three. *That's* old."

Anaya chuckled.

"I wish it was *my* birthday," Aaishi said dreamily. "I love when it's my birthday."

Anaya did too. From the time she was old enough to remember, Mama would wake her up, a steaming pile of homemade pancakes on a plate in her hand. She'd sing her "Happy Birthday," and then she'd sit on the edge of Anaya's bed and tell her all about the day she was born and how she got her name while Anaya smothered those pancakes in syrup.

Names were a big deal in her family.

Anaya's meant "God answered." Darius's meant "upholder of the good," like King Darius from the Bible. Auntie Trill called him Lil King until he turned ten and Darius didn't want to be called little anymore. Her mama's name was Latasha because she was born on Christmas Day, and Daddy's parents named him Jeremiah because they needed to believe that the Lord would lift them up.

She looked around at her students and set her hands on her hips.

"You know what? I have a fun idea."

They all perked up.

"Today we are going to study our names."

●●●●●

"I don't like my name," Paige announced as she climbed into the backseat after school.

Camille frowned. "You have a lovely name."

"Do you know what it means?"

"Uh . . . something from a book?"

"That's p-a-g-e, Mom. Not p-a-i-g-e."

"Right. Sorry." She waited for Paige to click her seat belt into place, then pulled away from the curb. Snow crunched under the tires. "How did the rest of Miss Jones's birthday go? Did Mr. Kelly remember to bring in the cupcakes after lunch?"

Camille was quite proud of herself for all she'd put together for Anaya's birthday. In fact, she was positive that after today, Miss Jones would change her mind about what a horrible person she must be.

"You really didn't look up the meaning of my name before you named me?"

"No, I really didn't."

"Then why did you give me the name?"

"I liked the way it sounded."

Paige shook her head, like she couldn't believe how utterly shallow her own mother was. "It means 'little servant.'"

Camille bit her lip to keep from smiling. Paige seemed very upset about the meaning of her name. Camille would not laugh at her.

"Do you want to know what Sarah's name means?"

"What?"

"Princess. Why didn't you name me Sarah?"

"Because, my darling dear, in this family, we appreciate a nice bit of irony."

Paige scrunched her nose. "What's irony?"

"The meaning of your name."

When they got home, her youngest went in search of the baby name book Camille told her she purchased a long time ago, when she was pregnant with Austin. It was probably somewhere in the basement storage room. She didn't think Paige would actually find it. But lo and behold, she did.

She brought it with her to the dinner table.

"Austin's name means 'magnificent' and Taylor's means 'tailor.'"

"Well that's boring," Taylor said.

"Daddy's name means 'champion.'"

Camille stuffed a bite of buttered tilapia into her mouth. If she couldn't say anything nice, she wouldn't say anything at all.

"But it also means 'cloud.'"

Now that was more appropriate.

"Mom, your name means 'perfect.'"

"I quite like that, thank you."

Taylor rolled her eyes.

"And also . . . a noble virgin?"

Austin almost spewed his milk all over the table.

Taylor smirked into her napkin.

Paige looked up from the book. "What's a noble virgin?"

"Something I hope you will be until you're married."

•€•⁶•

The next day, the kids took turns sharing about their names after the morning read-aloud time.

Nia told the class her name meant "bright." And then she told the class that her mother's name meant "a slender young tree," which made her mama laugh and laugh and laugh like it was the funniest darn joke she ever heard.

Jubilee was practically glowing when she said, in her heavily accented voice, "My name mean 'joy' and 'celebration.' Papa said he and Mama gave me da name Jubilee because I am joy and celebration."

Anaya called on Aaishi next. She'd been raising her arm ramrod straight in the air with such excited stillness Anaya could tell she was using every bit of focus not to wave it around. Her students learned quickly that they wouldn't get called on when they were *ooo-ooo-oooo*-ing and bouncing around in their seats.

But Aaishi didn't talk about her name.

"Miss Jones, are you Hindu like me?"

The question came out of left field.

"No, Aaishi, I'm not."

"Oh." Her shoulders slumped.

"Why did you think I was Hindu, sweetheart?"

"Because I wanted to look up your name last night, and my mom said that it was Hindu."

"Really?"

"Uh-huh. She has a cousin in India named Anaya."

Hindu.

Anaya had no idea, and she couldn't get it out of her head, either. While the rest of the kids shared what their names meant, she kept thinking about her own.

According to Mama, she came eight days late, after twenty-seven hours of hard labor. Every time that nurse told her to bear down, she'd cry out fervently and with much volume for God's deliverance. Finally, Anaya came—in a knot of umbilical cord, tiny arms flailing to fight free, nearly strangled before life could touch her.

It took a whole day before Daddy named her, and when he did, Mama's head fell back against the hospital bed and she let out a hoot of laughter. If ever a name fit, it was this one. Anaya. Hebrew for "God has answered." "He sure did. But it woulda been nice," Mama said, "if He answered a little bit sooner."

Anaya knew her name was also Nigerian, Ibo to be precise. In that translation, it meant "Look up to God," which Mama loved just as much, if not more, than the Hebrew one. But in all those years hearing that story, nobody said a thing about *Anaya* being Hindu.

As soon as she dropped her students off at their art special, she sat at her computer and began to search.

It turned out, Aaishi's mom was right.

Anaya was Hindu too, and in Sanskrit the meaning was different. In Sanskrit, Anaya meant "completely free."

It reminded her of what her dad would say after her track meets.

"You run like you got wings on your back, Anaya. You run like you're free. When I watch, I feel like I am too."

Forty-Five

Channel 6 News online:

> The unaccredited South Fork School District has been buckling under the financial weight of Missouri's school transfer law, and on Thursday the Missouri Board of Education voted unanimously to take financial control.
>
> "The amount of money South Fork is spending on transfer tuition is 1.5 times more than it receives in per-student state aid," says Deputy Education Commissioner Clint Fultz. "The potential for bankruptcy isn't a matter of if; it's a matter of when."
>
> Many residents of South Fork want to know what this means, including Mercy Ward, a mother of three students who have been attending school in the Crystal Ridge district. "People keep talking about dissolving the district, giving it a different name. Which is all well and good, unless they're trying to stop my kids from transferring to a better school. If that's the case, then we're going to take it to the court all over again."
>
> The latest in local sports: Two Crystal Ridge track stars are breaking records, and one has come out of nowhere. Get the full story here.

* * *

Late March in Missouri could never make up its mind. Hot, cold. Warm, cool. Sometimes all in a single day. It remained indecisive while a cluster of people stood at a graveside, setting flowers in front of a tombstone.

It was impossible to believe that it had been three years.

Three years since the smell of peach cobbler became forever tainted by grief. Three years since an entire church community stuffed itself inside Anaya's childhood home to eat that peach cobbler and reminisce about a man who'd been taken much too young. Three years since Granny's lament—an unbroken wail that joined the birds as she beat the ground with its insatiable appetite for black bodies.

She would never forget Mama's phone call or the hysterical sound of her voice on the other end. It came in the middle of Anaya's Title 1 practicum. Thirty minutes later she was sprinting through a hospital parking lot, desperate to get to her daddy. When she arrived, she found him in bed surrounded by beeping monitors, getting a verbal lashing from Mama.

"Your diet's gonna change," she said, wagging her finger. "No more bacon. No more french fries. No more donuts."

"Latasha, if I can't have bacon, I'd rather the good Lord take me now."

Mama threw her hands in the air and told Anaya to talk some sense into him. Then she kissed Daddy's cheek and left the two of them to talk alone. Daddy patted the bed, and she sat beside him, sandwiching his large hand between both of hers, alarmed at its coldness.

"I'm proud of you," he said.

She dipped her chin, because she already knew that. Daddy told her every day. And whenever he introduced her to anyone, it wasn't just, "This is my daughter, Anaya." It was, "This is my daughter, Anaya. She's on a full-ride track-and-field scholarship. One day she's gonna win gold for Team USA. Just you wait."

"Anaya." His eyes found hers, and they held all the world's gravity. "Anaya, Anaya, Anaya."

"Well, are you gonna say something, or are you just gonna keep repeating my name?"

He chuckled, and coughed. And then his eyes got serious again. "It's your birthright, baby. I want you to live it."

Her brow had furrowed. What was her birthright? And what did Daddy want her to live? But before Anaya could ask the question, a nurse bustled in to check his vitals and her brow furrowed too.

And then quicker than Anaya could blink, Daddy's heart attacked again. She was ushered out of the room while medical staff hurried in. No matter how many times the doctor shocked his heart, it refused to be revived.

For months and months afterward, her father's curious words repeated in her mind.

It's your birthright, baby. I want you to live it.

But how was she supposed to live it when she didn't know what it was?

Well, are you gonna say something, or are you just gonna keep repeating my name?

Her name.

Anaya.

All of a sudden, the confounding advice stepped into clarity. Her father had named her. He was a man who studied religion at Howard University.

And in Hindu, *Anaya* meant "completely free."

Forty-Six

April: Two Months Before the Color Run

Jen could run for thirty minutes without dying. She didn't think it possible at first, when she was contending not only with debilitating stitches in her side but cold weather and icy roads and hills that made her want to take up swearing. But then the weather warmed, the sun stayed up longer, and the pair of jeans languishing at the bottom of her dresser drawer almost fit.

Slowly she worked her way up to two miles without walking, and today she didn't even get a stitch. Now, as she stretched her legs in the backyard where Nick had the grill heating up for dinner, she experienced a rare wave of optimism.

Maybe this was a runner's high.

The screen door opened behind her. Nick walked outside and shot her a wink, a plate of raw chicken in his hand. He nodded toward their daughter. Jubilee sat beneath the shade of an oak tree, rocking her exorbitantly expensive American Girl doll in her arms. She was singing softly.

Jen had to lean closer to hear, and when she did, she was struck by the unmistakable sound of a sweet, familiar melody—one that was intricately tied to waiting. Jen had listened to the song on repeat while she prayed and prayed and prayed for her daughter to come home. Then God answered her prayer, and Jen stopped listening. Now Jubilee was sitting in the backyard rocking her doll, singing lyrics that brought her back to that place of acute longing so fast she nearly hissed at the sharpness of it.

The thing was, Jen had no idea where Jubilee would have learned it. Not at their new church. They played contemporary music there.

Jen came out of her stretch and walked across the freshly mowed lawn. "That's a pretty song you're singing to your baby."

Jubilee ran her flat palm over Baby's curly hair.

Jen sat beside them and plucked up a blade of grass. "Where did you learn it?"

"He sang it to me in the dark, when the doors went shut."

When the doors went shut.

She was talking about the orphanage.

And suddenly, this felt like holy ground, a burning bush, and Jen should take off her running shoes. Jubilee didn't like to talk about the orphanage. Any time she or Nick tried to bring it up, Jubilee got agitated.

Jen exchanged a look with Nick, whose ears were perked up and listening. "Who sang it to you?" Jen asked.

"I didn't know his name, Mama. He never told me."

"But he sang that song to you?"

"Uh-huh. He sang it whenever I got afraid."

Goose bumps marched up Jen's arms. Men were not allowed inside at night. The orphanage director locked the girls in, and if a man did come, it wouldn't be to sing. Certainly not this song.

"He would sing to me"—Jubilee threw her arms over her head, Baby lifted toward the sky—"and all the scary things would fly away!"

A knot tied in Jen's throat. She and Nick looked at each other again, and then they looked at their daughter sitting in the grass. She was singing. Their Liberian daughter was singing the words to an old Christian hymn—one a mysterious man sang to her in the dark when the doors went shut and she was most afraid.

"It is well . . . with my soul."

"It is well, it is well with my soul."

Forty-Seven

Jen used the scissor blade to slice through the tape and pulled the lid of the box open. There was a sticky note on top:

I was doing some spring cleaning and finally mustered up the courage to tackle the dreaded storage room. Your father is so proud! Don't throw any of this away! If you don't want it, I will put it back in storage. You just can't tell your father! XOXO

Jen stuck the sticky note on the counter and pulled out a small, neatly folded, tattered afghan, its pale pink having gone a dull gray years ago. Mom had called it her lovey, and Jen slept with it balled beneath her chin every night until she gave it up to go to a weeklong church camp the summer after sixth grade.

She pressed her nose against the knitted wool. It smelled like moth balls.

Underneath the blanket was a picture she'd made of a frog on a lily pad, drawn with the pastel set she got from her Aunt Meg on her tenth birthday. It won a spot in her elementary school art show. Mom framed it in one of those cheap plastic frames they sold at the dollar store. There were two soccer trophies from her short-lived soccer career. Baseball cards from her tomboy phase, carefully tucked inside plastic protector sheets. A plastic baggie of stray board-game pieces—the metallic thimble from Monopoly, some Battleship pegs, the pink and blue plastic cars from Life. A bare-bottomed troll with a jewel in its belly. This one had rainbow-colored hair and a black beard drawn on his chin with permanent marker. She remembered naming him Fred. There were a few children's books too. Jen smoothed her hand over the one on top—*The Velveteen Rabbit*.

"What is that?" Jubilee asked, coming into the kitchen with Baby tucked under her arm. She carried her everywhere these days.

"This," Jen said, tickling Fred's fluffy hair against Jubilee's cheek, "is some of my old stuff from when I was your age."

"Really?" She stood on her tiptoes and peeked inside.

"Really." Jen pulled out the last item at the very bottom. It was a scrapbook her mother made. "You can look through it if you want."

"Really?" Jubilee said again.

Jen helped her get the box into the living room. Then she returned to the kitchen and brushed her hand over the deep-purple cloth cover of the scrapbook, wiping away the dust.

It cracked when she opened it.

There was a pile of wrinkled, loose papers tucked in the front. Award certificates. Report cards. More pastel-inspired artwork. A third-grade writing assignment titled "Jennifer's Big Fortune," written and illustrated by Jennifer Newlin. She'd drawn a picture of a crystal ball on the front. The story itself was five pages long, and it was all about her future. How she would marry Joey Turner, a boy in class who had a mullet everyone thought was so cool. He chased all the girls with earthworms at recess, and if he caught you, he'd try to make you kiss it. Jen remembered wanting to kiss Joey instead. In "Jennifer's Big Fortune," Joey was the lead guitarist for a punk band and she was a veterinarian. They lived in Alaska and had four children—two sets of twins, boys and girls.

There was a crayon drawing on the final page. Her with a stethoscope around her neck and Joey with his impressive mullet and a guitar, along with a dog, and a cat, and a rabbit, and a horse, and their four peach-colored children. Two blond-headed identical boys and two brown-haired identical girls.

Shaking her head, Jen set the loose papers aside and began turning pages, wondering if Mom looked through them too, surprised that she hadn't removed the pictures of Brandon—actual evidence that he did exist. Photograph after photograph of the two of them, one with his arm slung around her shoulder in a pumpkin patch. Even then, he had the kind of eyes people commented on—big and blue with dark, long eyelashes. Girls loved them in high school, just like they loved his easygoing smile and his fun-loving personality. That was the Brandon she would always remember.

Not the Brandon drugs had turned her brother into.

She turned another page and ran her fingers over the one on top.

The four of them in their church clothes beneath the weeping willow out front, the two children splattered with mud. It was an after-church potluck pic. They went to every one because Daddy was an elder, and he loved all the food. She and Brandon were usually bored to death. Only this time, the Trenton boys found a mud puddle and dared Brandon to jump in. He did, of course, and then in a moment of impulsivity, Jen jumped after him—terrified and delighted at the squish of mud against her Mary Janes. Before she knew it, all the kids were jumping in. Stomping about. Laughing and screaming and swinging around on the willow branches like Tarzan.

Then their father snapped his fingers, and it was like jolting awake from a dream.

Mrs. Bother held up the camera slung around her neck. She was an old lady with bouffant hair who loved church hats and designated herself their church's official photographer. She snapped the picture—Brandon and Jen covered in mud from head to toe—and smiled fondly at Daddy with a nostalgic sparkle in her eye. "Oh, to be young again."

Daddy had smiled back.

And Jen felt a tsunami of relief.

Oh, good, she thought. *He's not mad.*

But then they climbed into the car, and the back of his neck got red like a beet, and as they drove out of sight, he said in a deep growl, "Don't you ever embarrass me like that again, do you hear?"

They both had to scrub their clothes clean when they got home.

Jen never jumped in another mud puddle again.

She closed the scrapbook. She tucked it under her arm to bring it up to her room when something slipped out from the pages and fluttered to the floor. It looked like an old newspaper article, yellowed with age.

Jen unfolded it.

It wasn't about her or Brandon. In fact, it was dated before she and Brandon were born. 1977, the year her parents got married. Daddy was 32 and principal at the local high school. This was before he was a superintendent. Mama was only nineteen and head-over-heels in love. The news article contained a black-and-white picture of the two of them. Mama smiling. Daddy looking serious. But it wasn't from their wedding day. Jen's attention moved upward, to the headline.

Oakdale Principal Opposes Integration

He called integration a political agenda. He said it was more damaging then it was beneficial. In his experience, kids learned best with their own kind.

Their own kind.

Her *father* said these words.

Jen pressed the ringing phone against her ear and paced in the small upstairs bathroom. She locked herself inside while Jubilee went through the nostalgia downstairs.

When Mom answered, she didn't say hello. She sang into the line—all southern honey and sunshine—like she'd been watching for Jen's phone call. "I take it the booooox arrrriiiived!"

Jen looked at the article clasped in her hand.

Their own kind.

"Isn't it a hoot? I'd forgotten all about those trolls. Oh, those hideous trolls. And the board-game pieces! Remember when you use to make artwork out of them? It made your daddy fit to be tied, but Mrs. Orwille thought it was creative. Remember her? Your old art teacher."

"Mama."

"She used to say to me, *Carol, you better get that girl in classes over the summer. She has an eye, and I'll die if I see it go to waste.* That's what she called it too. *An eye.* She was always so dramatic. And I would tell her—"

"Mama!"

The excited jabbering stopped.

Jen's mouth felt like cotton. "I found a newspaper article in the scrapbook."

"I'm sure you did. I put all kinds of things in there. Did you see that old story you wrote? 'Jennifer's Big Fortune.' That ridiculous crystal ball sure embarrassed your father. And Joey Turner. I wonder whatever happened to Joey Turner?"

"The article was about Dad."

"Oh. Well, it must have slipped in by accident. Lord knows, the man had enough of them. He was always making the papers." Porcelain clanked on the other end. Water ran. Mom was doing the dishes. "What was this one about? Some award he won, probably."

"It says he opposed integration."

The dishes stopped clanking.

Jen waited. She waited for her mother to explain. The journalist misquoted him. Dad sued for slander. But that wasn't what her mother said.

"Oh sugar, that was a long time ago. It was a different mind-set back then."

A different mind-set.

This was her explanation.

"Politicians were using children to push their agendas. To be honest, Jennifer, integration was a nightmare back then. People were pushing it too fast. There were so many problems. It needed to happen organically."

Organically.

And how did she suppose that would happen?

Or maybe she saw the one or two black kids in every classroom and thought education already had integrated. Never mind districts like South Fork.

"Is this why you didn't want us to adopt?"

There was a moment of loud silence, and then, "How dare you say such a thing."

How dare she?

But it was true. Her parents had been nothing but ominous warnings when Jen and Nick made their announcement. Her father didn't come to the airport when Jubilee came home. He barely looked at his granddaughter over Christmas break, but then he barely looked at his daughter either, so Jen hadn't given it much thought. But maybe she should have.

Oakdale Principal Opposes Integration

Her father was a racist. He was a racist, and she didn't even know it.

"I love my granddaughter. I have been nothing but supportive ever since she came home. I have loved her and embraced her and given her everything I would have given my own flesh and blood. I would have given her more too, if you hadn't kept her away from us."

"We weren't keeping her away from you. We were cocooning!" Something her mother refused to understand. "We needed Jubilee to understand that we are her mom and dad."

"And I'm her grandmother. But I guess that doesn't count for anything."

Jen brought her hand and the article up to her face in a fist.

"I can't believe what I'm hearing right now, Jennifer. I send you something nice in the mail. Your father and I fly your whole family home for Christmas. I drove up there and helped y'all move in, and you have the audacity to accuse us of . . . of . . ." But Mama wouldn't say it. She wouldn't say what she thought Jen was accusing them of. "We deserve to be treated better than this."

Before Jen could take a breath, before she could even unclench her fist, the line went dead in her ear.

Her mother had hung up on her.

Jen stood in front of the toilet, staring at the crumpled newspaper clipping in her hand.

Milliken v. Bradley Revisited

Four short years after the *Milliken v. Bradley* decision in 1970, the Supreme Court overturned its previous ruling, blocking metro-wide plans to desegregate urban schools. The majority said they found no evidence that the government had encouraged segregation in the metro area. For all intents and purposes, this decision made *Brown v. Board of Education* null and void in isolated urban districts.

> Every time we hear of a Negro moving in, we respond quicker than you do to a fire.
>
> —ORVILLE HUBBARD, segregationist
> mayor of Dearborn, Michigan, from 1942–1978

Forty-Eight

A yawn split Jen's mouth as she uncapped Derek Royce's medication. He had such a severe case of ADHD, he needed to take a second dose after lunch. He wasn't the only one. In fact, her office was a zoo after lunch. He was simply the one who needed the most reminders, often in the form of a phone call to his fifth-period teacher.

"Derek needs to come down and take his meds."

Several minutes later, Derek would wander in. He was a skinny kid with big ears and pale skin and an unwavering stare. He didn't look anything like his father, and yet, every time he came, Jen remembered the way Leif and Nick squared off at Unpack Your Backpack night. She remembered the racist comments Leif made in front of Jubilee, in front of Anaya and Nia's mother. Now Jen wondered if she'd be able to look at Derek without thinking of her own father and that article.

Oakdale Principal Opposes Integration

She and Nick had stayed up past midnight talking about it, dissecting her childhood, trying to find evidence that she had missed. She wasn't sure what was harder to wrap her mind around—the fact that her father held those kinds of beliefs or the fact that she had no idea her father held those kinds of beliefs. That particular skeleton remained safely tucked away in the family closet.

"Excuse me, Mrs. Covington?"

Jen looked up.

Taylor Gray stood in her office doorway—a younger, taller, skinnier version of her mother. Jen and Camille hadn't done more than exchange pleasantries since the N-word incident. Paige wrote an apology. Jubilee accepted it. Nick encouraged her to play with kids like Nia and Sarah.

Derek popped the pill into his mouth and drank it down with the small Dixie cup of water Jen provided.

"Hi," he said to Taylor.

"Hi," she said back, her cheeks blushing under that discomforting, unrelenting stare of his.

"You can head back to class now, Derek," Jen said.

He squished the Dixie cup and slam-dunked it into the garbage can by the door. He stared at Taylor as he walked out. By the time he was gone, the blush in her cheeks had turned bright red.

"Do you and Derek know each other?" Jen asked.

"We've gone to school together for a long time." Taylor shrugged. "He gets teased a lot."

"Yes. I heard about . . . well. I heard about the incident last year in the locker room."

Taylor pressed her lips together disapprovingly.

It was her second time visiting Jen's office in the past two weeks. It also happened to be the second time Taylor visited her office all year.

"Is everything okay?" Jen asked.

"I have a headache."

Jen motioned toward one of her office chairs. Taylor sank into it, and Jen took her temperature, just in case. There wasn't a line of students at her door. Today had been relatively slow, so she had time to be thorough. "Do you get headaches a lot?"

"I don't usually, but I've been getting them lately."

The thermometer beeped. 97.7 degrees.

She gave Taylor a quick eye examination. Her vision was perfect.

Perhaps the sudden onset of headaches had something to do with Shanice Williams, the new track star. Although she didn't think they ran the same events and she saw them sitting together at lunch the other day. So maybe the headaches were wrapped up in her parents' separation—something Jen hadn't learned about until recently, when two teachers were gossiping in the lounge.

"I think they're divorced now," one of them said.

"They're just separated. But I heard he has a girlfriend."

When Jen realized who they were talking about, her jaw had nearly unhinged. She experienced that jolting feeling that came whenever she thought she had a person pegged but then they did something that drove the peg so far out of place she had to start all over again. Like the time her next-door neighbor in Clayton stuck a large Green Party sign in her lawn. Jen always thought her neighbor was Republican, and suddenly there was that sign. Her neighbors were passionately green. That was how it was with Camille.

Jen assumed she had the perfect life. Three well-mannered children. A giant house. An adoring husband. It turned out, her husband didn't adore her. The two were separated.

Perhaps Taylor Gray was feeling the strain.

Forty-Nine

One year. Jubilee Covington had been home with them for exactly one year. It was Gotcha Day, a term Jen and Nick couldn't bring themselves to use.

"It sounds like something a kidnapper would say," he'd said the night before.

"Or a practical jokester," she replied.

She hated practical jokes.

When they were kids, Brandon found old VHS recordings of *Candid Camera* in the storage room. Jen had no idea who was the fan—her mother or her father. Brandon watched every one—fast-forwarding through commercials and laughing hysterically at every prank. Jen sat through one episode, and it almost gave her hives. She didn't think it was funny. She thought it was horrible. In fact, afterward she had a short stint of recurring nightmares wherein she would suffer some sort of public humiliation right before Allen Funt jumped out of the bushes and shouted, "Surprise, you're on *Candid Camera*!"

She would always wake up with a gasp.

Gotcha!

It was a word someone yelled when they weren't laughing with you, but at you.

Jen and Nick agreed to call it Family Day instead. To celebrate, they let Jubilee pick the restaurant. She chose Osaka, because she loved sushi and she loved watching the chef with the tall white hat light onions on fire and fling bits of grilled shrimp at people's mouths.

The first time they went, the chef hit Nick right below the eye. Jubilee laughed hysterically, just like Brandon when he watched *Candid Camera*. Maybe she would have liked the term *Gotcha Day* after all.

A petite Japanese hostess brought them to their table around one of the hibachi grills. Jubilee slid into the booth first, then Nick, then Jen.

Jen set the small gift bag to her right by her purse. It was a Saturday night, which meant they wouldn't have the grill to themselves. The restaurant was crowded, filled with the sound of sizzling food and clinking silverware and lively conversation.

Jen wasn't feeling lively.

Fake it until you make it.

That was the advice espoused in many adoption circles. She just never thought she'd still be doing it at one year home. One year ago today, when Jubilee jumped into her arms, she didn't think she'd have to fake it at all. But somewhere along the line, after the honeymoon period wore off and reality set in and Jubilee started peeing her pants and lying and spitting in her face, the warm, fuzzy emotions went away. Today, Jen should be overwrought with them. She should put together a montage of pictures from their airport homecoming and post it on Facebook with heartfelt words of love and gratitude, like so many of her adoptive Facebook friends did on Gotcha Day.

Look at what the Lord has done!

Instead, all she could manage was the small gift bag.

Nick took her hand and gave it a squeeze, as though he could read her thoughts.

A family joined them. A matching, blond family. Ken and Barbie and two little Kens and a baby Barbie.

Jen didn't miss the way Barbie's attention flicked to Jubilee, who was happily unrolling her silverware, and then to Nick and herself. She was tired of that look—a constant reminder that they were different. A constant reminder of all the things she had to consider as Jubilee's mother.

She really needed to get off Facebook. She needed to stop reading all the articles posted in all the groups that left her with such a profound sense of inadequacy. There was too much to contend with. What were she and Nick thinking, taking on such a task? Trauma and attachment and the loss of so much—Jubilee's first family, Jubilee's culture. Hair care and skincare, because those were important things when it came to Jubilee's self-esteem. And they really should consider adopting another child with brown skin so Jubilee wouldn't be the only one in the family with brown skin and she could finally give her daughter bunk beds. Jubilee still wanted them. But how could Jen adopt again when she was barely handling the first one?

In a selfish grab at motherhood, Jen had torn her away from too much. They should have spent all the money they spent on the adoption working for something noble—like family preservation and reunification. Too many orphans were poverty orphans, a fact she didn't even know until they were ten thousand dollars in and matched with a little girl whose picture had stolen their hearts. And if they would have walked away for the sake of investing their time and money into family preservation, what would have happened to Jubilee? It was too late for her. She still would have grown up in an orphanage.

There were too many voices in Jen's head. Too many reasons for guilt. The latest being her racist father.

She had brought Jubilee into a family that wasn't safe. Not emotionally, anyway. If Jen were a good mother, she would cut him off. He probably wouldn't care—he probably wouldn't even notice—but her mother would. And how could she do that to her when her mother had already lost her eldest—a living ghost they refused to address because her family didn't talk about their problems. They pretended their problems didn't exist. They got upset when their problems were pointed out. How was anything going to change with that kind of mentality?

"From Liberia," Nick said.

He was talking with Barbie and Ken, telling them about Jubilee's big day. *Their* big day.

Barbie seemed very interested.

"What a lucky little girl," she said to Jubilee.

Jen cringed.

Jubilee was not lucky.

The three towheaded Ken and Barbie littles were lucky. Because they wouldn't have to deal with the things Jubilee would have to deal with as she grew from a little black girl to an adult black woman. They wouldn't be called racist names. They wouldn't have to wonder if the reason their grandfather didn't talk to them was because of their skin color. They all matched, and there wasn't any trauma, and they'd never had to sleep in an orphanage that locked them in a dark, hot room at night.

Was Jesus wit me in da orphanage?

He sang it to me in the dark, when the doors went shut.

The waitress came and took their drink orders.

"Can I open da present now?" Jubilee asked after she left.

Jen handed the small gift bag over the table, past Nick.

Jubilee tore the tissue paper away and pulled out the framed photograph inside. She placed it on the table and stared down at it. It was a picture Nick's brother's wife snapped, right as Jubilee jumped up in Jen's arms in the airport. A mother and a daughter, embracing for the first time. A picture that oozed with answered prayers and happy endings.

"We can hang it in your room, if you want," Jen said.

Jubilee nodded, like she would like that.

"That is so beautiful," Barbie said, her eyes dewy.

Jen's were Sahara desert dry.

She didn't understand it. She thought things were looking up. Her heart was a balloon, slowly and optimistically inflating. She felt better about herself now that she was running and cutting back on the candy bars. Jubilee was doing well in school. Last week, Jen actually went into her bedroom after she'd fallen asleep to kiss her forehead. She'd never gotten that urge before.

But sometime between then and now, something had taken a needle to her balloon. Was it discovering the article about her father? Or maybe it was the fight she had with her mom afterward. Or the black lady at the YMCA who kept staring at Jubilee's hair. It was in need of another visit to the salon. She could practically see the woman's thoughts.

Do you know what you're doing with that child?

For a moment, Jen had been filled with a sense of shame.

She thought about the warm, affectionate way Nia and her mother interacted. She thought about the boisterous, animated atmosphere in Trill's salon. A tiny taste of what Jubilee was missing. Then she came home with Jen.

Cold, dead, fake Jen.

The waitress returned with their drinks, and the man in the tall white hat came out to prepare the grill.

Jubilee clapped.

Jen stared.

Wake me up, Lord. Do something—anything—*to wake my heart up.*

Fifty

Rose: Thinking of you today, friend.
Camille: Thanks
Rose: You doing okay?
Camille: Getting a pedicure at the moment. Might spring for a professional massage later.
Rose: Good for you!
Camille: It's definitely not how I imagined I'd be celebrating 22 years of marriage.

•●●●●

To: jones.anaya@crystalridge.k12.mo.us
From: morrison.kael@missouristate.edu
Subject: re: New Talent
Date: Wednesday, April 24

Dear Miss Jones,

Thank you for your email regarding your runner, Shanice Williams. Her times are noteworthy, especially considering the fact that this is her first year participating in the sport. I'm pleased to hear that her work ethic matches her raw talent. I will most definitely be keeping an eye on her throughout the remainder of the season.

We are always looking for exceptional student athletes to add to our student body. I'm sure I'll be in touch.

Sincerely,
Kael Morrison
Track and Field
Missouri State

To: jones.anaya@crystalridge.k12.mo.us
From: coolidge.valerie@umstlouis.edu
Subject: re: New Talent
Date: Thursday, April 25

Dear Miss Jones,

What a pleasure to find your email in my inbox. I have to admit, I followed your collegiate career quite closely and was so disheartened when I learned of your injury. I can't imagine how it must have been for you. I love to see that you're coaching the sport that gave you so much joy.

The times you sent definitely made me sit up and pay attention. The glowing recommendation from someone like you is the cherry on top.

Thanks for attaching your schedule. As fate would have it, I was planning on coming to the Crystal Ridge Invitational next Saturday. I would love to see Shanice in action. Perhaps you could arrange an introduction afterward?

Best,
Val Coolidge
Track and Field
UMSL

Conversation Between Two Parents at the Crystal Ridge Track & Field Invitational:

> Did you see the coach from UMSL?
> Where?
> Right there. Front row, over to the left.
> Who do you think she's here to scout—Taylor or Shanice?
> Probably both. Did you hear what happened to Alexis?
> No.
> She got sick during warm-ups. Threw up all over the track. The coach is having Shanice run her event.
> *What?* I thought Shanice was a sprinter.
> Apparently she's good at the 1600 too.
> I wonder how Camille feels about that.

●●●●●

"Is Taylor gonna be in a bad mood?" Paige asked.

"I don't know," Camille answered.

"She's never lost the 800 before."

"She didn't lose; she got third."

"I never remember her getting third before."

"There's nothing wrong with third."

"In the Olympics, third place earns you a medal," Austin said.

"Not the gold one," Paige replied.

Camille set her fork down and pinched the bridge of her nose as her two youngest argued about the merits of third place. She couldn't stop picturing it. The panicked look on Taylor's face as she finished the 1600. She almost lost to Shanice, a sprinter who didn't run the 1600. She was hoping to beat her personal record. Instead, she came in five seconds slower. Then she bombed the 800. Racing against Shanice must have gotten in Taylor's head. Or maybe it was the coach from UMSL.

Of course, Camille hoped Taylor would choose a more prestigious college. It was too optimistic to hope for Brown. Taylor wasn't the type to follow in her or Neil's footsteps, but she had the grades and the drive to run for an Ivy

League school. Still, Camille burned inside every time she pictured Anaya Jones introducing Shanice to Valerie Coolidge after the meet while her daughter sat off to the side, unlacing her track shoes.

The front door slammed shut.

"Oooo," Paige said. "We aren't supposed to slam doors."

"I'd like the both of you to take your plates to the sink and go downstairs."

Paige let out a groan and banged her head against the table. "Austin is gonna make me play chess downstairs, and I'm gonna die of boredom."

"Right now," Camille said, tossing her napkin on the table and scooting back her chair.

In the foyer, Taylor was kicking off her shoes. They hit the wall with loud *thunk*s and dropped to the floor. She slammed her bag down by the door and stomped up the stairs.

"Taylor."

She kept going.

Stomp, stomp, stomp. Like when she was four and Camille made her clean her room before she could watch *Kim Possible* on Disney.

Camille went after her. "Honey, you have every right to be upset. I would be upset too."

Taylor stopped at the top of the landing and whirled around. "Upset about what?" Her face was red and twisted and sneering and filled with so much contempt, it took Camille back a step.

"Well . . . that Shanice was thrown into your event at the last minute. I understand why it would throw you for a loop."

Taylor was shaking her head. "You have no idea what you're talking about."

"Then tell me."

"I'm not fast anymore!"

"Of course you are."

"No, I'm not. I'm not pacing myself right. I'm doing something wrong, and thanks to *you,* my coach won't help me."

"What?"

"She hates me. She doesn't coach me."

"Well, that's not okay."

"I don't even blame her!"

"Taylor."

"After everything you said at the town meeting? What Paige said in her classroom? The neighbors calling the police on Darius? They never would have called the police on Cody!" Her face was alarmingly red now. Redder than Camille had ever seen. "I hate this entire family! I wish I wasn't a part of it!"

With that, she spun back around, marched into her room, and slammed the door. So loud, Camille was certain Paige would have something to say about it later.

PART III

Newton's Third Law: Every action has an equal and opposite reaction.

Fifty-One

It was Monday morning. Anaya was putting up a new bulletin board, and she felt good. Really, really good. She couldn't stop thinking about Saturday's track meet. The impressed look on Coach Coolidge's face after Shanice ran the anchor for the 400. The way Shanice's mother ran along the fence as her baby came in second place for an event she'd never run before. Three seconds behind a girl who would no doubt get a full-ride track scholarship. Tears had welled in her mother's eyes. Because Shanice's mother knew what a run like that meant.

Opportunity.

Anaya had handed Shanice opportunity. And for one glorious moment, she felt like she was exactly—precisely—where she was meant to be. Maybe she wasn't helping an entire community, but she was helping one person in that community, and it sure felt good.

A throat cleared behind her.

She turned around, and her good feelings took a hit.

Camille Gray stood in the doorway with her purse clutched securely in front of her. She hadn't seemed very pleased at the track meet on Saturday, and she didn't look very pleased now. "I'd like to speak with you, if it's a good time."

One glance at the clock said it was only thirty minutes before the morning bell would ring. So no, it wasn't a good time. This was her planning time. Now that she coached track, she didn't have time to plan after school. She needed every minute in the morning. But Camille Gray, room mother extraordinaire, was a woman unaccustomed to the word *no*.

She took a step inside and lifted her chin. "I'd like to speak with you about my daughter. I'd like to know what you're doing to help her."

"Which one?"

"Taylor. She got third place in the 800. She never gets third."

"She had an off day. It happens to all of us."

The words seemed to act as a trigger. Camille flinched ever so slightly. "I came here to make sure you're giving her the same opportunities you are giving everyone else on the team."

The same opportunities? Was she kidding? Taylor didn't need Anaya to give her opportunity. She had that handed to her on a silver platter. "I'm not sure I'm following."

"You introduced Shanice to a college coach on Saturday, but you didn't introduce Taylor."

"Coach Coolidge already knows Taylor. Taylor got fifth place in the 1600 at state last year as a sophomore. She's on plenty of radars. I'm making sure Shanice is too."

"My daughter was devastated after the meet on Saturday."

"I don't see why. Her time in the 1600 helped us get first place."

"Her time was awful. She's struggling, and is it any wonder? Her coach isn't giving her the time of day."

Anaya could feel the heat rising up her neck. That was hardly the truth. She was raising Shanice up, not pulling Taylor down. Camille simply couldn't handle the fact that a girl from South Fork was being set on an equal playing field with her daughter. "I am giving Taylor all the attention she needs."

"Well, she obviously needs more." A muscle twitched in Camille's jaw. "Look, you don't like me. That's fine. I'm okay with that. Just don't take it out on my children."

"Excuse me?"

"You are Paige's teacher and Taylor's coach. You can go on thinking I'm a horrible, racist person. That's your prerogative. But maybe, just maybe, you don't actually know the first thing about me!"

It was a loud, heated outburst.

A luxury Anaya couldn't afford, lest she be labeled an angry black woman.

And yet here was Camille Gray, pitching a fit in Anaya's classroom because her daughters weren't getting special treatment.

Anaya delivered her rebuttal with ice in every syllable. "And you, ma'am, don't know the first thing about me, either."

●●●●●

To: Undisclosed Recipients
From: graypartyof5@msn.com
Subject: Calling All Volunteers!
Date: Thursday, May 9

Greetings, Parents and Coaches,

We need your hands! Or should I say, we need your students' hands.

As you know, the Crystal Ridge Memorial Day 5K is just around the corner, and this year it's going to be a color run! To cut down on cost, we decided to fill the color ourselves. Which means we're in need of lots and lots of volunteers!

We thought this would be the perfect opportunity for our Crystal Ridge sports teams to give back to the community that supports them so well.

We will begin filling bottles on Monday, May 13. We're not sure how long it will take, but we figure this far in advance should give us plenty of time. The community center kindly offered their upstairs banquet room to get the job done. We will have everything ready to go with bottles to fill every weekday, from 4–8 p.m., and weekends, from 1–5 p.m. Encourage your players to come on down, and please join in the fun yourself. The more people we have helping, the quicker we can fill those bottles!

With Sincere Gratitude,
Camille Gray

Fifty-Two

Anaya walked into the back of the office. There were two doors—one for visitors and parents at the front, and one in the back for staff, right next to the copy machine and the mailboxes. It was nearing the end of the day, her kids were in gym class, and she almost forgot to make copies of the homework sheet they needed to take home with them.

She set the copier for twenty back-to-back copies, fed the paper through the tray, and hit the green Start button. She turned around and pulled the stack of items from her mailbox—a white envelope with her check stub, two Scholastic book-order magazines, and twenty bright-purple flyers paper-clipped together.

The Crystal Ridge Memorial Day 5K is getting technicolored! Don't let your child miss out on this fun event. Sign them up for the one-mile kids' run. Registration is online, and the early sign-up rate ends soon!

The flyer reminded her of Camille's email early this morning. That woman had a lot of nerve.

"Well, what did she expect?" Jan said.

Anaya looked over her shoulder.

Jan McCormick was talking with the resource teacher—a frizzy-haired woman who had an affinity for gypsy skirts.

"It's not like you were making up random rules to pick on her son. You were following a long-standing district policy."

"It isn't a policy she was very happy with."

Jan sighed loudly. "That's how it is with these South Fork mothers. Every time one comes into the office, I can expect an earful."

The copier beeped.

The printing job was complete.

Anaya stood there, unexpectedly gut punched.

She straightened her spine, grabbed her photocopies and the stack from her mailbox, and slipped out of the office, away from Jan and the resource teacher. But the conversation followed her. She kept trying to rub the hurt away, but the muscles in her neck and shoulders tightened.

Every time a South Fork mother . . .

In other words, every time a *black* mother.

It stung.

Anaya wasn't sure why. It wasn't like she hadn't heard the stereotype before, unfair as it was.

But even if it were true—even if there was a hint of truth to it—maybe there was a reason. Maybe it had something to do with the fact that for centuries, black women had been silenced. They were told where to go, what they could do. Years upon years, they learned that if they wanted their voices to be heard, then they'd better yell.

And how was direct confrontation any worse than the passive aggressiveness running rampant among Crystal Ridge mothers? Smiling to your face, tearing you down behind your back? A knife was still a knife, even when it was dipped in sugar.

She gritted her teeth and marched down the hallway, replaying Camille's outburst in her classroom. Just last week. What a luxury to have. She could rage all she wanted and somehow she would always be a good mother fighting for her child. The Jan McCormicks of the world would sit up and listen, because if Camille Gray was upset, then that policy must be very bad. A black woman did the same thing and she was dismissed as one of "those." She was either not there or too there, and the injustice of it all rankled.

Rub it out, Anaya. Just rub it out.

The phone in her classroom was ringing.

She wouldn't have time to check voice mails after school, so she hurried inside, plopped the papers on her desk, took a deep breath, and picked up the receiver.

"Hello, Miss Jones speaking," she said, her voice calm and measured. Nobody listening would know anything was wrong.

"Hi . . . *Anaya?*"

"Yes."

"This is Ellie Sorrenson. I got your extension from the staff directory."

"Ellie Sorrenson?" Anaya didn't have a Sorrenson in her class, and the voice was unfamiliar.

"Mr. Davis's student teacher. We met at the district-wide meeting back in January. I was hoping we could talk."

⁕⁕⁕

The temperature stretched into the upper eighties—unseasonably hot and humid for May. Anaya felt like a teakettle set on a burner, the pressure slowly building as a group of boys sat in the bleachers, loud and obnoxious while her girls practiced on the track.

Her thoughts were scattered. Her arms didn't feel connected to her body as she held a stopwatch in one hand, a clipboard in the other, trying to focus on Taylor as she came around the bend. Taylor was struggling. One look at the stopwatch made that pretty obvious. Anaya watched as Taylor slowed, slowed, slowed like a gasoline-starved car petering to a stop. Two-hundred yards from the finish line, she did.

"Gray!" Anaya called, walking toward her. "What are you doing?"

Taylor walked the rest of the way on wobbly legs—her face red from exertion. When she reached Anaya, she bent over her knees and sucked at the thick air.

"Are you taking care of yourself?" Anaya asked. "Drinking enough water?"

"I've been drinking tons of water."

"Are you eating?"

"All the time." Taylor shook her head and wiped at the beads of sweat on her brow.

"Why don't you go grab a water bottle and have a seat."

Anaya watched her go. Was she coming down with something? Zeke and Madison were both out sick today. The nurse said the stomach bug was making its rounds. Was Taylor going to get sick all over the track like Alexis did before the invitational?

A loud, sharp wolf whistle sounded from the bleachers.

It was a sound that had Anaya feeling like a dog with hackles raised.

"You're looking hot out there, Gray!"

The boys guffawed.

Taylor didn't pay them any attention. She grabbed a water bottle and sat on the long metal bench where the football players sat during the home games in the fall.

"Hey look, Malone. She's in your spot!"

The boys guffawed again.

Anaya pressed her lips together and turned her attention to her 400 relay team. They were practicing their handoffs. But the boys' voices carried, as if they purposefully wanted Taylor to hear. The problem was, Anaya could hear too, and the things they were saying turned the burner to high heat.

"Ouch, C. She won't even look at you."

"Whatever, man. My interests have shifted."

"Oh yeah. To who?"

After a small beat, the boys all laughed.

"Shanice?" one of them said. "Are you serious?"

The pressure in Anaya's chest began to bubble.

"I guess now that Taylor's trying chocolate, Cody wants to get a taste too."

Anaya whirled around.

A blond kid with longish hair and preppy white tennis clothes sat in the center of the group. Anaya knew his name was Cody Malone. Darius had taken his spot on the football team. He was rubbing his chin and smirking. "Do you think she's as fast off the track as she is on?"

"What did you just say?" Anaya yelled.

The boys covered their laughter and their smarmy smiles behind fisted hands.

And the bubbling pressure turned into a boiling steam that rushed past her lips. "You better shut your mouth if you know what's good for you!"

Cody stared back at her with a face full of insolence. "Was that a threat?"

She threw down her clipboard. She threw down her stopwatch. Steam screamed from her ears as she marched up the bleachers and got in Cody's face. "You better believe that's a threat! I won't tolerate that kinda talk, not at my track. Not about my girls. So unless you want me to go find your coach and your mama right now and tell them exactly what you been saying, then you best stand up and get out."

The boys had turned into statues—gaping-mouthed, wide-eyed statues.

"I said, get out!"

They scrambled away as the words echoed across the stadium.

Anaya's chest heaved, her lungs inhaling and exhaling the hot, humid air as everyone—all the runners, all the coaches, all the high jumpers and the shot putters—stopped what they were doing and stared.

Fifty-Three

Two teenage boys wrestled on the lawn. One raised his hand to wave at Darius. The other grabbed both the kid's legs and took him down. They started rolling around in the grass. As Anaya and Marcus and Darius and Shanice walked past, the kid on the bottom grunted, "I'm letting him win."

"Yeah, okay," Shanice said.

Marcus opened the front door of the community center.

Noise filtered down the stairs.

All four of them were on edge after the latest news about the South Fork School District. Mama was at home making phone calls. And Anaya was here.

One hour.

She could handle one hour. She would do her duty, and tomorrow, when someone inevitably came up to her with color-stained hands asking if she'd been to the community center to help yet, she could hold up her own hands and say yes, she had.

If only Camille Gray wasn't standing outside the banquet room, her attention flitting from Anaya to Darius as they came to the top of the stairs. The last time the three of them were together, Darius had his hands up in the air in Camille's yard. Anaya wondered if Camille was thinking about that moment too. Or maybe the pink tinge in her cheeks had everything to do with their last encounter in Anaya's classroom.

Whatever she was thinking about, she fixed a smile on her face and stuck out her hand to Shanice. "We haven't officially met yet. I'm Taylor's mom."

"Nice to meet you, Mrs. Gray."

"Oh, please call me Camille. Mrs. Gray sounds too much like my mother." She turned her fixed smile on Marcus. "And you are?"

"Anaya's boyfriend, Marcus."

"You brought your boyfriend. How wonderful. We certainly need all hands on deck. It's a much bigger undertaking than we anticipated. But there's no going back now, is there? All we can do is learn our lesson and hope and pray that we actually get these bottles filled in time. Something tells me a color run wouldn't be very fun without color." She handed each of them a pair of see-through plastic gloves. "You'll want to wear these if you don't want your palms stained for the next three days. It's surprisingly hard to get off skin, and yet somehow it washes out of clothes without any problem."

"Hey, Camille?" A tiny woman with a baby strapped to her chest interrupted Camille's overly cheerful welcome. "Do you know where that box of extra funnels went?"

"It's not in the concession room?"

"If it is, it's hiding very well."

With a look of relief, Camille thanked Anaya, Darius, Marcus, and Shanice again for coming and bustled inside like a woman on a mission.

Marcus gave Anaya a nudge and leaned close to her ear. "I didn't see any horns."

"That's because they're retractable."

He chuckled.

The four of them walked inside, Shanice and Darius in front.

Her brother didn't like taking the South Fork bus home from school. He said it took too long. More often than not, he hung around during track practice, and since Anaya gave Shanice a ride home afterward, it gave the two high schoolers plenty of travel time to get to know each other. They loved to argue about deep and meaningful things, like who was the best basketball player of all time—LeBron or Jordan—and their weapon of choice in case of a zombie apocalypse. That one might have been a conversation instigated by Anaya, and although she didn't think either of them would stand a chance against zombies, she did think they would make a cute couple. She suspected Shanice would agree. If only Darius would open his eyes and see the amazing girl right in front of him.

Instead, he was scanning the tables, searching the crowd.

For someone in particular, no doubt.

He found her in the back of the room, waving them both over.

"I guess now that Taylor's trying chocolate, Cody wants to get a taste too."

The week-old words still burned her up inside. So did the humiliating memory that came afterward, when she screamed at Cody and his posse to get out. They were the jerks, but everyone was gaping at her. She could see it happening, right there in all those open-mouthed stares. She had become an entertaining story they would tell later. Ripple after ripple, confirmation after confirmation. Of a stereotype she worked hard to disprove. All of it left her with a growing pit in her stomach.

After that practice, she had asked Taylor how she was feeling. Anaya was surprised when she said, "Better after you put Cody in his place."

She'd experienced a surge of affinity for the girl.

Anaya didn't have a problem with Taylor. But that didn't mean she wanted her brother to *be* with Taylor.

Darius slapped fives with some guys from his football team—big, burly linebackers who seemed genuinely happy to see him. There were girls on the track team too. They welcomed Shanice with smiles that didn't seem fixed or forced. And yet there was a brittleness in Anaya's heart as she watched them. A predisposition of distrust. She didn't want it to be there. These kids weren't villains. Sure, they were rich and white and most likely oblivious, but they didn't have horns—retractable or otherwise. She tried to force her muscles to relax, unwind. But then she spotted Cody.

He was sitting at a table right beside the one Darius had joined, and he was looking at Shanice in a lingering way that made Anaya's skin crawl. Just like that, the pit in her stomach opened back up, filling with sick. Sloshing, slurping sick.

"Do you think she's as fast off the track as she is on?"

She wanted to go over and stand between them. She wanted to take Shanice away to a place where boys like Cody didn't exist. Instead, she followed Marcus to a table and put on a pair of gloves and began doing her part for a race that would benefit a community that already had plenty of benefits, while Cody's words repeated on a loop in her mind. They repeated and repeated until she could no longer pour the color neatly into the funnel.

It spilled everywhere.

Marcus stopped his small talk with the gentleman across the table and gave her a concerned look.

She turned away in search of something to clean it with and nearly bumped into someone. "Excuse me, I wasn't . . ."

Kyle Davis stood in front of her, his face brightening. "Anaya! Hey. It's good to see you again." He glanced from her to Marcus. "And you're . . . Marcus, right?"

"Yeah, man. Sorry. I don't remember meeting."

"We haven't officially. But Anaya used to talk about you all the time, so I made a guess. I'm Kyle Davis." He shook Marcus's hand. "Anaya was my student teacher last year. Anaya, this is my girlfriend, Jenna."

Jenna was a blonde with blue eyes and a spray of freckles across her nose. She said hello with a voice both high and soft.

"Jenna's going to run with me this year."

"It's my first race ever," she said. "I never run."

"Did you sign up?" Kyle asked Anaya. "Or are you still recovering from that injury? I'm assuming your girls are all going to run. That Shanice will probably win the whole thing. Talk about a star."

Anaya didn't get a chance to respond.

She didn't even get a chance to breathe.

There was an explosion of noise and commotion behind them.

Girls shrieked and jumped out of the way.

Two boys were fighting, throwing punches and shoving each other. They upended a table. Smashed another against a wall. Bottles and funnels and colored cornstarch powder flew everywhere.

A baby started wailing.

Troy Brewin, the football coach, jumped on top of the two fighting boys and pried them apart. He held them by the scruff of their necks like two naughty pups, their chests heaving.

One was Darius.

The other was Cody Malone, and his nose was gushing blood.

A woman screamed.

She screamed as she ran over to Cody and grabbed his face. He jerked away, blood squirting everywhere. On him. On the floor. On the frantic woman trying to see where the blood was coming from. There was so much it looked like a scene from a horror film.

"Calm down," Troy said. "Nobody's dead."

"His nose is broken!" the woman shouted.

Someone handed Cody a wadded-up towel.

Cody pressed it against his face, but the blood kept coming—ten times worse than any of Gavin Royce's nosebleeds.

"You should take him to the hospital," someone said.

The woman—Cody's mother—snapped her fingers at two boys, younger versions of Cody. She took Cody's elbow and pulled him toward the door while he held the bloodied towel against the injury and the two boys followed like shell-shocked soldiers, staring with wide eyes at all the blood, their mother's face a mask of panic and fury.

It was the fury that made Anaya's heart turn cold.

The fury, and the words she called out in a shrill voice as she left. "You'd better believe we'll be pressing charges."

Fifty-Four

Marcus handed Darius a bag of frozen peas. He stood in the middle of the tiny kitchen and pressed it against his swollen eye. Mama was going to flip out when she saw it. Which was why they came here, to Marcus's apartment. Maybe if they stayed long enough, Mama would go to sleep and they could avoid her until the morning. And maybe, if they prayed hard enough, Darius's injury would miraculously heal. Or maybe, if Anaya closed her eyes, she would wake up in bed and all of this would be a horrible nightmare.

She and Marcus kept exchanging long, worried looks.

Darius threw the first punch. His football buddies were backing him up, saying Cody started it. But too many people in that room witnessed otherwise, and Anaya's heart would not stop racing. It fluttered like the wings of a hummingbird. Her brother started a fight and broke Cody's nose, and Cody's mother wanted to press charges.

That wasn't something they could hide from Mama.

"I don't understand what you were thinking, Dare," Anaya said. "Why did you do it?"

Her brother remained tight lipped.

Anaya looked at Marcus for help, but he didn't have any better luck. Darius refused to talk about the fight. He refused to tell either of them why he threw that first punch.

"You cannot afford to get into fights. A jerk like Cody Malone is not worth your future. Do you understand me?"

There was anger in his eyes when he looked at her. So much anger. But sadness and fear too. Because he wasn't stupid. He heard Cody's mother. He knew this wasn't good. He knew the law would take one look at him—a six-foot-two black male with a record—and draw its unfair conclusion. For a kid like Darius, the law would never be on his side.

"You have to be better than that. You have to be better than Cody." She sounded like her mother the morning after the town meeting.

"They feel like we're a threat, Anaya," Mama had said. "All we can do is show them we're not."

"We shouldn't have to show anyone anything. Did you hear that woman? *'No one ever asked us about the bussing,'*" Anaya mocked. "No one ever asked us what it's like to watch our schools fail. To have fewer resources than the families up the road. No one knows, because no one asks. They don't want our side. Why should we show them anything?"

"I know, baby. But it's the way it is. We have to be twice as good."

Twice as good.

It wasn't the first time Mama had said it. It wasn't the first time Anaya hated the sound of it. Just like she hated the sound of her own words now.

She expected Darius to walk away, dark and moody. Instead, he grabbed her arm and pulled her into a hug—so unexpected, so out of the blue, it took a second to respond. It was such an odd feeling, being completely engulfed by a little brother whose diapers you once changed. Anaya leaned her head against his broad chest—one that felt so much like their father's—and hugged him back with all the fierceness of her love.

●●●●●

Kathleen to Camille: He broke my son's nose. Bennett and Dane are a wreck. Rick's on his way. Cody said Darius started it. The doctor has to reset his bone. This is UNACCEPTABLE.

Fifteen Minutes Later

Rebecca just called me. That boy has a record. Unlawful use of a firearm.

●●●●●

It took two hours to calm everyone down and clean up the mess—all that color, all that blood. Horrendous for Camille—who had never in her life witnessed such a thing until tonight. Overly stimulating for Paige, who bounced around like a Ping-Pong ball afterward, trying to get the most accurate version of the events while Camille called Tamika and apologized profusely, but would she be able to come get Edison?

Now, Paige slept like a rock in the backseat while Austin stared out his window, oncoming headlights scrolling across his unreadable expression. Camille white-knuckled the steering wheel and shot glances at Taylor, who sat in the passenger seat, typing furiously into her phone.

"Who are you texting?" she finally asked, her voice stiff.

"Darius."

"That's rich, Taylor."

"*What?* He's my friend."

"He assaulted Cody!"

Taylor's nostrils flared, but she kept on texting.

Camille pulled over to the side of the road. "Give me your phone."

"What?"

She held out her hand. "Give me your phone."

"Why?"

"*Now, Taylor.*"

Taylor handed it over.

Camille scrolled through her text messages, reminded of the time she scrolled through Neil's. There were way too many between her and Darius. With a few deft movements, she deleted them all, and removed his contact from Taylor's phone.

Taylor shrieked. "What are you doing?"

"I don't want you hanging out with that boy anymore."

"Are you kidding me?"

"He just got into a fight."

"So did Cody!"

But Cody didn't break anybody's nose!

And Cody didn't have a record. Unlawful use of a firearm? What did that even mean?

Camille took a deep breath and swallowed her emotions. The more anger she showed, the deeper Taylor's heels would dig in. "Cody didn't start that fight."

"Yes, he did."

"So your brother's lying?" Austin had seen it. According to him, Darius threw the first punch.

Taylor gritted her teeth and looked away.

"I have known Cody since he was six years old. He's a good kid, and right now he's in the ER with a broken nose. A broken nose, Taylor. All I know about Darius is what I saw tonight, and tonight he showed serious signs of aggression and violence. Aggression and violence that your two younger siblings witnessed. I'm not comfortable with that."

"He's not violent! He was defending his sister." Taylor crossed her arms. She looked up at the roof of the Highlander and huffed so loudly, it was almost laughable. But there were tears too. Gathering in her eyes. Angry, upset tears. "Do you want to know why Darius threw that first punch? Do you want to know what that 'good kid'—the one you've known since he was six—said about Darius's sister?" Taylor told Camille exactly what Cody called Anaya. It was a word that made Camille wince, especially coming out of her daughter's mouth. "Oh, and he added *black* before it. But I guess that doesn't matter to you, does it, Mom? I guess you'd rather me date a stand-up guy like Cody."

● ● ● ● ●

Channel 6 News online:

> It's out with the old and in with the new as the Missouri School Board announced today that it will dissolve the South Fork School District and replace it with the South Fork Cooperative. What does this mean for their accreditation and the transfer law? That's exactly what concerned parents would like to know.
>
> Dion Johnson, a South Fork Parent, is rightfully concerned. "It isn't fair. My kids are doing well at their new school. My oldest made honor roll. Now the state is telling me they have to come back here in the fall just because this district has a new name? I want to know what's going on. If I got to fight for my children, then I want to know right now."
>
> It looks like tension is running high on all fronts.
>
> Several Crystal Ridge parents are concerned that the pandemonium at the Crystal Ridge Community Center, where volunteering turned violent, is related to the tensions this transfer law has caused.

Fifty-Five

Leah to Jen: Is it weird if I send your dad flowers? He doesn't seem like the flower type, but I want to send something, and I can't send food. I'm so sorry, Jen. Diabetes is the worst.

● ● ● ●

Her mother's silent treatment had dragged on for a month. Granted, Jen hadn't reached out to her either, but this was ridiculous. Her father went to the hospital—he had to start dialysis—and she only knew because of a text from Leah.

She picked up her phone and dialed her mom.

"This is Carol," her mother answered in a cold, aloof voice.

Jen wanted to scream.

Unless she deleted Jen's contact from her phone—which, she supposed, wasn't completely out of the question—her mother knew it was her.

"Hey, Mom," she said, a blandness in her tone that seemed to accentuate the prickly feeling in her chest.

"Oh, Jen. Hello."

Jen inhaled through her nostrils. "How's Dad?"

"He's fine."

"*Mom.*"

"What?"

"I heard from Leah that he had to start dialysis."

"Yes, he did."

"And you didn't think I'd want to know that?"

"I honestly have no idea what you want to know anymore."

"How's he doing?"

"Horrible. He's on dialysis. He's exhausted all the time."

"Is there anything I can do?"

"I don't see what, with y'all living up there." She said y'all. The offer to help was unthawing her icy tone. "How is Jubilee?"

"She's fine."

"Thanks for elaborating."

"What do you want to know?"

"How's school? How was her Gotcha Day? I hope it was okay that I sent a gift in the mail."

"Of course it was okay."

"I do love her, Jennifer."

"I know you do."

"And your father, I know he's not the best at, well . . . You can think what you want about him, Jennifer, but no parent wishes extra hardship on their child. He didn't want you to struggle in life more than you needed to. He doesn't want that for anyone."

And that, right there, was as close to talking about their fight and the news article and Jubilee as they were going to get.

●●●●●

"Mrs. Covington?"

Jen looked up from her lunch. She was eating in her office today, trying to organize her notes. She'd had a whirlwind of students—one after the other. She handed out medicine so quickly, she barely had enough time to write down who took what.

Taylor Gray stood in her doorway; she didn't look well. "I'm sorry for interrupting your lunch."

Jen set her fork down. "Don't worry about it."

Taylor's chin gave a small quiver. "My head hurts again."

"Come on in. Let me get you some Tylenol."

Taylor sat in one of the chairs and put her face in her hand. "I feel like everything is blurry."

Jen frowned. Was Taylor having a migraine? Sometimes migraines caused vision changes. Was that what was going on? This was the fourth time Taylor had visited her office in a month. Each time, she complained of a headache. According to teachers in the lounge, she was lethargic in class.

Anxiety caused headaches. Anxiety caused sleepless nights, which impacted school work. Anxiety caused a lot of things, and Taylor had plenty of cause for anxiety. Her parents were separated. She wasn't doing as well in track this year . . .

She wasn't doing as well in track this year.

Jen thought of her father, on dialysis.

"Taylor, have you been urinating a lot?"

The question seemed to take Taylor aback, but she was in too much pain for embarrassment. "What's a lot?"

"Do you have to use the restroom between classes?"

"Yes."

"All of them?"

Taylor nodded.

"Do you have to get up in the middle of the night?"

"Yeah. Sometimes twice."

Frequent urination. Lethargy. Headaches. It definitely painted a particular picture. "Taylor, I think I'd like to do another vision test."

•°•.°•

"Kathleen is so upset," Rose said.

Camille wiped down the counter, her phone pressed against her ear, trying hard not to feel snubbed by the fact that Kathleen had called Rose but not her.

"She wants to press charges, but Rick doesn't. I guess they got into a big fight about it last night."

Camille wanted to tell Rose what Taylor told her last night—about the thing Cody said to Darius. It was an awful thing to say. It didn't seem like Cody at all. At least, not the polite, handsome version she knew. But then, the bullying incident in the locker room last year with Derek Royce didn't fit her version of Cody either. Cody always claimed that Derek started it. That Derek was being gross and inappropriate. That wasn't a stretch. It was easy to believe Cody's side of the story. But what if Cody's side of the story wasn't true?

"Oh, and get this. Kathleen found out this morning that one of the teachers at Lewis and Clark is under investigation."

"*What?*"

"Jill told her about it this morning."

"Who is it?"

"She couldn't say."

"Who couldn't say—Kathleen or Jill?"

"Jill."

A call beeped on the other line. Camille pulled the phone away from her ear and frowned. It was the high school. She told Rose she'd call her back and clicked over. "This is Camille."

"Hi Camille, this is Jen Covington."

It was weird, hearing her voice after all this time. Especially weird hearing Jen use her first and last name, like Camille might have forgotten who she was.

"I have Taylor here in the office with me."

"Is everything okay?"

"Well, she's come to my office a few times over the past month or so . . ."

Camille straightened. A few times over the past month? And Camille was only hearing about it now?

"She's been complaining of headaches. I just did a vision test on her and her eyesight is blurry."

"So she needs glasses?"

"Possibly. I'd like to check her blood sugar."

"Her blood sugar?"

"It's a very easy test. I have a glucose meter here with me. It requires a little prick on her finger, and the results will show up in a few seconds."

"I don't understand. Why do you want to check her blood sugar?" And why was Jen using such a calm, professional-sounding voice?

"Well, she's been using the restroom more than usual, and she says she's very thirsty."

"She's a runner."

"Right. It could very well be nothing more than eyeglasses. But I'd like to rule out high blood sugar first."

High blood sugar.

The only thing Camille knew related to high blood sugar was diabetes.

"Is that okay with you?" Jen asked.

"Can you keep me on the phone?"

"Of course."

Camille shut her eyes and told herself that Taylor just needed glasses. The last time Camille took Taylor to the eye doctor had been in June. Almost eleven months. Eyes could change a lot in eleven months, and a person got headaches when they needed glasses. Neil had LASIK almost ten years ago, but before that his eyes were so bad he wore coke-bottle glasses to bed. It was very feasible that Taylor would take after him. In fact, it seemed reasonable that at least one of their children would have bad eyes.

Please, Lord, let it be glasses.

"Camille?"

Her eyelids fluttered open.

"Taylor's blood sugar is high."

Camille gripped the phone. "What does that mean?"

"I would like you to come pick her up now. She needs to see a doctor as soon as possible."

Fifty-Six

Taylor lay in a hospital bed with an IV stuck in her arm in a curtained-off triage room that only gave the illusion of privacy. Camille stepped away briefly. She paced in the hallway, trying to get ahold of Neil. The phone rang in her ear as she bit her thumbnail to a nub.

She was shuffled to voice mail again.

This time, she waited for the beep and left a heated message.

"Where are you? Why aren't you answering your phone? I'm at the hospital with our daughter. Her blood sugar is really high, and they're running all these tests. I need you to answer, Neil. I need you to get over here. I . . . I need you, okay?"

Camille hung up and squeezed the phone in her hand.

A slow-moving earthquake rippled through her body. It started in her extremities and radiated inward until everything was quivering.

Her phone buzzed.

She quickly answered, pressing it to her ear.

"Hey," Neil said, his voice breathless, like he'd just run up a flight of stairs. Maybe she interrupted an evening CrossFit class. "I didn't have my phone on me. I just got out of a meeting and saw all your missed calls. Is everything okay?"

"I'm in the ER with Taylor."

"What?"

Camille re-explained her previous message. "The school nurse called around lunchtime. She said Taylor's vision was blurry, so she tested her blood sugar. It was really high, so I called Dr. Porter's office, and he said to bring her straight here, to the hospital. There's an endocrinologist with her right now." Her voice broke.

A flood of emotion rushed past the breach in a pathetic squeak. Camille cupped her mouth with her hand, as if this might keep everything—all the spiraling panic—inside.

"I'm on my way right now." Keys jangled in the background. "Everything's going to be okay, all right? I'll get someone to pick up Paige and Austin after school, and I'll be right there."

Paige and Austin.

She had completely forgotten about Paige and Austin.

Camille turned in a circle in search of a clock. She had no idea what time it was. No idea if school was already dismissed for the day.

"I'll call Deb," Neil said. "She can get Paige, and Kathleen—"

"No, not Kathleen." Kathleen was too preoccupied with Cody, and honestly, if Cody really said what Taylor said he said, Camille didn't want Austin around him.

"You don't worry about Paige and Austin. I'll get it taken care of, all right? You focus on Taylor, and I'll be there."

"I'm really scared."

"I know. I'm on my way."

She hung up, and another squeak came. She tried to swallow it. She needed to get herself together. She needed to walk back into that curtained-off room and be strong for her daughter.

The endocrinologist stepped out into the hallway.

Camille grabbed his arm.

He wore a light-blue oxford button-down beneath a white lab coat. His hair was sparse and silver, and he had a closely shaved, matching mustache. He looked kind and calm, a man accustomed to having answers.

"I'm Camille Gray, Taylor's mother. Can you please tell me what's going on? Why is her blood sugar so high?"

"Your daughter has diabetes." He delivered the words so matter-of-factly. He didn't hem or haw or provide any sort of qualifier. No "I think" or "it looks like" or "might." He just said it as if stating a simple fact. The sun rises in the east. The grass is green. It rains a lot in Seattle. And your daughter has diabetes.

"Are . . . are you sure? I mean, couldn't it be a fluke? I made pancakes this morning for breakfast. Taylor practically uses half a bottle of syrup any time I make pancakes. Maybe if we wait a little bit and test her again, it will come back normal."

Compassion crinkled the corners of his eyes. "One of the nurses ran a test as soon as Taylor was admitted, Mrs. Gray. It gives us information on her average blood glucose levels over the past three months. The results are textbook diabetes. Honestly, I'm surprised she's been able to function as normally as she has been for so long.

"I know this is a lot to take in. The good news is, she's in excellent hands here. We're getting her the insulin she needs to get her glucose levels down. She'll start to feel better soon, and we'll get her admitted into a more comfortable room. Just sit tight and we'll get you more answers shortly."

•◦•◦•

Today had been a strange day. Jen couldn't get the image of a frantic Camille picking up a frightened Taylor out of her head. All afternoon she couldn't stop thinking about their life and what a giant curveball they'd been thrown. As she helped students with menstrual cramps and toothaches and asthma and gym injuries, an odd, foreign feeling grew inside of her. She couldn't pin it down at first, until suddenly she could.

She was antsy.

Jen was antsy for the work day to end so she could see Jubilee.

Now the two of them sat in the living room, waiting for Nick to come home, watching raindrops race down the picture window. Rain was in the forecast all week long. The Gray family would be at the hospital. Taylor's blood sugar had been alarmingly high. For a long time, Jen assumed Camille's life was perfect. She assumed she didn't know the first thing about hardship. But then she learned of Camille's separation. And now there was this.

Proof that everyone had struggles. Significant struggles.

Somehow the realization made her own feel less . . . isolating. Less . . . daunting.

The rain fell harder outside.

Jubilee stared out at the wet gloom, her arm resting over the back of the couch, her lips pressed against the crook of her elbow.

"Do you like watching the rain?" Jen asked.

Jubilee nodded. "I like when da clouds go boom."

"You do?"

"And da whole sky lights up."

Most kids didn't like thunderstorms. Jubilee did. Tonight there was no thunder or lightning. Tonight there was just a good, hard rain.

"Wanna go run in it?"

Jubilee slowly lifted her chin off her arm and turned to look at Jen with big, wide eyes, like she couldn't believe what she just heard.

Jen couldn't really believe it either. She wasn't the type to play in the rain. And Jubilee's hair would certainly be fuzzy when they were done, but she widened her eyes right back, her mouth tipping into a grin.

And just like that, the two of them dashed outside, the rain soaking their clothes. Jubilee held out her arms and scrunched up her shoulders and looked up at Jen with squinty eyes and an ecstatic, wonder-filled smile as the rain turned into a downpour. With matching squeals, mother and daughter ran to the driveway and splashed in the puddles while the cat with the luminous eyes watched them suspiciously from beneath the boxwoods across the street. They splashed like Brandon and Jen splashed in the mud all those years ago, before her dad got angry and told them "never again."

That's how Nick found them.

He didn't ask what they were doing. He didn't yell that they were going to catch a cold. He got out of the car and joined them, because Nick was nothing like Jen's father. He ran up behind Jubilee, and he stomped in the large puddle by the curb, and she shrieked so loud the cat across the street darted away.

Jen stopped and watched them below the glow of the streetlight overhead as drops of rain sprayed all around. It was a moment worth capturing. The kind people would upload to social media. The kind that would have her Facebook friends clicking Like, because here was a family that made them feel happy. What had the elderly lady at church called them the other day?

Inspiring.

At the time, Jen wanted to laugh.

She hadn't seen them before church, or the way Jen reacted when she realized Jubilee had stolen her makeup and ruined it all on Baby and stuffed the mess in the bottom drawer of her dresser, where it got on all her clothes.

People didn't see those moments.

To the watching world, the Covington family represented something. And a photograph of them now—in this particular wild and free moment—would encapsulate everything they represented. But it wouldn't say anything about their struggles. The things Jubilee had stolen. The things that had been stolen from Jubilee. Jubilee's big emotions, and Jen's big emotions. The tears and the battles and the fits. All of them very, very real. As wrong as her dad was about so many things, he was right about this one—the hardship.

Which was why Jen wouldn't take a picture now.

Because this was real too, and she didn't want to give the memory away. She didn't want to share it. This fleeting, perfect moment that was bound to pass, just like the rain.

But the memory?

That would remain.

That would be theirs—just theirs—forever.

●°●°●

To Camille:

> Deb: I sent an email to the ladies in my Tuesday morning Bible study. They're all praying. You know I'm happy to keep Austin and Paige for as long as you need. I'll take good care of them. Jeremiah 29:11, Camille. He's got you and Taylor.
>
> Rebecca: Patrick's cousin has a son who was diagnosed with diabetes three years ago. She knows a lot. Let me know if you want her number.
>
> Rose: Don't even think of worrying about the color run stuff. We have everything under control. And stay away from WebMD.
>
> Tamika Harris: Edison told me that Austin's older sister is in the hospital. Let me know if there's anything we can do.
>
> Mom: Your father just got Neil's message. Please call us.

Fifty-Seven

Sometime around six in the morning, Taylor's primary care nurse changed to a big-boned black woman named Liz. She had the magic touch, like Midas, only instead of turning Camille's arm to gold whenever she squeezed it, she kept the fuzzy, disorienting abyss at bay. It would slowly creep closer, like wispy tentacles ready to grab on, but then Liz would touch Camille's elbow or her wrist and the abyss would slink away.

Neil had to remind Camille to eat.

Camille was more focused on getting answers.

But now that they were finally getting them, everything felt like a million-piece jigsaw puzzle in a box, impossible to put together.

They hadn't seen the endocrinologist since Taylor was moved to her own room. One without curtains for doors. But a pharmacist had come. And a social worker too. The pharmacist talked about things like carb counting and fast-acting insulin and long-acting insulin and when to inject which. Lantus would regulate her blood sugar when she wasn't eating and Humalog would regulate her blood sugar when she was, and the Lantus might sting because it was acidic. The social worker talked about insurance coverage and glucose meters and how there was a Child Life specialist on hand in case Taylor's younger siblings needed someone to help them cope.

Now Camille sat with a heavy binder filled with information in her lap while Liz explained the signs of hypoglycemia and hyperglycemia and what to do in case of an emergency.

"I know this is very overwhelming," she said. "I want to keep things simple for now. You'll have so many more questions for the diabetes educator on Monday. Until then, here's an on-call number for you."

"Why do we need this?" Camille asked.

"In case of an emergency."

"But won't we be *here*?"

"Taylor will most likely check out this afternoon, Mrs. Gray."

Camille blinked. She couldn't seem to make sense of Liz's words.

"Isn't that a little soon?" Neil asked.

"She'll heal much faster at home, where she won't be poked and prodded by strangers at all hours of the night." Liz gave Taylor's arm the same comforting squeeze she'd given Camille.

Camille wondered if it grounded her daughter as much as it grounded her.

Liz unzipped the black kit she brought in with her and laid it open on Taylor's bed. She started talking about the things inside. The meter and testing strips. Quality control solution. Alcohol swabs. A lancet device. Liz walked Taylor through this foreign thing that needed to become a part of her daily routine. Washing her hands with warm water. Loading the lancet and setting it to a three, because Taylor's skin wasn't overly thick or thin. Marking the test strips with an "open" date because they didn't work after four months. How to put the strip into the monitor. How to clean her fingertip with the alcohol swab, making sure to massage it so the prick would produce enough blood. She showed Taylor where to place it on her finger, and then Taylor pressed the button.

The swift, sharp sound made Camille flinch.

She watched the blood bead up on Taylor's fingertip.

"You want to wipe the first drop away, so the alcohol doesn't mess with the reading. Then squeeze some more out, just like that. Now you can put it up to the test strip. See how it sucks it right up?"

They waited a few seconds, and the meter flashed.

One hundred seventy-nine.

When they arrived yesterday, it had been in the six hundreds.

"There you go. You just checked your own blood sugar. This kit is yours. You'll get another one to keep at school. You'll want to test your blood sugar before every meal and two hours after, anytime you're feeling off, and of course, upon waking."

Liz's words grew muffled.

Camille was sinking.

Down, down, down into the deep, fuzzy abyss.

"Is that good?" she heard Neil ask.

"Eventually we'll want her to be between eighty and one hundred twenty. One hundred seventy-nine isn't bad. Remember, her glucose levels didn't get sky high overnight. She's been dealing with this for a long time. We don't expect her body to jump down to normal right away."

Deeper and deeper.

"You'll want to record each reading in your log there. There's also a pretty handy app you can download on your phone."

Each reading. Because Taylor would have to do this multiple times a day. Which meant she would have to prick herself multiple times a day. Inject insulin into her stomach with a needle, multiple times a day. And she needed to remember to rotate the injection sites so they didn't get calcified with overuse.

The abyss began to spin.

Camille was forgetting to breathe.

Someone squeezed her hand.

She looked and saw that it was Neil.

"If you get a reading above two hundred, you'll have to check your urine for ketones. If there are ketones in the urine, that means your body is using fat cells for energy. You'll have to forgo exercise until you get things regulated."

"So I can still run?"

"Of course. Exercise is very good. We'll have to set up a plan with the dietician first, and you'll need to make sure to have your meter with you to see how your body is handling things. But ultimately, we encourage people with diabetes to get regular exercise. It helps channel that glucose into the cell, which is where we want it to go."

Taylor sat in the bed, her posture so straight it was almost regal. But tears gathered in her eyes. Taylor looked at Camille, sitting there at the bottom of the abyss, and her chin quivered in that way it did when she was five and had to miss the kindergarten carnival because she threw up in the van on the way to school. "What about the rest of track season?"

Sectionals was this weekend.

State was next.

Taylor had been training so hard.

Liz squeezed Taylor's arm again. "How about we focus on getting you better, and then you can start talking about track next year."

●❀●❀●

"Camille?"

She kept walking.

"Camille, where are you going?"

But she didn't turn around. She walked away like *he* walked away, down the long, white hallway, out through the front doors of the hospital, where she inhaled great gobs of air.

How long had it been since she breathed?

Did she stop when Taylor asked Liz her tremulous question?

Or was it when Dr. Porter's office told Camille to go straight to the ER?

Or was it before that, when Neil left?

Taylor had diabetes. This wasn't a dream. This wasn't something she could fix. Not with more money. Not with the right game plan. Not with more volunteers or a little more ingenuity. She could not hold this together. There wasn't a cure. It wasn't something that would go away. From now until the time Taylor died, her life would revolve around needles and lancets and insulin and carbohydrates. Her daughter had been suffering for months. *For months.* And Camille hadn't noticed.

She dug inside her purse and pulled out her keys.

Her phone had exploded with more text messages.

They wouldn't stop.

And Camille couldn't read them.

She didn't have any answers.

She needed to get away.

She dropped her phone in the grass and climbed in her car and drove as clouds thickened overhead and tiny raindrops began to blur the windshield. She drove as her wipers squeak-squeaked against the glass, smearing the raindrops dry. She drove as the abyss sucked her further and further away from the shore. She drove and she drove, sinking deeper into the void, until something rattled her awake.

A giant boom followed by a loud hiss as her Highlander jerked suddenly toward oncoming traffic. An electric jolt seized Camille's heart. She tightened her grip and wrestled the steering wheel right until her SUV was stopped on the side of the road and the rain turned into a downpour that pounded against the roof.

Camille sat in the driver's seat for a shocked moment, the wipers still squeaking.

Then she squeezed the steering wheel and shook it violently. Shake, shake, shake, like she wanted to rip it right off. A scream tore up her throat. A guttural scream as she shook and shook and shook.

She had a flat tire.

Her daughter was sick in the hospital.

Running would never be easy.

Camille was in the middle of nowhere without her phone.

She turned on her hazards, threw open her door, and stepped out into the rain, her purse still slung over her shoulder. She stood there—paralyzed— staring at her flat front tire with no idea what to do as rain soaked her hair and her clothes, plastering them to her body.

Where was the Lord?

Where was God in this mess of a year?

"Where are you?" she shouted at the rain.

A car door slammed shut.

Her head jerked up.

A car idled behind hers, its headlights shining through the downpour. And a man—a large, broad-shouldered black man with sagging jeans and a hood pulled over his head—walked toward her.

Fear grabbed her by the throat.

She took a step back, reaching inside her purse.

The man stopped and held up his hands, his attention darting to hers. He stood like Darius stood all those months ago in her yard. "I didn't mean to scare you," he said. "I just wanted to see if you needed some help."

Fear let go of her throat.

And she let go of her gun.

Fifty-Eight

The first week Taylor came home from the hospital as a newborn infant, Camille became compulsively obsessed with her daughter's breathing. Taylor would sleep for five-to-six-hour stretches at a time—making other moms groan with jealousy—but Camille couldn't enjoy it. She woke up every hour on the hour and found herself incapable of falling back asleep until she felt the soft, sure pat of baby breath against her fingertips.

She was so terrified that Taylor would die in her sleep.

The same fear seized her, only this time Taylor was seventeen and it wasn't a simple pat of breath that would reassure her. This time, reassurance came with blood.

Tonight Camille watched her daughter stick herself with a needle. Every muscle in Camille's body had tensed. It took everything inside her not to say something. Not to step forward and do it for her, because Taylor seemed to be holding the needle wrong and shouldn't she inject more to the left? Neil must have sensed it, because he placed his hand on Camille's shoulder, and she bit back the advice. Taylor was doing fine. It was the first night of all the rest of her nights. At 9:15 p.m. Through the summer. Through her senior year of high school. Through college. On her wedding night. When she was old and gray. This would be her daughter's routine. Her day would end with a needle.

Camille stood in Taylor's doorway, watching her sleep as rain continued to fall outside—a steady downpour that might not ever stop. A steady downpour that would forever remind her of a flat tire and a man with a hood and a gun in her hand and the day everything in the world turned upside down.

By the time she returned to the hospital, two hours had passed. Two hours, and Neil didn't say anything. Not about her soaking wet clothes. Not about her missing phone. He didn't ask any questions. He wasn't angry at her disappearance. He just invited her to sit down, and then they watched Liz show Taylor how to inject the Lantus at night.

Now he was at the grocery store, picking up food recommended in the binder, and Camille couldn't stop staring at Taylor. She was an infant all over again, only now Camille loved her even more. She loved her more now than she did when she was a tiny newborn. This little stranger who grew inside her body. She loved her so much, she felt like her heart was going to collapse.

Camille crept closer, as if a magnet irresistibly pulled her. If she climbed into her bed, Taylor would be annoyed. She would push Camille away. That was all she did anymore—push her away. But so what? Maybe that was part of being a mother. Being pushed, and pushing back.

Only this time Taylor didn't push. As soon as Camille eased under the covers, her daughter turned around and looked up at her through the dark with eyes so big and round, it was like they stepped inside Anaya Jones's time machine and traveled thirteen years into the past, when Taylor was four and terrified of the wild things, convinced they lived under her bed and if Camille left they would roar their terrible roars and gnash their terrible teeth and roll their terrible eyes.

"You have to stay with me, Mommy," she would say. "You have to fight them for me."

"Those monsters don't stand a chance against your mother," Camille had always said.

Only this monster was one Camille couldn't fight.

"I'm scared," Taylor whispered.

Camille tucked a strand of Taylor's hair behind her ear. "I'm scared too," she whispered back.

"What if I can't run anymore?"

What if . . .

Oh, Lord. What if?

Camille set her chin on top of Taylor's head and inhaled the scent of her strawberry shampoo. "Then we'll jump that hurdle together."

Taylor buried her face in her mother's chest and cried herself to sleep.

●●●●●

A raccoon was rustling through the garbage. Right in front of Camille. It kept rubbing its paws together, looking at her with gleaming, beady eyes—as if daring her to chase it away. When she didn't, it would dive back in.

Rustle, rustle, rustle.

Neil sighed heavily in his sleep.

But wait . . .

Camille wasn't lying beside Neil, and there wasn't a raccoon digging through the trash. She squeezed her eyes shut and opened them again. She was in Taylor's bed. The clock on her nightstand glowed 1:12 a.m., and cool air blew from the vents. She lay for a still second, waiting for Taylor to breathe again. When she did, Camille extricated herself with painstaking slowness from her daughter's long limbs, wincing every time the mattress squeaked.

The rustling sound continued.

Camille crept through the hall, down the stairs, into the kitchen.

Bags of groceries created a maze on the kitchen floor. The big, intimidating binder from the hospital lay open on the counter, and Neil was hunched over it, holding a green box of Nature Valley granola bars.

"What are you doing?"

He whirled around, brandishing a yellow highlighter. He exhaled a breath and set down the box of granola bars. A yellow mark highlighted the carbohydrate count on the nutrition label.

Camille's heart swelled with affection.

He was going through groceries, highlighting important numbers on nutrition labels at one in the morning, because he loved Taylor like she loved Taylor. No matter what happened between them, they would always have that. These children they'd made, and these children they loved.

"I can't believe you're still here," she said.

"I was trying to get things organized. Make meal planning a little easier." Neil put the cap on the highlighter and hitched his thumb awkwardly toward the foyer. "Do you want me to go?"

"No," she said. She wanted him to stay. She *needed* him to stay. With the foreign nature of this new diagnosis, she needed familiarity, and despite being gone for the last ten months, Neil was everything familiar. She sat on one of the kitchen stools, sliding her hands over the cool granite and then folding them together.

The world had gotten very small, like it did when they brought Taylor home from the hospital.

"I keep thinking about the day we brought Taylor home from the hospital," he said.

She looked up. "I was just thinking the same thing."

"We thought the nurse was so crazy, to let us leave with this tiny human being. I remember looking in the rearview mirror, watching you watch Taylor in her car seat, and feeling . . . utterly terrified." Neil ran his hand down his face, his palm scraping against whiskers—the stressful kind that grew in hospital waiting rooms. They were completely gray. When had Neil's whiskers turned so gray? "I felt the same way driving you two home from the hospital tonight."

"Me too."

"I keep wanting to go up to her room and check her blood sugar."

Camille smiled. And she blinked too. She blinked away moisture.

"Remember that bike we got her when she was five?" he said.

"Oh, do I remember."

Dora the Explorer.

"*Hola,* my name's Taylor!" She and Neil said it at the exact same time, with the same perfect intonation that five-year-old Taylor used to use as she walked around the house with that beloved, tattered Boots doll tucked under her arm.

They smiled at each other.

"She was so determined to learn how to ride it without training wheels. Remember that?"

Camille nodded. Taylor had stubbornly refused training wheels. Seven-year-old Joseph across the street did not ride his bike with training wheels, so Taylor would not either. It caused more than a few fights between her parents. Neil wanted to take them off. Camille thought Taylor would kill herself.

"I remember when it finally clicked, and she took off pedaling. She was riding so fast and getting so far away from me, and I was panicked, because I knew she was going to fall. I kept yelling, 'Slow down, Taylor. Slow down.'"

A lump rose in Camille's throat.

"But she didn't slow down. She flew off the curb and completely wiped out."

"Five stitches."

Neil nodded.

That had caused a fight too.

Camille remembered him carrying a wailing Taylor inside, a bloody gash in her knee. She remembered her words too, as she frantically searched for something to stanch the flow. "I told you not to take off those training wheels!" She was so sure, as she sat with Taylor on her lap in the waiting room of the ER—because *she* was going to handle this now—that it never would have happened on her watch. The truth was, on her watch, Taylor probably never would have learned to ride.

"Our daughter makes me feel that way a lot, you know? 'Slow down, Taylor. Slow down.' I'm her dad, and she's always having to drag me along."

"At least you don't stop her altogether."

Their eyes met.

Silence sat between them.

"Somehow," Neil said, "we're supposed to believe that this is for her good."

A puff of air escaped Camille's nose.

"It's what our faith says, anyway."

Our faith.

Camille had a hard time understanding how Neil could still share her faith. How could he leave and continue to worship a God who told husbands not to leave? But then . . . she thought about Cody, who went to Fellowship of Christian Athletes almost every Wednesday. And her uncle, who taught Paige a filthy word but went to church every Sunday. She thought about herself, who never once confronted Uncle Ray when he said it. And her neighbors across the street, who brought their children to Awana on Tuesday nights but called the police when they saw a black kid on her front lawn. They were all such hypocrites. Such broken, in-need-of-grace hypocrites.

"It's hard to wrap your mind around, isn't it?" Neil said.

Yeah. Just a little.

Camille wound her hand around the back of her neck. "I remember hearing that verse in church as a little girl—the one about all our days being ordained before one of them came to be. I used to picture these invisible numbers hovering over everybody's head, and every time the clock struck midnight, the number would tick down. I would look at people and think, *What's your number?* I never really thought about our days being marked with other things."

Like diabetes.

Like a husband leaving.

Like a tire blowing out on the road.

The man's name was Chris. He was nice, a father of two little girls. He stopped when nobody else stopped and changed her tire. And she almost shot him.

"The newspaper was right," Camille said. "I'm racist."

"What?"

"I almost shot someone tonight."

Neil jerked his head back, his eyes widening.

"That's where I was when I was gone. I was driving. I didn't even know where. Then my tire blew out. This man got out to help me. This really tall, really big black man."

She pictured him, holding his hands up like Darius. Another snapshot in her mind. One she would have with her until the day she died. Chris, with his hands in the air and the same fear in his eyes that she had seen in Darius's. Because he knew. He saw her hand reach inside her purse.

"He had his hood up because it was raining, and I got scared. I . . ." She shook her head. What if she had done it? What if he hadn't put his hands up in the right way or he'd been a little closer and she slightly more startled? What if she had yanked that gun out and pulled the trigger? That man would be dead. His invisible number would have been up. Or maybe she would have ended it early.

Camille shuddered.

"I'm sure it didn't have anything to do with his color," Neil said. "I'm sure you would have been afraid of any large, hooded man."

Maybe.

Maybe not.

Camille didn't know. And there was the rub. She honestly didn't know.

Neil reached across the counter and put his hand on hers.

His touch broke something inside her.

The lump in her throat gave way.

She put her head on her arm and wept.

Neil took his hand back, and for a second she felt abandoned all over again. Bereft and alone. But then suddenly, she wasn't. He wrapped her in his arms. He drew her head to his shoulder and absorbed her tears.

Fifty-Nine

Anaya didn't feel any more comfortable at Camille Gray's house the second time around, and Darius had the audacity to ask to come with her. Here, to this neighborhood where people assumed he was a prowler. She told him no, of course.

He was at home with Mama, who was so preoccupied and stressed with the South Fork news and where Darius would go to school next year that when she saw his black eye on Thursday morning, she held up her hands and said, "I don't even wanna know."

So far, no police officers had shown up on their door to read Darius his rights. So far, Cody Malone's mother hadn't followed through on her threat. The stress of waiting to see whether or not she would was starting to take its toll.

Anaya rang the doorbell and took a step back.

A few seconds later, the door swung open.

A tall, trim, middle-aged man with a receding hairline and Paige's bright blue eyes answered the door. Paige's father, she guessed. Only she thought Taylor's parents were divorced or separated. One of the two.

"I'm Anaya Jones, Taylor's coach."

The man shook Anaya's hand. "And Paige's teacher."

She held up the card and the small gift from the team. Yesterday was sectionals. Shanice and Alexis both qualified for state. The whole team felt Taylor's absence. Anaya did too. "I wanted to stop by and see how Taylor was doing."

He called inside the house for Taylor and invited Anaya into the foyer.

It was practically bigger than her entire house.

Taylor came down the stairs, looking normal and healthy. Her hair was wet, her skin freshly scrubbed. Anaya wasn't sure what she was expecting—some sort of diminished, sickly version? "Hey, Coach," Taylor said, looking from Anaya to her father.

"I'll leave you two to talk."

"Want to talk outside?" Anaya asked. "It's really nice."

"Sure."

The two of them sat on the front stoop.

Anaya handed her the card and the gift. "Just a little something from the team to let you know we're thinking about you."

Taylor opened the card. *Get Better Soon.* It seemed odd, but Alexis brought it to practice on Friday, and Anaya wasn't about to point out the fact that maybe it was a little insensitive. As far as she knew, people didn't get better from diabetes. Everyone signed it, wrote little notes. Taylor read them, then set the card aside and pulled out a coffee mug from the small gift bag. It had the words *Strong is the New Beautiful* written in colorful, swirly font.

"Thank you," Taylor said.

Anaya rested her elbows on her knees. "I know you had some big goals for state. You'll get 'em next year."

Taylor turned the mug over in her hands. She gazed inside, like whatever she was thinking so intently about sloshed around like coffee in a cup. "What if I can't?" she finally asked.

"Can't what?"

"Run."

"You still have your legs, don't you?"

"You know what I mean. What if I'm not good anymore? What if I try and I lose every race?"

Then the world would keep turning.

Taylor would still go to college.

Her mother wouldn't have to quit night classes and take a second job. Taylor's parents had plenty of money to send her to college without any need of a scholarship.

She'd find something else to motivate her.

She'd meet a guy. They'd fall in love and get married and have kids and live in a neighborhood like this one.

But Anaya couldn't say that.

She was a coach, and right now one of her runners was facing a really big hurdle that had been unexpectedly tossed in front of her. "I know what it's like to be the best at something and then have that taken away."

Taylor's attention flitted to Anaya's ankle. Did Darius tell Taylor what happened? Did Taylor know that once upon a time, Anaya thought she would be running for Team USA, not coaching track for Suburbia USA?

She picked up a small pebble and tossed it into her other hand. "I guess the question you need to ask yourself is, What do you really love? Running or winning? If it's running, then you're not really going to lose anything."

●◦●◦❀◦●

A glucose meter. Meter strips. A lancet device. Lancets. An insulin pen. Extra screw-on needles. A bag full of snacks and juice boxes with exactly fifteen grams of carbohydrates. It was Monday morning, and Camille was shuffling through the monogrammed tote she purchased at Rebecca's Thirty-One party two summers ago to make sure everything was there.

"You can put it in here," Jen said, showing her a row of cabinets at the back of her office. Each one had its own name: Melanie Kasamir. Kai Mahon. Isabel Keely. Jack Emery. And now, Taylor Gray.

Taylor had her own cabinet. Because Taylor was a diabetic.

All weekend long, Camille had to run the words over and over in her mind. So far, they refused to stick. They kept flitting away like moths, and then she would see Taylor pricking herself with the lancet or Austin reading the new book he got from the library—*Think Like a Pancreas*—and Camille would have to repeat the words to herself all over again.

Taylor was a diabetic.

This was their life now.

Not the state track meet this weekend. Not running fifty to sixty miles a week this summer in preparation for her senior year of cross-country.

But this.

Diabetes.

"She's set on coming to school tomorrow," Camille said, unloading the supplies. How was she supposed to focus on anything with Taylor at school? And once life resumed normalcy, what was going to happen between her and Neil? When he pointed his thumb toward the door and asked if she wanted him to go, she said no, and he stayed.

All weekend long.

He slept in the guest room, of course. But still, he stayed.

The kids were confused, probably. But she needed him there. She needed him as they got used to this new regimented diet. She needed him as they got used to the finger pricking and the injections. He'd taken the day off work because later they would drive back to the hospital and meet with a diabetes educator. Camille should have a long list of questions. Instead, she kept running the same words through her head.

Taylor is a diabetic.

"I'll make sure to keep a good eye on her," Jen said. "If you want, I'd be happy to text you updates throughout the day."

"I'd like that."

"It's going to be okay. I know it doesn't feel like it right now, but this is not the end of the world."

They were almost the exact same words Liz had spoken before they left the hospital, only Liz had taken Camille by the shoulders and looked firmly—almost sternly—into her eyes. Jen kept her distance, but Camille was as thankful for the words now as she had been on Friday.

She wanted to apologize—sincerely apologize—for everything. For blindsiding Jen on Paige's birthday party with the presents. For the awful thing Paige said the Monday after. For not responding immediately. For not marching Paige straight into Principal Kelly's office, because yes, her daughter had in fact said that word. Jubilee wasn't a liar. Neither was Nia. She should have banged on Jen's door until she answered so she could tell her face to face how terribly, horribly sorry she was.

She kept experiencing these flashes of vulnerability. This overwhelming feeling of nakedness, like a needy toddler without food or clothes. She wanted to grab Jen's hands and get down on her knees and beg her forgiveness.

Instead, she hitched the empty tote over her shoulder and said two simple words with all the sincerity in her heart. "Thank you."

Sixty

To: jones.anaya@crystalridge.k12.mo.us
From: kelly.timothy@crystalridge.k12.mo.us
Subject: a meeting
Date: Monday, May 20

Anaya,

Great job at sectionals this weekend! Your girls ran great. I'm sure they were a little shaken up about Taylor. That's such a tough break. Anyway, I'm emailing to see if you're free for a quick meeting this afternoon during your specials. HR will be there. No need to be alarmed! You're not in any trouble.

Best,
Tim Kelly
Principal
Katie O'Hare Elementary

Anaya stood inside the refrigerator box, quickly removing the pictures she'd hung two weeks ago at the start of a literacy unit on Faith Ringgold. She read *Tar Beach* and *Aunt Harriet's Underground Railroad in the Sky* to her students. The illustrations enthralled them, and as soon as she finished, they wanted to learn more. So they did what they'd done all year.

They traveled back in time.

Did a parent complain again? Was that why Mr. Kelly and someone from HR wanted to meet with her? He brought up track in his email. Maybe it had something to do with track. Maybe it was about her confrontation with Cody Malone on the track. Maybe it was about Darius.

She shoved the thought away.

Darius and Cody didn't get into a fight on school property. They didn't get into a fight during school hours. This couldn't be about her brother. So then . . . what? Did they want to talk to her about the South Fork transfer situation? The Crystal Ridge School Board was already discussing next year and what they would do should the South Fork Cooperative attain a new accreditation status. Maybe HR wanted Anaya's input as a teacher.

Anaya set the pictures on her desk and headed to the office.

Jan McCormick was there. She smiled at Anaya.

Ever since her commentary on South Fork mothers, Anaya had a hard time believing her authenticity.

It turned out, HR was a woman with almond-colored skin and silver hair—a sharp contrast that accentuated both.

"Renatta West," she said, giving Anaya's hand a firm handshake. "Tim mentioned I'd be joining you, I hope."

"Yes, he did."

"Please don't be nervous. I want to assure you that you aren't in any trouble."

The words weren't any more comforting in person, especially not in light of the recorder in Renatta's hand. Mr. Kelly hadn't said anything about a recorder. Anaya didn't like it. She kept thinking about her brother and Cody's broken nose and his mother's ominous threat. What if Anaya said the wrong thing? What if she implicated Darius in some way and they used it against him?

"Please have a seat," Mr. Kelly said. "This shouldn't take long."

"We have a few questions for you regarding a situation that has arisen in the district. We appreciate your discretion."

"Okay," Anaya said. It came out sounding more like a question.

Renatta turned the recorder on and set it on Mr. Kelly's desk. "Anaya, I was hoping you could tell me about your student teaching experience."

The words spun her in a circle. "My student teaching experience?"

"Yes." Renatta folded her hands over her knee. "Specifically, how did you get along with your cooperating teacher, Kyle Davis?"

•❀•❀•

A Conversation on Twitter:

Ashleigh Spellerman @spellAshleigh: OMG. My 3rd grade teacher is a total sex predator. So creeped out!

Brenna Brown @brenbrown *(replying to @spellAshleigh)*: It's a lie. But good job spreading gossip.

Ashleigh Spellerman @spellAshleigh: It's not a lie. My sister's in his class. She had a sub all last week.

Brenna Brown @brenbrown: Doesn't mean he's a sex predator.

Dax Peterson @daxdaman *(replying to @spellAshleigh)*: Something tells me that chick is just looking for attention.

Holly Jordan @HollyatMe *(replying to @daxdaman @spell Ashleigh)*: Excuse me? This isn't the kind of attention ANY "chick" wants. She's being publicly eviscerated. Nobody will hire her after this.

Dax Peterson @daxdaman: Eviscerated. Fancy word. But c'mon. Did you see those Snapchat pictures?

Justin Fox @justafox *(replying to @daxdaman)*: See them? I printed them out and hung them on the ceiling above my bed. #bowchickawowwow

Brenna Brown @brenbrown *(replying to @HollyatMe @daxdaman)*: Hooters will hire her.

Dax Peterson @daxdaman: Brenna!!! LOLOLOLOLOL

Holly Jordan @HollyatMe *(replying to @justafox @daxdaman @brenbrown)*: You're all disgusting. I hope he's fired.

Justin Fox @justafox: No way. Mr. D is legendary. Best teacher of all time.

Dax Peterson @daxdaman: Remember when he gave the whole class giant-size Snickers bars for Halloween. Holly's just bitter b/c she has a nut allergy.

Lauren Graham @notagilmore *(replying to @spellAshleigh @justafox @daxdaman)*: You all realize anyone can read this conversation, right?

Sixty-One

Over the next twenty-four hours, Anaya existed in two worlds. There was her life in Crystal Ridge as a teacher and a track coach, where the sensitive situation Renatta talked about in Mr. Kelly's office no longer called for Anaya's discretion because Ellie Sorrenson wasn't being discrete. And there was her life in South Fork, as Mama's daughter and Marcus's girlfriend and a volunteer at the youth center, where nobody knew nor particularly cared about Kyle Davis, because they had—as Daddy would have said—bigger fish to fry. The two worlds didn't intersect much, but a ghost called Guilt haunted her in both.

Shanice and Alexis went through a series of warm-ups on the track.

The two coaches for the boys' track-and-field team chatted nearby.

"I guess they found a loophole," one of them said.

"The board's already talking about next year. It doesn't look like the transfer students are going to stay."

"That's a shame."

Their conversation floated around her like the wind as her girls moved from high knees to groin stretches.

"Hey, how's Kyle doing?"

The question pricked Anaya's ears.

"Not so good. This has all blindsided him, you know?"

"There's no chance it could be true, is there?"

"I've known Kyle for years. He's a stand-up guy."

"Well, I think it's safe to say his career at Crystal Ridge is ruined."

"I don't know about that. A lot of parents are showing their support."

The world shrank.

It blackened into a pinprick. A focal point.

Ellie's phone call.

Her meeting with Renatta West.

Did you ever feel uncomfortable?

Snapchat pictures captured on someone's screen and shared all over social media.

A victim on trial.

Marcus.

We can wipe the slate clean and start fresh.

But the past happened, whether they acknowledged it or not.

It couldn't be erased, no matter how much someone wanted to erase it.

"Dax! Stop goofing around and start stretching." The coach crossed his arms. "Anyway, after those pictures leaked, I'm not sure a girl like her has much credibility."

A girl like her . . .

A girl like her . . .

A girl like her . . .

"Hey Coach," Shanice called. "Where are you going?"

Anaya didn't answer.

Anaya didn't know.

•●₀°₀•

She sat in the dark while crickets serenaded the night—an incongruous sound, peace when there was no peace—the gun heavy in her lap.

"What do you really love?" she had asked Taylor. "Running or winning?"

As a kid, Anaya didn't run to win. She ran because it brought her to life. She ran because she had invisible wings on her back that compelled her to run. She ran because when she did, she soared. She ran like her name.

Completely free.

But then Daddy died and life unraveled.

She was so angry. She was overcome with the emotion, but she had no target. At the end of the day, it wasn't the streets that took her father. It wasn't a police officer with a twitchy finger. It wasn't an all-too-eager prison system. It was the organ inside his chest, and how could she be angry at a heart she loved so dear?

Anaya poured the aimless, insatiable emotion into training.

Her wings no longer carried her around that track.

Anger did.

She trained with a ferocity that alarmed everyone, her coaches included. They told her to slow down. They gave her plenty of warning. But she ignored them all, breaking record after record until her record breaking broke her.

In one fell swoop, she lost it all. Her aspirations. Her scholarship. She buried her grieving family under a mountain of medical bills. Mama refused to let Anaya drop out. Not when she was one year away from a college degree. Her mother quit night classes and got a second job. And Anaya could no longer outrun her grief.

It engulfed her completely.

It swallowed her right up.

She lost who she was.

And Marcus became a convenient scapegoat for all that was wrong.

But her cooperating teacher? He was different. A shiny, new object who personified a world so wholly opposite from the one she lived in. He joked about things people didn't typically joke about. He made her laugh when her insides were brittle. He was charming and self-deprecating in a way she wasn't used to and so far removed from all that was bad in her life. Plus, he shared her affinity for all things geek. Granted, he thought DC was better than Marvel and *Star Trek* better than *Star Wars,* but that only made their conversations more engaging, more blessedly distracting.

Anaya squeezed her eyes shut.

But it was too late.

The past refused to stay buried. After all this time, it had turned into a rotten corpse. A zombie pushing its bony hand up through six feet of dirt, and there wasn't a machete or a sword or anything at all to fight it with.

The day was already a bad day. A horrible anniversary. The kind nobody wanted to celebrate. Two years without a father. And she was extra irritated because of a text message. It came from a former teammate—a girl who took her spot as anchor on the 200 relay.

On our way to take on Mizzou. Missing you like crazy!

It felt cruel.

She was spending the lunch hour in Kyle's classroom, organizing her afternoon lesson plans. He didn't like the lounge any more than she did, so he would spend it in his classroom too. He always blasted classic rock on his phone and did a really dorky impression of playing an air guitar. At the moment, he was doing an even dorkier robot dance to "Mr. Roboto" by Styx. Thanks to Kyle, Anaya knew *domo arigato* meant "thank you very much" in Japanese.

That was when the second text came through. This one from Marcus.

Meet me outside.

He drove all the way to Crystal Ridge with her favorite pizza. He came without giving her any sort of warning—her world colliding with this world—and instead of expressing thanks, she expressed annoyance. Her reaction hurt his feelings, which made her feel guilty, and then she got angry at him for making her feel guilty.

"I'm *sorry,* but I have to teach this afternoon," she said.

"I'm *sorry* for trying to do something nice for my girlfriend." He jabbed his hands on his hips, fisting the hem of his shirt, and shook his head. Anaya knew then that he didn't remember what today was. He'd forgotten a day she would never be able to forget. "I can't even get that right anymore. Apparently, everything I do is wrong."

"Don't make this a bigger deal than it is, okay? I don't have time to eat pizza right now. That's all."

He called her bluff. "Is that really all, Anaya?"

"I told you. I have to teach."

"Nah. This isn't about teaching. This is about us, in a relationship, and I'm the one pulling all the weight."

"Maybe that has something to do with the fact that my running career is over."

"I get that, but don't you think it's time to move on?"

The insensitive question—especially on this particular day—might as well have slapped her across the face. And when she recovered, all the anger in need of a target took its aim. "Move on, huh? It's that simple, is it Marcus?"

"Anaya . . ." She could see the regret pooling in his eyes. But it was too late. She was too revved up.

"I lost my scholarship. I lost my father. Two years ago *today,* by the way. I have a bum ankle that is worthless. And my mama is breaking her back to put me here, so excuse me if I don't wanna take a break to eat pizza!"

He stepped toward her.

But she stepped back. "You know what? You're right. You are pulling all the weight. Maybe it's time you stopped."

She threw his pizza in the garbage, and she cried in the bathroom. Angry tears. Sad tears. Frustrated tears, because she knew she was being awful, but she didn't know how to stop. That afternoon, she taught one of the worst science lessons in the history of all science lessons. When it was done and the bell rang and the kids were gone, Kyle sat on the edge of a nearby desk and she started to apologize for not being better prepared.

He held up his hand to stop her. "I think you need some therapy."

"Excuse me?"

"Therapy? I know some that comes highly recommended. It's called happy hour. It's the best therapy I know, actually."

She exhaled and rolled her eyes.

"Come on. I've never had a student teacher work as hard as you. Which is great, don't get me wrong. I hardly have to do anything. But at least let me do this." He dipped his chin and smiled at her. "Just one drink."

Anaya wasn't a drinker.

She could count on one hand the number of alcoholic beverages she'd had in her lifetime and not one of them had ever been a shot.

It burned her throat like fire.

She coughed and blinked back tears.

Kyle laughed. "The next one won't burn as much."

He was right.

It didn't.

By the time she had another one, her head was already swimming and her teeth felt pleasantly numb. Maybe soon her heart would too.

She forgot about Marcus. She forgot about her injury and the track meet against Mizzou that she wasn't running in. She forgot about Mama with bags under her eyes because no woman should have to work as much as she did. She forgot about the medical bills and Darius getting into trouble. She forgot about how much she missed her daddy.

And then she just forgot.

The night went black, with nothing but flickering bits of memory that wouldn't come until later.

The next thing she knew, she was waking up in a strange bed to the sound of a bird chirping outside a window, her tongue swollen, her head splitting, confusion grabbing hold. Panicked confusion. She didn't know where she was. She didn't know how she got there.

Until she saw the REO Speedwagon poster on the closed, wooden door.

"Shh," someone whispered behind it. "You're gonna wake her up."

She pulled the covers to her body.

Kyle's covers.

"Are you kidding me, dude? You have your student teacher in there?"

"Shh," he whispered again.

There was laughter—soft, but distinct. "How was she?"

Pause.

"Come on, man. You gotta give me something."

Another pause.

And then more laughter, louder this time. "*A girl like her?* No way! I thought black girls were supposed to be way better than that."

"Guess not."

Anaya lurched out of Kyle's bed. She scrambled into his bathroom and clutched the toilet. There was dried urine on the back of the seat, and dirty grout between the tiles. Her stomach emptied itself. She threw up in Kyle's bathroom. Demoralized. Degraded. Disgusted.

Disgusting.

The filth on her hands would never go away. It was there like a stain as she put on her clothes and grabbed her shoes and snuck out of Kyle's house. It was there still, no matter how often she begged forgiveness. It was there, and her wings were gone.

She lied.

Renatta West asked her if Mr. Davis ever made her uncomfortable, and she said no.

But he had. He'd made her feel worse than uncomfortable. He made her feel like she wasn't even human.

A light turned on in his kitchen.

A silhouetted shape moved around inside.

The Kyles of the world were multiplying, and the corpse was out now. It was awake. Resurrected. No longer buried. And its nails were sharp like talons.

The first time she heard the word—that awful no-good word. *You dirty little . . .*

Scratch.

Every racial slur she'd ever read on a bathroom stall.

Scratch.

All those angry parents at the town meeting.

Scratch.

The disparity between South Fork schools and Crystal Ridge.

Scratch.

Leif Royce at Unpack Your Backpack night and his carrying, awful voice.

Scratch.

The Confederate flag on Gavin's shirt.

Scratch.

Principal Kelly, sitting placidly behind his desk after Paige said that awful, no-good word to Jubilee.

Scratch.

Darius, with his hands raised in Camille's yard.

Scratch.

Jan McCormick talking about the South Fork moms.

Scratch.

Cody Malone.

Scratch.

Kyle Davis.

Scratch.

A girl like her . . .

A girl like her . . .

A girl like her . . .

Scratch. Scratch. SCRATCH.

Anaya picked up the gun with trembling hands, her heart howling in pain. At some point, the scratch had become a gaping, bleeding wound. And all the rubbing in the world would not make it better.

Sixty-Two

The house oozed with anxiety. Anaya could feel it like impending rain as soon as she walked through the door. She could feel the stillness too, as Mama, Granny, and Darius stood in the kitchen. Anaya walked inside with her hands stuffed inside the pockets of her hoodie, her heart detached from her body.

"Was that Latrell and Darnell I heard outside a second ago?" Granny said, taking Darius by the elbow. "Walk me next door so I can see if them boys have any Tabasco sauce. I'm fixing to fry me up some eggs, and I ain't eating no eggs without Tabasco sauce."

Granny might be old and frail, but she hardly needed Darius to escort her next door in search of Tabasco sauce. Their sudden departure had nothing to do with a hankering for fried eggs at ten at night and everything to do with the fact that for the past six hours, Anaya had dropped off the face of the earth. She left Shanice and Darius out to dry. She left Mama to sit in a pool of worry, and there was nothing that got Mama hotter under the collar than that.

"Where in the world have you been?"

Anaya pulled the gun out from her front hoodie pocket and set it on the table.

The house ticked with silence.

"Where did you get that?" Mama asked in a hushed voice that quavered.

"Uncle Jemar's glove box."

Mama winced. A sharp intake of breath, like Anaya had physically wounded her. It was a painful déjà vu. The first time Mama and Uncle Jemar got into a yelling match so loud, the whole neighborhood took cover.

It wasn't really Uncle Jemar's fault. He had every right to carry a gun in his glove box. Mama knew that. Just like she knew Darius wasn't stupid. He wasn't even irresponsible. He was just a fourteen-year-old kid in the middle of his overwhelming grief who got caught up with the wrong crowd and made the stupid, irresponsible decision to put that gun in his backpack and take it to school. It was a decision that came without grace. One that would follow him indefinitely.

Anaya sank into a chair at the table. She had never gotten out of her car. She was never actually going to do anything with the gun. She just wanted to hold it in her hand. She wanted to imagine for a moment that she held the power to make Kyle Davis and his roommate feel as small and worthless as they made her feel that day.

"Why?" Mama asked.

The story came tumbling out. So did the bitterness that came with it. Anaya told her mother the truth. She told her the truth about it all. The foolish thing she did. The horrible thing Kyle and his roommate said. Everything that happened afterward. She confessed it, and when she was finished and shame ravaged her body and tears of disgrace tumbled fast down her cheeks, Mama walked around the table and gathered Anaya up in her arms.

"You are not the sum of one bad decision, do you hear me?"

But it was such a big, bad decision. And Marcus didn't know. And she lied to Renatta West. Anaya wiped her nose. "I hate him. I hate him so much. Sometimes I start to feel like I hate all of them."

All of them.

Her mother didn't have to ask who she meant.

The confession hovered there above the table. It hovered above Uncle Jemar's gun.

"Hatred is a tasty morsel," Mama said, her face a mask of compassion—because maybe at one point, or several points, she hated *them* also. "It's poisonous too."

Anaya knew that for herself.

She was currently choking on its poison.

"It'll eat you from the inside, until all that's left of you is a husk of bitterness." She pulled out the chair beside Anaya. The legs scraped against the linoleum. She sat down and let out a long, loud sigh that filled the kitchen. "It ain't easy. Choosing to see the image of God in people who don't see the image of God in us? I think it's one of the bitterest pills I'll ever have to swallow. But, baby, those people? They aren't the real enemy. The minute we start believing they are, the real enemy wins, and our hearts turn hard."

Anaya's heart already felt hard—callused from a life's worth of scratches. But then, Mama had endured those same scratches too. And Granny before her. Two women with skin like steel but hearts that still bled.

"I know it's difficult. But every day, you gotta make the choice."

"The choice to what?"

"Forgive."

Anaya went silent. She sat back in the chair.

"Listen to me. You can't live your one life angry. Living angry means living caged, and I won't have that for my daughter. Not when so many people before you fought hard to set us free."

"But nobody's asking for forgiveness, Mama. They don't even know anything's wrong. We're supposed to just let them off the hook?"

"That hook don't belong to you, baby. It never did; it never will."

Anaya sniffed.

"And forgiveness isn't pardon for them. It's freedom for you. 'Vengeance is mine, says the Lord.' That don't mean we're silent for justice. That don't mean we aren't called to fight against all forms of oppression. But sin has a death grip on this world, Anaya. It is broken, with broken systems and broken people. And Jesus died for it all. The oppressor and the oppressed."

Mama reached into Anaya's lap and squeezed her hand. "Someday, somehow, He's gonna make all things new. Every chain gone and we'll dance on streets of gold. That's where I fix my eyes. But until then, I'll keep on forgiving. I'll forgive and I'll forgive and I'll forgive even when they don't ask, holding fast to a Jesus who didn't just put on flesh—He put on flesh and resided with the least of these, and He died for me when I was yet His enemy. He turned the world upside down. He made the last first. He blesses the weak. He made the despised Samaritan the hero of the story. Oh baby, He's a good God, and He don't want you walking around with your heart in a fist. It is for freedom that Christ has set us free."

Her heart pulled tight inside her chest.

Freedom.

Anaya.

Her name.

Her birthright.

And a verse from Galatians that hung above the television in their living room, cross-stitched by Granny before her arthritis got bad. It was the verse Hettie Horton taught Granny to hide in her heart when she was six years old. A verse Hettie Horton would have held on to fiercely because of what came next.

Stand firm, then, and do not let yourselves
be burdened again by a yoke of slavery.

Sixty-Three

Facebook statement from Ellie Sorrenson:

Up until last week, I was a student teacher at Lewis and Clark Elementary School in Kyle Davis's third grade classroom. At first, Mr. Davis was really nice and friendly. But then he started paying me compliments that seemed inappropriate. Several times, his body would brush against mine in a way that made me feel uncomfortable, but he would quickly apologize, like it was an accident, so I let it go.

What happened last week was not an accident. It wasn't funny, either. It was demoralizing. He ran his hand up my thigh beneath a table when he was supposed to be giving me feedback for my afternoon lesson plan. Afterward, he tried to act like it was a joke. I immediately went to my supervisor and reported the incident. Now Mr. Davis is saying it didn't happen at all.

It's not okay to put your hands on someone without their consent. I don't care if everyone thinks he's a nice guy or a good teacher. What he did was sexual harassment, and it was wrong.

⁕⁂⁕

Anaya's heart pounded in her ears. She sat in the same seat she sat in eleven months ago, before her interview for a second grade teaching position at Kate Richards O'Hare Elementary. Only now, she wasn't there to impress. She was there to confess.

She couldn't stop thinking about the cross-stitched verse hanging above the television in her living room or the meaning of her name.

Anaya.

Completely free.

According to her mother, freedom came with forgiveness. According to the Bible, it came with truth. Anaya hadn't been telling it. She wasn't truthful when Ellie Sorrenson called her on the phone two weeks ago, asking if Kyle Davis ever made her uncomfortable. And she wasn't truthful two days ago, when Renatta West asked the same question.

Maybe if she told the truth, the administration would be more inclined to believe Ellie's testimony.

Renatta walked out to the front desk with a small, perplexed furrow etched between her eyebrows. "Hello, Anaya," she said. It was more of a question than a greeting. "Is there something I can do for you this morning?

"I was wondering if you had a minute to talk."

"Of course. Come on back." She led the way past a row of cubicles that didn't lend themselves to much privacy. "We can talk in here."

It was the conference room where she'd had her interview. Her palms were just as sweaty as she sat in one of the chairs across from Renatta. This time, there wasn't a recorder.

"You asked me if Kyle Davis ever behaved inappropriately."

"And you said no."

"I was lying."

Renatta closed her eyes—barely longer than a blink. "Go on."

Anaya told her about Kyle's invitation to happy hour. She told her about the tequila shots and waking up in his bed. Renatta sat there listening, twisting one of her pearl earrings around and around and around.

"Was it consensual?" she asked.

It was a question without an answer at first. When Anaya woke up that awful morning, the entire night had been wiped from her memory. She remembered saying yes to happy hour. She remembered waking up in Kyle's bed. She remembered the things she overheard in Kyle's hallway. The rest was black. A blank slate, like Marcus wanted them to have. But slowly and intrusively, bits and pieces returned.

Laughing on the dance floor while Kyle did the robot.

Stumbling to his front door while he fumbled with his keys.

Standing in front of that REO Speedwagon poster while he kissed her neck, his stubble sharp and alien against her skin.

Not in one of the bits and pieces could she remember saying no.

The heat in her cheeks grew hotter. "I think so."

"Unfortunately, Anaya, if it was consensual, there's really not much we can do."

"But—"

"That's not to say he isn't a jerk. It's just to say that he's not in breach of contract. He wasn't in a supervisory role. You weren't one of his students."

"So he's going to get away with it all?"

Renatta frowned. "The only certain thing at this point is that he will no longer be getting student teachers."

It felt like another scratch.

"But he wrote me a letter of recommendation."

"Most cooperating teachers do."

"He implied he would as long as I didn't say anything." His exact words had been, *This wouldn't be good for either of us if anyone found out what happened. It's probably best to pretend it didn't. Oh, and don't let me forget. You need a letter of recommendation for your portfolio, right?* Then he winked. Anaya wasn't sure what was worse—that wink or the fact that she took his letter a week later. "He said I was the best student teacher he'd ever had."

How well she remembered those typed words.

Had the innuendo been intentional? Did he laugh with his roommate when he read them out loud? Did he know how they would make her feel when she read them? Like there wasn't enough hand sanitizer in the world to make her clean.

Renatta pursed her lips; then she folded her hands on the table. "I'm sorry you had to go through this, Anaya. By all accounts, you are a wonderful teacher. I appreciate your honesty, and we'll take this into consideration as we continue our investigation."

That was it.

Anaya's big confession was over.

It didn't make a difference in the end. Kyle Davis wouldn't pay for what he did. But Ellie was paying. And Anaya would, because now she had to tell the truth again. This time, she had to tell it to Marcus.

●◦●◦◉◦●◦

Marcus sat on the front stoop, laughing at something Granny said while she swung back and forth on the porch swing, one hand on her cane, the other wrapped around the rusty chain.

Anaya's tires rolled over the curb, up onto the driveway.

When Darius got out, Marcus stood and slapped him some skin. "What's up, bruh? You hanging in there?"

"I'll be better once I know where I'm going next year."

"Yeah. I hear you, man."

"Help an old woman to her feet," Granny said, reaching her hand out to Darius. She patted his arm. "Let me whip you up something good to eat. I'll have you forgetting next year in no time. Marcus, you stayin' too. And bring your appetite to my table. If you're gonna marry my great-granddaughter, then you best know how to eat."

The screen door squealed open, then thwacked shut, leaving Marcus and Anaya alone with the heat and chirping birds.

Marcus grinned. "Was that her way of giving me her blessing?"

A knot tied itself in Anaya's throat. She felt like she was waking up in Kyle's bed all over again, a feeling of doom sinking through her body. She knew this was going to happen. Ever since he took her to the homecoming game, she'd known. The other shoe was bound to drop. They couldn't keep pretending the past didn't exist. It went against everything she taught her second graders all year long. The past echoed into the present, and that echo could not be ignored.

Marcus looked at her, really looked at her. "You okay?"

She didn't deserve him. This man who had the same heart for youth as she did, the same heart for this community as her father did. He stuck by her side when she was at her worst. He apologized for things he never should have.

Anaya took his hand and sat on the stoop, pulling him down with her. A car without a muffler drove past, temporarily drowning out the sound of Mr. Johansen mowing his lawn five houses away.

She could feel Marcus looking at her, waiting for her to speak.

"You said you wanted to start fresh. Wipe the slate clean." She held on to his hand with both of hers, studying the lines of his palm like they might tell her something. "But you don't know what you're wiping away."

"What are you talking about?"

"I have to tell you something."

"Okay."

Anaya shook her head. "I don't even know how it happened, really. It was the day we got into that fight. The day you brought pizza to school. I was upset afterward, and Kyle Davis—

"The guy I met at the community center?"

Anaya nodded. "He convinced me to go out for a drink. He thought I needed to loosen up."

Marcus took his hand away.

Anaya's felt empty and cold. "I don't know what happened, Marcus. I don't drink, but one led to another, and I . . . I blacked out, and the next morning when I woke up, I was in his bed. And then you came over, and I couldn't tell you. I couldn't say it out loud. I didn't know how to make anything right."

She looked up into his eyes then, all the apology in the world in hers as his pupils expanded—black eating away at warm, chocolate brown. He leaned away like she was contagious. "Did you . . ." He blinked, like he was speaking a foreign language he didn't know he knew how to speak. "Did you sleep with him?"

Anaya closed her eyes.

"Did he force you?"

"I don't know."

"You don't know?"

"I don't think so."

And Marcus was up and away.

She stood up too. "Where are you going?"

But he kept walking.

She hurried after him. "I'm so sorry. I was lost. And the alcohol went to my head so fast. I didn't even know what I was doing. I wasn't myself. I wish more than anything I could take it back. Please. Don't go." She reached for his arm. "It was a mistake."

He stopped, jerking away from her touch. He shook his head, his nostrils flaring. "A mistake?"

"A really horrible one."
"Tell your grandmother I'm sorry I couldn't stay."
"Marcus, please."
He held up his hands. "I need to go right now, Anaya."

Sixty-Four

Support 4 Parents of Diabetics Facebook Group:

May 24 at 12:12 p.m.

Camille Gray: Hello, everyone. I guess I should introduce myself. My name is Camille. My oldest was diagnosed with type 1 diabetes one week ago today. According to her A1C test, she's been living with really high blood sugar levels for months. I feel horrible that I didn't notice something was wrong sooner. They released her from the hospital on Friday. They sent us home with a gigantic binder of information. We met with a diabetes educator on Monday. She went back to school on Tuesday. We've had to tweak her Lantus injection at night a couple times. She's had one reading over 200, but there weren't any ketones in her urine. She had a small breakdown the night she came home from the hospital. But since then, she seems to be doing fine. I keep waiting for all of this to sink in. Taylor has always been a big runner. Cross-country and track. She's had college coaches watching her since her freshman year. I'm completely overwhelmed. Meanwhile, she seems steady as a rock.

Mary Crawford: Welcome to the group! And welcome to life with diabetes. Those first few months are the hardest. Hang in there. Everyone feels overwhelmed one week in. Repeat after me: this is not a death sentence. Your daughter is going to be

okay. And before you know it, that binder they sent you home with? You'll be an expert on everything in there.
Likes: 19

Tabitha Rogers: Your daughter sounds like mine. I was a train wreck. Bethany took the whole thing in stride. That's not to say there haven't been hard days. With diabetes, those are inevitable.
Likes: 12
> **Bonnie Kent:** I think you mean with life, those are inevitable. ;-)
> **Mary Crawford:** Everyone reacts differently. My son was okay at first too. But it really got to him later, after the novelty of it all wore off. Keep asking how she's doing. Be a safe space if she's not okay.

Erin Harwood: Have her download the Sugar Sense Diabetes App! Such a lifesaver, especially if she goes away to camp or some sort of overnight. You share an account, so that way, you know what her blood sugar is every time she checks.
Likes: 5
> **Tabitha Rogers:** I second that!
> **Jason Holmes:** I third it!

Sharon Neff: Welcome, Camille! You're not alone! You said Taylor is your oldest. How are your other kiddos doing?
Likes: 3
> **Camille Gray:** They seem to be doing okay. Austin is twelve. He's my investigator, so he checked out a book at the library and learned all about insulin. Paige is eight. She's asked some questions but seems mostly uninterested.

Bonnie Kent: My daughter was diagnosed at 17 too. She just got married last week. It's gonna be okay, Mama!
Likes: 7

Dennis McVay: She can still run. My son is running in college right now on a scholarship. He was diagnosed when he was 11.
Likes: 10

> **Janelle Rodriguez:** My DD (26 yesterday) is a runner too. She just finished her first marathon. Here's what diabetes has taught me: our children are amazing. The best advice I ever got was from her primary care nurse the day after diagnosis. "Follow her lead." So far, it hasn't led me astray.

●●●●●

Color Run Meeting:

Rebecca: Rick thinks she's overreacting. He says it was a typical high school fight and there's no way they're pressing charges.

Rose: Isn't it a little too late to press charges now, anyway?

Rebecca: Not even close. The statute of limitations for assault is two years.

Rose: You're telling me that in two years, if Cody suddenly wanted to press charges, he could?

Rebecca: Yep. I'm not sure anyone would take him very seriously at that point, but he definitely could. Anyway, she's got all these things going on. Cody's graduation party, this mess with Dane's teacher . . .

Deb: Isn't that awful?

Rebecca: If it's true. I guess the sub they hired to replace him doesn't know what he's doing. This morning Kathleen told me she's going to send the boys to Lakemont next year.

Deb: How do they feel about that?

Rebecca: She hasn't told them yet. But I'm sure they won't be very happy when they find out.

Deb: Man, this has been such a rough year for both of them.

Rebecca: Kathleen was really hurt that Camille didn't call her about Taylor.

Rose: I hope she cuts her some slack on that one.

Rebecca: It's not about cutting her slack. She thought it was weird. I mean, Camille called you.

Rose: *I* called *her*. We were talking when she got the phone call from the school nurse. I wanted to make sure everything was okay. She told me what was going on, so I offered to text everyone. I'm sure Camille would have called Kathleen if I hadn't.

Deb: Did Neil really move back in?

Rose: Not technically, but he's been over a lot.

Rebecca: Do you think they're getting back together?

Deb: Wouldn't that be wonderful?

Rose: Yes, it would. We should probably talk about packet pickup this weekend. If everyone waits until Sunday night, it's going to be a zoo at the community center.

Rebecca: Everyone always waits until Sunday night. Oh, I almost forgot. Guess who came to the station yesterday demanding cones for her yard?

Deb and Rose: Juanita Fine.

Sixty-Five

Leah to Jen: We're all packed and ready to go! I cannot wait to hug your neck!

●●●●●

Taylor: Good luck today. Run hard for me.
Shanice: Thx, girl. U know I will.
Taylor: I wish I was there.
Shanice: You will be next year. 1st place all the way.
Taylor: You think so?
Shanice: I know so. C U Monday, right?
Taylor: I don't know.
Shanice: Did someone cut off your legs?
Taylor: I'd probably have to walk the whole thing.
Shanice: Big deal. Then we'll walk. Darius will walk too. C'mon.
There's no way I'm dressing in a tutu unless you are too.

●●●●●

Taylor studied the label on the back of the turkey bacon with the same, small concentrated furrow she wore when she was learning to tie her shoelaces—a task she completed one week to the day before she turned five. Not because she was particularly gifted but because she was fiercely independent.

Her first three-word phrase wasn't "I love you" or even "I did it." It was "I *do* it," quickly followed by another three-word phrase—"all by myself." Austin hardly uttered either of them, and Paige was so prone to fits of frustration when she couldn't figure something out right away that her "I do it" quickly became a hysterical "I can't do it!" Taylor, on the other hand, would sit patiently and try and try, a slight pucker in her forehead, until she figured it out.

Austin didn't learn how to tie his shoes until halfway through first grade and that was only because Camille forced him. She had been convinced something was severely wrong with him, even when Kathleen assured her over and over again that five years old was really quite young to tie shoes—to which Camille would respond, "She was technically four."

And now that once-four-year-old was tackling diabetes with the same focused determination.

As Camille sat at the counter finishing her yogurt parfait, her throat swelled with sudden and unexpected emotion. It was similar to the feeling she got whenever she watched Taylor break away from a pack of runners. And yet, different too, because this came without any sense of pride, as if Camille deserved credit for her daughter's speed. This was wholly removed from Camille altogether.

She was a mother in awe.

Taylor dialed her insulin pen.

Her daughter was supposed to be on a bus, headed for the state track meet right now. Instead, she was giving herself pricks and shots in her kitchen.

"You amaze me, you know that?" Camille said.

Taylor looked up, her pucker smoothing away. It softened with surprise, as though she didn't actually know it at all. As though Camille had just told her—for the first time—that she loved her. As though Camille wasn't the type of mother to say things like that. But of course she was. She was generous with her hugs, even when Taylor didn't want them. She was generous with her "I love yous," even when Taylor rarely said them back.

Taylor knew how much Camille loved her.

But did she know she believed in her?

The question came like a slap.

From the Dora bike to driving a car and every other message in between, Camille's actions and concerns all said the same thing. *You can't do it, Taylor. I don't believe in you, Taylor.* She needed to stop. She needed her children to know that she didn't just love them, she believed in them too. Because she did. Oh my goodness, she did.

"The way you have handled all of this has been nothing short of astounding."

A pink blush blossomed in Taylor's cheeks. She looked away, but not before Camille saw it. It wasn't embarrassment sparkling in her eyes; it was pleasure. She unscrewed the needle from her pen and put it inside the empty coffee canister on the counter. "I want to run on Monday."

"What's that?"

"In the 5K. I was supposed to do it with some friends. I think I still want to."

Camille wanted to laugh. Her diagnosis was only nine days old. They were just getting used to shots and pricks and carb counting. Running in a 5K nine days after being hospitalized for hyperglycemia was . . . well, it was downright irresponsible. It was the training wheels all over again. This was too soon. Taylor was going to fall, and this time she'd need more than five stitches.

"The diabetes educator said that if I'm consistently below two hundred, exercise is good for me. My blood sugar's been below two hundred." Taylor zipped her insulin kit closed. "I'm still a runner, Mom. I don't want this to change that."

Slow down, Taylor. Slow down.

"I want to at least try."

It went against every one of Camille's motherly instincts to nod and say, "I'll give the diabetes educator a call. She'll probably want to talk to you first."

* * *

ReShawn: Finally got my behind to church & you nowhere. SMH. Where you at, girl? And why Marcus look like he fixing to kill someone in the Lord's house?

Anaya: I'm giving him space.

ReShawn: Why does he need space?

Anaya: It's a long story.

ReShawn: I'll come pick you up. You can tell me about it over tacos.

Sixty-Six

The sun shone hot on Camille's back as she lifted another box from the bed of the truck and carried it over to a long foldout table in front of Rick Malone's law office. Fleat Family Auto loaned them four trucks altogether, one for each of the three stations along the route and another for the start and finish line. A team of volunteers had loaded the back of each one with boxes of color-filled bottles.

Kathleen and Camille were supposed to set up the pink station.

So far, there was no sign of Kathleen.

It was just Camille and Neil, Austin, and Paige—who was smeared from head to toe in colored cornstarch, a medal hanging proudly around her neck. She skipped back and forth from the truck to the table with items she could carry, like wet wipes and paper towels and sponsor signs and water guns and the first-aid kit. This morning's kids' run had gone off without a hitch, with blasts of color and excited children making for excellent photo ops that would work perfectly for next year's advertisement.

Paige loved every second of it. She especially loved the fact that her mother and her father had stood next to each other while they cheered her on.

Camille barely had to do anything. Since Taylor's diagnosis, the Crystal Ridge Memorial Day 5K planning committee did such a good job picking up her slack, they made her obsolete. It was the same thing with the year-end carnival at O'Hare. Usually, this time of year Camille spun a thousand plates in the air. It turned out, those plates spun just fine without her.

A screen door slammed shut.

She turned around and saw Juanita Fine marching across her front lawn with a stack of orange cones. She started placing them around the periphery of her yard.

Camille waved, overly cheerful—her typical response when it came to miserable people. They grumbled and frowned. She chirped and beamed. "Hello, Mrs. Fine. How are you doing today?"

"I'll be better once this race is over and my lawn survives."

"I think those cones should do the trick!"

Juanita harrumphed.

Neil grabbed the last box from the back of the truck.

He was wearing a gray T-shirt and khaki cargo shorts, his forearms tan and well defined. It made her think about CrossFit. It made her think about Jasmine Patri. Was she still in her husband's life? And if so, in what capacity? These were the questions she'd wanted to ask at least a hundred times over the past ten days, but every time she opened her mouth to ask one, the words got stuck. Taylor's diabetes had thrown them out onto thin ice together, and as precarious as it was, she wanted to stay there.

"I hope you don't play your music too loud!" Juanita yelled.

"Not any louder than the marching band will be, I assure you," Camille called back, holding up one of two portable speakers, her smile as bright as the sun.

She caught Neil's eye. He was hiding a grin. She could tell by the shy dimple in his left cheek, the one that only made an appearance when he was working really hard to tuck away his amusement. For a brief moment, it distracted her from the heavy feeling she went to sleep with. The heavy feeling she woke up with. Neil found her response to cranky Juanita Fine funny.

It drummed up a euphoria that lingered until Kathleen arrived.

She drove down the road in a golf cart with Bennett in the passenger seat, a large water rifle strapped in front of his chest. She pulled to a stop beside Juanita Fine's cones. The old woman had taken a seat on her rocker and watched them all with beady eyes.

Any other year, Camille and Kathleen would have shared a smile over her scrutiny. This year, Kathleen seemed to be working hard to avoid Camille's eye altogether.

Paige tore off the medal hanging around her neck and shoved it in Bennett's face. "I beat your brother in the race this morning!"

He jerked away.

"Paige," Camille barked.

"What? I did. I beat Dane. He's one year older than me. *And* he's a boy."

Neil cupped Paige's shoulder. "Humility's never been her strong suit."

Kathleen didn't seem offended. "In another year, you'll probably be able to beat Bennett."

Bennett rolled his eyes, then hopped out of the cart and aimed his water rifle at Austin. A stream of pink shot from the gun and almost hit him in the face.

Austin held up his hand and ducked away.

"Sorry we're so late," Kathleen said, setting her purse on the table. "We got cornered by Mr. Ripple. You know how he is when he gets going."

"Good old Mr. Ripple," Neil said before turning to Camille. "I'm gonna run to the house quick with Paige. Check in on Taylor."

The heavy feeling in Camille's gut returned with full force. It was eerily similar to the one she woke up with on September 11 after a horribly prophetic dream.

Neil kept telling her it was going to be okay. Taylor's numbers were fine, and she promised to take it easy. She would have honey packets on her if she started to feel low. She would listen to her body, and if it told her to stop, she would stop.

The thing was, it wasn't in Taylor's nature to stop.

There would be medical personnel on site, but Camille didn't want Taylor to have to use any of them.

Neil and Paige climbed into the truck. Her daughter pulled the seat belt strap in front of her chest. Neil rolled down his window. "You almost forgot this," he said, holding out Camille's purse.

"Oh, right." She stepped forward and took it.

He smiled, his eyes squinty against the sun.

And without realizing what she was doing, Camille leaned in for a quick peck on the lips, an error born from years' and years' worth of habit. It was like the time they moved into their house when Camille was six months pregnant with Paige. She kept turning down Locust when she needed to stay straight on Pine. It was this automatic thing she did, and every time, Taylor would yell from the backseat, "Mo-om, you did it again!"

Right, they no longer lived off Locust.

And Camille no longer kissed her husband.

As soon as it happened, the world stuttered to a halt.

Paige stared.

Austin stared.

Kathleen and Bennett stared.

Camille's cheeks caught on fire. She laughed a little nervously, a little awkwardly. They apologized at the same time. Neil rubbed the back of his neck, and then he drove away.

"So," Kathleen said. "Did Taylor's diabetes cure your marriage?"

Her tone was acidic, like she didn't want their marriage cured. It hurt Camille's feelings. How could she say such an insensitive thing about Taylor's diabetes? "Nothing's cured. We're all adjusting to the diagnosis. It's thrown us for a loop, I guess."

"A good one, by the looks of it."

Camille set her purse beside Kathleen's, her shoulders tense.

The sun passed behind a white cloud and lost some of its intensity.

"I'm sorry. Ignore me," Kathleen said. "I'm in a bad mood."

Camille glanced at Bennett, who was a safe distance away, trying to shoot Austin with the water rifle again. "Are you really sending the boys to Lakemont next year?"

"Yes."

Camille sighed. "Look, Kathleen. I know you're hurt that I didn't call you about Taylor. I'm sorry, but I was a little . . . out of my mind."

"I understand that. I would have been too. But you didn't even call me the next day. Your daughter was in the hospital, Camille, and I had to hear it from Rose. What's going on with us?"

"Nothing's going on with us." And she'd been even more out of her mind the next day. The next day, she nearly shot a man on the side of the road. "I was trying to process everything, and I knew you had a lot going on with Cody. I didn't want to bother you."

"It wouldn't have bothered me, and there *is* a lot going on with Cody. This whole year's been a nightmare. I'm not sure what's been more of a highlight—when my nine-year-old son asked me if his teacher was a rapist—"

"I heard about Kyle Davis. That's awful."

"Or when my eighteen-year-old son was attacked by your daughter's boyfriend."

"Darius isn't her boyfriend." And it wasn't an attack. They got into a fight.

One that was provoked by Cody. But somehow Camille doubted Cody divulged that part of the story to his mother. She wanted to tell Kathleen exactly why Darius broke her son's nose. But some part of her couldn't say the words. Some part of her knew that if she did, everything would change between them. She'd be taking a side, and it wouldn't be Cody's, and they'd never be able to pretend that her son hadn't said such an awful thing. As strained as they were now, Camille wasn't ready for that.

"You're letting her hang out with a boy who broke Cody's nose. You're letting her hang out with a boy who has a record."

"We don't know all the facts, Kathleen."

Kathleen looked at her like she couldn't believe what she was hearing.

Then Bennett hopped inside the golf cart and started driving it in circles.

Juanita Fine stood up from her rocker and glared.

"Get out of there, Bennett!" Kathleen yelled.

"I don't want to run in this stupid race," he yelled back.

"You promised your dad."

"If Cody's not running in it, then why do I have to?"

Kathleen rolled her eyes and let out a frustrated growl. She crossed her arms and looked at Camille. "Look, I care about Taylor, okay? She's had a rough year, and I would hate to see her get hurt."

Sixty-Seven

Starting Line Conversations:

"Wait, is that . . . He's allowed to be here?"
"It's not technically a school event."
"Wow. That takes a lotta nerve."
"Not if he didn't do it."
"Do you think he did?"
"I don't know, but look at his girlfriend. She looks miserable."
"I can't imagine they're going to last."

"There she is."
"Where?"
"Look, buddy, right there. She's waving at us. See her waving?"
"Mommy! Mommy, look! We made you a sign!"

"Oh my goodness, look at Evan's onesie. 'Mommy's favorite running partner'?"
"PJ was saving it from the color this morning. He bought it on Amazon."
"That is adorable."
"They're acting like I'm running a marathon."
"Hey, some days it felt like a marathon."
"We should get one of those little stickers for our rear windshields. Only instead of 26.2 it will say 3.1."
"People will be very impressed."
"I think so."

"Hi, Mrs. Covington!"
"Oh, hey Taylor. You're running today, huh?"
"Just jogging. I promised my mom I wouldn't run."

"I promised myself I wouldn't walk."

"Well, good luck."

"You too. And, uh . . . I like your outfit."

"What in the world is that boy wearing?"

"A tutu."

"Why is he wearing a tutu?"

"He's in high school, Mama. High schoolers think that sort of thing is
  funny."

"It ain't funny. He looks like a fool. And who's that girl he with? Are they
  holding hands?"

"Her name's Taylor."

"I ain't ever hear him talk about no Taylor."

"Happy Memorial Day, Crystal Riiiiiidge! I'm Lonnie from 106.3, but
this isn't lunchtime, folks, it's race time. Who's ready to have some fuuuun? . . .
Come on, you can do better than that. I said, who's ready to have some *fun*? . . .
That's more like it! Just a quick reminder to stay off lawns and private property,
pay attention to the cones, and drink plenty of water. Now let's get those color
packets ready, because we're about to get colorful! Runners take your mark . . .
get set . . ."

BOOM!

●◉●◉●

The gun exploded. Color burst like clouds above the runners.

Camille kept her eyes pinned on Taylor through all that raining cornstarch, her stomach tying into a gigantic knot. She was more nervous today
than at all of Taylor's important running meets combined, and there had been
a lot of them through the years.

"C'mon, Mom. We need to get back to our station," Austin said.

"It's pink!" Edison exclaimed.

The boys fell into a fit of laughter, like Edison's comment was worthy of a
Jimmy Fallon late night routine. They'd spent the last five minutes tossing
color at each other—leftover packets they snagged from unclaimed registration

bags. They were delirious with excitement and frozen lemonade and the anticipation of shooting water guns at people.

Paige, on the other hand, wanted to stay, because the foam machines were
at the starting line and once all the runners cleared away, she and Faith would
get to play in it.

"I'll stay here with Paige," Neil said. "You'd better get these boys to the
pink station."

She nodded.

Neither of them mentioned the kiss from earlier.

It wasn't really a kiss, anyway. Certainly no steamier than the kind of
greeting someone might give their grandmother. And yet, Camille couldn't get
it out of her head. When it came to today, there were a lot of things she couldn't
get out of her head.

Taylor's blood sugar.

The way Darius whispered in her daughter's ear just now, before the gun
went off. The way Taylor leaned closer and laughed at whatever he said.

All the tension between her and Kathleen.

Neil's lips.

"Mom!" Austin called.

He and Edison were already sitting in the back of the golf cart, not-so-
patiently waiting.

She slid behind the wheel and put her purse beside her.

Austin reached for it as she hit the gas. "Can I have some gum?"

Camille's hand clamped on to his like a snake. "I'll get it, Austin." He
knew very well that he was not—under any circumstances—to dig inside her
purse.

Sixty-Eight

The pink station was rocking, and it only got better when the high school marching band showed up—their loud cymbals clashing, their drum line booming, trumpets blasting the Crystal Ridge fight song.

Camille kept her eye out for Taylor. The pink station was at the 3 km mark in the race. Usually, Taylor would have passed by now. Usually, she would be close to finishing. Then she would untie the chip from her shoe, rehydrate herself, and search for something yummy to eat. There was plenty of it to be had, all right there, half a block past the finish line. Ice cream and sherbet pops from Molly's Emporium. Mouthwatering chocolate-chunk cookies from the Pickle Pie Deli. Granola bars and small bags of kettle-cooked chips and juice boxes from Schnucks. Ice-cold lemonade and chicken nuggets from Chick-fil-A. A hot dog and brat stand. And of course, beer. There was always lots of beer. Camille suspected that three-fourths of the runners ran for an excuse to drink it afterward.

So far, though, there was no sign of Taylor—which made her simultaneously relieved, because that meant she wasn't pushing herself, and terrified, because what if she was pushing herself and she collapsed and there was a team of medical personnel frantically working on her right now? Did they know to squirt the honey packet beneath her tongue, where the membranes were the most porous? Of course they did, they were medical professionals.

She told herself to relax and filled more water cups.

"Mom!"

Camille turned around at the sound of the angry call, but it wasn't Austin. It was Bennett. Like the other boys, he wore a pink headband advertising Malone & Strut Law Firm around his forehead. "Those guys are saying I'm going to Lakemont next year."

Kathleen stopped. She'd been removing bottles of color from one of the boxes underneath the table.

A couple of kids with water guns, along with Edison and Austin, stood in a huddle, peeking glances at them. Camille really hoped it wasn't Austin who'd said anything. She knew he heard her talking on the phone with Rose about it. She told him not to say anything. Usually, she could count on him to obey. He wasn't her defiant one.

"We'll discuss that later, Bennett," Kathleen said.

"Mom!" His cheeks turned bright red; his eyes darkened. "Are you sending me to Lakemont?"

"Yes, honey. But now's not the time to talk about this. Later, okay?"

His mouth twisted, and his eyes narrowed. It was the same expression he got whenever he struck out in baseball. The same expression he used to get when he was little and Kathleen made him wear a life vest if he wanted to swim in the pool.

Kathleen shot an accusatory glance at Camille, then carried a handful of bottles to the volunteers.

The knot in Camille's stomach tied tighter as she turned her attention back to the passing runners.

Sixty-Nine

A forty-three-year-old woman with a blond bob attempted to fix a kid's faulty squirt gun.

Her angry friend handed out water cups and pretended not to be angry.

The marching band marched away, taking their boisterous clamoring with them. Volunteers continued to slaughter the passing runners in clouds of pink. There was so much pink. It stained hands, smeared faces. By the time the runners got through the tunnel of volunteers, their skin was completely covered in it.

Neither of the women were paying attention when the boy reached inside the purse. Nobody saw that but a twelve-year-old kid with a hint of acne. It was the same twelve-year-old kid who'd told the boy what was inside the purse at their final baseball game the season before.

The boy's hand closed around cold metal. He shoved the weapon in the waistband of his shorts, his face a mask of fury.

The twelve-year-old met the boy halfway. "What are you doing?"

"I'm not going to Lakemont." His attention narrowed on the twelve-year-old's friend, who was shooting a water gun. "He can go. They all can go. This isn't even their school."

"Put that back, or I'm going to tell my mom."

A group of laughing teenagers approached. Some were jogging. Some were skipping. All were wearing tutus.

One felt good. Great, actually. And it filled her with optimism. An overwhelming determination that she could do this. She wasn't going to lose something she loved.

Another had broad shoulders and muscular arms, the kind that could throw a football like a rocket.

The sight of him turned the boy's cheeks beet red. His chest caved in with hatred. That particular teenager took his brother's spot on the football team.

He stole his brother's girlfriend. He broke his brother's nose. He humiliated him in front of all his friends, and he wasn't going to have to pay for any of it.

It was *his* fault the boy had to go to Lakemont.

For a delicious second, the boy imagined he would make him pay. He was only going to imagine.

It wasn't in him to actually pull the trigger.

But how was the twelve-year-old supposed to know that? Especially when the boy pulled the gun from his waistband and held it up and squinted his eye, as though taking aim.

The twelve-year-old lunged.

The boy jerked the gun away.

The two of them fell to the grass, wrestling.

Seventy

Jen and Leah were less than a block away from Juanita Fine's house when the gun exploded. Two blocks before that, they passed PJ and Nick and the kids with their proud, glittery signs, jumping and cheering as soon as their mothers waved at them from the street.

At first, Jen thought it was a firecracker. A loud firecracker somebody had set off a month prematurely. It was too loud to belong to the marching band receding in the distance beyond the wall of pink haze up ahead. But then it happened again, followed by an unmistakable wave of panic.

It was like somebody flipped the channel, and suddenly you realized that the happy, high-energy sounds that typically accompanied a race had turned sharp and shrill. The noise morphed into hysteria.

Runners began to run in the wrong direction.

"Somebody's shooting a gun," one of them yelled.

People screamed and ducked to the pavement.

Jen's blood ran cold.

Her eyes caught Leah's, their pupils expanding in matched confusion. They turned and ran with everyone else. They ran toward their husbands, toward their children. In some distant part of Jen's mind, she heard a woman screaming. Screaming and screaming and screaming until it got swallowed up in the cacophony.

The farther they ran, the more the panic turned into confusion.

"A shooter?"

"Someone was shot?"

"Where?"

Then Nick was there and PJ too. PJ had scooped Lila into his arms, and baby Evan was wailing, and Noah was clinging to his father's leg, their signs long gone, trampled underfoot somewhere along the side of the road. Leah grabbed Lila, and PJ picked up Noah, and Nick spun in a circle, as though noticing what Jen was noticing at the exact same time.

Where's Jubilee?

"She was just with me," he said, scanning the crowd.

All the confused panic turned into an ice pick that stabbed Jen's heart—jolting it wide and unmistakably awake.

"Jubilee!" she yelled.

Leah and PJ joined.

Jen's panic rose.

She pushed through the crowd, every face the same—smeared with color, wide with fear, because who was shooting and where were they shooting and what was going on?

Sirens sounded in the distance.

Jubilee was nowhere.

"Jubilee!" she yelled again.

She couldn't have gotten far, Jen told herself. She had to be close by. So why wasn't she answering? Where could she have gone? How could Nick have let her go?

"Please help; I can't find my daughter," Jen yelled at nobody, at everybody. She grabbed a man's shoulder. "Have you seen a little girl? A little black girl with beads in her hair?"

"No, sorry."

Jubilee ran when she was scared.

Jubilee's flight response was strong.

They learned that early.

And there were people everywhere. All kinds of people.

"Jubilee!" Jen yelled.

"Jubilee!" Leah yelled beside her.

The scene had turned into a nightmare. Jen pushed through a small group of people huddled close together. What if the shooter was still on the loose? What if Jubilee was kidnapped? If she was scared and the wrong person offered her a hug, she would gladly take it. Indiscriminate affection. Jubilee on the woman's lap at the party. Jubilee clinging to the lady at church. All the times Jubilee had succumbed ran through Jen's mind.

Please help.

She scanned the street with frantic eyes, past a row of cars as the sirens got louder behind her. Loud, scary sirens that would scare any little girl, but especially her little girl. She couldn't bear the thought of her being afraid. She couldn't bear it.

Please help.

Suddenly, Leah's grip tightened.

Because suddenly, there she was.

Her daughter.

Squatting down behind a bench across the street with her hands clamped over her ears.

"Jubilee!" Jen yelled.

Somehow it got through.

Jubilee's hands slid down the sides of her color-streaked face. Her big brown eyes found her mother's through all that confusion. Jen's knees buckled. She dropped to the cement, and she held up her arms, and she watched as Jubilee stood and ran straight into them. Like she had in an airport terminal over a year ago.

Their bodies collided, knocking Jen back. But she didn't fall. She absorbed the impact as Jubilee wrapped her arms around Jen's neck and her legs around Jen's waist.

Jen stood to her feet and pressed her daughter against her, burying her face in Jubilee's neck. This time, the weight of her wasn't new. Jen was familiar with the contours of her body, the sweet, nutty smell of her skin, the coarseness of her hair.

"I'm not gonna let go," Jen whispered into her ear. "You're okay. I'm not gonna let go."

"She's over here," Leah called.

And then Nick was with them too, wrapping his arms around them as the police began clearing everyone away.

●◦●◦◦●◦

Late-breaking news from Channel 6:

> Reporter: I'm here at the Crystal Ridge Memorial Day 5K finish line, not far from where the shooting took place. As you can see by

the people behind me, this has been a most shocking event. Police officers have assured us that the situation is under control. So far, the identity of the shooter isn't being released, and it doesn't look like any arrests have been made. Again, one person was shot and rushed to the hospital. We don't know yet in what kind of condition, but we hope to be informed of that soon. Our thoughts and prayers go out to the family. Please stay tuned for more.

Seventy-One

His blood was on her hands. No matter how frantically she scrubbed, it wouldn't come off. It was a permanent stain.

Just like the memory . . .

Her eyes trained on Taylor, healthy and smiling, jogging beside Darius, both in those silly tutus. The flood of relief that came at the sight of her. And then the blast of noise, so loud Camille jumped.

There was a moment of startled confusion. And then another sharp, deafening crack.

That's when the realization hit, and then the panic.

A gun.

Someone was shooting a gun.

Runners screamed. Volunteers scattered. The table upended. Self preservation kicked in. But not for Camille. Not for Kathleen. It wasn't themselves they wanted to protect.

Their eyes met in a shared moment of pure, unadulterated terror.

Taylor. Austin. Bennett.

Where were Taylor and Austin and Bennett?

Camille searched the scrambling crowd through a cloud of hazy pink. She'd lost sight of Taylor. She couldn't see Taylor. She turned toward the kids with water guns. Edison had hit the ground. He'd thrown his hands over his head. But Austin wasn't beside him.

Where was Austin?

Then she saw them, tangled up on the edge of the grass, a familiar gun on the curb. Blood everywhere.

No. No, no, no.

No, no, no, no!

Kathleen must have seen them at the same time, because she sprinted with her. Whose blood was it? Who was bleeding? One of the boys pushed himself up. But it wasn't her son.

It was Bennett—pale, small, shaking Bennett.

Camille dropped to her knees.

Blood was everywhere.

So much blood.

Her son's blood.

"Somebody help!" she screamed. "Somebody call 911!"

And then she just screamed. She cradled her son's head in her lap, and she tried to stop the blood, and she screamed and she screamed and she screamed.

"Camille?"

She turned around.

Neil was leaning inside the hospital ladies' room.

"I can't get it off," she said. "It won't come off."

And she couldn't breathe.

Her knees buckled just as Neil reached her.

○●●●

Tamir Rice was twelve like Austin. He had the audacity to play with a pellet gun at a park, similar to the water guns the boys at the pink station were excited to play with. The police arrived and two seconds later one of the officers shot his gun.

Two seconds.

For the next four minutes, that twelve-year-old boy lay on the snow-covered ground while the man who shot him—a man who was supposed to protect him—did nothing. Tamir died the next day in a hospital like this one.

A twelve-year-old kid, gone from the world.

A twelve-year-old kid like Austin.

Anaya couldn't wrap her mind around it as she sat in that hospital waiting room, filled with guilty relief because Darius was safe beside her. Anaya and Mama had been standing at the finish line when it happened. They'd been waiting to cheer for Darius and some of Anaya's runners.

They didn't hear the gunshots from where they were, not with the high school marching band between them and those two blasts.

But the panic spread like ripples in a pond.

Someone's shooting a gun!

Somebody's been shot!

For eight agonizing minutes, Anaya and her mother had no idea if that somebody was Darius. When they finally found him, he was sitting on the curb in his ridiculous tutu, covered in color. The ambulance had already pulled away. The police were trying to clear everybody out, including a couple of reporters. Darius was in a state of shock.

"Taylor's brother," he finally said. "Taylor's little brother was shot."

Anaya drove Mama home so she could reassure Granny, since the news was already getting out, and then she and Darius sped to the hospital while their phones blew up with text messages.

Now she was here, in the waiting room. Darius to her left. Taylor to his left. She didn't care that they were holding hands. She was too relieved that he was next to her, whole and healthy, able to hold anyone's hand at all.

The sliding doors whooshed open.

Marcus walked in, his eyes wide as they locked onto Anaya's.

She stood.

They hadn't spoken since she told him the truth about Kyle Davis. And now here he was, looking as wrecked as he looked the morning after the second anniversary of her father's death, when he knocked on her front door and apologized.

He came toward her and wrapped her in a hug, burying his face in her neck. "I'm so glad you're okay."

●●●●●

Camille clutched Neil's hand as they sat in the crowded waiting room. Taylor and Darius. Anaya and Marcus—the young man who came to the community center to help fill bottles. Shanice and Alexis. Edison and his mother, Tamika, who kept squeezing Camille's shoulders like Liz, the big-boned nurse who kept Camille grounded when it was Taylor in a hospital bed. Rose and Joe and their daughter, Rebecca and Patrick, and several people from church. Deb was at home with Paige, but her husband was there. Jen Covington too. She came shortly after Marcus. She came with her husband, Nick, and she looked fit. It was an odd thing for Camille to notice. But she did.

They all made for an interesting sight, with half of them covered in colored cornstarch and a few dressed in tutus.

Camille clutched Neil's hand like a life raft, staring hard at his thumbnail. The lunula on his thumbnail—that white half circle she noticed when he was a nervous TA and she was a homesick freshman and they never ever would have guessed that one day they'd be here.

She looked down the line of chairs.

Taylor's hand in Darius's hand.

Anaya's hand in Marcus's hand.

Edison's hand in Tamika's hand.

All of them with lunula too.

A doctor walked out into the waiting room.

Camille and Neil stood at the same time. They joined the man in the white coat right in front of the hallway, Camille's heart in her throat.

Taylor was standing, but she didn't join them. She stood there like a frozen doe after the cock of a rifle.

"Your son came out of surgery just fine."

Neil grabbed Camille's elbow.

"We were able to stop the bleeding. The bullet got his gall bladder, so we went ahead and removed it. I'm not sure how, but every other major organ is intact. He's in stable condition, and you'll be able to see him soon."

Camille's entire body convulsed.

A sob tore up her throat.

She turned and looked at Taylor. Her face crumpled. She cupped her mouth and nodded as Taylor hurried over.

"He's okay. He's going to be okay."

The three of them fell into a hug.

Neil's shoulders shook. They chugged like the engine of a freight train as he held up his wife and his daughter.

Seventy-Two

Two thin purple veins intersected on Austin's left eyelid. Camille studied them, watching him like she had when he was a baby. She had a hard time leaving his bedside, even now when he was out of rocky waters. Tomorrow or the next day he would be ready to come home. They would have a lot to bring with them—cards and flowers and picture after picture from his little sister, Paige, who thankfully had been spared the whole traumatic ordeal.

She was playing with Faith in the colored foam when it happened. Later, Camille learned that Neil got the two girls out of there immediately, as soon as he heard about a shooter. Then he spent the next twenty minutes calling Camille and Taylor and Austin, over and over again, losing his mind—until Taylor called him and told him the kind of news no father ever wanted to hear.

Paige didn't find out what happened to Austin until after he came out of surgery. By then, the scariness had taken on an air of intrigue. Camille's beautiful, eight-year-old girl had been spared nightmares. But not Taylor. And not Camille. For the rest of their lives, they would be able to conjure the image with astounding clarity at the drop of a hat—Austin, lying in the grass, covered in blood. Another one of those snapshot photographs.

But praise the Lord, it wasn't the last image they would have of him. Praise the Lord, for He had spared her son.

"Knock, knock," someone said.

It was Anaya Jones. She stood hesitantly in the doorway of Austin's hospital room, holding a collection of brightly colored balloons and a black teddy bear with a sign that said Get Well Soon.

Camille joined her out in the hall.

"I wanted to come earlier, but I kept getting sidetracked with all the end-of-the-year craziness."

Camille cupped her forehead. The end of the school year. Over the past few days, she'd lost track of time completely. It could be Christmas and she'd be none the wiser. "I didn't get you anything."

"What?"

"For the end of the school year. Paige didn't get you anything."

Anaya waved her hand. "You have much more important things to worry about right now."

Still. She would have liked to get her something.

Camille motioned toward the bench by the wall. "Do you want to sit?"

"Sure. I have a minute." She set the balloons and the teddy bear on the shiny, white linoleum and the two women sat shoulder to shoulder as a nurse walked down the hallway. She smiled at them as she passed.

"I met your mother in the cafeteria the other day," Camille said.

"Oh."

"She's lovely. You look a lot like her."

"My dad used to say I was her little twin."

Used to say.

She wondered why he stopped.

She wondered if he was dead.

She wondered if she should tell Anaya what she knew.

Bennett was aiming for Darius.

He told Kathleen later that he wasn't going to shoot anyone. He was overcome with anger because he had to go to Lakemont in the fall. So he took the gun Camille had purchased to protect herself and her children from a burglar. The one her neighbors assumed was Darius.

But it wasn't a burglar who hurt Austin. It wasn't a transfer student from South Fork. It was her best friend's son—with Camille's own weapon.

She shuddered every time she thought about it, how close she came to losing him.

Bennett wasn't arrested.

He was a twelve-year-old kid with an anger problem. A twelve-year-old kid who made a really impulsive, foolish choice in the midst of that anger. Camille couldn't help but wonder if Bennett would have received the same amount of grace had he looked more like the boy he was aiming at.

The thought taunted her. And yet she couldn't escape it.

As much as she wished it weren't true, as much as she wished she had the confidence to say the same thing she said in the town meeting back in July— *this has nothing to do with skin color!*—she just wasn't sure anymore. How could she be, with all those photographs from this past year in her head? Darius on her front lawn, with his arms raised, when Cody had wandered around her front yard plenty of times without ever having the cops called on him. Chris, the nice man who changed her tire, with his hands up in the rain. The fear she felt the second she saw him walking toward her and what that fear almost drove her to do.

It's about trash, Leif Royce had yelled.

God forgive her, Camille had been annoyed. Not because his words might have wounded real, live people in that gymnasium. But because his words reflected poorly on her. She didn't give the people a second thought.

Paige, I don't care about skin color. It's what's in a person's heart that matters.

Maybe that ought to be true, but was it how the world worked?

But Mommy, all of them have brown skin.

Camille closed her eyes against an onslaught of emotion. Another blinding flash of vulnerability—naked and needy, with no clue which way was up anymore—and an overwhelming desire to beg for forgiveness. It was the same urge she had with Jen Covington in her office, and the same urge she kept experiencing at random moments with Neil.

Only this time, she didn't resist it.

Camille grabbed Anaya's hand.

Anaya's eyes went wide, slightly alarmed.

"I'm so sorry," Camille said. "I'm sorry for everything."

It wasn't enough—not even close—but maybe it was a good place to start.

Seventy-Three

The house felt large and foreign as she stepped inside, her arms laden with too much stuff. Over the past week, she'd been sleeping on a cot in Austin's hospital room. Neil stayed at home with Taylor and Paige. This afternoon, Austin was being discharged.

They wanted to set up a temporary room in the small office off the foyer so he wouldn't have to climb the staircase right away. So Neil rolled the trundle from the laundry room while Camille walked upstairs to deposit all the cards and the plants and the balloons.

Austin especially liked the plants.

She set them on his windowsill in the sunlight, where he kept a small collection of geodes. One was a gift from Kathleen, something she saw at a gift shop when she and Rick went to Branson last spring.

Rose called earlier today.

Bennett had started mandatory counseling, and the Malones put their house up for sale. They were moving to Minnesota to be closer to Rick's family. They were hoping it could happen as quickly as possible.

"Rebecca said Kathleen wants to call you," Rose had said. "But she isn't sure what to say."

Camille didn't know how to respond to that. In truth, there was nothing Kathleen could say. In truth, it seemed it might be best for the Malones to move, and their families to move on.

It was strange, after all they'd been through together. Baseball and swimming lessons and camping trips and beach vacations and Bible study and, of course, every single one of the Crystal Ridge Memorial Day 5Ks. They'd been friends since Cody and Taylor were in kindergarten and first grade. They potty-trained Bennett and Austin together. For years, the screen saver on Camille's laptop had been a picture of both boys standing side by side in Kathleen's backyard, their bare butts exposed for all the world to see as they peed in the green grass. Taylor and Cody were in the picture too, and they were laughing hysterically. Kathleen and Camille used to dream that one day, those laughing children would get married. They never ever imagined that one day, the little boy on the left would shoot the little boy on the right.

Kathleen and Camille had been friends—best friends. The Malone family wasn't a threat. Those transfer students were the threat, and together, they worked hard to keep them out.

Now that friendship had hurt her son—almost killed her son—and nobody was certain if the transfer students would be able to return to Crystal Ridge in the fall. Camille would fight, only this time, she was going to fight to make sure they could stay. This time, Austin's best friend was a transfer student, and Taylor's . . . well, Camille wasn't sure what Darius was to Taylor. But whatever he was, he was helping her get through a really rough month. It turned out, her family benefited from something she had diametrically opposed, from something she had absolutely feared.

Camille bundled up Austin's bedding and carried it downstairs. She finished making his bed, and she and Neil stepped out into the foyer.

"Do you have everything you need?" he asked.

"I think so."

He snapped his fingers, one after the other, and clapped his palm over his fist. "I'd be happy to drive Taylor to her appointment with the diabetes educator tomorrow morning. It's pretty early, isn't it?"

"Don't you have CrossFit?"

He blushed. "I haven't gone to CrossFit in a while."

"Oh. Well, you still look like you're in shape."

"I've been jogging again. Doing some lifting at the apartment."

Not *home.*

Not even *his apartment.*

Just *the apartment.*

"Do you think we should throw a party?" Camille asked.

"A party?"

"For Austin. It seems like he deserves a party. I'm sure your mom would love to come."

"She's always up for a good excuse to get out of the retirement center."

"How's she doing?"

"Oh, you know."

Another wave hit—that vulnerable, broken wave that shanghaied all her anger and struck her with an acute desire to apologize. For yelling at him when Taylor was five and fell off her Dora bike. For dismissing him so decidedly when he said he wasn't happy at his job. For all the ways she made him feel insignificant and not needed. "I'm sorry that I wasn't there for her that day."

"What day?"

"The closing."

His cheeks turned red again. He shook his head and looked down at his shoes. "You don't have to apologize for that. I was going through . . . I don't know what I was going through."

A midlife crisis, she wanted to say.

For a while she'd suspected a brain tumor.

Instead she said, "It's been a crazy year, hasn't it?"

He laughed a soft sort of laugh and rubbed the back of his neck. "Maybe a little."

It had been a season of upheaval. Painful. Like breaking a bone. But sometimes bones had to be broken for the purpose of resetting them. Sometimes they had to be broken so they could heal the right way. "It's going to be a hard summer . . . with Austin's physical therapy and Taylor dead-set on training."

"Yeah."

"I think they're going to need their dad."

"I'm available, Camille. Any time. Just say the word."

"I mean they're going to need their dad here, at the house."

He looked at her expectantly, hopefully, as if all this time he'd just been waiting for her invitation.

There would have to be counseling. Neil would still sleep in the guest room. But maybe this was their chance to start healing. "I need him too."

"Really?"

Camille nodded. "Really."

Seventy-Four

Anaya and Marcus held hands as they strolled up the pathway that cut across an all-too-familiar lawn. They held hands like two people taking their first tentative steps into a relationship—one that was fragile and new but you desperately wanted to work.

Darius walked ahead of them.

Yesterday she finished packing up her classroom. The two bulletin boards were bare. The desks were empty and pushed off to the side so José could clean the carpet. She had disassembled the time machine, packed all the books, bins, and knickknacks, and tucked them away into cabinets. Her Funko Pop figures were back on the dresser in her bedroom. To anyone who passed by, it would be like the last year didn't happen.

But to Anaya, the walls spoke. They brimmed with memories of Nia and Dante and Zeke and Sarah and Jubilee and Aaishi and Gavin and Paige and all the other bright, shining faces she saw every morning for one-hundred-eighty days—students from two very different worlds, brought together in this fancy district she never wanted to teach in.

Be the change where you're at.

Anaya hoped she had been.

Taylor opened the front door, her smile bright as Darius came forward and wrapped her in a bear hug. The two of them had gotten close. Going through what they had tended to do that to people. Anaya worried it was too close, too fast, and too intense for a couple of seventeen-year-old kids, but Darius had told her to mind her own business, and Mama had invited Taylor over for dinner tomorrow night.

That ought to be interesting.

Taylor said hello to Anaya and Marcus and held the door open, inviting them inside the large foyer. "The party's out back."

Anaya took a deep breath.

They were only going to stay for thirty minutes. Forty-five, tops.

"It's not winning," Taylor said.

Anaya turned around. "What's that?"

"Don't get me wrong. Winning is fun. But it's not why I run." Taylor shrugged, her long blond hair swept over her shoulder. "Thanks for helping me see that."

●❀●❀●

Jen experienced a major bout of déjà vu as Jubilee walked in front of her, down the wooden stairs to the patio below. It turned out that when Jen and Nick were frantically searching the crowd for their missing daughter, Camille Gray was kneeling in the grass with her son's head in her lap while he bled all over. She was the one who had screamed and screamed.

When Jen found out that the victim was a sibling of Taylor's, Leah and PJ took Jubilee and their children to Nick and Jen's house, and Nick and Jen went to the hospital. Now Taylor's brother was home, and they were all invited to celebrate.

Camille and a tall, trim man greeted them as they came down the final step.

"I'm so glad you came," Camille said.

The man reached out and shook Jen's hand. Nick's too. "You're Mrs. Covington, right?"

Jen nodded. "You can call me Jen."

"I'm Neil. Thanks for all your help with Taylor. She speaks very highly of you."

"Well, she makes my job easy. She's a great kid."

"We think so." Neil slid his arm around Camille's waist. It would seem that their separation had ended. They made a handsome couple. In fact, they reminded Jen of Ken and Barbie from Osaka on Jubilee's Family Day celebration, when Jen had felt dull and a little dead and prayed that God would wake her up.

When the gun went off and Jubilee went missing, God certainly had. For a few moments, she had been every inch a normal mother, a frantic parent who lost sight of her child and was desperate to find her. It was good to know—a relief to know—that at the end of the day, she wanted Jubilee in her arms.

"I'm glad Austin is doing so well," Jen said.

"We have a lot of physical therapy ahead of us, but the doctors are saying he should make a full and complete recovery."

Jen's eyes got a little glossy. "It could have been so much worse."

Jubilee tugged on the hem of Jen's shirt. "Mama?"

"Yes, sweetheart?"

"I wanna jump in da bounce house."

"You can go."

"I want you to jump with me."

It was a request she made before, in a scene eerily similar to this one—with the large, landscaped backyard and tables full of food. Only this time, Nick was with her and there weren't any presents or a bunch of girls running around with American Girl dolls, and it wasn't just Taylor manning the bounce house but Taylor and Darius Jones, and instead of Paige being the center of attention, it was Austin—a tall, lanky boy sitting in a chair in the shade, playing chess with a shorter, equally lanky boy with skin like Jubilee's.

Back then, Jen had been too concerned about how she might look in front of all the fancy mothers to say yes. So she watched through black mesh windows as her daughter jumped.

In the span of time they waited to bring Jubilee home, Jen and Nick went to an Empowered to Connect conference. They learned all about the fundamentals of attachment and the impact of a child's history and the role fear played in behavior and the importance of meeting sensory processing needs and establishing healthy neurological pathways. That last one was done largely by something called the do-over.

Let's try that again.

What's another way to say that?

How can we do that differently?

As Jen looked down at Jubilee, she felt like she was being given one now. A giant do-over, as though they could travel back in time and establish a different way. A new route. Where she wasn't a spectator of her daughter's joy, but a participant.

She took Jubilee's hand, and together they walked to the bounce house.

Taylor smiled at Jen, and Darius slapped Jubilee a five as they slipped off their shoes and climbed inside. It was hot and kind of loud, and Jen stood there a little awkwardly as Jubilee began to jump.

"Come on, Mama! Like 'dis!"

Jen watched her daughter—beaming from ear to ear with a crooked-toothed smile—jumping like a pogo stick, and her heart went warm and soft in her chest as she slowly began to bounce.

"Does it hurt?" asked the Rabbit.

"Sometimes," said the Skin Horse, for he was always truthful. "When you are Real you don't mind being hurt."

For some people, attachment came right away. But for Jen, it hadn't. For Jen, it would come like this. In a journey filled with jumps and bumps, fits and starts. Maybe someday that journey wouldn't feel so jolting. Maybe someday being Jubilee's mother would be as natural as breathing.

"Higher!" Jubilee sang, lifting her arms above her head as her beads clacked together. Lifting her arms above her head like she had in the backyard, when she'd told Jen and Nick about the man who sang to her in the night when the doors went shut. "Higher and higher!"

Maybe someday.

But until then, they had this moment, right here.

Jubilee grabbed Jen's hands, and they jumped higher and higher, until their smiles turned into giggles, and then Jen slipped and they fell and Jubilee laughed from deep in her belly. And Jen was laughing too.

Oh, she was laughing.

So hard and free, tears tumbled past her temples, into her hair.

She and Jubilee? They were *becoming,* like the velveteen rabbit, and along the way, her hair would be loved off and her eyes would drop out and she would get loose in the joints and very shabby. But it wouldn't matter. Not one piece of their journey—not one bump or bruise or struggle—would be ugly. Because all of it made them Real, and when you were Real, you couldn't be ugly, except to the people who didn't understand.

Jubilee rolled over on top of her and stopped suddenly with a soft gasp. "Mama, are you sad?"

Jen wiped at the tears and pulled Jubilee close—so thankful, so filled-to-the-brim thankful, because in that moment, she wasn't sad at all. In that moment, she was something else altogether.

"Not all tears are the sad kind," she said, and then she whispered into Jubilee's ear something that was wonderfully true. "I'm so glad I get to be your mama."

●●●●●

Anaya double knotted the laces on her shoes and peered down the length of the track. It had been two years since her injury. Two years since she laced up these particular shoes.

There had been a lot of dust.

She stood and shook out each leg, one at a time. She tested her ankle. It didn't throb or smart or ache. It felt just fine.

She spread her feet and stretched to the left.

This time next year, Darius would be a high school graduate getting ready for college. Hopefully, South Fork Cooperative would have its accreditation. They learned today that until then, her brother would be able to finish his high school career in Crystal Ridge. She also learned today that Kyle Davis would no longer be teaching third grade at Lewis and Clark Elementary. He would now be working at the Crystal Ridge administration building.

The man had gotten a pay raise.

Anaya stretched to the right.

Next year, she would continue to drive Darius to school each morning. She would teach at O'Hare and coach track in the spring. Mama would finish her night classes and hopefully find a supervisory position in food management. They'd pay off more of their debt, and maybe the year after, Anaya could work in the district her daddy had taught in for so many faithful years.

You run like you got wings on your back, Anaya. You run like you're free.

At some point, those wings got clipped.

Or maybe, like her heart, they had bunched into an angry fist, refusing to unfurl, lest the pain be too severe.

She shook out her hands, bounced on her toes, found the inside lane, and began to jog around the track. Slow at first. Hesitant, almost—like a person doing something they shouldn't be doing.

Marcus had forgiven her.

Maybe it was time to forgive herself.

Maybe it was time to forgive *them.*

She lengthened her stride and imagined herself releasing the death grip she had on a hook that didn't belong to her. Camille Gray and Leif Royce and every angry parent at that awful town meeting last July. Jan McCormick. The liquor store owner next to Auntie Trill. Kyle Davis and his roommate.

Forgiveness isn't pardon for them. It's freedom for you.

And she was more than the sum of one bad decision.

She ran faster, the wings on her back unfurling, stretching wide behind her, the shackles that had bound them falling away. She rounded the bend, picking up speed. She could see him, right there at the fence. Her daddy, smiling proudly, clapping his large hands in that staccato beat.

"Anaya, Anaya, Anaya," he said. "It's your birthright, baby. I want you to live it."

It was his final gift to her, and she would.

She would live free, even when it felt impossible. She would make the hard choice every single day to keep her heart soft. She would make the hard choice to forgive even when forgiveness wasn't asked. She would be the change where she was at. She would keep running this race called life, even when it broke.

Especially when it broke.

The ground raced past her in a blur.

She would live it for him, and she would live it for herself, and she would live it for every girl like her. The ones who came before and made the wings on her back possible. The ones who would come after and were counting on her to keep running.

One day she would fly free. Completely free, just like her name.

Until then she would run.

Author's Note

In the summer of 2016, when Alton Sterling and Philando Castile became hashtags, I came across an episode on *This American Life* called "The Problem We All Live With." It was about segregation in modern American education. In the episode, investigative reporter Nikole Hannah-Jones shared an integration story that happened in the Saint Louis area in 2013.

Normandy and Riverview Gardens, two school districts composed almost entirely of black and brown students, lost their accreditation. Both districts were severely underresourced and understaffed and had a high concentration of students from poverty. The loss of accreditation triggered a Missouri transfer law that gave any student at a failing district the option of transferring elsewhere. The failing school was not only responsible for transfer tuition; they had to provide transportation as well. Normandy chose to bus students to Francis Howell, a mostly white, affluent district in a neighboring county.

The pushback and resistance as told in the episode of *This American Life* was disturbing.

I listened to snippets of the town meeting in Francis Howell's high school gymnasium with my heart in my throat and my stomach churning. Despite everything I'd been learning about racism in America, I still couldn't believe that the sound bites were from 2013.

Every time I opened my laptop to work on the novel I was supposed to be writing, my mind would wander to those sound bites. I couldn't stop imagining what it must've been like to be a Normandy parent or a Normandy student sitting in that gymnasium.

It reminded me of a book assigned by one of my professors when I was an education major at the University of Wisconsin, Madison: *Savage Inequalities* by Jonathan Kozol. Schools like Normandy and Riverview Gardens and others included in that book don't happen in a vacuum. They are a product of our past, a history riddled with injustice, and real children attend them. The racial disparity in our country's education system is alarming, and I couldn't get any of it out of my head.

So I went out on a limb and sent an email to my editor, explaining the episode I'd listened to and the idea forming in my mind. Was there any way I might be able to write this story instead? Lo and behold, my editor said yes, and I dove in.

I read every obscure article written about the Normandy transfer situation. I found a timeline of events. I pulled up radio-show archives. I listened to a recording of the town meeting in its entirety. I looked for ways to incorporate fact into fiction and quickly learned that like most things in life, the situation was complicated with differing opinions on all sides.

It turned out to be the most challenging novel I've ever written.

I'm aware that I have stepped into a sensitive space. I'm a white girl. I have a black daughter; even so, I'll never truly understand what it's like to be black in America. I'm aware that there are a plethora of black authors out there writing stories that absolutely need to be read. But the Lord has pressed a hot iron against my heart. He has shown me an injustice that I can never unsee, and as I wrestle with what to actually *do*—there has been a common refrain I hear from many in the black community: "If you want to do something to fight racial injustice, talk to your people about it."

You, dear reader, are my people. And story is a powerful medium. It speaks to hearts in ways facts and articles cannot. Through it, we get to live someone else's experience. We get to put on someone else's skin and walk a mile in their shoes, which makes it the best possible breeding ground for empathy.

That is my hope for this story. When you close this book and the characters and the plot fade away, I pray that empathy would remain. That empathy would grow. That conversations would be had. And maybe, the hot iron pressing against my heart might press against yours too. Maybe you will go and talk to your people and maybe they will go and talk to their people. And somehow something as big and systemic and as seemingly unmovable as this might actually start to change.

If you're unsure where to start, here are some excellent resources to help you on your way:

- *Pass the Mic,* the official podcast for the Witness, a Black Christian Collective, cohosted by Tyler Burns and Jemar Tisby. Seriously. Subscribe. And then listen to every single episode.
- *Just Mercy* by Bryan Stevenson. If you want to better understand the systemic nature of racism in our criminal justice system, this book will blow your eyes wide open. Also, Bryan Stevenson is the founder and executive director of EJI (Equal Justice Initiative). The website alone is a wealth of information.
- *Why Are All the Black Kids Sitting Together in the Cafeteria?* by Beverly Daniel Tatum
- *Divided by Faith* by Michael O. Emerson and Christian Smith
- *13th,* a documentary on Netflix that explores the intersection of race, justice, and mass incarceration in the United States

He has told you, O man, what is good;
and what does the LORD require of you
but to do justice, and to love kindness,
and to walk humbly with your God?

—MICAH 6:8

Readers Guide

1. This novel opens with a quote by Claudia Rankine from her book *Citizen: An American Lyric.* "The world is wrong. You can't put the past behind you. It's buried in you; it's turned your flesh into its own cupboard." Do you think this quote is true? Why or why not? In what ways does the quote apply to this story? In what ways does this quote apply to our country?

2. From captivity to freedom, from ignorance to awareness, from counterfeit to real. Those are just some of the journeys that happen in this novel. What other journeys did the characters go on? Which journey impacted you the most and why? Who did you relate to the most? Are the two the same?

3. The title of this book is first used by Camille during the town meeting. Later, we see it again, only this time it's from Anaya's point of view. What did Anaya think and how did she feel about Camille's complaints from the town meeting? Can you think of how the title might apply to Jen or Jubilee?

4. While reading a memoir called *The Grace of Silence* by Michele Norris, I came across an analogy, wherein racial trauma was compared to a repeated scratch on the back of a person's hand. One scratch was tolerable. But the accumulation of scratches caused the trauma. When I read it, I immediately thought of the term *microaggression*. According to *Merriam-Webster*, a *microaggression* is "a comment or action that subtly and often unconsciously or unintentionally expresses a prejudiced attitude toward a member of a marginalized group (such as a racial minority)." What are some of the microaggressions Anaya experiences throughout the story? Did these "scratches" surprise you, or could you relate to them?

5. What were Anaya's father's final words to her? How did they take on new meaning for Anaya as the story progressed? What do you think

it means to be completely free? What did Anaya's mother have to say about freedom?

6. There is a scene where Anaya is remembering the death of twelve-year-old Tamir Rice. What did her college roommate have to say about Tamir's death? Why was that hurtful to Anaya? Do you agree with the observation Anaya's grandmother made about it? What's your reaction when a black person turns into a hashtag? Why do you think this is your reaction?

7. Adoption plays a role in this story, particularly transracial adoption. While Jen and Jubilee's story certainly isn't everyone's adoption story, the first year home is almost always a very difficult and often isolating one. What insights—if any—did Jen and Jubilee's relationship give you into adoption?

8. What does Jen's brother, Brandon, represent in the story? Why do you think Jen's mother doesn't like to talk about Brandon? Is pointing to or talking about a problem the same as creating the problem? Why do you think racism is a topic so many would rather avoid?

9. There is a scene before Christmas when Camille is sitting in church, wondering how Neil could still bring the kids to church. She doesn't understand how he can sit there and not feel the weight of his sin. Later, after Taylor is diagnosed with diabetes, Neil and Camille are sitting in the kitchen together in the middle of the night and Neil mentions his faith. Camille wrestles with the same question all over again, only this time her perspective has changed. How so? What do you think about her observation?

10. Kyle Davis sexually harasses his student teacher, Ellie Sorrenson. What happens to her after she comes out and publicly announces what Kyle did? What happens to Kyle? Can you think of other instances in our culture when the victim is turned into a villain?

11. As I wrote this story, I was very aware of the "white savior" trope, wherein a white person "rescues" people of color. It's prevalent in both literature and film. Can you think of examples of books or movies that utilize this trope? Why is this trope problematic? Is anyone "rescued" in *No One Ever Asked*?

12. Extra credit: Listen to the podcast episode that inspired the novel. *This American Life: The Problem We All Live With*. Follow investigative reporter, Nikole Hannah-Jones on Twitter (@nhannahjones). She covers race in America—more specifically segregation in modern-day American education. Find a time line on the history of segregation in our country's education system. Was this a problem you were aware of before reading *No One Ever Asked*? Discuss Nikole's work, as well as the podcast.

Acknowledgments

This book holds a very special place in my heart, and I am so grateful to everyone who had a hand in making it happen.

Thank you, Terri Haynes, Charlene Guzman, Bonnie Calhoun, and Jamie Lapeyrolerie for your time and your feedback. This book tackles a whole lot of sensitive issues, race being one of them. I am forever grateful for your input.

Thank you to all the people who helped me with the various aspects of this novel I knew little to nothing about.

Yolanda Waters, for answering my salon questions. Paige Chinn and Debbie Whitten, my go-to gals for all things nursing and diabetes. Leigh Bowman and Kathy Ruggerberg, for your expertise in school administration, especially as it related to that dastardly Kyle. Kristi McFate and Julie Martin, for helping me understand the ins and outs of a color run. Jen and Jay Montgomery, for answering my clueless gun questions. Courtney Walsh and Laura Glynn Weaver, who know all about track and cross-country. And of course, my fellow adoptive mamas on Facebook, many of whom have adopted older kiddos like Jubilee. Y'all helped me bring authenticity to Jen's story. Thank you for being Real.

Thank you to everyone who kept me functional as I wrote.

Paul and Lisa Glynn, for opening your home so I could work uninterrupted. Mary Weber, for not just being a friend as I grappled with fear and doubt but for being a sounding board too. Your heart is gold, and I love our deep conversations. Betsy Haddox (it's so fun to write *Haddox*!), for encouraging me when this book was just a bean of an idea. The Inkettes, for some wonderful brainstorming in Washington, DC. Becky Wade and Courtney Walsh. Oh girls, how do I count the ways? And how in the world did I survive as a writer—as a person—before our three-way conversation on Voxer began? Melissa Gilroy, as always, for your unwavering support. And my husband, Ryan Ganshert. I couldn't do any of this apart from you.

Thank you to everyone on my team.

Rachelle Gardner, my fabulous agent, for believing in this story. My brilliant editor, Shannon Marchese, for not just saying yes when I came to you with an idea that wasn't part of the contract but for championing this project. You let me follow my heart. You let me write what the Lord was pressing there, and I am so grateful. Cover designer, Mark Ford. Boy, did you earn your keep on this one! I'm not sure how many versions we went through, but I'm sure thrilled with where we landed. Hopefully the process didn't give you too many gray hairs. Lissa Halls Johnson, for your attention to detail and putting up with my angst. (Why does it always come during line edits?) My production editor, Laura Wright. Jamie Lapeyrolerie and Chelsea Woodward and everyone else at WaterBrook and Penguin Random House, for getting this into the hands of readers.

A special thank you to Jemar Tisby and Tyler Burns from *Pass the Mic,* for the tireless work you do in opening eyes like mine. I pray that God would bless you and keep you and make His face shine upon you as you continue onward.

And of course, thank you, Reader. Without you, this would be nothing but a bunch of words on a page. Thank you for picking it up. Thank you for bringing this story to life.

About the Author

KATIE GANSHERT is the author of eight novels and several works of short fiction. She has won both the Christy and Carol Awards for her writing and was awarded the RT Reviews Reviewers Choice for her novel, *The Art of Losing Yourself*. Katie makes her home in eastern Iowa with her family.

●●●●●

You can connect with Katie at
katie@katieganshert.com
www.katieganshert.com
Twitter: @KatieGanshert
Facebook: www.facebook.com/AuthorKatieGanshert